Lynne Graham was born in Northern Ireland and has been a keen romance reader since her teens. She is very happily married to an understanding husband who has learned to cook since she started to write! Her five children keep her on her toes. She has a very large dog, who knocks everything over, a very small terrier, who barks a lot, and two cats. When time allows, Lynne is a keen gardener.

Kim Lawrence lives on a farm in Anglesey with her university lecturer husband, assorted pets who arrived as strays and never left, and sometimes one or both of her boomerang sons. When she's not writing she loves to be outdoors gardening, or walking on one of the beaches for which the island is famous—along with being the place where Prince William and Catherine made their first home!

THE SECRET VALTINOS BABY

BY
LYNNE GRAHAM

THE GREEK'S ULTIMATE CONQUEST

BY
KIM LAWRENCE

MILLS & BOON

First Published in Great Britain 2018
by Mills & Boon, an imprint of HarperCollins*Publishers*
1 London Bridge Street, London, SE1 9GF

The Secret Valtinos Baby © 2018 by Lynne Graham

The Greek's Ultimate Conquest © 2018 by Kim Lawrence

ISBN: 978-0-263-93518-9

MIX
Paper from
responsible sources
FSC® C007454

This book is produced from independently certified FSC™ paper
to ensure responsible forest management.
For more information visit www.harpercollins.co.uk/green.

Printed and bound in Spain
by CPI, Barcelona

THE SECRET
VALTINOS BABY

CHAPTER ONE

THE GREEK BILLIONAIRE, Angel Valtinos, strode into his father's office suite to find both his brothers waiting in Reception and he stopped dead, ebony brows skating up. 'What is this? A family reunion?'

'Or Papa is planning to carpet us for something,' his Italian half-brother, Prince Vitale Castiglione, commented with perceptible amusement because they were all beyond the age where parental disapproval was a normal source of concern.

'Does he make a habit of that?' Zac Da Rocha demanded with a frown.

Angel met Vitale's eyes and his jawline squared, neither passing comment. Zac, their illegitimate Brazilian sibling, was pretty much a wild card. As he was a new and rather mysterious addition to the family circle his brothers had yet to fully accept him. And trust came no more easily to the suspicious Angel than it did to Vitale.

Vitale grinned. 'You're the eldest,' he reminded Angel. 'You get top billing and first appearance.'

'Not sure I want it on this occasion,' Angel conceded, but he swiftly shrugged off the faint and comically unfamiliar sense of unease assailing his innately rock-solid confidence.

After all, Charles Russell had *never* played the heavy father in his sons' lives, but even without exercising that authority he had still been a remarkably decent father, Angel conceded reflectively. Charles had not stayed married to either his or Vitale's mother for very long but he had taken a keen interest post-divorce in fostering and maintaining a close relationship with his sons. Angel had often had cause to be grateful for his father's stable approach to life and the shrewd business brain he suspected he had inherited from him. His mother was a thoroughly flighty and frivolous Greek heiress, whose attitude to childcare and education would have been careless without his father's stipulations on his son's behalf.

Charles Russell crossed his office to greet his eldest son. 'You're late,' he told him without heat.

'My board meeting ran over,' Angel told him smoothly. 'What's this all about? When I saw Zac and Vitale in Reception I wondered if there was a family emergency.'

'It depends what you call an emergency,' Charles deflected, studying his very tall thirty-three-year-old eldest son, who topped him in height by several inches.

A son to be proud of, Charles had believed until very recently when the startling discovery of certain disquieting information had punctured his paternal pride. To be fair, Angel also carried the genes of a fabulously wealthy and pedigreed Greek family, more known for their self-destructiveness than their achievements. Even so, Charles had prided himself on Angel's hugely successful reputation in the business world. Angel was the first Valtinos in two generations to make more money than he spent. A very astute high-achiever and a loyal and loving son, he was the very last child Charles had expected to disappoint him. Nonetheless, Angel had let him down by revealing a ruthless streak of Valtinos self-interest and irresponsibility.

'Tell me what this is about,' Angel urged with characteristic cool.

Charles rested back against his tidy desk, a still handsome man with greying hair in his early fifties. His well-built frame was tense. 'When do you plan to grow up?' he murmured wryly.

Angel blinked in bewilderment. 'Is that a joke?' he whispered.

'Sadly not,' his father confirmed. 'A week ago, I learned from a source I will not share that I am a *grandfather*...'

Angel froze, his lean, extravagantly handsome features suddenly wiped clean of all animation, while his shrewd dark eyes hardened and veiled. In less than a split second, though, he had lifted his aggressive chin in grim acknowledgement of the unwelcome shock he had been dealt: an issue he had hoped to keep buried had been unexpectedly and most unhappily disinterred by the only man in the world whose good opinion he valued.

'And, moreover, the grandfather of a child whom I will never meet if you have anything to do with it,' Charles completed in a tone of regret.

Angel frowned and suddenly extended his arms in a very expansive Greek gesture of dismissal. 'I thought to protect you—'

'No, your sole motivation was to protect *you*,' Charles contradicted without hesitation. 'From the demands and responsibility of a child.'

'It was an accident. Am I expected to turn my life upside down when struck by such a misfortune?' Angel demanded in a tone of raw self-defence.

His father dealt him a troubled appraisal. 'I did not consider *you* to be a misfortune.'

'Your relationship with my mother was on rather a different footing,' Angel declared with all the pride of his wealthy, privileged forebears.

A deep frown darkened the older man's face. 'Angel... I've never told you the whole truth about my marriage to your mother because I did not want to give you cause to respect her less,' he admitted reluctantly. 'But the fact is that Angelina deliberately conceived you once she realised that I wanted to end our relationship. I married her because she was pregnant, *not* because I loved her.'

Angel was startled by that revelation but not shocked, for he had always been aware that his mother was spoilt and selfish and that she could not handle rejection. His luxuriant black lashes lifted on challenging and cynical dark golden eyes. 'And marrying her didn't work for you, did it? So, you can hardly be suggesting that I marry the mother of *my* child!' he derided.

'No, marrying Angelina Valtinos didn't work for me,' Charles agreed mildly. 'But it worked beautifully for *you*. It gave you a father with the right to interfere and with your best interests always at heart.'

That retaliation was a stunner and shockingly true and Angel gritted his even white teeth at the comeback. 'Then I should thank you for your sacrifice,' he said hoarsely.

'No thanks required. The wonderful little boy grew up into a man I respect—'

'With the obvious exception of this issue,' Angel interjected tersely.

'You have handled it all wrong. You called in the lawyers, those Valtinos vulture lawyers, whose sole motivation is to protect you and the Valtinos name and fortune—'

'Exactly,' Angel slotted in softly. 'They protect me.'

'But don't you *want* to know your own child?' Charles demanded in growing frustration.

Angel compressed his wide, sensual mouth, his hard bone structure thrown into prominence, angry shame engulfing him at that question. 'Of course, I do, but getting past her mother is proving difficult.'

'Is that how you see it? Is that who you are blaming for this mess?' the older man countered with scorn. 'Your lawyers forced her to sign a non-disclosure agreement in return for financial support and you made no attempt at that point to show enough interest to arrange access to your child.'

Angel went rigid, battling his anger, determined not to surrender to the frustrating rage scorching through him. He was damned if he was about to let the maddening baby business, as he thought of it, come between him and the father he loved. 'The child hadn't been born at that stage. I had no idea how I would feel once she was.'

'Your lawyers naturally concentrated on protecting your privacy and your wealth. Your role was to concentrate on the *family* aspect,' Charles asserted with emphasis. 'Instead you have made an enemy of your child's mother.'

'That was not my intention. Using the Valtinos legal team was intended to remove any damaging personal reactions from our dealings.'

'And how has the impersonal approach worked for you?' Charles enquired very drily indeed.

Angel very nearly groaned out loud in exasperation. In truth, he had played an own goal, getting what he'd believed he wanted and then discovering too late that it wasn't what he wanted at all. 'She doesn't want me to visit.'

'And whose fault is that?'

'Mine,' Angel acknowledged fiercely. 'But she is currently raising my child in unsuitable conditions.'

'Yes, working as a kennel maid while raising the next Valtinos heiress isn't to be recommended,' his father remarked wryly. 'Well, at least the woman's not a gold-digger. A gold-digger would have stayed in London and lived the high life on the income you provided, not stranded herself in rural Suffolk with a middle-aged aunt while working for a living.'

'My daughter's mother is *crazy*!' Angel bit out, betraying his first real emotion on the subject. 'She's trying to make me feel bad!'

Charles raised a dubious brow. 'You think so? Seems to be a lot of sweat and effort to go to for a man she refuses to see.'

'She had the neck to tell my lawyer that she couldn't allow me to visit without risking breaching the non-disclosure agreement!' Angel growled.

'There could be grounds for that concern,' his father remarked thoughtfully. 'The paparazzi do follow you around and you visiting her *would* put a spotlight on her and the child.'

Angel drew himself up to his full six feet four inches and squared his wide shoulders. 'I would be discreet.'

'Sadly, it's a little late in the day to be fighting over parental access. You should have considered that first and foremost in your dealings because unmarried fathers have few, if any, rights under British law—'

'Are you suggesting that I marry her?' Angel demanded with incredulity.

'No.' Charles shook his greying head to emphasise that negative. 'That sort of gesture has to come from the heart.'

'Or the brain,' Angel qualified. 'I could marry her, take her out to Greece and then fight her there for custody, where I would have an advantage. That option *was* suggested at one point by my legal team.'

Charles regarded his unapologetically ruthless son with concealed apprehension because it had never been his intention to exacerbate the situation between his son and the mother of his child. 'I would hope that you would not even consider sinking to that level of deceit. Surely a more enlightened arrangement is still possible?'

But *was* it? Angel was not convinced even while he assured his concerned father that he would sort the situation out without descending to the level of dirty tricks. But was an access agreement even achievable?

After all, how could he be sure of anything in that line? Merry Armstrong had foiled him, blocked him and denied him while subjecting him to a raft of outrageous arguments rather than simply giving him what he wanted. Angel was wholly unaccustomed to such disrespectful treatment. Every time she knocked him back he was stunned by the unfamiliarity of the experience.

All his life he had pretty much got what he wanted from a woman whenever he wanted it. Women, usually, adored him. Women from his mother to his aunts to his cousins and those in his bed worshipped him like a god. Women lived to please Angel, flatter him, satisfy him: it had always been that way in Angel's gilded world of comfort and pleasure. And Angel had taken that enjoyable reality entirely for granted until the very dark day he had chosen to tangle with Merry Armstrong…

He had noticed her immediately, the long glossy

mane of dark mahogany hair clipped in a ponytail that reached almost to her waist, the pale crystalline blue eyes and the pink voluptuous mouth that sang of sin to a sexually imaginative male. Throw in the lean, leggy lines of a greyhound and proximity and their collision course had been inevitable from day one in spite of the fact that he had never before slept with one of his employees and had always sworn *not* to do so.

Merry's fingers closed shakily over the letter that the postman had just delivered. A tatty sausage-shaped Yorkshire terrier gambolled noisily round her feet, still overexcited by the sound of the doorbell and another voice.

'Quiet, Tiger,' Merry murmured firmly, mindful that fostering the little dog was aimed at making him a suitable adoptee for a new owner. But even as she thought that, she knew she had broken her aunt Sybil's strict rules with Tiger by getting attached and by letting him sneak onto her sofa and up onto her lap. Sybil adored dogs but she didn't believe in humanising or coddling them. It crossed Merry's mind that perhaps she was as emotionally damaged as Tiger had been by abuse. Tiger craved food as comfort; Merry craved the cosiness of a doggy cuddle. Or was she kidding herself in equating the humiliation she had suffered at Angel's hands with abuse? Making a mountain out of a molehill, as Sybil had once briskly told her?

Sadly the proof of that pudding was in the eating

as she flipped over the envelope and read the London postmark with a stomach that divebombed in sick dismay. It was another legal letter and she couldn't face it. With a shudder of revulsion laced with fear she cravenly thrust the envelope in the drawer of the battered hall table, where it could stay until she felt able to deal with it...*calmly.*

And a calm state of mind had become a challenge for Merry ever since she had first heard from the Valtinoses' lawyers and dealt with the stress, the appointments and the complaints. Legally she seemed mired in a never-ending battle where everything she did was an excuse for criticism or another unwelcome and intimidating demand. She could feel the rage building in her at the prospect of having to open yet another politely menacing letter, a rage that she would not have recognised a mere year earlier, a rage that threatened to consume her and sometimes scared her because there had been nothing of the virago in her nature until her path crossed that of Angel Valtinos. He had taught her nothing but bitterness, hatred and resentment, all of which she could have done without.

But he had also, although admittedly *very* reluctantly, given her Elyssa...

Keen to send her thoughts in a less sour direction, Merry glanced from the kitchen into the tiny sitting room of the cottage where she lived, and studied her daughter where she sat on the hearth rug happily engaged with her toys. Her black hair was an explosion of curls round her cherubic olive-toned face, highlighting striking ice-blue eyes and a pouty little mouth. She had her father's curls and her mother's eyes and mouth and was an extremely pretty baby in Merry's opinion, although she was prepared to admit that she was very biased when it came to her daughter.

In many ways after a very fraught and unhappy pregnancy Elyssa's actual birth had restored Merry to startling life and vigour. Before that day, it had not once occurred to her that her daughter's arrival would transform her outlook and fill her to overflowing with an unconditional love unlike anything she had ever felt before. Nowadays she recognised the truth: there was nothing she would not do for Elyssa.

A light knock sounded on the back door, announcing Sybil's casual entrance into the kitchen at the rear of the cottage. 'I'll put on the kettle…time for a brew,' she said cheerfully, a tall, rangy blonde nearing sixty but still defiantly beautiful, as befitted a woman who had been an international supermodel in the eighties.

Sybil had been Merry's role model from an early age. Her mother, Natalie, had married when Merry was sixteen and emigrated to Australia with her husband, leaving her teenaged daughter in her sister's care. Sybil and Merry were much closer than Merry had ever been with her birth mother but Sybil remained very attached to her once feckless kid sister. The sanctuary had been built by her aunt on the proceeds of the modelling career she had abandoned as soon as she had made enough money to devote her days to looking after homeless dogs.

In the later stages of her pregnancy, Merry had worked at the centre doing whatever was required and had lived with her aunt in her trendy barn conversion, but at the same time Merry had been carefully making plans for a more independent future. A qualified accountant, she had started up a small home business doing accounts for local traders and she had a good enough income now to run a car, while also insisting on paying a viable rent to Sybil for her use of the cottage at the gates of the rescue centre. The cottage was small and old-fashioned but it had two bedrooms and a little garden and perfectly matched Merry and Elyssa's current needs.

In fact, Sybil Armstrong was a rock of unchanging affection and security in Merry's life. Merry's mother, Natalie, had fallen pregnant with her during an affair with her married employer. Only nineteen at the time, Natalie had quickly proved ill-suited to the trials of single parenthood. Right from the start, Sybil had regularly swooped in as a weekend babysitter, wafting Merry back to her country home to leave her kid sister free to go out clubbing.

Natalie's bedroom door had revolved around a long succession of unsuitable men. There had been violent men, drunk men, men who took drugs and men who stole Natalie's money and refused to earn their own. By the time she was five years old, Merry had assumed all mothers brought different men home every week. In such an unstable household where fights and substance abuse were endemic she had missed a lot of school, and when social workers had threatened to take Merry into care, once again her aunt had stepped in to take charge.

For nine glorious years, Merry had lived solely with Sybil, catching up with her schoolwork, learning to be a child again, no longer expected to cook and clean for her unreliable mother, no longer required to hide in her bedroom while the adults downstairs screamed so loudly at each other that the neighbours called the police. Almost inevitably that phase of security with Sybil had ended when Natalie had made yet another fresh start and demanded the return of her daughter.

It hadn't worked, of course it hadn't, because Natalie had grown too accustomed to her freedom by then, and instead of finding in Merry the convenient little best friend she had expected she had been met with a daughter with whom she had nothing in common. By the time Keith, who was younger than Natalie, had entered her life, the writing had been on the wall. Keen to return to Australia and take Natalie with him, he had been frank about his reluctance to take on a paternal role while still in his twenties. Merry had moved back in with Sybil and had not seen her mother since her departure.

'Did I see the postman?' Sybil asked casually.

Merry stiffened and flushed, thinking guiltily of that envelope stuffed in the hall table. 'I bought something for Elyssa online,' she fibbed in shame, but there was just no way she could admit to a woman as gutsy as Sybil that a letter could frighten and distress her.

'No further communication from He Who Must Not Be Named?' Sybil fished, disconcerting her niece with that leading question, for lately her aunt had been very quiet on that topic.

'Evidently we're having a bit of a break from the drama right now, which is really nice,' Merry mumbled, shamefacedly tucking teabags into the mugs while Sybil lifted her great-niece off the rug and cuddled her before sitting down again with the baby cradled on her lap.

'Don't even think about him.'

'I don't,' Merry lied yet again, a current of self-loathing assailing her because only a complete fool would waste time thinking about a man who had mistreated her. But then, really, what would Sybil understand about that? As a staggeringly beautiful and famous young woman, Sybil had had to beat adoring men off with sticks but had simply never met one she wanted to settle down with. Merry doubted that any man had ever disrespected Sybil and lived to tell the tale.

'He'll get his comeuppance some day,' Sybil forecast. 'Everyone does. What goes around comes around.'

'But it bothers me that I hate him so much,' Merry confided in a rush half under her breath. 'I've never been a hater before.'

'You're still hurting. Now that you're starting to

date again, those bad memories will soon sink into the past.'

An unexpected smile lit Merry's heart-shaped face at the prospect of the afternoon out she was having the following day. As a veterinary surgeon, Fergus Wickham made regular visits to the rescue centre. He had first met Merry when she was off-puttingly pregnant, only evidently it had not put him off, it had merely made him bide his time until her daughter was born and she was more likely to be receptive to an approach.

She *liked* Fergus, she enjoyed his company, she reminded herself doggedly. He didn't give her butterflies in her tummy, though, or make her long for his mouth, she conceded guiltily, but then how important were such physical feelings in the overall scheme of things? Angel's sexual allure had been the health equivalent of a lethal snakebite, pulling her in only to poison her. Beautiful but deadly. Dear heaven, she hated him, she acknowledged, rigid with the seething trapped emotion that sent her memory flying inexorably back sixteen months...

CHAPTER TWO

MERRY WAS FULL of enthusiasm when she started her first job even though it wasn't her dream job by any stretch of the imagination. Having left university with a first-class honours degree in accountancy and business, she had no intention of settling permanently into being a front-desk receptionist at Valtinos Enterprises.

Even so, she had badly needed paid employment and the long recruitment process involved in graduate job applications had ensured that she was forced to depend on Sybil's generosity for more months than she cared to count. Sybil had already supported Merry through her years as a student, helping her out with handy vacation jobs at the rescue centre while always providing her with a comfortable home to come back to for weekends and holidays.

Her job at Valtinos Enterprises was Merry's first step towards true independence. The work paid well and gave her the breathing space in which to look for a more suitable position, while also enabling her to base herself in London without relying on her aunt's financial help. She had moved into a room in a grotty apartment and started work at VE with such high hopes.

And on her first day Angel strode out of the lift and her breath shorted out in her chest as though she had been punched. He had luxuriant black curls that always looked messy and that lean, darkly beautiful face of his had been crafted by a creative genius with exotic high cheekbones, a narrow, straight nose and eyes the colour of liquid honey. Eyes that she had only very much later discovered could turn as hard and cutting as black diamonds.

'You're new,' he commented, treating her to the kind of lingering appraisal that made her feel hot all over.

'This is my first day, Mr Valtinos,' she confided.

'Don't waste your smiles there,' her co-worker on the desk whispered snidely as Angel walked into his office. 'He doesn't flirt with employees. In fact the word is that he's fired a couple of his PAs for getting too personal with him.'

'I'm not interested,' Merry countered with amusement, and indeed when it came to men she rarely was.

Growing up watching her mother continually search for the man of her dreams while ignoring everything else life had to offer had scared Merry. Having survived her unsettled childhood, she set a high value on security and she was keen to establish her own accountancy firm. She didn't take risks…

ever. In fact she was the most risk-averse person she had ever met.

That innate caution had kept her working so hard at university that she had taken little part in the social whirl. There had been occasional boyfriends but none she had cared to invite into her bed. Not only had she never felt passion, but she had also never suffered from her mother's blazing infatuations. Watching relationships around her take off and then fail in an invariably nasty ending that smashed friendships and caused pain and resentment had turned Merry off even more. She liked a calm, tidy life, a *quiet* life, which in no way explained how she could ever have become intimate with a male as volatile as Angel, she acknowledged with lingering bewilderment.

But it was the truth, the absolute truth, that on paper she and Angel were a horrendous match. Angel was off-the-charts volatile with a volcanic hot temper that erupted every time someone did or said something he considered stupid. He wasn't tolerant or easy to deal with. In the first weeks of her employment she regularly saw members of his personal staff race out of his office as though they had wings on their feet, their pale faces stamped with stress and trepidation. He was very impatient and equally demanding. He might resemble a supermodel in his fabulously sophisticated designer suits, but he had the temperament of a tyrant and an overachiever's appetite for work and success. The only thing she admired about him in those initial weeks was his cleverness.

Serving coffee in the boardroom, she heard him

dissect entire arguments with a handful of well-chosen words. She noticed that people listened when he spoke and admired his intellect while competing to please and impress him. Occasionally beautiful shapely blondes would drift in to meet him for lunch, women of a definite type, the artificial socialite type, seemingly chosen only for their enviable faces and figures and their ability to look at him with stunned appreciation. Those who arrived without an invite didn't even get across the threshold of his office. He treated women like casual amusements and discarded them as soon as he got bored, and the procession of constantly changing faces made it obvious that he got bored very quickly and easily.

In short, nothing about Angel Valtinos *should* have attracted Merry. He shamelessly flaunted almost every flaw she disliked in a man. He was a selfish, hubristic, oversexed workaholic, spoiled by a life of luxury and the target of more admiration and attention than was good for him.

But even after six weeks in his radius, dredging her eyes off Angel when he was within view had proved impossible. He commanded a room simply by walking into it. Even his voice was dark, deep and smoulderingly charismatic. Once a woman heard that slumberous accented drawl she just had to turn her head and look. His dynamic personality suffused his London headquarters like an energy bolt while his mercurial moods kept his employees on edge and eager to please. Valtinos Enterprises felt dead and flat when he was abroad.

When one of Angel's personal assistants left and the position was offered internally, Merry applied, keen to climb the ladder. Angel summoned her to his office to study her with frowning dark golden eyes. 'Why is a candidate with your skills working on Reception?' he demanded impatiently.

'It was the first job I was offered,' Merry admitted, brushing her damp palms down over her skirt. 'I was planning to move on.'

Rising to his feet, making her uneasily aware of his height, he extended a slim file. 'Find somewhere quiet to work. You're off Reception for the morning. Check out this business and provide me with an accurate assessment of its financial history and current performance. If you do it well, I'll interview you this afternoon.'

That afternoon, he settled the file back on the desk and surveyed her, his wide, sensual mouth compressing. 'You did very well but you're a little too cautious in your forecasts. I *enjoy* risk,' he imparted, watching with amusement as she frowned in surprise at that admission. 'You've got the job. I hope you can take the heat. Not everyone can.'

'If you shout at me, I'll probably shout back,' Merry warned him warily.

And an appreciative grin slashed his shapely lips, making him so powerfully attractive that for a split second she simply stared, unable to look away. 'You may just work out very well.'

So began the most exciting phase of Merry's working life. Merry was the most junior member of Angel's personal staff but the one he always entrusted with figures. Sybil was thrilled by the promotion her niece had won but would have been horrified by the long hours Merry worked and the amount of responsibility she carried.

'The boss has got the hots for you,' one of her male co-workers told her with amusement when she had been two months in the job. 'Obviously you have something all those long tall blondes he parades through here don't, because he's always watching you.'

'I haven't noticed anything,' she said firmly, reluctant to let that kind of comment go unchallenged.

But even as she spoke she knew she was very carefully impersonal and unobtrusive in Angel's vicinity because she was conscious of him in a way she had not been conscious of a man before. If she was foolish enough to risk a head-on collision with his spectacular liquid honey eyes, her tummy somersaulted, her mouth dried and she couldn't catch her breath. Feeling like that mortified her. She knew it was attraction and she didn't like it, not only because he was her boss, but also because it made her feel out of control.

And then fate took a hand when Merry firmly believed that neither of them would ever have made any sort of a move. A highly contagious flu virus had decimated the staff and as his employees fell by the wayside Merry found herself increasingly exposed to working alone with Angel. At the office late one evening, he offered her a drink and a ride home. She said no thanks to the drink, deeming it unwise, and yes to the ride because it would get her home faster.

In the lift on the way down to the underground car park, Angel studied her with smouldering dark golden eyes. She felt dizzy and hot, as if her clothes were shrink-wrapped to her skin, preventing her from normal breathing. He lifted a long-fingered brown hand and traced his fingertips along the full curve of her lower lip in a caress that left her trembling, and then, as though some invisible line of restraint had snapped inside him, he crushed her back against the mirrored wall and kissed her, hungrily, feverishly, wildly with the kind of passion she was defenceless against.

'Come home with me,' he urged in a raw undertone as she struggled to pull herself back together while the lift doors stood open beside them.

Her flushed face froze. 'Absolutely not. We made a mistake. Let's forget about it.'

'That's not always possible,' Angel breathed thickly. 'I've been trying to forget about the way you make me feel for weeks.'

Disconcerted by that blunt admission as he stepped out of the lift, Merry muttered dismissively, 'That's just sex. Ignore it.'

Angel stared back at her in wonderment. '*Ignore* it?'

As the lift doors began to close with her still inside it, he reached in and held them open. 'Come on.'

'I'll get the Tube as usual.'

'Don't be childish,' Angel ground out. 'I am fully in control.'

Merry wasn't convinced, remembering that mad, exciting grab and the slam of her body back against the lift wall, but that instant of hesitation was her undoing because without hesitation Angel closed a hand over hers and pulled her out of the lift. 'I'll drop you home.'

'There are boundaries that shouldn't be crossed,' she told him with precision on the way to his car.

'Don't preach at me,' Angel sliced back in a driven undertone. 'I don't have a history of making moves on my staff. You are a one-off.'

'And it won't happen again now that we're both on our guard so let's forget about it,' Merry counselled, sliding breathlessly into a long silver low-slung bullet of a vehicle that she suspected was worth many times more than her annual salary. 'I prevented you from making a mistake.'

'You're preaching again,' Angel derided. 'If I hadn't stopped kissing you we'd still be in the lift!'

'No. I would've pushed you away,' she insisted with cool assurance.

She gave him her address, although he didn't seem to need it, and the journey through heavy traffic was silent, tense and unnerving. He pulled up at the kerb outside the ugly building where she lived. 'You could afford to live in a better area than this,' he censured.

'I have a healthy savings account,' she told him with pride, releasing her seat belt at the same time as he reached for her again.

His wide sensual mouth crushed hers with burning hunger and no small amount of frustration. Her whole body leapt as though he had punched a button detonating something deep down inside her, releasing a hot surge of tingling awareness in her pelvis that made her hips squirm and her nipples pinch painfully tight.

Angel lifted his tousled dark head. 'I'm still waiting on you pushing me away. You're all talk and no action,' he condemned.

'I don't think you'd appreciate a slap,' Merry framed frigidly, her face burning with mortification.

'If it meant that you ditched the icy control I'd be begging for it,' Angel husked suggestively, soft and low, the growl of his accent shaking her up.

Merry launched out of his sports car as though jet-propelled, uncharacteristically flustered and shaken that she had failed to live up to her own very high principles on acceptable behaviour. She should've pushed him away, slapped him, thumped him if necessary to drive her message home. Nothing less would cool his heels. He was a highly competitive, aggressive male, who viewed defeat as an ongoing challenge.

His car stayed at the kerb until she stalked into the building and only then did she breathe again, filling her compressed lungs and shivering as though she had stepped out of a freezing snowstorm. She felt all shaken up, shaken up and *stirred* in a way she didn't appreciate and almost hated him for.

The feel of his mouth on hers, the *taste* of it, the

explosive charge of heat hurtling at breakneck speed down into her belly and spreading to other, more intimate places she never ever thought about. How dared he do that to her? She would lodge a complaint of sexual harassment! Didn't he know what he was risking? But being Angel, he wouldn't care, wouldn't even stop to consider that he was playing with fire. Indeed, the knowledge would only energise and stimulate him because he loved to push the limits.

She curled up tight in her bed that night, overwhelmed by her first real experience of sexual temptation. When he kissed her she couldn't think, couldn't breathe. A kiss had never had that effect on her before and she was unnerved by the discovery that a kiss could be that influential. She toyed with the idea of complaining about sexual harassment, pictured Angel laughing fearlessly in the face of such a threat and finally decided that she didn't want the embarrassment of that on her employment record. Particularly when such a claim would fail because she hadn't pushed him away, hadn't given him an immediate rejection.

The next day she was very nervous going into work, but Angel didn't do or say anything that was different and she was strangely irritated by that reality: that he could act as though he had never offered to take her home to bed for the night and, afterwards, simply treat her like everyone else. But those same moments of intimacy had carried a higher price for *her*. It was as though he had stripped away her tough outer layer and chipped her out of her cautious shell to ensure that she began feeling physical and emotional responses she had comfortably held at bay until she'd met him.

During the week that followed she was feverishly aware of Angel to a degree that sent her temperature rocketing. When he looked at her, it was as if a blast of concentrated heat lit her up inside and her bra would feel scratchy against her tender nipples and a dull ache would stir between her thighs, her every tiny reaction in his presence like a slap in the face that shamed her. It was a terrible destructive wanting that wouldn't go away. He had lit the spark and she seemed stuck with the spread of the fire licking away at her nerves and her fierce pride.

At the end of that week, Angel asked her to stay behind after everyone else had left to go for drinks.

'Next on the agenda...*us*,' Angel murmured sibilantly.

Merry shot him a withering appraisal. 'There is no us.'

'Exactly,' Angel pronounced with satisfaction. 'Scratch the itch and it goes away and dies, ignore it and it festers.'

'Your seduction vocabulary needs attention,' Merry quipped, standing straight in front of him, grudging amusement dancing in her crystalline eyes.

Angel grimaced. 'I don't do seduction.'

'I don't do one-night stands.'

'So if I make it dinner and sex I'm in with a chance?' A sardonic ebony brow elevated.

'No chance whatsoever,' Merry contradicted with

pleasure. 'I'm a virgin and I'm not trading that for some sleazy night with my boss.'

'A virgin?' Angel was aghast. *'Seriously?'*

'Seriously,' Merry traded without embarrassment, reflecting on how her mother had fallen pregnant with her and determined to make every choice that took her in the opposite direction. 'Sex should mean something more than scratching an itch.'

Angel sprang upright behind his desk, all supple, graceful motion, the fine, expensive fabric of his suit pulling taut over powerful thigh muscles and definable biceps. Her mouth ran dry, her eyes involuntarily clinging to his every movement. 'It's never been anything more for me,' he admitted drily. 'But I take offence at the word "sleazy". I am never sleazy and… I don't do virgins.'

'Good to know,' Merry breathed tightly, watching his shirt ripple ever so slightly over his muscular chest as he exhaled while cursing her intense physical awareness of him. 'May I go home now?'

'I'll drop you back.'

'That's not necessary,' she told him coolly.

'I decide what's necessary around here,' Angel pronounced, throwing the door wide and heading for the lift. 'You realise you're as rare as a unicorn in my world? Are you holding out for marriage?'

Involuntarily amused by his curiosity, Merry laughed. 'Of course not. I'm just waiting for something *real.* I'm not a fan of casual or meaningless.'

Angel lounged back fluidly against the wall of the lift, all naked predator and jungle grace. 'I'm casual but I'm very real,' he told her huskily, his deep dark drawl roughening and trickling down her taut spine like a spectral caress.

'Oh, switch it off,' Merry groaned. 'We're like salt and pepper except you can't mix us.'

'Because you've got too many rules, too many barriers. Why is that?'

'Like you are actually interested?' Merry jibed.

'I *am* interested,' Angel growled, dark golden eyes flashing as the lift doors sprang back. 'I want you.'

'Only because you can't have me,' Merry interposed drily, her skin coming up in gooseflesh as he flashed her a ferocious appraisal capable of flaying her skin from her bones. 'That's how basic you are.'

'You're becoming rude.'

'Your persistence is making me rude,' Merry told him.

'I want to see your hair loose,' Angel bit out impatiently. 'It's unusually long.'

'My mother kept on cutting it short when I was little because it was easier to look after. Now I grow it because I can,' she said truthfully, her stomach flipping as he shot a sudden charismatic smile at her, his lean, darkly beautiful face vibrant with amusement.

'You're a control freak,' he breathed lazily. 'Takes one to know one, *glikia mou*.'

'That's why we don't get on,' Merry pointed out.

'We don't get on because you have a very annoying sort of pious vibe going,' Angel contradicted. 'You're smug.'

'No, I'm not,' she argued instantly as they crossed the half-empty car park.

'You think you're superior to me because you're not at the mercy of your hormones…but you *were* when I touched you,' Angel breathed, caging her in against the passenger door of his car, the heat of his lean, powerful body perceptible even through the inches separating them and the rich, evocative scent of husky male and exotic cologne filling her nostrils. His hands braced either side of her, not actually touching her quivering length, and her knees turned weak at the thought that he *might* touch her. 'You can hardly breathe when I'm this close to you. I *see* that, I *know* that…every time I try to step back, it sucks me back in.'

He was like an impenetrable force field surrounding her. She knew she could push him away, she knew he wouldn't fight, she knew he wouldn't do anything she didn't want him to do and a weird sense of unexpected power engulfed her. He was still coming back at her because he couldn't resist the pull between them and she couldn't resist it either. It was a weakness deep down inside her that she couldn't suppress. Nobody had ever made her feel the way he was making her feel and that was a thrill on its own, a shot of adrenalin in her veins to match the feverish pound of her heartbeat. She wanted him. The knowledge ploughed through her like a battering ram, casting everything she had thought she knew about herself into a broken jumble of messy pieces.

'You're not my type,' she whispered in dry-mouthed protest.

'You're not my type either,' Angel admitted thickly. 'But I'd still have sex in a car park with you any time you cared to ask.'

'Not about to ask,' Merry confided shakily. 'Take me home…back off.'

'You're making a major production of this again,' Angel accused, flashing his key fob to open the car. 'Stop doing that. It's…it's bizarrely unnerving.'

She climbed into his car in a daze, the throb between her legs angry and unsettling, the sensual smoulder in the air almost unbearable, every nerve ending painfully aware of it. She didn't know how he did that using only words and looks. It was terrifying. He had wiped her mind clean, made her feel stuff she didn't want to feel, rocked the foundations of her security.

'I don't like you,' she admitted.

'*Thee mou*…you don't have to like me, you only have to want me…and you do.'

And it was agonisingly true, she registered in dismay. Her brain didn't seem to have anything to do with the equation. She thoroughly disapproved of everything he was and yet the chemistry between them was wild and dominant.

'We have one night together and sate the craving. Then we put it away and bury it,' Angel intoned in a driven undertone.

'I thought you didn't do virgins.'

'Evidently you were born to be my single exception.'

'Is this an actual negotiation?' Merry enquired incredulously.

'We have to sort this out. You're taking my mind off work,' Angel complained. 'I can't handle watching you all day and fantasising about you all night. It's bad for business.'

'What's in it for me?' Merry whispered unevenly.

'I'm superlative at sex.'

'Oh…' Her lashes fluttered, her tummy somersaulting again as she wondered if she really was about to do what he wanted her to do, what *she* herself wanted to do. And that was the answer there and then when she was least expecting to see or understand it.

He would make a great introduction to sex for her, she thought dizzily. It would end the insane craving he had awakened inside her and maybe then she could return to her normal tranquil self. That prospect had huge appeal for her. The need would be satisfied, the intolerable longing ended. All right, it wasn't the big romance with hearts and flowers that she had dimly envisioned, but then possibly that had never been a very practical aspiration. What he was offering was basic and honest even if it was casual and uncommitted and everything she had once sworn she would never participate in. It was not as though she had been saving herself for a wedding ring. She had been saving herself for love, but love hadn't happened.

'So, you're suggesting that I just use you,' Merry remarked grittily as he pulled into another underground car park.

'We use each other,' Angel exhaled in a rush and, killing the engine, stretched out a long powerful arm to enclose her in almost the same moment.

His mouth crashed down on hers with a hunger that blew her away. Somehow he made it that she didn't remember getting out of the car, didn't remember getting into a lift or emerging from it. There was only that insane, greedy melding of their mouths and the frantic impatient activity of their hands in a dimly lit hall. Her coat fell off or maybe he helped it. His jacket disappeared at similar speed. She kicked off her shoes. He wrenched off his tie and cannoned into a door as he lifted her off her feet.

'We have to slow down,' he told her roughly, dark golden eyes shimmering like gold ingots, his sexual excitement patent. 'Or I'll screw this up for you.'

He laid her down on a wide, comfortable mattress and stood over her, stripping without inhibition. All she wanted was his mouth on hers again, that magical escape from the limits of her own body that sent her flying higher than she had ever known she could fly. He shed his trousers and her attention locked warily on the very obvious bulge in his boxers while she struggled to accept that she could, even briefly, be with a man who was chronically untidy and dropped clothes in a heap on the floor. Not her type, not her type; she rhymed it like a mantra inside her head, her bulwark against getting attached in any way. It was sex and she didn't want to regard it as anything else.

He unzipped her dress and flipped her over to

remove it with deft precision and release her bra, before pausing to carefully unsnap the clasp in her hair and let his skilled mouth roam across her pale shoulders. He tugged her round and up to him then, long fingers lifting to feather her curtain of dark coffee-coloured hair round her shoulders, thready shimmers of lighter caramel appearing in the light filtering in from the hall.

'You have amazing hair,' he muttered intently, gazing down into blue eyes as pale as an Arctic sky.

'Is that a fetish of yours?'

'Not that I've noticed, but that prissy little smile of yours turns me on no end,' Angel confided, disconcerting her.

'I do *not* have a prissy smile.'

'Talking too much,' Angel growled, crushing her ripe mouth beneath his again, running his hands down the sides of her narrow ribcage to dispose of her bra and let his hands rise to cup the small delicate mounds of her breasts.

As his thumbs grazed her sensitive nipples a gasp parted Merry's lips, and when his hungry mouth followed there she fell back against the pillows and dug her fingers into his thick tangle of curls. Heat arrowed in stormy flashes right to her core, leaving her insanely conscious of how excited she was becoming. Her thighs pressed together, her hips dug into the mattress as she struggled to get a grip on herself, but it was as if her body were streaking ahead of her and no matter how hard she tried to catch it, she couldn't.

He shifted position, ran his tongue down over her

straining midriff to her navel, parted her from her knickers without her noticing, traced her inner thighs with a devil's expertise until she was splayed out like a sacrifice. And then the flood of crazy pleasure came at her in breathless, jolting stabs that shocked and roused her to a level that was almost unbearable. She was shaken by what she was allowing him to do and how much her body craved it and how very little she could control her own reactions. She twisted and turned, hauled him back to her at one point and kissed him breathless, wanting, needing, trembling on the edge of something she didn't understand.

The tight bands in her pelvis strained to hold in the wild searing shots of pleasure gripping her and then her control broke and she writhed in a wild frenzy of release. The sound of her own gasping cry startled her, her eyes flying wide, and Angel grinned shamelessly down at her like a very sexy pirate, a dark shadow of stubble merely accentuating his fantastic bone structure.

'You're staying the whole night,' he told her thickly.

'No,' Merry muttered, head rolling back on the pillows as he crawled up her body like the predator he truly was. 'Once it's done, it's over.'

'You are so stubborn,' Angel groaned in frustration, nipping up her slender throat to find her swollen lips again, teasing and tasting and letting his tongue plunge and twin with hers until she was beyond thought and argument again. He donned protection.

He eased into her slowly, very slowly, and impatience assailed her. She didn't want or need to be treated like fine china that might shatter or like that rare unicorn he had mentioned. Her body was slick and eager again, the pulse at the heart of her racing with anticipation. She tilted under him, angling up her hips, and the invitation was too much for his control and he jerked over her and plunged deep. A brief burning sting of pain made her stiffen and gasp.

'That's your own fault,' Angel growled in exasperation. 'If you would just lie still.'

'I'm not a blow-up doll.'

'I was trying not to hurt you.'

'I'm not breakable either,' Merry argued, every skin cell on red alert as she felt her body slowly stretch to enclose his, tiny little shimmers of exquisite sensation flying through her as he began to move, hinting that the best was yet to come. 'Don't stop.'

And he didn't. He sank deep into her with a shuddering groan of pleasure and the pace picked up, jolting her with waves of glorious excitement. She arched her body up, suddenly needy again, hungry again, marvelling at the limitless capacity of her body to feel more and yet more. But this time the climb to pleasure was slower and she writhed, blue eyes lighting up with impatience and a need she had never expressed before. Her heart raced, her pulses pounded and that sweet, seductive throb of delight grew and grew inside her until she could contain it no longer. Every barrier dropped as her body exploded into an ecstatic climax that left her limp and stunned.

Angel released her from his weight but made a move to pull her under his arm and retain a hold on her. Quick as a flash Merry evaded him, her whole being bent on immediate escape. They had had sex but she didn't want to hang around for the aftermath. Dignity, she told herself staunchly, dictated an immediate departure. She slid out of the other side of the bed, bending down to scoop up her discarded clothes.

'I asked you to stay,' Angel reminded her.

'I'm going home,' she said as he vaulted out of bed and headed into what she presumed was a bathroom, his lean, powerful body emanating impatience and annoyance in perceptible waves.

She would have liked a shower but she was determined not to linger. With a grimace, she pulled her clothes back on and was out in the hall cramming her feet back into her shoes and hurriedly calling a taxi when Angel reappeared, bronzed and still unashamedly naked in the bedroom doorway. 'I don't want you to leave.'

'I've already ordered a taxi.' Merry tilted her chin, her long hair streaming untidily round her flushed heart-shaped face. 'We agreed and it's better like this.'

'I asked for one night—'

'You can't have everything your way,' Merry declared flatly. 'I enjoyed myself but all good things come to an end.'

Angel swore in Greek. 'You drive me insane.'

'What's your problem? According to your fore-cast, we're done and dusted now,' she pointed out helplessly.

Yet for all her proud nonchalance in front of him, Merry travelled home in a daze of mounting panic. Back at her apartment she had to wait until the shower was free. She felt shell-shocked by what she had done. Her body ached but her brain ached almost as much, trying to rationalise the fleeting madness that had overtaken her. She tried to ex-amine it from Angel's unemotional point of view, but that didn't work for her when her own emo-tions were throwing tantrums and storming about inside her as much as if she had killed someone. *Done and dusted, forget about it now,* she reminded herself doggedly. He had much more experience in such encounters than she had, had to know what he was talking about. The curiosity and that unnatural hunger had been satisfied and now it would all die a natural death and become an embarrassing mem-ory that she'd never ever share with anyone, she told herself with determination.

Only in the days that followed Merry slowly came to appreciate that, for all his evident experi-ence, Angel Valtinos had got it badly wrong. Feed a cold, starve a fever was a saying she had grown up with, and before very long had passed she knew that it had been a serious mistake to *feed* the fever. She saw it in the way Angel's stunning dark eyes locked on her like magnets, heard it in the terseness of his instructions to her and she felt the pull of him inside herself as if he had attached a secret chain to her. Excitement crashed over her when he was close by, her temperature climbing, her heart thumping. Slowly, painfully, she came to appreciate that she was infatuated with him and very nearly as giddy and mindless as a silly schoolgirl in his vicinity. The suspicion that she was more her mother's daughter than she had ever dreamt she could be appalled her.

Was that the real explanation of why she had slept with Angel Valtinos? She had asked herself again and again why she had done that, why she had made such an impulsive decision that went against everything she believed, and now she was being faced with an answer that she loathed. At some point in their relationship she had begun getting attached to him, possibly around the time she had started admiring his intellect and shrewd business instincts. That attachment was pitiful, she decided with angry self-loathing, and in haste she began to look for another job, desperate to leave Angel and Valtinos Enterprises behind her.

Two weeks after their first encounter, Angel showed up at her apartment one evening without the smallest warning. The same angry frustration that powered him was running through her.

'What are you doing here?' she demanded, far from pleased to be surprised in her cotton pyjamas, fresh from the shower and bare of make-up.

Angel grimaced, his lean, darkly handsome features taut and troubled as he leant back against her bedroom door to close it. 'My car brought me here.'

'What on earth—?' she began, disconcerted by his sudden appearance in a place where she had never imagined seeing him.

Angel settled volatile dark golden eyes on her angrily. 'I *can't* stay away,' he grated rawly, his beautiful mouth compressing.

'B-but…we agreed,' she stammered.

'Massive fail,' Angel framed darkly. 'Biggest bloody mistake of my life!'

Merry almost laughed and fortunately killed the urge. It was simply that Angel's innate love of drama not only amused her, but somehow touched her somewhere down deep inside, somewhere where she was soft and emotional and vulnerable even though she didn't want to be. He had come to her even though he didn't want to. He resented his desire for her, had tried to stamp it out and failed. She grasped immediately that that weakness for her infuriated him.

'I want to be with you tonight.'

'Angel—'

He came down on the bed beside her and framed her face with long, cool brown fingers. 'Say my name again,' he demanded.

'No,' she said stubbornly. 'I don't do what you tell me to do outside working hours.'

'*Thee mou*…stop challenging me,' he groaned, tilting her head back to follow the long, elegant column of her throat down to the slope of her shoulder, nipping and kissing a tantalising path across her sensitised skin while she quivered. 'This isn't me. This isn't what I'm about.'

'Then why are you here?' she whispered weakly.

'Can't stay away.' He carried her hand down to where he was hot and hard and wanting and groaned without inhibition as she stroked him through the fine, crisp fabric of his well-cut trousers.

Heat coursed through her in molten waves, the hunger unleashed afresh. Simply touching him inflamed her. She tried to fight it, she tried to fasten it down and ground herself, but Angel smashed any hope of control by welding dark golden eyes to hers and kissing her with barely contained ferocity. Not a single thought passed her mind beyond the thrillingly obvious reality that he needed her and couldn't stay away. That knowledge vanquished every other consideration. She kissed him back with the same uncontrollable, desperate passion.

'I intended to take you out to dinner,' Angel admitted breathlessly as he fought with her pyjamas, his sleek, deft skills with feminine clothing deserting him.

'You hungry?' she gasped, almost strangling him with his own tie in her struggle to loosen it.

'Only for you,' he growled fiercely against her swollen mouth. 'Watching you round the office all day, being unable to touch, even to look.'

And then they were naked in her bed, naked and frantic and so tormentingly hungry for each other that she writhed and squirmed and he fought to hold her still. He produced a condom, tore it from the wrapper with his teeth. 'We don't want an accident,' he said unevenly.

'No, no accidents,' she agreed helplessly, lying there, shocked by what she was doing but participating all the same, quite unable to deny him. Their clothes lay festooned all around them and she didn't care. Angel had come to her and she was happy about that, there in her pin-neat room made messy by his presence.

He drove into her yielding flesh with a heartfelt sound of satisfaction and she wrapped her legs round him, arching up and gasping at every fluid stroke. The excitement heightened exponentially, the pulsing pound of intolerable desire driving them off the edge fast into a hot, sweaty tangle of limbs and shuddering fulfilment.

Angel pressed his sensual mouth against her brow and eased back, only to grate out a curse in Greek. 'I broke the condom!' he growled in harried explanation as she stared up at him, recognising the stress and anxiety in his expressive gaze.

As if a simultaneous alarm bell had sounded, Angel flipped back from her and slid fluidly out of bed while Merry hurriedly hid her fast-cooling body under the duvet they had lain on. Her eyes were wide with consternation.

'This has never happened to me before,' Angel assured her, hastily getting back into his clothes.

Merry pondered the idea of mentioning that dinner invite and discarded it again. She had nothing comforting to say to him, nothing likely to improve his mood. She wasn't on the pill, wasn't taking any contraceptive precautions, a reality that now made her feel very foolish. Why hadn't she rethought her outlook the minute she'd ended up in bed with Angel Valtinos? Wasn't a woman supposed to look after herself?

'I'm not on anything,' she admitted reluctantly.

Angel dug out his wallet and flipped out a card. 'Come in late tomorrow. See this doctor first. He's a friend of mine. He'll check you out,' he told her, setting the card down by the bed.

And within a minute he was gone. *Wham-bam—no, thank you, ma'am,* she acknowledged with a sinking heart and a strong need for a shower.

If only she could shower the thoughts out of her head and the feelings in her heart as easily, she concluded wretchedly. She felt sick, humiliated and rejected. She also hated herself. A contraceptive accident had sent Angel into a nosedive, his horror unconcealed. Did she hold that against him when trepidation had seized her by the throat as well?

But luckily, that night she had no grasp at all of the nightmare that was waiting to unfold and the many months of unhappiness that would follow as punishment for her irresponsibility. In effect, she was still a complete innocent then. She was hopelessly infatuated with a man who only lusted after her and with a lust that died the instant a condom failed. That was why she had held herself back from casual sex, seeking the feelings and the certain amount of safety that came with them...

Her first wake-up call to what she was truly dealing with came early the next morning. She went, as instructed, to see the suave private doctor, who ran a battery of tests on her and then casually offered her the morning-after pill. She didn't want it, hadn't ever even thought about whether or not she approved of that option, but when it was suggested to her, it grated on her, and even though she could see the doctor's surprise at her refusal she saw no reason to explain her attitude. Had such a possibility been available to her mother, she reckoned that she herself would never have been born and that was a sobering acknowledgement. Had Angel sent her to that doctor quite deliberately to ensure that she was offered that option? She planned to have that out with him the instant she got a moment alone with him.

Unfortunately what she didn't know then was that it would be many, many weeks before she had the opportunity of a moment alone with Angel again and even then she only finally achieved that meeting by stalking him to one of his regular retreats.

When she finally arrived at work after seeing the doctor she was sent straight into one of the meeting rooms where a senior HR person and a company lawyer awaited her. There she was presented with a compromise agreement by which, in return for substantial compensation, she would immediately cease working for Valtinos Enterprises and leave without disclosing her reasons for doing so to anyone.

The shock and humiliation of that meeting marked Merry long after the event. As soon as she realised that Angel wanted her out of the building and away from him, no matter what it cost him, she felt sick

CHAPTER THREE

'FERGUS ASKED ME where he should take you tomorrow,' Sybil volunteered, shooting Merry straight back into the present with that surprising announcement. 'I thought that was a bit wet of him. I mean, doesn't he have any ideas of his own? But obviously he wants you to enjoy yourself.'

A bit wet sounded all right to Merry, who was still reeling from the consequences of Angel's me-me-me approach to life. A macho, self-assured man was hugely impressive and sexy only until he turned against you and became an enemy, armed to the teeth with legal sharks.

'I suggested a trip to the seaside for you and Elyssa. I know you love the beach,' Sybil mused. 'Fergus does like children.'

'Yes,' Merry agreed quietly, scooping Elyssa off the older woman's lap to feed her while wondering what it would have been like to have a father for her daughter. Would he have helped out with their child? Taken a real interest? She suppressed the thought, knowing it probably came from the reality that *she*

had had to grow up without a father. She had, however, visited her father once, but his enraged betrayed
wife had been present as well and the visit had been
a disaster. Her father had only asked to see her on
that one occasion and then never again.

The next morning, Merry finished drying her
hair and took the time to apply a little make-up because Elyssa was having her morning nap. Pulling on
skinny jeans and a vibrant cerise tee, she dug her feet
into comfy shoes. She was heading downstairs again
with Elyssa anchored on her hip when the phone
rang. Breathless, she tucked it under her chin while
she lowered her daughter to the hearth rug.

'Yes?'

'I'm in the office,' her aunt told her curtly. 'Elyssa's father is here demanding to see her. I'll keep
him here with me until you come.'

Shock and disbelief engulfed Merry in a dizzy
tide. She snatched Elyssa back off the rug and wondered frantically what to do with her daughter while
she dealt with Angel, because she didn't want him
to see her. Her mind was a chaotic blur because she
couldn't imagine Angel travelling down to Suffolk
just to see the child he had once done everything possible to avoid and deny. It was true that since he had
been informed of Elyssa's birth he had made repeated
requests to meet his daughter, but Merry had seen no
good reason to cater to his natural human curiosity
and she herself wanted nothing more to do with him.

After all, as soon as Angel had learned that she
was pregnant he had brought his lawyers in to han-

dle everything. They had drawn up a legal agreement by which Merry was paid a ridiculous amount of money every month but only for as long as she kept quiet about her daughter's parentage. Merry currently paid the money into a trust she had set up for Elyssa's future, reckoning that that was the best she could do for her daughter.

She left the cottage with Elyssa tucked into her well-padded pushchair, her toy bunny clutched between her fingers. Walking into the rescue centre, she saw a long black limousine sitting parked and she swallowed hard at the sight of it. Angel didn't flaunt the Valtinos wealth but even at the office she had seen occasional glimpses of a world and lifestyle far different from her own. He wore diamond cufflinks and his shirts had monograms embroidered on the pockets. Every garment he wore was tailored by hand at great expense and he thought nothing of it because from birth he had never known anything else.

She pushed the buggy into the barn, where the kennel staff hung out when they took a break. 'Will you watch Elyssa for me for ten minutes?' she asked anxiously of the three young women, chattering over mugs of coffee.

'Can we take her out of the pram and play with her?' one of them pressed hopefully.

A smile softened Merry's troubled face. 'Of course...' she agreed, hastening out again to head for the rescue centre office.

What on earth was Angel doing here? And how could she face him when the very idea of facing him again made her feel queasy with bad memories? They had last met the day she'd tracked him down to tell him that she was pregnant. Those liquid-honey eyes had turned black-diamond hard, his shock and distaste stark as a banner.

'Do you want it?' he had asked doubtingly, earning her hatred with every syllable of that leading question. 'Scratch that. It was politically incorrect. Naturally I will support you in whatever choice you make.'

How could she come back from that punishing recollection and act normally? She thought of Elyssa's innocent sweetness and the reality that her father didn't want her, had *never* wanted her, and the knowledge hurt Merry, making her wonder if her own father had felt the same about her. Even worse, she was convinced that allowing any kind of contact between father and daughter would only result in Elyssa getting hurt at some later stage. In her opinion, Angel was too selfish and too spoiled to be a caring or committed parent.

As she rounded the corner of the tiny office building a startling scene met her eyes. Poised outside the door, Sybil had her shotgun aimed at Angel, who was predictably lounging back against the wall of the kennels opposite as though he had not a care in the world.

'Will you call this madwoman off me?' Angel demanded with derisive sibilance when he heard her footsteps and without turning his arrogant dark head. 'She won't let me move.'

'It's all right, Sybil,' Merry said tautly. 'Elyssa is in the barn.'

Angel's arrogant dark head flipped, the long, predatory power of his lean, strong body suddenly rippling with bristling tension. 'What's my daughter doing in a barn? And who's looking after her?' he demanded in a driven growl.

Sybil lowered her shotgun and broke it open to safely extract the cartridges. 'I'll take her back home with me,' she declared, entirely ignoring Angel.

'Come into the office and we'll talk,' Merry framed coldly as his dark eyes locked on her tense face.

'I'm not very good at talking,' Angel acknowledged without embarrassment as he straightened. 'That's why I use lawyers.'

In an angry defensive movement, Merry thrust wide the door of the little office before spinning back round to say, 'What the hell are you doing here?'

'I warned you that I intended to visit,' Angel bit out impatiently.

Merry thought about the letter she had bottled out of opening and uneasily looked at him for the first time in months. The sheer power of his volatile presence made her tummy turn hollow and her legs wobble. He was still so wickedly beautiful that he made her teeth clench with fierce resentment. It wasn't fair that he should look so untouched by all that had passed between them, that he should stand there perfectly at his ease and glossily well groomed, sheathed in his elegant charcoal-grey designer suit. It was especially unfair that he should still have the nerve to voice a demand for a right he had surrendered entirely of his own volition before their daughter was even born. 'And I've already told your lawyers that I won't accept *any* kind of visit from you!'

'I won't accept that, not even if I have to spend the rest of my life and yours fighting you.' Angel mapped those boundaries for her, wanting her to know that there would be no escape from his demands until he got what he wanted. He would not accept defeat, regardless of what it cost him. He had lost his father's respect and he was determined to retrieve it and get to know his child.

Frowning, black brows lowering, he studied Merry, incredulous at her continuing defiance while marvelling at the quiet inner strength he sensed in her, which he had never noticed in a woman before. She had cut her hair, which now fell in glossy abundance to just below her shoulders. He was ridiculously disappointed by that fashion update. There had been something ultra-feminine about that unusually long hair that he had liked. She was also thinner than she had been and there had not been much of her to begin with, he conceded reflectively. She looked like a teenager with her long, coltish legs outlined by distressed denim and with her rounded little breasts pushing at the cotton of her top so that he could see the prominent points of her lush nipples. He went hard and gritted his teeth, furious with himself for that weakness but... *Thee mou*, shorn of her conservative office apparel, she looked ridiculously sexy.

'Why can't you simply move on from this and forget we exist?' Merry demanded in fierce frustration. 'A year ago, that's what you wanted and I gave it to you. I signed everything your legal team put in front of me. You didn't want to be a father. You didn't want to know anything about her and you didn't want her associated with your precious name. What suddenly changed?'

Angel's lean, hard jaw line took on an aggressive slant. 'Maybe I've changed,' he admitted, sharply disconcerting her.

Merry's tense face stiffened with suspicion. 'That's doubtful. You are what you are.'

'Everyone is capable of change and sometimes change simply happens whether you want it to or not,' Angel traded, his lean, dark features taut. 'When you first told me that you were pregnant a year ago, I didn't think through what I was doing. Gut instinct urged me to protect my way of life. I listened to my lawyers, took their advice and now we've got…now we've got an intolerable mess.'

Merry forced herself to breathe in deep and slow and stay calm. He sounded sincere but she didn't trust him. 'It's the way you made it and now you have to live with it.'

Angel threw back his broad shoulders and lifted his arrogant dark head high, effortlessly dominating the small cluttered room. Even though Merry was a comfortable five feet eight inches tall, he was well over six feet in height and stood the tallest in most gatherings. 'I can't live with it,' he told her with flat finality. 'I *will* continue to fight for access to my daughter.'

The breath fluttered in Merry's drying throat,

consternation and fury punching up through her, bringing a flood of emotion with it. 'I *hate* you, Angel! If you make any more threats, if you bombard me with more legal letters, I will hate you even more! When is enough *enough*?' she hurled at him with bitter emphasis.

'When I can finally establish a normal relationship with my daughter,' Angel responded, his lean, strong face set with stubborn resolve. 'It is my duty to establish that relationship and I won't shirk it.'

'The way you shirked everything else that went with fatherhood?' Merry scorned. 'The responsibility? The commitment? The caring? I was just a pregnant problem you threw money at!'

'I won't apologise for that. I was raised to solve problems that way,' Angel admitted grittily. 'I was taught to put my faith in lawyers and to protect myself first.'

'Angel…you are strong enough to protect yourself in a cage full of lions!' Merry shot back at him wrathfully. 'You didn't *need* the lawyers when I wasn't making any demands!'

A ton of hurt and turbulent emotion was sucking Merry down but she fought it valiantly. She was trying so hard not to throw pointless recriminations at him. In an effort to put a physical barrier between them she flopped down in the chair behind the desk. 'Did you ever…even once…think about *feelings*?' she prompted involuntarily.

Angel frowned at her, wondering what she truly wanted from him, wondering how much he would be willing to give in return for access to his daughter. It wasn't a calculation he wanted to do at that moment, not when she was sitting there, shoulders rigid, heart-shaped face stiff and pale as death. 'Feelings?' he repeated blankly.

'My feelings,' Merry specified helplessly. 'How it would feel for me to sleep with a man one night and go into work the next day and realise that he couldn't even stand to have me stay in the same building to do my job?'

Angel froze as if she had fired an ice gun at him, colour receding beneath his bronzed skin, his gorgeous dark eyes suddenly screened by his ridiculously luxuriant black lashes. 'No, I can't say I did. I didn't view it in that light,' he admitted curtly. 'I thought separation was the best thing for both of us because our relationship had crossed too many boundaries and got out of hand. I also ensured that your career prospects were not damaged in any way.'

Merry closed her eyes tight, refusing to look at him any longer. He had once told her that he didn't do virgins and it seemed that he didn't do feelings either. He was incapable of putting himself in her shoes and imagining how she had felt. 'I felt…absolutely mortified that day, completely humiliated, *hurt*,' she spelt out defiantly. 'The money didn't soften the blow and I only took it because I didn't know how long it would take for me to find another job.'

Angel saw pain in her pale blue eyes and heard the emotion in her roughened voice. Her honesty unnerved him, flayed off a whole layer of protective skin, and he didn't like how it made him feel. 'I had no desire to hurt you, there *was* no such intent,' he countered tautly. 'I realised that our situation had become untenable and in that line I was guiltier than you because I made all the running.'

It was an acknowledgement of fault that would once have softened her. He had created that untenable situation and brutally ditched her when he had had enough of it but his admission didn't come anywhere near soothing the tight ball of hurt in her belly. 'You could have talked to me personally,' she pointed out, refusing to drop the subject.

'I've never talked about stuff like that. I wouldn't know where to begin,' Angel confessed grimly.

'Well, how could you possibly forge a worthwhile bond with a daughter, then?' Merry pressed. 'The minute she annoys you or offends you will you turn your back on her the way you turned your back on me?'

Angel flashed her a seethingly angry appraisal. 'Not for one minute have you and that baby been out of my mind since the day you told me you were pregnant! I did not turn my back on you. I made proper provision for both of you.'

'Yeah, you threw money at us to keep us at a safe distance, yet now here you are breaking your own rules,' Merry whispered shakily.

'What is the point of us wrangling like this?' Angel questioned with rank impatience. 'This is no longer about you and I. This involves a third person with rights of her own even if she is still only a baby. Will you allow me to meet my daughter this afternoon?'

'Apart from everything else—like it being immaterial to you that I hate and distrust you,' Merry framed with thin restraint, 'today's out of the question. I've got a date this afternoon and we're going out.'

Angel tensed, long, powerful muscles pulling taut. He could not explain why he was shocked by the idea of her having a date. Maybe he had been guilty of assuming that she was too busy being a mother at present to worry about enjoying a social life. But the concept of her enjoying herself with another man inexplicably outraged and infuriated him and the vision of her bedding another man when he had been the first, the *only*, made him want to smash something.

His lean brown hands clenched into fists. 'A date?' he queried as jaggedly as if he had a piece of glass in his throat.

Merry stood up behind the desk and squared her slim shoulders. 'Yes, he's taking us to the beach. You have a problem with that as well?'

Us? The realisation that another man, some random, unknown stranger, had access to his daughter when he did not heaped coals of fire on Angel's proud head. He snatched in a stark breath, fighting with all his might to cage his hot temper and his bitterness. 'Yes, I do. Can't you leave her with your aunt and grant me even ten minutes with my own child?' he demanded rawly.

'I'm afraid there isn't time today.' Merry swallowed

the lump in her throat, that reminder that Elyssa had rights of her own still filtering back through her like a storm warning, making her appreciate that every decision she made now would have to be explained and defended to satisfy her daughter's questions some years down the road. And just how mean could she afford to be to Angel before her daughter would question her attitude? Question whether her mother had given her daughter's personal needs sufficient weight and importance? Her tummy dive-bombed, her former conviction that she was totally in the right taking a massive dent.

Nobody was ever totally in the right, she reminded herself reluctantly. There were always two sides to every story, every conflict. She was letting herself be influenced by her own feelings, not looking towards the future when Elyssa would demand answers to certain tough questions relating to her father. And did she really want to put herself in the position of having refused to allow her daughter's flesh and blood to even *see* her? Dully it dawned on her that that could well be a step too far in hostilities. Angel had hurt *her*, but that was not indisputable proof that he would hurt his daughter.

'Pick another day this week,' she invited him stiffly, watching surprise and comprehension leap like golden flames into his vivid eyes. 'But you make your arrangements with me, not through your lawyers. You visit for an hour. Let's not raise the bar too high, let's keep it simple. I won't let you take her out

anywhere without me and I don't want you arriving
with some fancy nanny in tow.'

His dramatic dark eyes shone bright, a tiny muscle
jerking taut at the corner of his wide, sensual mouth.
He swung away, momentarily turning his back on
her before swinging back and nodding sombrely in
agreement with her strictures. But in those revealing few seconds she had recognised the stormy flare
of anticipation in his stunning gaze, finally registering that he *had* been serious in his approach and that
he did genuinely want to meet his infant daughter.

'Tomorrow morning, then,' Angel pronounced
decisively. 'We'll take it from there.'

Take what from where? she almost questioned but
she ducked it, worn out by the sheer stress of dealing
with him. Inside herself she was trembling with the
strain of standing straight and unafraid and hiding
her fearful anxiety from him because she knew that
Angel would pounce on weakness like a shark catching the scent of blood. 'About ten,' she suggested
carefully. 'I have someone to see at half eleven.'

Angel gritted his even white teeth, wanting to ask
if she was seeing the boyfriend again, but he had no
intention of being foolish enough to ask questions
he had no right to demand answers to. She had been
under covert surveillance for weeks and he would
soon identify the boyfriend from the records he had
yet to examine. His mouth quirked because he knew
she would be outraged if she knew he was paying a
private firm to watch her every move.

But, when it came to protecting a member of the

Valtinos family, Angel had no inhibitions. Hired security was as much a part of his life as it was for his mother. Safety came first and his daughter would be at risk of kidnapping were anyone to work out who had fathered her. It was his duty to safeguard his child and he would not apologise for the necessity.

Merry opened the office door to urge him out and followed him to where the limousine sat parked. 'I live in the cottage at the front gate,' she informed him.

'I thought you lived with your aunt,' Angel admitted with a frown.

'When I became a mother I thought it was time for us to get our own space. Sybil practically raised me. I didn't want her to feel that she had to do the same for my daughter,' Merry confided ruefully.

In the summer sunlight she studied Angel's lean, strong face, marvelling at the sleek symmetry of the hard cheekbones and hollows that enhanced his very masculine features. He was a literal work of art. It was little wonder that she had overreacted to his interest and refused to accept how shallow that interest was, she told herself squarely, struggling to calm the stabs of worry that erupted at the prospect of having any further dealings with him.

She would cope. She *had* to cope. So far she had contrived to cope with everything Angel Valtinos had thrown at her, she reminded herself with pride. As long as she remembered who and what he was, she would be fine…wouldn't she?

CHAPTER FOUR

'LETTING ELYSSA'S FATHER visit is the right way to go,' Fergus opined, scrutinising her troubled face with concern before turning to gaze out to sea. 'He treated you badly but that doesn't automatically mean he'll be a bad father. Only time will answer that.'

Merry went pink. As Fergus had combined picking her up with an examination of the latest arrival at the rescue centre, he had heard about the fuss created by Angel's visit earlier in the day and had naturally asked her about it. She looked up at Fergus, drawn by his calm and acceptance of her situation, wondering if it was possible to feel anything or even trust a man again. Fergus stood about an inch under six feet. He had cropped brown hair and cheerful blue eyes and she had never heard him so much as raise his voice while she had already witnessed his compassion and regret when he was treating abused animals.

'Are you over him?' Fergus asked her bluntly.

Merry vented a shaken laugh. 'I certainly hope so.'

And then he kissed her, wrapping her close in the

sea breeze, and she froze only momentarily in surprise. Suddenly she found herself wanting to feel more than she actually felt because he was a good guy, ostensibly straightforward and as different from Angel as day was to night. Angel was all twists and turns, dark corners and unpredictability and she had never had any genuine hope of a future with him. Furthermore, Angel had never been her type. He wasn't steady or open or even ready to settle down with conventional expectations. Feelings were foreign and threatening to Angel yet he bristled with untamed emotion. As Fergus freed her mouth and kept an arm anchored to her spine she realised in horror-stricken dismay that she'd spent their entire kiss thinking about Angel and her face burned in shame and discomfiture.

Angel sat in his limo and perused the photo that had been sent to his phone while he angrily wondered if he was a masochist or, indeed, developing sad stalker tendencies. But no, he had to deal with the situation as it was, not as he would've preferred it to be. Even worse, Merry had just upped the stakes, ensuring that Angel had now to raise his game. He wanted to stalk down to that beach and beat the hell out of the opposition. Because that was what Fergus Wickham was: opposition, *serious* opposition.

And naturally, Angel was confident that he was not jealous. After all, with only one exception, he had never experienced jealousy. He had, however, once cherished a singularly pathetic desire for his mother to take as much of an interest in him as she took in her toy boys. He *had* only been about seven years old at the time, he reminded himself forgivingly, and a distinctly naïve child, fondly expecting that, his having spent all term at boarding school, his mother would make him the centre of her loving attention when he finally came home.

Well, he wasn't that naïve now, Angel acknowledged grimly. From his earliest years he had witnessed how fleeting love was for a Valtinos. A Valtinos *bought* love, paid well for its upkeep, got bored in exactly that order. His mother ran through young men as a lawnmower ran through grass. By the time Angel was in his twenties he was dealing with blackmail attempts, compromising photos and sordid scandals all on his mother's behalf. His mother had tremendous charm but she remained as immature and irresponsible as a teenager. Even so, she was the only mother he would ever have and at heart he was fond of her.

But he didn't get jealous or possessive of lovers because he didn't ever get attached to them or develop expectations of them. Expectations *always* led to disappointment. Merry, however, was in a different category because she was the mother of his daughter and Angel didn't want her to have another man in her life. That was a matter of simple good sense. Another man would divide her loyalties, take her focus off her child and invite unflattering comparisons…

'You heard the pitter patter of tiny feet and literally ran for the hills,' his brother Vitale had summed up a week earlier. 'Not a very promising beginning.'

No, it wasn't, Angel conceded wrathfully while endlessly scrutinising that photo in which his daughter appeared only as a small indistinct blob anchored in a pram. He had screwed up but he was a terrific strategist and unstoppable once he had a goal. He didn't even need an angle because his daughter was all the ammunition he required. Was Merry sleeping with that guy yet? Angel smouldered and scowled, beginning for the first time to scroll through the records he had studiously ignored to respect Merry's privacy. To hell with that scruple, he thought angrily. He had to fight to protect what was *his*.

'So, how are you planning to play it with Elyssa's father tomorrow?' Sybil asked that evening, having tried and failed to get much out of her niece concerning the date with Fergus.

Merry shrugged. 'Cool, calm...'

'He's impossibly headstrong and obstinate,' her aunt pronounced with disapproval. 'I only cocked the gun because I didn't want him landing on your doorstep unannounced but he wouldn't take no for an answer.'

'He isn't familiar with the word no,' Merry mused ruefully. 'I do wish I'd treated him to it last year.'

'Do you really wish you didn't have Elyssa?'

Merry flushed and, thinking about that, shook her head in dismissal. 'I thought I would when I was pregnant but once she was here, everything changed.'

'Maybe it changed for Angel as well. Maybe he wasn't lying about that. He does value family ties,' Sybil remarked.

Merry frowned. 'How do you know that?'

Sybil reddened, her eyes evasive. 'Well, you told me he meets up with his father twice a month and never cancels…and naturally I've read about his mother, Angelina's exploits in the newspapers. She's a real nut-job—rich, stupid, fickle. If he's still close to her, he has a high tolerance threshold for embarrassment. She's not far off my age and the men in her bed are getting younger by the year.'

Merry's eyes widened. 'I had no idea.'

'Shallow sexual relationships are all he saw growing up, all he's ever had as an example to follow. It's hardly surprising that he is the way he is. I won't excuse him for the way he treated you but I do see that he doesn't know any better,' Sybil completed, recognising Merry's surprise. 'But you could teach him different.'

'I don't think you can domesticate a wild animal.'

Sybil rolled her eyes. 'Elyssa has enough charisma to stop a charging rhinoceros.'

Merry tossed and turned in her bed, despising herself for her nervous tension. Angel had cast a long shadow over her afternoon with Fergus, depriving her of relaxation and appreciation. She had made hateful, unforgivable comparisons. On some secret, thoroughly inexcusable level, she still craved the buzz of excitement that Angel had filled her with and that unsettled and shamed her. After all, once the excitement had gone she had been left pregnant and alone and now her memory trailed back fifteen months...

Discovering that she was pregnant had proved a real shock for Merry because she had not seriously considered that that single accident was likely to result in conception and had hoped for the best. She had barely settled into a new and very challenging job, and falling pregnant had seemed like the worst possible news. She had suffered from severe morning sickness and at one stage had even feared she was on the brink of having a miscarriage. She had waited until she was over three months along before she'd even tried to contact Angel to tell him that she was carrying his child. She had never had his personal mobile number and had never got to speak to him when she'd phoned the office, suspecting that calls from her were on some discreet forbidden list. The prospect of sending a letter or an email that would probably be opened and read by a former colleague had made her cringe. In the end she had used her working knowledge of Angel's diary and had headed to the hotel where he met his father for lunch twice a month.

That unwise but desperate move had put in motion the most humiliating, wounding encounter of Merry's life. Angel had had a very tall and beautiful blonde with him when he entered the bar, a blonde with bare breasts on display under a gauzy see-through dress. She had looked like the sort of woman who didn't ever wear underwear and every man in the place had stared lustfully at her, while she'd clung to Angel's arm and giggled and touched him with easy confidence. Just looking at her, Merry had felt sick and ugly and plain and boring because pregnancy had not been kind to her. Her body had already been swelling and thickening, her eyes had been shadowed because she couldn't sleep and the smell of most foods had made her nauseous. She had stayed concealed in the bar behind a book and round a corner while Angel, his companion and eventually his father had sat down to lunch on an outside terrace.

If Angel had not reappeared at the bar alone, she would probably simply have gone back to work without even trying to achieve her goal. But when she'd seen him she had forced herself up out of her seat and forward.

'I have to speak to you in private,' she had said. 'It's very important. It will only take five minutes.'

He had spun back from the bar to appraise her with cool, guarded eyes. 'I'm listening.'

'Could we go out into the foyer?' she had pressed, very conscious of the number of people around them. 'It would be more private.'

He had acquiesced with unconcealed reluctance. 'What is this about?' he had demanded as soon as they'd got there.

And then she had made her announcement and those expressive beautiful eyes of his had glittered like cold black diamonds, his consternation and annoyance obvious.

'Do you want it?' he had asked doubtingly, earning her hatred with every syllable of that leading question. 'Scratch that. It was politically incorrect. Of course, I will support you in whatever choice you make.' He had drawn out a business card and thrust it into her unwilling hand. 'I will inform my lawyers. Please provide them with contact details and I will make provision for you.'

And that had been Angel's knee-jerk response to unexpected fatherhood: brief and brutal and wholly unemotional and objective. *Go away and I'll give you cash to keep you quiet and at a distance.*

Remembering that encounter, Merry shuddered and tears stung her eyes afresh. That was the final moment when she had faced the reality that she had given her body to a ruthlessly detached man without a heart. How could she let such a man come within ten feet of her precious, loving daughter? That question kept her awake until dawn. Suddenly keeping the peace and giving Angel another chance seemed the stuff of stupidity.

Having done his baby research diligently before his visit, Angel believed he was prepared for all eventualities. His second cousin had six-month-old twins and a toddler and lived in London. It was hard to say who had been most startled by his interest: his cousin at the shock of his curiosity or Angel at finding himself festooned in wriggling babies, who cried, pooped and threw up while poking and pulling at him. There were loads of babies in his extended family circle but Angel had always given them a very wide berth.

He put on his oldest jeans for the occasion and, after consulting his cousin, he purchased only one modest gift. Merry wouldn't be impressed by a toyshop splurge. She was already saving every penny he was giving her into a trust for their daughter. Merry and her endless rainy-day fund, he thought incredulously, deeming her joyless, fearful attitude to spending money depressing. She was a natural-born hoarder of cash. If only his mother suffered from the same insecurity, he conceded wryly.

From upstairs, Merry watched the sleek, expensive car pull into the driveway. She had dressed smartly that morning. After all she had a potential new client coming at half eleven and she needed to look professional, so her hair was freshly washed, her make-up was on and she wore a summer dress that clung to her slender curves. What she wore had nothing whatsoever to do with Angel's visit, except in so far as looking smart lifted her confidence, she told herself soothingly.

Angel sprang fluidly out of his car, his lean, powerful body clad in black jeans and a green sweater that was undoubtedly cashmere. He found English summers cold. She carried Elyssa downstairs. Her daughter wore one of the fashionable baby outfits that Sybil often bought her, a pretty blue floral tunic and leggings that reflected her eyes. The door knocker rapped twice and she hastily settled Elyssa down on the rug before rushing breathlessly back to the door, scolding herself for the unmistakeable sense of anticipation gripping her.

Angel stepped in and his stunning dark golden gaze locked to her with the most electrifying immediacy. Tension leapt through Merry along with a growing unease about the decision she had made. He looked amazing. He *always* looked amazing, she reminded herself mockingly, striving not to react in any way. But it was impossible. Her breath shortened in her tightening throat and her breasts tingled and a sensual warmth made her thighs press together.

Angel's scrutiny roamed from the glossy bell of her dark hair, down to the modest neckline of the dress that clung to the delectably full swell of her breasts, before skimming down over her waist to define the feminine swell of her hips. He didn't let himself look at her legs because she had fantastic legs and the heat pooling in his groin didn't need that added encouragement. He didn't know how she had contrived to get skinnier and at the same time more interestingly curvy but he especially didn't like the feeling of being sexually drawn against his will.

'Elyssa's in here,' she framed stiffly.

'That's a Greek name.'

'Yes, she's entitled to a Greek name,' Merry proclaimed defensively.

'I wasn't…criticising.' Angel registered the white-knuckled grip she had on the edge of the door and recognised that he would be treading on eggshells every time he spoke. He gritted his teeth on the awareness but as Merry pushed the door fully open he finally saw his daughter and for several timeless moments stayed rigid in the doorway drinking in the sight of her.

'She's got my hair,' he almost whispered, moving forward and then dropping down onto the rug a couple of feet from his daughter. 'But curls look cute on her...'

Merry watched him closely, registering that he had enough sense not to try to get too familiar too fast with a baby that didn't know him. No, Angel was far too clever to make an obvious wrong move, she reflected bitterly, before catching herself up on that suspicious but hardly charitable thought and crossing the room to go into the kitchen. 'Coffee?'

'If it's not too much trouble.'

'Don't go all polite on me,' she said drily.

'What do you expect?' Angel shot her a sardonic glance of rebuke. 'I know you don't want me here.'

Merry paled at that blunt statement. 'I'm trying not to feel like that.'

She put on the kettle and watched him remove a toy from his pocket, a brightly coloured teething toy, which he set on the rug at his feet. It was a strategic move and Elyssa quickly fulfilled his expectations by extending the toy she held to him in the hope of gaining access to the new and more interesting one. Angel accepted it and handed over his gift. Elyssa chortled with satisfaction and bestowed a huge smile on him before sticking the new toy into her mouth and chewing happily on it.

'She has your eyes,' Angel remarked. 'She's incredibly pretty.'

In spite of her desire to remain unmoved, Merry flushed with pride. 'I think so too.'

'She's also unmistakeably mine,' Angel intoned with unashamed approval.

'Well, you already knew that,' Merry could not resist reminding him. 'She was DNA tested after she was born.'

Angel winced. 'I never once doubted that the child you were carrying was mine but in view of inheritance rights…and us not being married…it was best to have it legally confirmed.' He hesitated before turning his classic bronzed profile to study her levelly. 'But I let the lawyers take over and run the whole show and that was a mistake. I see that now.'

Merry jerked her chin in acknowledgement, not trusting herself to speak.

'I didn't know any other way to handle it,' Angel admitted grimly. 'I took the easy way out… unfortunately the easy way turned out to be the wrong way.'

Taken aback by that admission, Merry dragged in a ragged breath and turned away to make the coffee. A fat burst of chuckles from her daughter made her flip back and she saw Elyssa bouncing on the rug, held steady by Angel's hands and revelling in both the exercise and the attention.

When Elyssa tired of that, Angel turned out her

toy box for her. Tiger slunk out from under the chair where he had been hiding since Angel's arrival and moved hesitantly closer to investigate.

'*Diavolos!*' Angel exclaimed in surprise. 'Where did the dog come from?'

Startled by Angel's deep voice, Tiger shot back under the chair.

'He's been here all along. His name's Tiger.'

'Kind of nervous for a dog called Tiger and hardly a stream-lined predator.'

'OK. He's fat, you can say it. He's addicted to food and he wasn't socialised properly when he was young. He came from a puppy farm that was closed down,' Merry volunteered, extending a cup of black coffee to Angel as he vaulted lithely upright, suddenly dominating the small room with his height and the breadth of his shoulders.

'I didn't know you were keen on dogs.'

'I practically grew up helping in the rescue centre.' Merry could hear herself gabbling because her heart was pounding wildly in her chest as Angel moved towards her and even breathing was a challenge beneath the onslaught of his gleaming dark golden eyes. 'I—'

'Tell it like it is,' Angel urged sibilantly.

Her smooth brow furrowed. 'What are you talking about?'

'You still want me as much as I want you,' he breathed huskily, sipping his coffee as if he were merely making casual conversation.

'I don't want to have that sort of discussion with

you,' Merry told him curtly, colour burnishing her cheeks as she wondered if he really could tell that easily that she was still vulnerable around him. Not that she would do anything about it or let *him* do anything about it, she reasoned with pride. Attraction was nothing more than a hormonal trick and, in her case, a very dangerous misdirection.

'Avoid? Deny?' Angel derided, his beautiful wilful mouth curling, his smouldering gaze enhanced by unfairly long black lashes welded to her fast-reddening face. 'What's the point?'

'If you continue this I'm going to ask you to leave,' Merry warned thinly.

And genuine amusement engulfed Angel and laughter lit up his lean, dark features. 'I'm not about to pounce on you with our daughter watching! Believe me, while she's around, you're safe,' he assured her smoothly.

Inexplicably that little exchange made Merry feel foolish and rather as though she had ended up with egg on her face, which was burning like a furnace. Even now, many months after the event, she couldn't laugh about what had happened between them. Looking back, it was as if blinding sunlight overlaid and blurred the explosive passion she couldn't begin to explain and never wanted to experience again. Unfortunately for her, her body had a different ambition. One glimpse of Angel's darkly handsome face and long, sleek, muscular frame and she was as tense as a bowstring, caught between forbidden pleasure at his sheer physical beauty and angry self-loathing at her susceptibility to it.

'I brought lunch with me,' Angel revealed, startling her.

Her eyes widened. 'But I have a client due.'

'I'll return in an hour. You know we need to talk about Elyssa and how we move on from here,' Angel pointed out as if it were the most reasonable and natural thing in the world when in truth they had never ever talked about anything.

'Yes…yes, of course,' she muttered uneasily, because she could see that a talk made sense and it was surely better to get it all over in one go and in one day, she told herself soothingly. 'I should be free in an hour, but—'

'I'll make it an hour and a half,' Angel cut in decisively as he moved towards the door.

Merry skimmed his arm with an uncertain finger to attract his attention. 'I'm afraid Elyssa has… er…stained your sweater,' she told him awkwardly.

His amused grin flashed perfect white teeth and enhanced the sculpted fullness of his wide, sensual mouth. 'It's not a problem. I brought a change of clothes with me.'

'My goodness, you were organised,' she mumbled in surprise as he strode down the path and leant down into his car, straightening to peel off the offending sweater and expose the flexing muscles of his bronzed and powerful torso. Her mouth ran dry and she stared, watching him pull on another sweater, black this time, before she closed the door.

She ignored her reeling senses to concentrate on what was truly important. Angel was unpredictable, she reminded herself worriedly, devious to a fault and dangerously volatile. What did he truly want from her? Why was he putting himself to so much trouble? *Lunch?* All of a sudden he was bringing her lunch? Merry was stunned by the concept and the planning that must have gone into that. Did Angel really want access to his daughter *that* badly? Did he have sufficient interest and staying power to want a long-term relationship with his daughter? And where did that leave her when she really didn't want Angel to feature *anywhere* in her life?

You should've thought of that before you let him visit, Merry told herself in exasperation. Possibly Angel was only trying to smooth over the hostilities between them. And possibly she was a suspicious little shrew, still bitter and battered from her previous encounters with him. At the very least she ought to acknowledge that she would never ever second-guess Angel Valtinos and that he would always take her by surprise. After all, that was how he did business and how he thrived in a cut-throat world.

CHAPTER FIVE

MERRY SHOOK HANDS with her new client, who had got into a mess with his tax returns, and promised to update him on the situation within the week. Soon she would have to try to fit in a refresher course to update her knowledge of recent legislative changes, she reflected thoughtfully, incredibly keen to think of anything other than the awareness that Angel was sliding supple as a dancer out of his car as her visitor departed.

Sybil had swooped in to take enthusiastic charge of Elyssa soon after Angel's earlier departure. Hearing of the lunch plan, she had laughed and drily observed, 'He's treating you to a charm offensive. Well, if you must have a serious talk with him, it'll be easier not to have Elyssa grizzling for her lunch and her nap in the midst of it. Phone me when you want to steal her back.'

And once again, Merry had reflected how very, very lucky she had always been to have Sybil in her life, standing by her when life was tough, advising and supporting her, in short being the only caring mother figure that she had ever known. Sybil had cured the hurts inflicted by her kid sister's lack of interest in and impatience with her child and, although Merry knew her aunt had been disappointed when she became pregnant without being in a serious relationship, she had kept her disappointment to herself and had instead focused her attention on how best to help her expectant niece.

'Lunch,' Angel told her carelessly, carting a large luxurious hamper in one hand.

'I've got a terrace out the back. Since it's sunny, we might as well eat there,' Merry suggested, preferring the idea of that casual setting in which she thought Angel would be less intimidating.

'This is unexpectedly pleasant,' Angel remarked, sprawling down with innate grace on a wrought-iron chair and taking in the pleasant view of fields and wooded hills visible beyond the hedge.

'This was Sybil's Christmas surprise for us,' Merry explained. 'Her last tenant was elderly and the garden was overgrown. Sybil hired someone to fix it up and now Elyssa will have somewhere safe to play when she's more mobile.'

'You're very close to your aunt,' Angel commented warily. 'She doesn't like me.'

Crystalline blue eyes collided with his in challenge. 'What did you expect?' she traded.

Angel had not been prepared to meet with a condemnation that bold and unapologetic and his teeth clenched, squaring his aggressive jaw, the faint dark shadow of stubble already roughening his bronzed skin accentuating the hard slant of his shapely mouth.

'Yes, you ensured I had enough money to survive but that was that,' Merry stated before he could remind her of the reality.

Angel sidestepped that deeply controversial issue by ignoring it. Instead he opened the hamper and stacked utensils and dishes on the table and asked where his daughter was. After all, what could he say about his treatment of Merry? The facts were the facts and he couldn't change them. He knew he had done everything wrong and he had acknowledged that. Didn't his honesty and his regret lighten the scales even a little? Was she expecting him to grovel on hands and knees?

'Wow…this is some spread,' Merry remarked uneasily as she set out the food and he uncorked the bottle of wine and filled the glasses with rich red liquid. 'Where did it come from?'

'From one of my hotels,' Angel responded with the nonchalance that was the sole preserve of the very rich.

Merry placed a modest selection of savoury bites on her plate and said tensely, 'What did you want to discuss?'

'Our future,' Angel delivered succinctly while Tiger sat at his feet with little round pleading eyes pinned to the meat on his fork.

'Nobody can foretell the future,' Merry objected.

'I can where we're concerned,' Angel assured her, every liquid syllable cool as ice. 'Either we spend at least the next ten years fighting it out over Elyssa in court *or*…we get married and *share* her.'

Merry studied him over the top of her wine glass with steadily widening pale blue eyes, and then gulped in more wine than she intended and coughed and spluttered in the most embarrassing manner as she struggled to get a grip on her wildly fluctuating emotions. First he had frightened the life out of her by mentioning a court battle over her beloved daughter, and then he'd sent her spinning with a suggestion she had never dreamt that she would hear from his lips.

'*Married?*' she emphasised with a curled lip. 'Are you crazy or just trying to unnerve me?'

Having forced himself to pull the pin on the marriage grenade straight away, Angel coiled back in his chair and savoured his wine. 'It's an unnerving idea for me as well. Apart from my mother, who wanders in and out of my properties, I've never lived with a woman before,' he admitted curtly. 'But we do need to think creatively to solve our current problems.'

'I don't have any problems right now. I also can't believe that you want Elyssa so much after one little meeting that you would sink to what is virtually blackmail,' Merry framed coldly, eyes glinting like chipped ice in the sunlight.

'Oh, I would sink a lot lower than that and I think you know it,' Angel traded without shame, unyielding dark golden eyes steady with stubborn resolve. 'I will do whatever I have to do to get what I want…

or in this case to ensure that my daughter benefits from a suitable home.'

'But Elyssa already *has* a suitable home,' Merry pointed out, working hard to stay calm and appear untouched by his threat of legal intervention. 'We're happy here. I have work that I can do at home and we have a decent life.'

'Only not by my standards. Elyssa is my heir and will one day be a very wealthy woman. When you're so prejudiced against spending my money, how do you expect her to adapt to my world when she becomes independent?' he demanded with lethal cool.

Merry compressed her sultry mouth and lifted angrily out of her seat. 'I'm not prejudiced!' she protested. 'I didn't want to *depend* on your money. I simply prefer to stand on my own feet.'

Angel dealt her a perceptive appraisal that made her skin tighten uneasily over her bones. 'Like me, you have trust issues and you're very proud.'

'Don't you tell me that I have trust issues when you know absolutely nothing about me!' Merry practically spat back at him in her fury. 'Newsflash, Angel…we had two sexual encounters, *not* a relationship!'

Angel ran lingering hooded dark eyes over her slender figure and her aggressive stance, remembering that fire in bed, how it had stoked his own and resulted in a conflagration more passionate than anything he had ever known. As a rule, she kept that fire hidden, suppressed beneath her tranquil, prissy little surface, but around him she couldn't manage that feat and he cherished that truth. Anger was much more promising than indifference.

Merry planted her hands on her curvy hips and flung him a fierce look of censure. 'And don't you *dare* look at me like that!' she warned him, helplessly conscious of that smouldering sexual assessment. 'It's rude and inappropriate.'

Angel shifted lithely in his chair, murderously aware of his roaring arousal and the tightness of his jeans and marvelling at the reality that he could actually be enjoying himself in her company, difficult though she was. A slow-burning smile slashed his lean, strong face. 'The burn is still there, *glyka mou*,' he told her. 'But let's concentrate our energies on my solution for our future.'

'That wasn't a solution, that was fanciful nonsense!' Merry hissed back at him. 'You don't want to marry me. You don't want to marry anybody!'

'But I'll do it for Elyssa's benefit because I believe that she needs a father as much as she needs a mother,' Angel asserted levelly. 'A father is not expendable. My father was very important in my life, even though he wasn't able to be there for me as much as he would have liked.'

Unprepared for that level of honesty and gravity from a man as naturally secretive and aloof as Angel, Merry was bemused. 'I never said you were expendable, for goodness' sake,' she argued less angrily. 'That's why I let you finally visit and meet her.'

'How much of a relationship did you have with your own father?' Angel enquired lethally.

Merry's face froze. 'I didn't have one. My mother, Natalie, fell pregnant by her boss and he was married. I met him once but his wife couldn't stand the sight of me, probably because I was the proof of his infidelity,' she conceded uncomfortably. 'He never asked to see me again. When it came to making a choice between me and his wife, naturally he chose his wife.'

'I'm sorry.' Angel disconcerted her with a look of sympathy that hurt her pride as much as a slap would have done.

'Well, I'm not. I got by fine without him,' Merry declared, lifting her chin.

'Maybe you did.' Angel trailed out the word, letting her know he wasn't convinced by her face-saving claim. 'But others don't do so well without paternal guidance. My own mother grew up indulged in every financial way, but essentially without parents who cared enough about her to discipline her. She's well past fifty now, although she doesn't look it, but she's still a rebellious teenager in her own head. I want my daughter to have stability. I don't want her to go wild when she becomes an adult with the world at her feet along with every temptation.'

Involuntarily impressed by that argument, Merry shook her head. 'That's a long way off and if I don't stand in the way of her having a relationship with you now, you'll still be around.'

Angel lounged back in his chair and crossed an ankle over one knee, long, powerful thigh muscles flexing below tight, faded denim. He looked outrageously relaxed, as if he were posing for a publicity shot, and drop-dead gorgeous from the spill of glossy black curls to the golden caramel brilliance of his eyes. Merry dragged her guilty gaze from his thighs and his crotch, sudden heat rising inside her and burning her cheeks. His hard-boned, thoroughly raunchy masculine beauty broke through her defences every time she looked at him and it made her feel like a breathless fan girl.

'But the bottom line is that unless we marry I won't be around *enough*,' Angel intoned with grim emphasis. 'I spend at least fifty per cent of the year abroad. I want her to meet my relatives and learn what it means to be a Valtinos…'

He could have said nothing more calculated to cool Merry's fevered response to him. Dismay filled her because she understood the message he was giving her. As soon as Elyssa was old enough, Angel would be spiriting her out to Greece, taking her away from her mother, leaving Merry behind, shorn of control of what happened in her child's life. It was a sobering prospect.

'Did you mean it…what you said about fighting me in court?' Merry prompted angrily.

'For once in my life I was playing it straight,' Angel declared.

'But where the heck did all this suddenly come from?' Merry demanded in heated denial. 'You didn't want anything to do with us last winter!'

'It took time for me to come to terms with how I felt about fatherhood. At first I thought the most important objective was to conserve my world as it was. I thought I could turn my back on you and my child but I found that I couldn't,' Angel breathed in a roughened undertone as though the words were being extracted forcibly from him. 'I couldn't stop thinking about her...or you.'

'Me?' Merry gasped in sharp disbelief. 'Why would you have been thinking about me?'

Angel lifted and dropped a broad shoulder in questioning doubt. 'So, I'm human. Learning that a woman is carrying your child is an unexpectedly powerful discovery—'

'Angel,' Merry cut in without hesitation, 'let's come back down to earth here. Learning that I was pregnant sent you into retreat so fast you left a smoke trail in your wake!'

'And all I learned was that there was no place to run from reality,' Angel countered with sardonic bite. 'I fought my curiosity for a long time before I finally gave way to it and asked to see her. You said no repeatedly but here we are now, supposedly acting like adults. I'm *trying* to be honest... I'm *trying* not to threaten you but I've come to see marriage as the best option for all three of us.'

'You threatened me quite deliberately!' Merry slung at him furiously.

'You need to know that I'm serious and that this is not some whim that will go away if you wait for long enough. I'm here to stay in your lives,' Angel intoned harshly.

'Well, that's going to be rather awkward when it's

not what I want and I will fight you every step of the way!' Merry flung back at him. 'You wanted me out of your life and I got out. You can't force me back.'

'If it means my daughter gets the future she deserves, I will force you,' Angel bit out in a raw, wrathful undertone as he plunged upright, casting a long dark shadow over the table. 'You need to accept that this is not just about you and me any more, it's about *her*!'

Merry paled. 'I do accept that.'

'No, you don't. You're still set on punishing me for the selfish decisions I made and that approach isn't going to get us anywhere. I don't *want* to go to court and fight but I *will* if I have no alternative!' Angel shot at her furiously, dark golden eyes scorching, his Greek accent edging every vowel with piercing sibilance in the afternoon stillness. 'When I asked you to marry me I was trying to show respect!'

'You wouldn't know respect if it bit you on the arse!' Merry flamed back at him with helpless vulgarity. 'And I am so sorry I didn't grovel with gratitude at the offer of a wedding ring the way you obviously expected.'

'No, you're not sorry!' Angel roared back at her equally loudly. 'You enjoyed dragging me over the coals, questioning my motivation and commitment, and not for one minute did you seriously consider what I was offering...'

'Stop shouting at me!' Merry warned him, reeling in shock from that sudden volatile surge of anger from him, not having appreciated that that rage could lie so close to his seemingly cool surface.

'I've said sorry every damn way I know how but you're after revenge, not a way forward, and there's nothing I can do to change that!' Angel growled, throwing open the back door to go back into the house and leave.

There was sufficient truth in that stormy welter of accusations to draw Merry up short and make her question her attitude. 'I'm not after revenge…that's ridiculous!' she protested weakly, closing a staying hand over his arm as he shot her yet another murderous smouldering glance before turning back to the door.

Sorry every damn way I know how rang afresh in her ears and tightened her grip on his muscular forearm. 'Angel, please…let's calm down.'

'For what good reason would I calm down?' Angel raked down at her. 'This was a pointless attempt on my part to change things between us.'

Her teeth were chattering with nerves. 'Yes, I can see that but you storming off in a rage is only going to make things worse,' she muttered ruefully. 'Maybe I haven't been fair to you, maybe I haven't given you a decent hearing, but you came at me with this like a rocket out of nowhere and I don't adapt quickly to new ideas the way you do!'

'You adapted fast enough to me in bed!' Angel husked with sizzling clarity.

'That's your massive ego talking!' Merry launched back at him irately.

'No, it's not,' Angel growled, yanking her up against him, shifting his lithe hips, ensuring she recognised how turned-on he was. 'You make me want you.'

'It's *my* fault?' Merry carolled in disbelief even as her whole body tilted into his, as magnetised by his arousal as a thirsty plant suddenly placed within reach of water. Little tremors were running through her as she struggled to get a grip on the prickling tightness of her nipples and the heat building between her thighs. An unbearable ache followed that she positively shrank from reliving in his vicinity. She wanted to slap herself, she wanted to slap him, she wanted to freeze the moment and replay it *her* way, in which she would draw back from him in withering disgust and say something terribly clever and wounding that would hold him at bay.

'You just can't bring yourself to admit that you're the same,' Angel gritted, bending his arrogant dark head, one hand meshing into the tumble of her hair to drag her head back and expose her throat. His mouth found that slender corded column and nipped and tasted up to her ear, awakening a shower of tingling sensation, and she was electrified and dizzy with longing, wanting what she knew she shouldn't, wanting with a hunger suppressed and denied for too many months, craving the release he could give.

And then he kissed her, crushing her ripe mouth, his tongue plunging and retreating, and she saw stars and whirling multicoloured planets behind her lowered lids while her body fizzed like a firework display, leaving her weak with hunger. She kissed him back, hands rising to delve into the crisp luxuriance of his hair, framing, holding, *needing*. It was frantic, out of control, the way it always was for them.

Angel wrenched her back from him, long brown fingers biting into her slim shoulders to keep her upright and gazing up into his blazing liquid-honey eyes. 'No, I'm not a one-trick pony or a cheap one-night stand. You'll have to marry me to get any more of that,' he told her with derision as he slapped a business card down on the table. 'My phone number...should you think better of your attitude today.'

When he was gone, Merry paced back and forth in her small sitting room, facing certain realities. She hadn't seriously considered Angel's supposed solution. But then that was more his fault than her own. Warning her that he intended to trail her into court and fight for access to their daughter had scarcely acted as a good introduction to his alternative offer. She was angry and bitter and she wasn't about to apologise for the fact, but possibly she should have listened and asked more and lost her temper less.

In addition, Angel's visit had worsened rather than improved their relations because now she knew he was prepared to drag her through the courts in an effort to win greater access to Elyssa. And what if his ambitions did not stop there? What if he intended to try and gain sole custody of their daughter and take Elyssa away from her? Paling and breathing rapidly, Merry decided to visit her aunt and discuss her mounting concern and sense of being under threat with her.

Sybil, however, was nowhere to be found in the comfortable open-plan ground floor of her home and it was only when Merry heard her daughter that she realised her aunt and her daughter were upstairs. She was disconcerted to walk into Sybil's bedroom where Elyssa was playing on the floor and find her aunt trailing clothes out of the wardrobes to pile into the two suitcases sitting open on the bed.

'My goodness, where are you going?' Merry demanded in surprise.

Sybil dealt her a shamefaced glance. 'I meant to phone you but I had so many other calls to make that I didn't get a chance. Your mother's in trouble and I'm flying out to Perth to be with her,' she told her.

Merry blinked in astonishment. 'Trouble?' she queried.

Sybil grimaced. 'Keith's been having an affair and he's walked out on your mother. She's suicidal, poor lamb.'

'Oh, dear,' Merry framed, sinking down on the edge of the bed to lift her daughter onto her lap. She was sad to hear that news, but her troubled relationship with her dysfunctional parent prevented her from feeling truly sympathetic and that fact always filled her with remorse. Not for the first time she marvelled that Sybil could be so forgiving of her kid sister's frailties. Time and time again she had watched her aunt wade into Natalie's emotional dramas and rush to sort them out with infinite supportive compassion. Sometimes, too, Merry wondered why it was that she, Natalie's daughter, could not be so forgiving, so tolerant, so willing to offer another fresh chance. Possibly that could be because Merry remembered Natalie's resentment of her as a child too strongly, she told herself guiltily. Natalie hadn't wanted to be anyone's Mummy and her constant rejections had deeply wounded Merry.

'Oh, dear, indeed,' her aunt sighed worriedly. 'Natalie was distraught when she phoned me and you *know* she does stupid things when she's upset! She really shouldn't be alone right now.'

'Doesn't she have any friends out there?' Merry prompted.

Sybil frowned, clearly finding Merry's response unfeeling. 'Family's family and you and her don't get on well enough for you to go. Nor would it be right to subject Elyssa to that journey. Natalie wouldn't want a baby around either,' she conceded ruefully.

'She really can't be bothered with young children,' Merry agreed wryly. 'Do you *have* to go?'

Sybil looked pained by that question. 'Merry, she's got nobody else!' she proclaimed, sharply defensive in both speech and manner. 'Of course, that means I'm landing you with looking after things here…will you be able to manage the centre? Nicky is free to take over for you from next week. I've already spoken to her about it. Between minding Elyssa and running your own business, you're not able to drop everything for me right now.'

'But I would've managed,' Merry assured the

older woman, resisting the urge to protest her aunt's decision to call on the help of an old friend, rather than her niece. Seeing the lines of tension and anxiety already indenting Sybil's face, Merry decided to keep what had happened with Angel to herself. Right now, her aunt had enough on her plate and didn't need any additional stress from Merry's corner.

That evening, once Elyssa was bathed and tucked into her cot, Merry opened a bottle of wine. Sybil had already departed for the first flight she had been able to book and Merry was feeling more than a little lonely. She lifted her laptop and put Angel's name into a search engine. It was something she had never allowed herself to do before, deeming any such information-gathering online to be unhealthy and potentially obsessional. Now drinking her wine, she didn't care any more because her spirits were low and in need of distraction.

A cascade of photos lined up and in a driven mood of defiance she clicked on them one after another. Unsurprisingly, Angel looked shockingly good in pictures. Her lip curled and she refilled her glass, sipping it while she browsed, only to freeze when she saw the most recent photo of Angel with the same blonde he had brought to lunch with his father the day Merry had told him that she was pregnant. That photo had been taken only the night before at some charitable benefit: Angel, the ultimate in the socialite stakes in a designer dinner jacket, smooth and sleek and gorgeous, and his blonde companion,

Roula Paulides, ravishing in a tight glittering dress that exposed an astonishing amount of her chest.

She was Greek too, a woman Angel would presumably have much more in common with. Merry fiercely battled the urge to do an online search on Roula as well. What was she? A stalker?

She finished her glass of wine and grabbed the bottle up in a defiant move to fill the glass again. Well, she was glad she had looked, wasn't she? The very night before he proposed marriage to Merry, Angel had been in another woman's company and had probably spent the night in her bed. Even worse the sexy blonde was clearly an unusual woman, being one who was an enduring interest in Angel's life and not one of the more normal options, who swanned briefly on scene and then was never seen again with him.

Merry fought the turbulent swell of emotion tightening her chest, denying that it hurt, denying that it bothered her in the slightest to discover that Angel was still seeing that same blonde all these many months later. But denial didn't work in the mood she was in as she sat sipping her wine and staring into the middle distance, angry bitterness threatening to consume her.

How *dared* he propose to her only hours after being in another woman's company? How *dared* he condemn her for not taking him seriously? And how dared he come on to her as he had out on the terrace before he'd left? Didn't he have any morals at all?

Any conscience? And how could she even begin to
be jealous over such a brazen, incurable playboy?

And yet she *was* jealous, Merry acknowledged
wretchedly, stupidly, pointlessly jealous of a thoroughly fickle, unreliable man. Rage flared inside her
afresh as she recalled that careless suggestion that
they marry. Oh, he had played that marriage proposal
down, all right, shoving it on the table without ceremony or even a hint of romance. Was it any wonder that she had not taken that suggestion seriously?

In a sudden movement Merry flew out of her
seat and stalked out to the kitchen to lift the business card Angel had left with her. She was texting
him before she had even thought through what she
wanted to say...

Do you realise that if you married me you would
have to give up other women?

Angel studied the screen of his phone in disbelief.
He was dining with his brother Vitale and the sudden text from an unfamiliar number that belonged
to Merry took him aback. He breathed in deep, his
wide, sensual mouth compressing with exasperation.

Are you finally taking me seriously? If I married you
there would be NO OTHER WOMEN.

Merry had texted him in shouty capitals.
'Problems?' Vitale hazarded.
Angel shook his dark head and grinned while won-

dering if Merry was drunk. He just could not imagine her being that blunt otherwise. Merry of all women drunk-dialling him, Merry who was always so careful, so restrained. A sudden and quite shocking degree of wondering satisfaction gripped Angel, washing away his edgy tension, his conviction that he had made a fatal misstep with her and a hash of their meeting.

And no other men for you either.

He pointed this out with pleasure in his reply.

That wasn't a problem for Merry, who was stunned that he was replying to her so quickly. In truth, she had never ever wanted anyone as much as she wanted Angel Valtinos. All thoughts of kindly and dependable Fergus flew from her mind. She didn't like the fact and certainly wasn't proud of it. Indeed, she wouldn't have admitted it even if Angel slow-roasted her over an open fire but it was, indisputably, the secret reality she lived with.

'Who are you texting?' his brother demanded.

'My daughter's mother.' Angel shot his sibling a triumphant glance. 'I believe that you will be standing up at my wedding for me as soon as I can get it arranged.'

Vitale frowned. 'I thought you crashed and burned?'

'Obviously not,' Angel savoured, still texting, keener yet to get a clear response.

Exclusivity approved. Are you agreeing to marry me?

* * *

Merry froze, suddenly shocked back to real life and questioning what she was doing. What *was* she doing? Raging, burning jealousy had almost eaten her alive when she saw that blonde with him again.

We'd have to talk about that.

I'm a doer, not a talker. You have to give me a chance.

But he'd had his chance with her and wrecked it, Merry reminded herself feverishly. He didn't do feelings or proper relationships outside his own family circle. Yet there was something curiously and temptingly seductive about proud, arrogant Angel asking *her* to give *him* another chance.

She decided to give him a warning.

One LAST chance.

YES! WE HAVE A DEAL!

Angel texted back with amusement and an intense sense of achievement.

He had won. He had gained his daughter, the precious chance to bring Elyssa into his life instead of losing her. In addition, he would be gaining a wife, a very unusual wife, who didn't want his money. Another man would have celebrated that reality but, when it came to women, Angel was always suspi-

cious, always looking out for hidden motives and secret objectives. Women were complicated, which was
why he never got involved and never dipped below
the shallow surface with his lovers…and Merry was
infinitely *more* complicated than the kind of women
he was familiar with.

Could such a marriage work?

Only time would tell, he reflected with uncharacteristic gravity. No other women, he pondered ab-
stractedly. Well, he hadn't been prepared for that
demand, he acknowledged ruefully, having proposed marriage while intending the union as more
of a convenient parental partnership than anything
more personal. After all, he knew several couples
who contrived to lead separate lives below the same
roof while remaining safely married. They stayed
together for the sake of their children or to protect
their wealth from the damage of divorce, but nothing more emotional was involved.

In reality, Angel had never seen anything positive
about the marital state. The official Valtinos outlook
on marriage was that it was generally disastrous and
extremely expensive. His own mother's infidelity had
ensured that his parents had parted by the time he
was four years old. His grandparents had enjoyed an
equally calamitous union while shunning divorce in
favour of living in separate wings of the same house.
Nor was Angel's attitude softened by the number of
cheating spouses he had met over the years. In his
early twenties, Angel had automatically assumed
that he would never marry.

But, self-evidently, Merry had a very different take on marriage and parenthood, a much more conventional take than a cynical and distrustful Valtinos. Here she was demanding fidelity upfront as though it was the very bedrock of stability. And maybe it *was*, Angel conceded dimly, reflecting on the constant turmoil caused by his mother's rampant promiscuity. He thought equally hard about the little scene of apparent domestic contentment he had glimpsed at his cousin's house, where a husband rushed into his home to greet a wife and children whom he obviously valued and missed. That glimpse had provided Angel with a disturbing vision of another world that had never been visible to him before, a much more personalised and intimate version of marriage.

And Merry, it seemed, had chosen to view his suggestion of marriage as being personal, *very* personal, rather than practical as he had envisioned. Beneath his brother's exasperated gaze, Angel lounged back in his dining chair, his meal untouched, and for the first time in his life smiled with slashing brilliance at the prospect of acquiring a wife and a wedding ring…

by his ruthlessness, having seen how he operated on the business front.

Angel would undoubtedly hurt her but when push came to shove she had decided that she would infinitely rather have him as a husband than not have him at all. He would be hers with a ring on his finger and she would have to settle for that level of commitment, was certainly not building any little fantasies in which Angel, the unfeeling, would start doing feelings. She was trying to be realistic, trying to be practical about their prospects and she would have been happier on her wedding day had she not somehow contrived to have a massively upsetting row with Sybil about her plans.

Quite how that dreadful schism had opened, Merry had no very clear idea. Her aunt had been understandably shocked and astonished when Merry had phoned her in Australia to announce that she was getting married. Sybil had urged her to wait until she got home and could discuss that major step with her. But Merry, fearful of losing her nerve to marry a man who did not love her, had refused to wait and Sybil had taken that refusal to wait for her counsel badly. The more Sybil had criticised Angel and his reputation as a womaniser, the stiffer and more stubborn Merry had become. She was very well acquainted with Angel's flaws but had not enjoyed having them rammed down her throat in very blunt words by her protective aunt. It was all very well, she had realised, for *her* to criticise Angel, but inexplicably something else entirely for anyone else to do it.

And throughout the past tumultuous and busy two weeks, Angel had been terrific in trying to organise everything to ensure that Merry could cope with the gigantic life change he was inflicting on her. Unfortunately, it was also true that between their various commitments they had barely seen each other. Handing Tiger over to the new owner Sybil had approved had been upsetting because she had become very fond of the little dog and only hoped that his quirks would not irritate in his new home.

Angel had had so much business to take care of while Merry had been engaged in closing down her own business and packing. Even so, Angel had managed to meet with her twice in London to see Elyssa and in his unfamiliar restraint she had recognised the same desire not to rock the boat that beat like an unnerving storm warning through her every fibre. He had been very detached but playful and surprisingly hands-on with Elyssa. It was clear to her that Angel didn't want to risk doing anything that could potentially disrupt their marital plans and deprive him of shared custody of their daughter.

Of course it would take time for Angel to adapt to the idea of marriage and a family of his own and Merry appreciated that reality. He wasn't going to be perfect from the word go, but the imperfect that warned her that he was trying hard was enough to satisfy her…admittedly somewhat low…expectations. She couldn't set the bar too high for him at the start, she told herself urgently. She had to compromise and concentrate on what was truly important.

And what could be more important than Elyssa and seizing the opportunity to provide her daughter with a father? Merry knew what it was like to live with a yawning space in her paternal background. She had never known her father and, unpleasant though it was to acknowledge, her father hadn't cared enough to seek her out to get to know her. But Angel *was* making that effort, right down to having interviewed nannies with Merry to find the one he thought would be most suitable. Entirely raised by nannies before boarding school, Angel had contrived to ask questions that wouldn't even have occurred to Merry and she had been impressed by his concern on their daughter's behalf and his determination to choose the most caring candidate.

So what if his input on the actual wedding and their future relationship had been virtually nonexistent? He had hired a wedding organiser to take care of the arrangements and hadn't seemed to care in the slightest about the details that had unexpectedly consumed Merry. Was that just Angel being a man or a dangerous sign that he couldn't care less about the woman he was about to marry? Merry stifled a shiver, rammed down the fear that had flared and contemplated her manicured fingernails with rampant nervous tension. She had made her choice and she had to live with it when the alternative was so much worse and so much emptier. Surely it was better to give marriage a chance?

It had been embarrassing to tell Fergus that she was marrying Angel but he had taken the news in good part, possibly having already worked out that she was still far from indifferent to her daughter's father.

The first shock of Merry's wedding day was the unexpected sight of Sybil waiting on the church steps, a tall, slender figure attired in a very elegant blue dress and brimmed hat. Eyes wide with astonishment, Merry emerged from the limousine that had ferried her to the church from the hotel where she had stayed the night before and exclaimed in shaken disbelief, *'Sybil?'*

'Obviously I couldn't miss your big day, darling. I got back in the early hours,' Sybil breathed with a revealing shimmer in her eyes as she reached for Merry's hand. 'I'm so sorry about the things I said. I overstepped, *interfered—*'

'No, I was too touchy!' Merry slotted in, stretching up on tiptoe to press a forgiving kiss to the older woman's cheek. 'You were shocked, of course you were.'

'Yes, especially as you're contriving to do what I never managed…you're getting married,' Sybil murmured fondly. 'And you didn't do too badly at all picking that dress without my advice. It's a stunner.'

Her heartache subsiding in the balm of her aunt's reassuring presence, Merry grinned. 'Your voice was in my head when I was choosing. Tailored, *structured*,' she teased, stepping into the church porch. 'Where's Angel's father? He offered to walk me down the aisle, which I thought was very kind of him.'

'Yes, quite the charmer, that man,' Sybil pronounced a shade tartly, evidently having already met

Charles Russell. 'But I told him he could sit back down because I'm here now and I'll do the long walk.'

'I think you'd rather take a long walk off a plank,' Merry warned the older woman gently.

Sybil squeezed the hand she was gripping and smiled warmly down at the young woman who had been more her daughter than her niece, only to stiffen nervously at the prospect of the confession that she knew she *had* to make some time soon. Natalie had asked her to tell Merry the truth and Sybil was now duty-bound to reveal that family secret. Sadly, telling that same truth had shattered her relationship with Natalie when Natalie was eighteen years old and she could only hope that it would not have the same devastating effect on her bond with Merry and her child.

Gloriously ignorant of that approaching emotional storm, Merry smoothed down her dress, which effortlessly delineated the high curve of her breasts and her neat waist before falling softly to her feet, lending her a shapely silhouette. Straightening her slight shoulders, she lifted her head high, her short flirty veil dancing round her flushed face, accentuating the light blue of her eyes.

Even before she went down the aisle, she heard Elyssa chuckling. Her daughter was in the care of her new nanny, a lovely down-to-earth young woman from Yorkshire called Sally, who had impressed both Merry and Angel with her genuine warmth and interest in children. Merry's eyes skimmed from her daughter's curly head and waving arms as she danced on Sally's knee and settled on Angel, poised at the altar with an equally tall dark male, Vitale, whose resemblance to Angel echoed his obvious family relationship to his brother. But Angel had the edge in Merry's biased opinion, the lean, beautiful precision of his bronzed features highlighting the shimmering brilliance of his dark eyes and his undeniable hold on her attention.

Her breath caught in her dry throat and butterflies ran amok in her tummy, her chest stretched so tightly that her lungs felt compressed. Her hand slid off Sybil's arm, suddenly nerveless as she reached the altar to be greeted by the Greek Orthodox priest. Angel gripped her cold fingers, startling her, and she glanced up at him, noticing the tension stamped in his strong cheekbones and the compressed line of his wide, sensual mouth. Yes, getting wed had to be a sheer endurance test for a wayward playboy like Angel Valtinos, Merry reflected with rueful amusement, but it was an unfortunate thought because she started wondering then whether he would find the tedious domestic aspects of family life and the unchanging nature of a wife a trial and a bore. The service marched on regardless of her teeming anxiety. The vows were exchanged, an ornately plaited gold wedding ring that she savoured for its distinctiveness and his selection of it slid onto her finger and then a matching one onto his.

And then, jolting her out of the powerful spell that Angel cast, Charles Russell surged up to her to kiss her warmly on both cheeks, closely followed by Sybil, who strove to conceal her shotgun attitude to Angel with bright, determined positivity. Elyssa, seated in a nearby pew on Sally's lap, held out her arms and wailed pathetically for her mother.

'That little chancer knows how to pick her moment,' Sybil remarked wryly as Merry bent to accept her daughter and hoisted her up, only to be intercepted by Angel, who snagged his daughter mid-manoeuvre, saying that the bride could scarcely cart a child down the aisle.

'Says who?' Merry teased, watching Elyssa pluck at his curls and his tie with nosy little hands, watching Angel suddenly slant a grin at his lack of control over the situation. Once again she found herself suppressing her surprise at his flexibility when at the mercy of a wilful baby.

Angel maintained a grip on his daughter for the handful of photos taken on the church steps. Merry watched paparazzi wield cameras behind a barrier warded by security guards, their interest visibly sharpened by her daughter's first public appearance. Her eyes widened in dismay when she finally recognised how much her life and Elyssa's were about to change. For years, Angel's every move had been fodder for the tabloid press. He had his own jet, his own yacht and the glitzy lifestyle of great wealth and privilege. His very marked degree of good looks and predilection for scantily dressed blonde beauties only added to his media appeal. Naturally his sudden marriage and the apparent existence of a young child were worthy of even closer scrutiny. Merry

wondered gloomily if she would be denounced as a
fertile scheming former Valtinos employee.

As they were moving towards the limousine to de-
part for the hotel another limo drew up ahead of them
and a tiny brunette on skyrocketing heels leapt out in
a flurry of colourful draperies and a feathered hat.
She was as exquisite as a highly sophisticated and
perfectly groomed doll. 'Oh, Charles, have I missed
it?' she exclaimed very loudly while all around her
cameras began to flash.

Angel murmured something very terse in Greek
while his father moved off to perform the welcome
that his son clearly wasn't in the mood to offer to
the late-arriving guest. Angel relocated Elyssa with
Sally and swept Merry into their vehicle without
further ado.

'Who was that?' Merry demanded, filled with curiosity, glancing out of the window to note that the
brunette was actually lodged at the security barriers
exchanging comments with the paparazzi while posing like a professional. 'Is she a model or something?'

'Or something,' Angel breathed with withering
impatience. 'That's Angelina.'

'Your *mother*?' Merry gasped in disbelief. 'She
can't be! She doesn't look old enough.'

'And it's typical of her to miss the ceremony. She
hates weddings,' Angel divulged. 'At a wedding the
bride is the centre of attention and Angelina Valtinos cannot bear to be one of the crowd.'

Merry frowned. 'Oh, I'm sure she's not as bad as
that,' she muttered, chiding him.

'No doubt you'll make your own mind up on that score,' Angel responded wryly, visibly reluctant to say any more on the topic of his mother.

'Is she likely to be the interfering mother-in-law type?' Merry prompted apprehensively.

'*Thee mou*, you have to be kidding!' Angel emitted a sharp cynical laugh. 'She couldn't care less that I've got married or who I've married but she'll be furious that I've made her a grandmother because she will see that as aging.'

Merry could not comprehend the idea of such an attitude. Sybil had approached maturity with grace, freely admitting that she found it more relaxing not to always be fretting about her appearance.

'I love the dress.' Swiftly changing the unwelcome subject, Angel enveloped Merry in a smouldering appraisal that somehow contrived to encompass the ripe swell of her breasts below the fitted bodice. 'You have a spectacular figure.'

Heat surged into Merry's cheeks at that unexpected and fairly basic compliment. His fierce appraisal emanated raw male appreciation. Her stomach performed a sudden somersault, a shard of hunger piercing her vulnerable body with the stabbing accuracy of a knife that couldn't be avoided. He could do that to her simply with a look, a tone, a smile. It always, *always* unnerved her, making her feel out of control.

The reception was being held at a five-star exclusive city hotel. Merry met her mother-in-law for the first time over the pre-dinner drinks. By then Angelina Valtinos had a young and very handsome Italian man on her arm, whom she airily introduced as Primo. She said very little, asked nothing and virtually ignored her son, as though she blamed him for the necessity of her having to attend his wedding.

'She's even worse in person than I expected,' Sybil hissed in a tone most unlike her.

'Shush…time will tell,' Merry said with a shrug.

'I wish that wretched man would take a hint,' Sybil complained as Charles Russell hurried forward with a keen smile to escort her aunt to their seats at the top table.

Merry tried not to laugh, having quickly grasped that Angel's father had one of those drivingly energetic and assured natures that steamrollered across Sybil's polite lack of interest without even noticing it. But then she had equally quickly realised that she liked her father-in-law for his unquestioning acceptance of their sudden marriage. His enthusiastic response to Elyssa had also spelled out the message that he was one of those men who absolutely adored children. He exuded all the warmth and welcome that his ex-wife, Angelina, conspicuously lacked.

Angel's brother, Prince Vitale, drifted over to exchange a few words. He was very smooth, very sophisticated and civil, but Merry was utterly intimidated by him. From the moment Angel had explained that his half-brother was of royal birth and the heir to the throne of a small, fabulously rich European country, Merry had been nervous of meeting him.

A slender blonde grasped Merry's hand and, look-

ing up at the taller woman, Merry froze in consternation. Recognition was instant: it was the *same* blonde
she had twice seen in Angel's company, a slender,
leggy young woman in her early thirties with sparkling brown eyes and an easy, confident smile.

'Merry…allow me to introduce Roula Paulides,
one of my oldest friends,' Angel proffered warmly.

With difficulty, Merry flashed a smile onto her
stiff lips, her colour rising because she was mortified by her instant stiffening defensiveness with the
other woman. An old friend, she should've thought
of that possibility, she scolded herself. That more
than anything else explained Angel's enduring relationship with the beautiful blonde. Unfortunately,
Roula Paulides was stunning and very much Angel's
type. Even worse and mortifyingly, she was the same
woman who had been lunching with Angel on the
dreadful dark day when Merry had had to tell him
that she was pregnant.

It was only when Sally retrieved Elyssa to whisk
her upstairs for a nap that Angel's mother finally approached Merry. A thin smile on her face, she said,
'Angel really should have warned me that his bride
already had a child.'

'He should've done,' Merry agreed mildly.

'Your daughter is very young. Who is her father?'
Angelina demanded with a ringing clarity that en-
couraged several heads to turn in their direction. 'I
hope you are aware that she cannot make use of the
Valtinos name.'

'I think you'll find you're wrong about that,' Sybil

declared as she strolled over to join her niece with a protective gleam in her gaze. 'Elyssa is a Valtinos too.'

Angel's mother stiffened, her eyes widening, her rosebud mouth tightening with disbelief. 'My son has a child with you?' she gasped, stricken. 'That can't be true!'

'It is,' Merry cut in hurriedly, keen to bring the fraught conversation to an end.

'He should've married Roula... I always thought that if he married anyone, it would be Roula,' Angelina Valtinos volunteered in a tone of bitter complaint.

'Well, tact isn't one of her skills,' Sybil remarked ruefully when they were alone again. 'Who's Roula? Or don't you know?'

Merry felt humiliated by the tense little scene and her mother-in-law's closing comment about Roula Paulides. Roula, evidently, was something more than a harmless old friend, she gathered unhappily.

Meanwhile, shaken by what she had learned and very flushed, Angelina stalked to the end of the table to approach her son, who was talking to Vitale. A clearly hostile and brief dialogue took place between mother and son before the older woman careened angrily away again to snatch a glass of champagne off a passing waiter's tray and drop down into her chair.

Sybil's eyes met Merry's but neither of them commented.

'Your mother's all worked up about Elyssa,' Merry acknowledged when Angel sank fluidly down into his seat by her side. 'Why?'

'The horror of being old enough to be a grandparent,' Angel proffered wryly.

'Are you serious?'

'There's nothing we can do about it. She'll have to learn to deal.'

'Do you see much of your mother?' Merry probed uneasily.

'More than I sometimes wish. She makes use of all my properties,' Angel admitted flatly. 'But if she wants that arrangement to continue she will have to tone herself down.'

As the afternoon wore on Merry watched Angel's mother drink like a fish and then put on a sparkling display on the dance floor with Primo. She did not behave like a woman likely to tone her extrovert nature down. Merry also saw Angelina seek out Roula Paulides and sit with the blonde for a long time while enjoying an animated conversation. So, she was unlikely to be flavour of the month with her mother-in-law any time soon, Merry told herself wryly. Well, she could live with that, she decided, secure in the circle of Angel's arms as they moved round the dance floor. His lean, powerful body against hers sparked all sorts of disconcerting responses. The prickly awareness of proximity and touch rippled through her in stormy, ever-rolling waves. She rested her head down on his shoulder, drinking in the raw, evocative scent of him like a drug she could not live without and only just resisting the urge to lick the strong brown column of his masculine throat.

Early evening, the newly married couple flew out

to Greece and the Valtinos home on the island of Palos where Angel had been born. Merry was madly curious about the small island and the darkness that screened her view of it frustrated her. Serried lines of light ascending a hillside illuminated a small white village above the bay as the helicopter came in to land. A pair of SUVs picked them up, ferrying them up a steep road lined with cypress trees to the ultra-modern house hugging the promontory. Like a giant cruise ship, the entire house seemed to be lit up.

They stepped out into the warmth of a dusky evening and mounted the steps into the house. Staff greeted them in an octagonal marble hall ornamented by contemporary pieces of sculpture.

'Sally will take Elyssa straight to bed,' Angel decreed, closing his hand over Merry's before she could dart off in the wake of her daughter. 'She's so tired she'll sleep. This is *our* night.'

Merry coloured, suddenly insanely conscious of the ridiculous fact that she had barely acknowledged that it was their wedding night. She was tempted to argue that she had to take care of Elyssa, but was too well aware of their nanny's calm efficiency to tilt at windmills. Even so, because she was accustomed to being a full-time mother, she found it difficult to step back from the role and accept that someone else could do the job almost as well. Her slender fingers scrabbled indecisively in the grip of Angel's large masculine hand until she finally followed his lead and the staff already moving ahead of them with their bags.

'Supper has been prepared for us. We'll eat in our room,' Angel told her lazily. 'I'm glad to be home. You'll love it here. Midsummer it can be unbearably hot but in June Palos is lush with growth and the air is fresh.'

'I didn't realise that you were so attached to your home,' Merry confided, running her attention over the display of impressive paintings in the corridor.

'Palos has been the Valtinos base for generations,' Angel told her. 'The original house was demolished and rebuilt by my grandfather. He fancied himself as something of an architect but his design ambitions were thwarted when he and my grandmother split up and she refused to move out. His house plan was then divided in two, one half for him, the other half for her and it's still like that. Some day I hope to turn it back into one house.'

Merry was frowning. 'Your grandparents divorced?'

'No, neither of them wanted a divorce, but after my mother's birth they separated. He was an incorrigible Romeo and she couldn't live with him,' Angel admitted as carved wooden doors were spread back at the end of the corridor. 'I never knew either of them. My grandfather didn't marry until he was almost sixty and my grandmother was in her forties when my mother was born. They died before my parents married.'

On the threshold, Merry paused to admire the magnificent bedroom. An opulent seating area took up one corner of the vast room. Various doors led

off to bathroom facilities and a large and beautifully fitted dressing room where staff were already
engaged in unpacking their cases. A table sat beside
patio doors that led out onto a terrace overlooking
a fabulous infinity swimming pool lit with underwater lights. In the centre of the room a giant bed
fit for Cleopatra and draped in spicy Mediterranean
colours sat on elaborate gilded feet. Her expressive
face warmed, her pulses humming beneath her calm
surface because she ached for him, and that awareness of her own hunger embarrassed her as nothing
else could because she was mortifyingly conscious
that she had no control around Angel.

'Let's eat,' Angel suggested lazily.

A slender figure clad in loose linen trousers and
an emerald-green top with ties, Merry took a seat.
She had dressed comfortably for the flight and had
marvelled that, even in designer jeans and a black
shirt, Angel could still look far more sleek and sophisticated than she did. No matter what he wore, he
had that knack, if there was such a thing, of always
looking classy and exclusive.

Wine was poured, the first course delivered. It
was all food calculated to tempt the appetite, nothing
heavy or over spiced and, because she hadn't eaten
much at the wedding, Merry ate hungrily. During
the main course, she heard splashing from the direction of the pool and then a sudden bout of high-
pitched giggling. She began awkwardly to twist her
head around to look outside.

'*Diavole!*' Angel swore with a sudden frown, flying upright to thrust open the doors onto the terrace.

Merry rose to her feet more slowly and followed him to see what had jerked him out of his seat as though rudely yanked up by invisible steel wires. She was very much taken aback to discover that the source of the noise was her mother-in-law and her boyfriend, both of whom appeared to be cavorting naked in the pool. She blinked in disbelief while Angel addressed the pair in angry Greek. Primo reacted first, hauling himself hurriedly out of the water and yanking a towel off a lounger to wind it round his waist. Angelina hissed back at her son in furious Greek before leaving the pool by the steps, stark naked and evidently quite unconcerned by that reality. Her companion strode forward to toss her a robe, his discomfiture at the interruption unhidden. Angel's mother, however, took her time about covering up, her tempestuous fury at Angel's intrusion fuelling a wealth of outraged objections.

Merry swallowed hard on her growing embarrassment while Angel stood his ground, his dark deep voice sardonic and clipped with derision as he switched to English. 'You will not use this pool while I, my wife or my daughter are in residence.'

'This is my home!' Angelina proclaimed. 'You have no right to make a demand like that!'

'This house belongs to me and there are now rules to be observed,' Angel sliced back harshly. 'If you cannot respect those rules, find somewhere else to stay on the island.'

And with that final ringing threat, Angel swung back and pressed a hand to Merry's shoulder to guide her firmly back indoors. His mother ranted back at him in Greek and he ignored the fact, ramming shut the doors again and returning to their interrupted meal.

Unnerved by what she had witnessed, Merry dropped heavily back into her chair, her face hot with unease. 'I think your mother's had too much to drink.'

Angel shot her a grim glance. 'Don't make excuses for her. I should have told her that she was no longer welcome here *before* we married. Her conduct is inappropriate and I refuse to have you or Elyssa subjected to her behaviour in what is now your home.'

Merry sipped at her wine, stunned by the display she had witnessed and wondering helplessly what it had been like for him to grow up with so avant-garde a mother. Angelina seemed to have no boundaries, no concept of what was acceptable. It must have been a nightmare to grow up in the care of so self-indulgent a woman. For the first time she understood why Angel was so close to his father: he only had one parent, he had only *ever* had one parent. Parenting had been something that Angelina Valtinos had probably never done and she understood why Angel had been placed in a boarding school at a very young age.

As silence reclaimed the pool beyond the terrace, Angel audibly expelled his breath, the fierce tension in his lean, darkly handsome features and the set of his wide shoulders fading. He was determined that Merry would not be embarrassed by his mother's attention-grabbing tactics. Merry was too prim to comfortably cope with the scenes his mother liked to throw. In any case, his wife was entitled to the older woman's respect. Angelina could dislike her all she wished but, ultimately, she had to accept that her son's wife was the new mistress of the house and had the right to expect certain standards of behaviour.

'How is it that the family home belongs to you and not to your mother?' Merry asked curiously.

'My grandmother survived my grandfather by several months. She was never able to control her daughter and once she realised that Angelina was pregnant, she left this house to my mother's descendants rather than to her,' he advanced.

Merry frowned. 'That's kind of sad.'

'Don't feel sorry for Angelina. My grandfather adored her and endowed her with a massive trust fund. All her life she has done exactly what she wanted to do, regardless of how it harms or affects others. At some stage, there's got to be a price to pay for that,' Angel declared with dry finality. 'I have long wished that my mother would buy her own property where she could do as she likes without involving me.'

'Why doesn't she do that?' Merry asked with genuine curiosity.

'The ownership of property involves other responsibilities. Hiring staff, maintenance, running costs…all the adult stuff,' he pointed out with a sardonic twist of his wide, sensual mouth. 'My mother avoids responsibility of any kind. May we drop this subject?'

'Of course,' Merry conceded, a little breathless while she collided with smouldering dark eyes and sipped at her wine. Her mind, however, remained awash with conjecture about her mother-in-law and her disconnected and antagonistic relationship with her son. At the same time she wasn't worried about Angelina causing trouble between them because she could see that Angel had few illusions about his parent and intended to protect her from any fallout. And that made her a little sad, made her wonder what it must have been like for him to be saddled with a spoilt heiress of a mother, a party girl, who flatly refused to accept responsibility and grow up. A mother who, from what she could see, had never behaved like a normal mother. Surely that truth must've lessened his respect for women and his ability to trust her sex, she reasoned helplessly.

'Let's concentrate on us,' Angel suggested with emphatic cool.

She felt overheated and her mouth ran dry. Her entire body tensed, tiny little tremors shimmying through her pelvis, tremors of awareness, arousal and anticipation. She was embarrassed by the level of her sheer susceptibility, shaken by the power he had over her, suddenly wondering if he too knew the full extent of it…

CHAPTER SEVEN

ANGEL GRASPED HER HAND and eased her up out of her seat. 'I have a special request,' he admitted almost harshly.

Enthralled by the golden glimmer of his intense appraisal, Merry moistened her dry lips with the tip of her tongue. 'And what would that be?'

Long fingers flicked the silken bell of hair that fell to just below her shoulders. 'You cut your hair. I loved it the way it was. Will you grow it again for me?' he asked levelly.

Surprise darted through Merry, who had wondered if he had even noticed that she had shortened her hair. 'I suppose that could be arranged,' she breathed shakily.

'Why did you cut it?' he demanded. 'It was really beautiful.'

Even more taken aback by that blunt question and the compliment, Merry coloured. She couldn't tell him the truth, couldn't afford to dwell on unfortunate memories at this stage of their marriage or mention truths that he might think were aimed at reproaching him. But when she had been pregnant and struggling against an unending tide of exhaustion and sickness to get through every day, the amount of care demanded by very long hair had simply felt like an unnecessary burden.

'It was too much work to look after when I was pregnant,' she muttered awkwardly.

'Fortunately, you no longer have to look after your own hair,' Angel informed her lazily. 'Add a stylist to your staff—'

Merry opened pale blue eyes very wide. 'I'm to have my own staff?' she gasped.

'Of course. You'll need a social secretary to take care of your calendar, someone to shop for you… unless you want to do it yourself,' Angel volunteered doubtfully. 'I've started you off with a new wardrobe—'

'Have you indeed?' Merry cut in jerkily.

'It's a wedding present. I wasn't sure you'd want to be bothered,' Angel volunteered, a fingertip tracing the quivering fullness of her lower lip, sending a shiver through her taut, slender body. 'You've never struck me as being that interested in clothes or appearances.'

'I'm not,' she agreed almost guiltily. 'Sybil was always trying to persuade me that shopping was enjoyable.'

'I don't want you having to do things you don't want to do,' Angel told her huskily. 'I don't want you to change who you are to fit into my world, so it's easier to have someone else take care of the less welcome aspects for you.'

Her heartbeat was thumping hard and fast inside her tightening chest. 'You like me the way I am?'

'Very much,' Angel asserted. 'You're unusual and I value that.'

A smile slowly tilted and softened the tense line of her mouth. 'And you have a fetish for very long hair?'

A wolfish grin slashed his expressive mouth, cutting his dark male beauty into high-cheekboned perfection and interesting hollows while his intense gaze held hers fast. 'Only from the first moment I saw you.'

Warmth flushed through Merry, leaving her breathless. 'That must be the most romantic thing you've ever said to me.'

'I don't do romantic, *koukla mou*,' Angel told her uneasily, a frown line building between his fine ebony brows as he stared down at her in frustration. 'For me, it was a sexual charge and instantaneous…'

And if she was honest, Merry reflected ruefully, it had been the same for her that first day, a powerful instant physical reaction that had only deepened with repeated exposure.

Lean brown hands dropped to the sash at her waist and jerked it loose so that her breath hitched in her throat. She could feel her breasts swelling inside her bra, her nipples prickling into feverish prominence, the sense of melting at her feminine core. She was trembling, awake on every level even before he picked her up against him and crushed her ripe mouth hungrily under his.

'*Thee mou*… I want you even more now than I wanted you then,' Angel intoned rawly. 'And that's saying something. But then I've never had to be patient before.'

'You don't have any patience,' she whispered through reddened lips. 'You want everything yesterday.'

'Once I got you back I didn't want to be too demanding in case it made you change your mind. Before the wedding, I felt like I was in a straitjacket around you, forced to be on my best behaviour,' he complained.

Merry laughed, riveted to appreciate that she had read his uncharacteristic restraint correctly. She knew him better than she had believed, she thought victoriously, and his admission thrilled her. He hadn't wanted to risk driving her away and losing her. Losing *them*, she corrected with a sudden inner flinch of dismayed acceptance, the thrilled sensation swiftly dying again. He had practised patience with Elyssa's mother for Elyssa's benefit, fearful of losing access through their marriage to his daughter, which put a very different slant on his attitude.

'Unhappily for me, I am a naturally demanding man,' Angel admitted thickly, long, deft fingers twitching the buttons loose on her top, parting the edges, pushing them off her slim, taut shoulders until the garment dropped to the tiled floor. 'No good at waiting, no fan of deferred gratification either…'

Her ribcage tensed as she snatched in a sustaining breath, ridiculously self-conscious standing there in her simple white lace bra. Although they had been intimate twice before, on the first occasion they had been in semi-darkness and on the second they had both been so frantic that she hadn't had the time or space to feel remotely shy. But now, her face burned as Angel released the catch on her bra and her breasts tumbled free, plump and swollen and heavy.

'I have died and gone to heaven,' Angel intoned, scooping her up and carrying her across to the bed. 'I love your curves.'

'I'm pretty much stuck with them,' Merry pointed out, resisting a very strong urge to cup her hands over the swells that pregnancy had increased in size.

Angel cupped the burgeoning creamy swells, gently moulded and stroked them before leaning back to peel his shirt off over his head. Tangled black curls, glossy below the discreet lights, tumbled over his brow, his lean, strong face taut with hunger, dark golden eyes glittering like polished ingots. A thumb teased a quivering pink nipple until it hardened into a tight bud and throbbed, her breath escaping from her parted lips in an audible hiss of quaking response.

'You *should* tremble… I want to eat you alive,' Angel warned her, settling his hands to her waist to extract her from her linen trousers, yanking them off with scant ceremony and trailing off her last garment with brazen satisfaction. 'But we've never taken the time to do this properly. We were always in a ridiculous hurry to reach the finishing line. It won't be like that tonight.'

Merry felt the dampness between her thighs and reddened fiercely, wildly aware that her body was even now ready for him, surging impatiently ahead without shame to that finishing line he had mentioned. He made her single-minded and greedy and shameless, she thought helplessly. He turned everything she thought she knew about herself on its head and he had done that from the outset.

Watching her, Angel sprang upright again to strip off what remained of his clothes. He was, oh, so beautiful that she stared, taking in the long, bronzed flexing torso lightly sprinkled with black curling hair, the superb muscle definition, the long, powerful, hair-roughened thighs and the bold, eager thrust of his erection. Her belly fluttered, her mouth ran dry, her body flexed with sinful eagerness.

He returned to her again, all smouldering sexual assurance and with eyes that ravished her as she lay there. His hands found her curvy hips, his mouth locked to a rosy crest, and she simply gasped while he played with the puckered buds until they throbbed almost unbearably. A finger trailed through her slick folds and her spine arched, another sound, a plea for more that she couldn't help, dragged from her. He spread her thighs to invade her body with skilful fingers and slid down her pale body to explore her most tender flesh.

Merry was already so aroused that she could barely contain herself. He toyed with her, brought his mouth to her and licked and teased until she writhed helplessly beneath his ministrations, her body alight like a forest fire, hot and twitchy and excited beyond bearing. It was as though every nerve ending had reached saturation point, thrusting her higher and higher with every passing second until her body shattered in an ecstatic climax without her volition. A high keening cry fell from her, her body jerking and gasping with the intensity of her relief as the long, convulsive waves of pleasure rippled through her again.

'You really needed that,' Angel husked knowingly, his brilliant gaze locked to her hectically flushed and softened face. 'So did I. I needed to see you come for me again. I need to know I'm the only man to see you like this.'

'Why?' she asked baldly, taken aback by that admission.

Angel shrugged a broad shoulder. 'I don't know,' he admitted, quite unconcerned by his own ignorance of what motivated him. 'But when I saw you kissing that vet guy I wanted to wipe him off the face of the earth.'

Merry sat up with a start and hugged her knees in consternation. 'How did you see that?'

'You and Elyssa have had a security detail discreetly watching over you for months. It's standard in this family and not negotiable,' Angel told her without apology. 'I needed to know you were both safe. I was sent a photo of you kissing him. I didn't need to see that. I didn't ask for it. I hated it.'

Merry sat there frozen, shock and resentment momentarily holding her fast. 'Standard?' she queried.

'It's my job to keep you both safe,' he delivered flatly. 'But sometimes you don't want the details. Did you have sex with him?'

'None of your business!' Merry framed jaggedly, swinging her legs off the bed and standing up. 'How many women have you been with since the night Elyssa was conceived?'

The silence simmered like a kettle suddenly pushed close to noisy boiling point.

Merry swung back to him, too angry to even care that she was naked. 'I thought that would shut you up!'

'After our little contraceptive mishap it was months before I was with anyone again. I couldn't get you or that accident out of my head. I still wanted you but I *had* to stay away from you,' Angel ground out with suppressed savagery, his lean, dark features rigid with remembered frustration and resentment. 'Every other woman turned me off. You destroyed my sex drive until I got very, very drunk one night and finally broke the dry spell.'

Well, that was blunt and very Angel brutal, Merry acknowledged, stalking into the bathroom with hot stinging tears brimming in her eyes. And she still wanted to kill him, rake jealous fingernails down over his beautiful face and draw blood in punishment. Jealousy and hatred ate her alive, threatening to rip her asunder because she had no defence against such honesty. Of course, she had guessed there would be other women, other flings and sexual dalliances while they were apart, but guessing and *knowing* were two very different things.

Inside the bathroom, Angel closed two strong arms round her to hold her fast. 'It was the worst sex I've ever had.'

'Good!' she bit out with raw sincerity.

'It wasn't like you and me. It wasn't what I really wanted but I couldn't *have* what I wanted and celibacy made me feel like a weakling,' he groaned against the damp nape of her neck. 'The sexual hold you had over me unnerved me right from the beginning. It felt toxic, dangerous...'

'Thanks... I think,' Merry framed weakly as he wrapped his strong arms even more tightly round her, imprisoning her in the hard, damp heat of his lean, powerful body.

'It was the same for you. You fought it as well,' he reminded her.

And that was true, she conceded grudgingly. That overpowering hunger had scared her, overwhelmed her, made her all too aware of her vulnerability. Could it really have been the same for him?

'Even if the condom hadn't broken that night, I'd have run like a hare,' Angel admitted in a driven undertone. 'I felt out of control. I couldn't live like that.'

'Neither could I,' she confessed unevenly.

'But now that I've got that ring on your finger, everything feels different,' Angel stated, his breath fanning her shoulder, his hands smoothing up her body in innate celebration of the possessiveness roaring through him. 'You're mine now, *all* mine.'

'Am I?' she dared.

An appreciative laugh vibrated through him and his hands swept up over her breasts, moulding the ripe swells, tugging at the still-distended peaks, sending a piercing arrow of sweet shuddering sensation right down to the moist heart of her. 'If you don't know that yet, I'm doing something very wrong,' he growled, lifting her off her feet to carry her back into the bedroom.

'You have a one-track mind, Mr Valtinos,' Merry condemned helplessly as he spread her on the bed and hovered over her body, brazenly eager for more action.

'No, I have a wife to claim,' Angel declared urgently, sliding between her slender thighs, gathering them up and plunging into her with ravenous sexual dominance. 'And tonight nothing will keep me from you. Not my mistakes, not my clumsy efforts to make amends, not your disappointment in me, not my inability to live up to your impossibly high ideals. We are married and we will do the best we can with that challenge.'

His sudden intrusion into her honeyed depths stretched her tight and then sent a current of melting excitement surging through Merry. She closed her eyes as he moved, her head falling back, her body an erotic instrument in his charge, glorious sensation spilling through her, washing away the hurt and the disillusionment. Oh, later she would take out the hurt again and brood on it and hate herself, but just then she couldn't hold onto that pain, not when a delicious flood of exquisite feeling clenched her core with his every sensual movement. He felt like hers for the first time, and as an explosive orgasm lit her up from inside out and he groaned with passionate pleasure into her hair she was soothed, quieted and gratified to be the source of that uninhibited satisfaction.

CHAPTER EIGHT

MERRY AND ANGEL lay side by side in the orange grove above the private beach. Day after day had melted into the next with a curiously timeless quality that had gradually teased all the tension from Merry's bones and taught her how to relax. She could hardly credit that they had already spent an entire month on the island. Her body ached from his demands, not that she wasn't willing, but she was still in shock at the extent of Angel's ravenous hunger for her.

It was sex, only sex, she told herself regularly, and then in the dark of the night when Angel wasn't his sardonic know-all self she snuggled up to him, revelling in the intimacy that now bonded them. Maintaining a controlled distance wasn't possible with a man as unashamedly physical as the one she had married. Angel had no limits. He would go and work for a couple of hours in his home office and then sweep down on her wherever she was and cart her off to bed again as if he had been parted from her for at least a month.

'I missed you,' he would say, replete with satisfaction while her pulses still pounded and her body hummed in the aftermath.

'I could work *with* you,' she would say.

'You're my wife, the mother of my child, no longer an employee.'

'I could be a junior partner,' she had proffered pathetically.

'We can't live in each other's pockets twenty-four-seven,' Angel had pointed out drily. 'It would be unhealthy.'

No, what Merry sometimes thought was unhealthy was the sheer weight of love that Angel now inspired in her. That was a truth she had evaded as long as possible: she *loved* him.

Only because she loved him and her daughter had she been willing to give Angel one last chance, she acknowledged ruefully. There were still a thousand things she wanted to punish him for, but she knew that vengeful, bitter thoughts were unproductive and would ultimately damage any hope of their having a stable relationship. In that line, she was sensible, very sensible, she acknowledged ruefully. Unfortunately, she only became stupid when it came to Angel himself.

Sometimes she had to work uncomfortably hard to hide her love. She would see him laughing over Elyssa's antics in the bath, amusement lightening and softening his lean, darkly handsome features, and she wouldn't be able to drag her eyes from him. He had taken her down to the village *taverna* above the harbour and dined with her there, introducing her to the locals, more relaxed than she had ever seen him in company, his usually razor-edged cynicism absent. He had tipped her out of bed to climb the highest hill on the island to see in the dawn and told her off for moaning about how tired she was even though he had drained her energy at the summit with *al fresco* sex. But of course she was tired, making love half the night and half the day, physically active in all the hours between as she strove to match his high-voltage energy levels.

Ironically, complete peace had engulfed the Valtinos house the day after the wedding once Angel had revealed that his mother and her boyfriend had departed at dawn for an unknown destination, leaving the other half of the house in a fine mess for the staff to deal with. Merry had felt relieved and then guilty at feeling relieved because, like it or not, Angel's challenging and difficult mother was family and had to somehow be integrated into their lives or become a continuing problem.

They had gone sailing on the yacht, visiting other islands, shopping, picnicking. They had thrown a giant party at the house attended by all Angel's relatives, near and distant. She had met his second cousin who lived in London and had heard all about Angel's visit to her home before he first met Elyssa, and Merry had laughed like a drain when she'd recognised how wily he had been to find out a little more about babies before he'd served himself up as a new father to one.

'What's your favourite colour?' she asked drowsily.

'I'm not a girl. I don't have a favourite,' Angel parried with amusement.

'Birth sign?'

'Look at your marriage certificate, lazy-bones,' he advised. 'I'm a Scorpio, but I don't believe in that sh—'

'Language,' she reminded him, resting a finger against his parted lips.

'Prim, proper, prissy,' Angel labelled without hesitation.

'Your first lover? What age were you?' she pressed, defying that censure while wondering how on earth he could still think of her that way after the time they had spent together.

'Too young. You don't want to know,' Angel traded.

'I *do* want to know,' Merry argued, stretching indolently in the drenching heat, only vaguely wondering what time it was. They had spent the morning swimming and entertaining Elyssa on the beach and then Sally had come down to collect their daughter and take her back up to the house for lunch and a nap. Now the surf was whispering onto the shore a hundred yards below them while the cane forest that sheltered the orange grove from the coastal breezes concealed them entirely from view.

'I was fourteen. She was one of my mother's friends,' Angel admitted grimly.

Frowning, Merry flipped over to stare at him. *'Seriously?'*

'You're still so naïve,' Angel groaned, lifting up on his elbows to study her, hard muscles flexing on his bare bronzed torso, the vee at his hipbones prominent above the low-slung shorts as he leant back. Just looking at that display of stark masculine beauty made her mouth run dry and her heart give a sudden warning thud, awareness thundering through her at storm-force potency.

'What do you think it was like here when I was an adolescent with Angelina in charge?' he chided. 'I came home for the summer from school and there were no rules whatsoever. Back then it was all wild, decadent parties and the house was awash with people. Believe it or not, my mother was even less inhibited in those days and, being an oversexed teenager, I naturally thought the freedom to do anything I liked was amazing and I never let my father know how debauched it was.'

'So, your first experience was with an older woman,' Merry gathered, determined to move on past that sordid revelation and not judge, because when he had been that young and innocent she believed he had been more sinned against than he had been a sinner.

'And the experience was disappointing,' Angel admitted with derisive bite. 'It felt sleazy, not empowering. I felt used. When the parties here got too much I used to go down and camp out with Roula's family for a few days.'

'She lived here on the island back then?' Merry said in surprise.

'Still does. Roula was born and bred on Palos, like me. This is her home base too. She runs a chain of beauty salons, comes back here for a break. Unlike me, she had a regular family with parents who were still married and their home was a little oasis of peace and normality… I loved escaping there,' he confided. 'Rules and regular meal times have more appeal than you would appreciate.'

'I can understand that,' Merry conceded ruefully. 'My mother was very disorganised. She'd want to eat and there'd be nothing in the fridge. She'd want to go out and she wouldn't have a babysitter arranged. Sometimes she just left me in bed and went out anyway. I never told Sybil that. But when I was with Sybil, everything was structured.'

'*Thee mou*… I forgot!' Angel exclaimed abruptly. 'Your aunt phoned to ask me if there was any chance we'd be back in the UK in the next couple of weeks because your mother's coming over to stay with her for a while and she wants to see you. I said I'd try to organise it.'

Merry frowned, reluctant to get on board with yet another reconciliation scene with her estranged mother. Natalie enjoyed emotional scenes, enjoyed asking her daughter why she couldn't act more like a normal daughter and love and appreciate her, not seeming to realise that the time for laying the foundation for such bonds lay far behind them. They had missed that boat and Merry had learned to get by without a mother by replacing her with the more dependable Sybil.

'You're not keen,' Angel gathered, shrewd dark golden eyes scanning her expressive troubled face. 'Sybil made it sound like it was really important that you show up at some stage. I think she's hoping you'll mend fences with her sister.'

Merry shrugged jerkily. 'I've tried before and it never worked. Sybil's a peacemaker and wants everyone to be happy but I always annoy Natalie by saying or doing the wrong thing.'

'Try giving her another chance,' Angel urged, surprising her. 'I don't get on with my mother either, but then she doesn't make any effort to get on with me. At least yours is willing to make the effort.'

'And when it goes pear-shaped, she blames me every time,' Merry said bitterly.

'You can be an unforgiving little soul when people fail your high expectations,' Angel murmured softly. 'I know you haven't forgiven me yet for running out on you.'

Her face froze. 'What makes you think that?'

'Be honest. I'm still on probation. You're always waiting for me to do something dreadful and show my true colours,' Angel told her impatiently. 'You hold back. You watch everything you say and do and always give me the carefully sanitised version.'

Merry clashed in shock with hot dark golden eyes and recognised his exasperation. Guilty dismay pierced her and she was even more taken aback by how very clearly he saw through her pretences to her fearful desire to keep the peace. He lifted a hand and traced the full, soft curve of her lower lip as she caught it between her teeth.

'I don't mean to be like that,' she admitted uncomfortably.

'I'll have to work that pessimistic streak out of you. By all means, set the bar high because I do rise to a challenge,' Angel assured her. 'But don't drown me before I can even begin in low expectations.'

'I *don't* have low expectations,' Merry protested breathlessly, flipping over to face him, her colour high.

Angel grasped her hand and spread her fingers low on his belly with a glittering smile of disagreement. 'Go on, tell me you're too tired or just not in the mood for once,' he urged.

Her small fingers flexed against his sun-warmed skin and then pulled defiantly free to trace the furrow of silky hair that ran down from his navel to vanish beneath the waistband of his shorts. Heat uncoiled and spread low in her belly. 'You don't get it, do you?' she whispered, flicking loose the first metal stud separating her from him. 'No matter how tired, I can't help always being in the mood for you,' she confided unsteadily. 'It's not fake, it's not me trying to please.'

She heard the startled catch of his expelled breath as she attacked the remaining studs, felt too the hardness of the arousal he couldn't possibly hide from her and she thrilled at his unashamed need for her. She had assumed that initial enthusiasm would die a death once she was no longer a novelty in his bed but he hadn't flagged in the slightest. She jerked the shorts down and reached for him.

Angel watched her in fascination. Here she was again taking him by surprise, defying his own expectations with a bold counter-attack, despite her inexperience. And he treasured her ability to disconcert him, revelling in the reality that she appeared to have more interest in his body than she had in the new wardrobe he had bought for her. She was quite unlike any other woman he had ever been with, gloriously unimpressed by his wealth and what he could buy her. Her shy fingers found him, stroked him and the sweet swell of shattering pleasure washed over him. His breath hissed out between his even white teeth. He lay back, giving her control without hesitation.

Merry licked the long, strong column of him, swiping with her tongue, eager to return the favour of his attention even if it meant she delivered a less than polished performance. The muscles on his abdomen rippled, his tension building, his hips rising as a sexy sound of reaction escaped his parted lips and she smiled, loving his responsiveness, his unexpected willingness to let her take charge for a change. She closed him between her lips and he groaned out loud, long fingers knotting into her hair, urging her on, controlling the rhythm.

'Enough!' Angel bit out abruptly, pulling her back and slotting her deftly under him, rearranging her for what he really wanted and needed.

Splayed beneath him starfish-mode, Merry cried out as he plunged straight into her, all ferocious urgency and unleashed passion, his lean hips rising and falling between her slender thighs to send jolt after jolt of hot, sweet pleasure surging in waves through her. Her excitement climbed exponentially and when he flipped her over onto her knees and slammed into her again and again while the ball of his thumb stroked against her, he sent her flying into an explosive orgasm that left her sobbing for breath and control in the aftermath.

'No, that definitely wasn't fake or you trying to please me,' Angel murmured with roughened satisfaction in her ear as he gently tugged her hair back from her hot face and planted a lingering kiss there.

At some stage of the night, Angel shook her awake and her eyes flew open to focus on him in drowsy surprise. He was already fully dressed, sheathed in a sleek business suit, freshly shaven. He sank down on the side of the bed. 'I'm heading back to London. There's a stock-market crisis and I prefer to handle it on the spot with my staff around me. I've made arrangements for you to fly back first thing tomorrow morning…you need your sleep right now,' he said, stroking her cheekbone with unexpected tenderness. 'Once you've seen your aunt and your mother you can come and join me.'

Angel stared down at his wife, more than a little unnerved by the guilt sweeping him when he noticed the shadows below her eyes and the weary droop of her eyelids. He had been too demanding. He couldn't get enough of her in or out of bed and she was so busy being the perfect wife and perfect mother that she wasn't taking time out for her own needs. He was selfish, had always been selfish, was trying in fits and starts to be less selfish, but when he wanted her with him it was a challenge to defy his own need. Leaving her to sleep the night through was a sacrifice when he would sooner have had her by her side.

'It drives me mad when you make decisions for me!' Merry groaned in frustration. 'I could have flown back with you.'

'It wouldn't be fair to take Elyssa out of bed in the middle of the night and you're already tired out. I suggest that you leave her here with Sally unless you're planning to stay with your family for a few days,' Angel opined with an ebony brow rising in question on that score.

Merry sighed, unenthusiastic about the prospect of seeing her mother again. 'Not very likely. After a couple of hours catching up I'll probably be glad to escape,' she forecast ruefully.

Angel sprang upright again, all lithe, sexy elegance and energy, holding her gaze like a live flame burning in the darkness. 'And I'll be glad to have you back,' he declared with a flashing smile that tilted her heart inside her and made her senses hum.

Merry recalled that brief snatch of dialogue over coffee on the terrace the following morning. It was Sally's day off and Elyssa had just gone upstairs for her nap, leaving her mother free to relax in the sunshine. She smoothed a hand down over the bright red sundress she wore, preventing it from creeping any further up her slender thighs because she didn't want to flash the gardener engaged in trimming the edges of the lawn.

Angel had bought her a new wardrobe and it had very much his stamp on it. She thought the hemlines were too short, the necklines too revealing or snug in fit and the colour choices too bold, but then she wasn't used to showing off her figure or seeking attention. Maybe that had been Angel's nefarious plan all along, she reflected with wry amusement; maybe he hoped to drive her out shopping by landing her with a selection of garments she considered too daring. She certainly wouldn't put such scheming past him. The lingerie, however, was a superb fit and very much to her taste, plain and comfortable rather than provocative or elaborate.

One of the maids walked onto the terrace to announce a visitor and a moment later Roula Paulides strolled out to join Merry, a wide smile of greeting pinned to her beautiful face. 'I heard Angel's helicopter taking off during the night and thought this would be a good opportunity for us to get better acquainted,' she admitted.

Determined to look welcoming, Merry smiled and ordered fresh coffee. Roula was one of Angel's most long-standing friends yet Merry was also conscious of the possessive vibe that flared through her whenever she relived how she had once felt seeing her husband in the glamorous blonde's company.

Roula took a seat, very self-assured in her designer casuals, her blonde hair secured in a stylish twist, her brown eyes bright as she smiled again. And something about that second smile warned Merry that her visitor wasn't half as relaxed as she was trying to appear.

'I want to make it clear that I won't make a habit of visiting like this,' Roula assured her smoothly as she lifted her coffee cup. 'We're both entitled to our privacy. We'll only occasionally meet when Angel holds a big party because that is the only time he invites me to his home.'

'You're welcome to visit any time you like,' Merry responded easily, wondering if, in a roundabout, devious way, she was being accused of being a jealous, possessive wife likely to resent and distrust any female friend of her husband's.

'Oh, that wouldn't do. Angel wouldn't allow that,' Roula declared. 'He wouldn't consider that appropriate in the circumstances. I thought he would've mentioned our arrangement by now but, although he never justifies his lifestyle, he's like most men: keen to avoid conflict.'

Merry's eyes had steadily widened throughout that speech as she struggled to work out what the other woman was talking about. 'What arrangement?' she heard herself ask baldly. 'I'm afraid I don't know what you're referring to.'

Roula Paulides settled cynically amused brown eyes on her. 'I'm Angel's mistress. I have been for years.'

For a split second, Merry didn't believe that she had heard that announcement because it struck her like a blow, freezing her brain into incredulous inactivity, leaving her staring back at her companion in blank disbelief.

Roula lifted and dropped a thin shoulder in acknowledgement. 'It's how he lives and I have never been able to refuse Angel anything. If you and I can reach an accommodation that we can both live with, all our lives will run much more smoothly. I'm not the jealous type and I hope you aren't either.'

Merry sucked in a shuddering breath. 'Let me get this straight. You came here today to tell me that you're sleeping with my husband?'

'Oh, not recently. Angel has no need of me right now with a new wife in his bed,' the Greek woman declared drily. 'But in time, when you are no longer a novelty, he will return to me. Other women have always come and gone in his life. I accept that. I've *always* accepted that and if you are wise and wish to remain his wife you will accept it too. You can't own him, you can't cage him.'

Merry looked beyond Roula, unnerved by the sudden throbbing intensity of her low-pitched voice and the brash, hard confidence with which she spoke, the suggestion that *she* knew Angel better than anyone else. On the hill above the village sat the Paulides home, a rather boxy modern white villa, which Angel had casually identified as being where Roula lived. Shock was winging through Merry in giddy waves of increasingly desperate denial, her fingers curling into defensive claws on her lap. It couldn't be true, it couldn't possibly be true that Angel had some permanent, non-exclusive sexual arrangement with the other woman that he had remained silent about.

'You seem shocked, but why? We were childhood friends and have always been very close. We understand each other very well,' Roula told her calmly. 'In the same way I accepted that after your child was born, Angel would inevitably end up marrying you. He doesn't love you any more than he loves me but he will do his duty by his daughter. I'm here now only to assure you that I will never try to interfere in your marriage in any way and that I hope you will not be spiteful and try to prevent Angel from seeing me.'

Merry swallowed hard at that unlikely hope. 'What's in this weird arrangement for you?' she asked bluntly.

Roula vented a laugh and tossed her head. 'I have a share of him. I'm willing to settle for that. I've loved him since I was a girl. He rescued my father from bankruptcy and financed the set-up of my beauty salons. When I was younger I hoped that he would eventually see me as a possible wife, but of course that hasn't happened. Marrying the mistress isn't in the Valtinos genes.'

Nausea stirred in Merry's tummy. Swallowing her coffee without choking on it was a challenge. Roula managed to make it all sound so normal, so inevitable. She loved Angel, unashamedly did what it took to hold onto her small stake in his life while accepting that there would be other women and eventually a wife she would have to share him with.

But such acceptance was nowhere within Merry's grasp. She was an all-or-nothing person. She had told Angel before she agreed to marry him that he could have no other women in his life and that she expected complete fidelity. He had agreed to that boundary. Had he lied? Had he expected her to change her mind? Or had he been planning to be so discreet that she never found out that he sometimes slept with Roula Paulides?

Shock banging through her blitzed brain, Merry struggled to relocate her reasoning powers. Did she simply accept that the blonde was telling her the truth? Why would Roula lie about such a relationship? Could she simply be trying to cause trouble in Merry's marriage? But what would be the point of that unless she was already engaged in an affair with Angel with something to gain from his marriage breaking down?

And then, according to Roula, Angel had not been *with* her recently? Or simply since his marriage? Merry's head was spinning. She wanted to pack her bags, gather up her daughter and run back to the UK to establish a sane and normal life where a blonde beauty did not calmly stroll into her home one morning to announce that she was in love with Merry's husband and keen to continue having hassle-free sex with him.

Stark pain sliced through Merry, cutting through the numbness of shock. She had been happy, she registered wretchedly, hopelessly, helplessly happy with Angel and their marriage as it was. She had seen nothing to question, nothing to rouse her suspicions. She had believed his promise of fidelity, believed that they had a future, but if she believed Roula her future with Angel could only be a deceitful and fragile farce because she would never ever accept him betraying her with another woman. Nor would she ever share him.

'Well, you've said your piece. Now I think you should leave,' Merry told Roula quietly, her self-discipline absolute because wild horses could not have dredged a more vulnerable reaction from her.

'I do hope I haven't upset you,' the Greek woman said unconvincingly. 'I suspected you didn't know and that wasn't right.'

As far as Merry was concerned there was nothing right about Roula's attitude to either Angel or his marriage or even his wife. Roula had developed her own convictions based on what she wanted. Roula, it seemed, lived to please Angel. Merry loved Angel but she had never been blind to his flaws. Had he discounted his intimate relationship with Roula in the same way as he had once ignored the reality that his pregnant former employee might need more than financial support from him?

It would have been uncomfortable for Angel to overcome his own feelings back then and offer Merry his support, and he had been unable to force himself to go that extra mile for her benefit. In the same way being honest about his relationship with Roula would have put paid to any hope of Merry marrying him and sharing their daughter. Was that why he had kept quiet? Or was it possible that he believed the relationship with Roula was at an end? But then wouldn't Roula know that? Had Angel lied to Merry to get her to the altar? Was he that ruthless?

Oh, yes, a little voice chimed inside her head.

CHAPTER NINE

'MRS VALTINOS INSISTED that she had to make an immediate departure from the airport,' Angel's driver repeated uneasily. 'I did tell her that you were expecting her to join you for lunch before she left London but she said—'

'That she didn't have time,' Angel slotted in flatly.

'I took her to Foxcote Hall at two and then an hour later dropped her off at her aunt's house. She said she'd call when she needed to be picked up again,' the older man completed.

Angel breathed in slow and deep. Something was wrong. His wife had flown back to London with their daughter and mounds of luggage even though she had only been expecting to remain in the UK for forty-eight hours at most. She had blown him off for lunch. She wasn't answering his calls or his texts. Such behaviour was unlike her. Merry wasn't moody or facetious and she didn't play games. If something had annoyed her, she was more likely to speak up straight away. His growing bewilderment was starting to give way to righteous anger and an amount of unfamiliar apprehension that only enraged him more.

What could possibly have happened between his departure and her arrival in London? Why the mounds of luggage? Wasn't she planning to return to Greece? Was it possible that she was leaving him and taking their daughter with her? But why would she do that? He had checked with the staff on Palos. Merry had had only one visitor and that was Roula, and when he had phoned Roula she had insisted that Merry had been perfectly friendly and relaxed with her. His lean brown hands knotting into fists, his tension pronounced, Angel resolved to be waiting at Foxcote when Merry got back.

Merry emerged from the rambling country house that she had not until that day known that Angel owned and climbed into the waiting limousine. She had left Elyssa with Sally, deeming it unlikely that her mother was likely to be champing at the bit to meet her first grandchild because Natalie had never had much time for babies. Furthermore, if Natalie was likely to be chastising her daughter and creating one of her emotionally exhausting scenes it was better to keep Elyssa well away from the display because Merry always lost patience with the older woman. What did it matter after all these years anyway? Natalie hadn't even made the effort to attend her daughter's wedding. But then she hadn't made the effort to attend Merry's graduation or, indeed, any of the significant events that had marked her daughter's life.

Obsessed with the recollection of Roula's sleazy allegations, Merry was simply not in the mood to deal with her mother. Landing in London to discover that Angel had arranged to meet her for lunch had been unsettling. Merry was determined to confront him but only in her own time and only when she had decided exactly what she intended to say to him. Not yet at that point, she had ducked lunch and ignored his calls and texts. Let him fester for a while as she had had to fester while she'd run over Roula's claims until her head had ached and her stomach had been queasy and she had wept herself empty of tears.

Angel hadn't asked her to love him, she reminded herself as the limo drew up outside Sybil's house. But he had asked her to trust him and she had. Now that trust was broken and she was so wounded she felt as though she had been torn apart. She had trailed all her belongings and her daughter's back from Greece but she still didn't know what she would be doing next or even where she would be living. While she had been getting married, life had moved on. The cottage now had another tenant and she didn't want to move in with her aunt again. Nor did she want to feel like a sad, silly failure with Angel again.

'So glad you made the time to come,' Sybil gabbled almost nervously as Merry walked through the front door into the open-plan lounge where her mother rose stiffly upright to face her. Natalie bore little resemblance to her daughter, being small, blonde and rather plump, but she looked remarkably young for her forty odd years.

'Natalie,' Merry acknowledged, forcing herself forward to press an awkward kiss to her mother's cheek. 'How are you?'

'Oh, don't be all polite and nice as if we're strangers. That just makes me feel worse,' her mother immediately complained. 'Sybil has something to tell you. You had better sit down. It's going to come as a shock.'

Her brow furrowing in receipt of that warning, Merry sank down into an armchair and focused on her aunt. Sybil remained standing and she was very pale.

'We have a big secret in this family, which we have always covered up,' Sybil stated agitatedly. 'I didn't see much point in telling you about it so long after the event.'

'No, you never did like to tell anything that could make you look bad,' Natalie sniped. 'But you *promised* me that you would tell her.'

Sybil compressed her lips. 'When I was fifteen I got pregnant by a boy I was at school with. My parents were horrified. They sent me to live with a cousin up north and then they adopted my baby. It was all hushed up. I had to promise my mother that I would never tell my daughter the truth.'

Merry was bemused. 'I—'

'I was that adopted baby,' Natalie interposed thinly. 'I'm not Sybil's younger sister, I'm her *daughter* but I didn't find that out until I was eighteen.'

Losing colour, Merry flinched and focused on Sybil in disbelief. 'Your *daughter*?'

'Yes. Then my mother died and I felt that Natalie had the right to know who I really was. She was already talking about trying to trace her birth mother, so it seemed sensible to speak up before she tried doing that,' Sybil explained hesitantly.

'And overnight, when that truth came out, Sybil went from being my very exciting famous big sister, who gave me wonderful gifts, to being a liar, who had deceived me all my life,' Merry's mother condemned with a bitterness that shook Merry.

'So, you're actually my grandmother, not my aunt,' Merry registered shakily as she studied Sybil and struggled to disentangle the family relationships she had innocently taken for granted.

'It wasn't my secret to share after the adoption. I gave up my rights but when I came clean about who I really was, it sent your mother off the rails.'

'Lies…the gift that keeps on giving,' Natalie breathed tersely. 'That's part of the reason I fell pregnant with you, Merry. When I had that stupid affair with your father, I was all over the place emotionally. I had lost my adoptive mother and then discovered that the sister I loved and admired was in fact my mother…and I didn't like her very much.'

'Natalie couldn't forgive me for putting my career first but it enabled me to give my parents enough money to live a very comfortable life while they raised my daughter,' Sybil argued in her own defence. 'I was grateful for their care of her. I wasn't ready to be a mother.'

'At least, not until *you* were born, Merry,' Natalie slotted in with perceptible scorn. 'Then Sybil interfered and stole you away from me.'

'It wasn't like that!' Sybil protested. 'You *needed* help.'

Merry's mother settled strained eyes on Merry's troubled face and said starkly, 'What do you think it was like for me to see *my* birth mother lavishing all the love and care she had denied me on my daughter instead?'

Merry breathed in deep and slow, struggling to put her thoughts in order. In reality she was still too upset about Roula's allegations to fully concentrate her brain on what the two women were telling her. Sybil was her grandmother, *not* her aunt and Merry had never been told that Natalie was an adopted child. She abhorred the fact that she had not been given the full truth about her background sooner.

'The way Sybil treated you, the fuss she made of you, made me *resent* you,' Merry's mother confessed guiltily. 'It wrecked our relationship. She came between us.'

'That was never my intention,' Sybil declared loftily.

'But that's how it was…' Natalie complained stonily.

Merry lowered her head, recognising that she saw points on both sides of the argument. Sybil had only been fifteen when she gave Natalie up to her parents for adoption and she had been barred from admitting that she was Natalie's birth mum. Merry refused to condemn Sybil for that choice but she also saw how devastating that pretence and the lies must've been for her own mother and how finding out that truth years afterwards had distressed her.

'You *say* you want a closer relationship with me and yet you still had no interest in coming to my wedding or in meeting my daughter,' Merry heard herself fire back at her mother.

'I couldn't afford the plane fare!' Natalie snapped defensively. 'Who do you think paid for this visit?'

'How do you feel about this?' Sybil pressed anxiously.

'Confused,' Merry admitted tightly. 'Hurt that the two of you didn't tell me the truth years ago. And I hate lies, Sybil, and now I discover that you've pretty much been lying to me my whole life.'

In actuality, Merry felt as if the solid floor under her feet had fallen away, leaving her to stage a difficult balancing act. Her grandmother and her mother were both regarding her expectantly and she didn't know what she was supposed to say to satisfy either of them. The sad reality was that she had always had more in common with Sybil than with Natalie and that, no matter how hard she tried, she would probably never be able to replicate that close relationship with her mother.

'All I ever wanted to do was try to help you still have a life as a single parent,' Sybil told her daughter unhappily. 'You were so young. I never wanted to come between you and Merry.'

'I'd like to meet Elyssa,' Natalie declared. 'Sybil's shown me photos. She is very cute.'

And Merry realised then that she had been guilty of holding her own unstable childhood against her mother right into adulthood instead of accepting that Natalie might have changed and matured. 'I will bring her over for a visit,' she promised stiffly. 'How long are you staying for?'

'Two weeks,' Natalie told her. 'But now that Keith's gone and we've split up, I'm thinking of moving back to the UK again. I'd like to meet your husband while I'm here as well.'

Tears suddenly stinging her hot eyes, Merry nodded jerkily, not trusting herself to speak. She understood why her mother had wanted the story told but wasn't at all sure that she could give the older woman the warmer relationship she was clearly hoping for. But then too many of her emotions were bound up in the bombshell that had blown her marriage apart, she conceded guiltily. Roula's confession had devastated her and at that moment having to turn her back on the man she loved and her marriage was still all she could really think about. It was the thought, the terrifying awareness, of what she might have to do next that left room for nothing else and paralysed her.

She shared photos of the wedding and Elyssa with both women, glossed over Sybil's comment that she seemed very pale and quiet and returned to Foxcote

Hall as soon as she decently could, having promised to bring Elyssa back for a visit within a few days. The limo travelled at a stately pace back up to the elegant country house that had the stunning architecture of an oversized Georgian dolls' house. Informal gardens shaded by clusters of mature trees spread out from the house and slowly changed into a landscape of green fields and lush stretches of woodland. Foxcote was a magnificent estate and yet Angel had not even mentioned that he owned a property near her aunt's home.

She had originally planned to go to a hotel from the airport, but when she had yet even to see and speak to Angel such a statement of separation had seemed a tad premature. Walking into the airy hall with its tall windows and tiled floor, she heard Elyssa chuckling and stringing together strings of nonsense words and she followed the sounds.

Several steps into the drawing room, she stopped dead because Angel was down on the floor with Elyssa, letting his daughter clamber over him and finally wrap her chubby arms round his neck and plant a triumphant noisy kiss on his face. He grinned, delighting in the baby's easy trusting affection, but his smile fell away the instant he glimpsed Merry. Suddenly his lean, darkly handsome features were sober and unsmiling, his beautiful dark eyes wary and intent.

'You never mentioned that you owned a house near Sybil's,' Merry remarked in a brittle voice as he vaulted lithely upright with Elyssa clasped to his chest.

'My father bought the estate when he was going through a hunting, shooting, fishing phase but he soon got bored. Angelina used it for a while when she was socialising with the heir to a local dukedom. It should really be sold now,' Angel contended, crossing the room to lift the phone and summon their nanny to take charge of their daughter.

A current of pained resentment bit into Merry when Elyssa complained bitterly about being separated from her father. That connection, that bond had formed much sooner than she had expected. Elyssa had taken to Angel like a duck to water, revelling in his more physical play and more boisterous personality. If her father was to disappear from her daily life, their daughter would miss him and be hurt by his absence. But then whose fault would that be? Merry asked herself angrily. It certainly wouldn't be *her* fault, she told herself piously. She had played by the rules. If their marriage broke down, it would be entirely Angel's responsibility.

'So, what's going on?' Angel enquired, taking up a faintly combative stance as Sally closed the door in her wake, his long powerful legs braced, shoulders thrown back, aggressive jaw line at an angle. 'You blew me off at lunch and all day you've been ignoring my calls and texts…*why*?'

Merry sucked in a steadying breath. 'I'm leaving you…well, in the process of it,' she qualified stiffly, her face pale and set.

'Why would you suddenly decide to leave me?' Angel demanded, striding forward, all brooding intimidation, dark eyes glittering like fireworks in the night sky. 'That makes no sense.'

Anger laced the atmosphere, tensing every defensive muscle in her body, and she cursed the reality that she was not mentally prepared for the confrontation about to take place.

'Roula told me everything.'

Angel looked bemused. 'Everything about… *what*?' he demanded with curt emphasis.

'That she's been your mistress for years, that you always go back to her eventually.'

'I don't have a mistress. I've never had one. Before you, I've never wanted repeat encounters with the same woman,' Angel told her almost conversationally, dark golden eyes locked to her strained face. 'You must've misunderstood something Roula said. There's no way that she told you that we were lovers.'

'There was no misunderstanding,' Merry framed stiffly. 'She was very frank about your relationship and about the fact that she expected it to continue even though you were married.'

'But it's not true. I don't know what she's playing at but her claims are nonsense,' Angel declared with harsh emphasis. 'Is this all we've got, Merry? Some woman only has to say I sleep with her and you swallow the story whole?'

Merry clasped her trembling hands together and tilted her chin, her spine rigid. 'She was very convincing. I believed her.'

'*Diavolos!* You just judge me out of hand? You believe her rather than *me*?' Angel raked at her in a burst of incredulous anger, black curls tumbling across his brow as he shook his head in evident disbelief. 'You take her word over mine?'

'She's your friend. Why would she lie about such a thing?'

'How the hell am I supposed to know?' Angel shot back at her. 'But she *is* lying!'

'She said you'd been lovers for years but that you've always had other women,' Merry recounted flatly. 'I will not accept you being with other women!'

Angel settled volatile eyes on her and she backed away a step at the sheer heat she met there.

'Then try not to *drive* me into being with them!' he slammed back. 'I have not been unfaithful to you.'

'She did say that you hadn't been with her since you got married but that eventually you would return to her because apparently you always do.'

'You are the only woman I have *ever* returned to!' Angel proclaimed rawly. 'I can't believe we're even having this stupid conversation—'

'It's not a conversation, it's an argument,' she interrupted.

'I promised you that there would be no other women,' Angel reminded her darkly. 'Didn't you listen? Obviously, you didn't believe—'

'Your reputation goes before you,' Merry flung back at him bitterly.

'I will not apologise for my past. I openly acknowledge it but I have never cheated on any woman I have been with!' Angel intoned in a driven undertone. 'I grew up with a mother who cheated on all her lovers and I lived with the consequences of that kind of behaviour. I know better. I'm honest and I move on when I get bored.'

'Well, maybe I don't want to hang around waiting for you to get bored with me and move on!' Merry fired back with ringing scorn. 'Maybe I think I'm worth more than that and deserve more respect. That's why I'm calling time on us now before things get messy!'

'You're not calling time on us. That's not your decision to make,' Angel delivered with lethal derision. 'We got married to make a home for our daughter and if we have to work at achieving that happy outcome, then we *work* at it.'

A cold, forlorn hollow spread like poison inside Merry's tight chest as she recognised how foolish and naïve she had been to dream that Angel could eventually come to care for her. He had only married her for Elyssa's sake. She would never be important to him in her own right, never be that one special woman in his eyes, never be anything other than second best to him. He could have had any woman, and a woman like Roula Paulides, who shared his background and nationality as well as a long friendship with him, would have had infinitely more to offer him. He wouldn't have had to talk about having to *work* at being married to anyone else. In fact her mind boggled at the concept of Angel being prepared to do anything as dully conventional and sensible as *work* at a relationship.

'I don't want to work at it,' she heard herself say, and it was truthfully what she felt at that moment because her pride could not bear the idea of him having to suppress his natural instincts before he could accept being married to her and staying faithful.

'You don't get a choice,' Angel spelled out grimly. 'We'll fly back to Palos in the morning—'

'No!' she interrupted. 'I'm not returning to Greece with you!'

'You're my wife and you're not leaving me,' Angel asserted harshly. 'That isn't negotiable.'

Merry tossed her head, dark hair rippling back from her flushed cheeks, pale blue eyes icy with fury. 'I'm not even trying to negotiate with you... I already know what a slippery slope that can be. Our marriage is over and I'm staying in the UK,' she declared fiercely. 'I'll move out of here as soon as I decide where I'm going to be living.'

Angel stared back at her, his hard bone structure prominent below his bronzed skin, his eyes very dark and hard. 'You would just throw everything we've got away?' he breathed in a tone of suppressed savagery that made her flinch. 'And what about our daughter?'

Merry swallowed with difficulty, sickly envisioning the likely battle ahead and cringing from the prospect. 'I'll fight you for custody of our daughter here in the UK,' she told him squarely, shocked at what she was saying but needing to convince him that she would not be softened or sidelined by threats.

Angel froze almost as if she had struck him, black

lashes lifting on grim dark eyes without the smallest shade of gold, his lean, strong face rigid with tension. 'You would separate us? That I will not forgive you for,' he told her with fierce finality.

Ten seconds later, Merry was alone in the room, listening numbly to the roar of a helicopter taking off somewhere nearby and presumably ferrying Angel back to London. And she was in shock, her head threatening to explode with the sheer unbearable pressure that had built up inside it, her stomach churning sickly. Tears surged in a hot stinging tide into her eyes and she blinked furiously but the tears kept on coming, dripping down her face.

Their marriage was over. Hadn't she always feared that their marriage wouldn't last? Why was she so shocked? Yes, he had denied that Roula Paulides was his mistress but she hadn't believed him, had she? When she had packed her bags on the island she had known she wasn't coming back and certainly not to a marriage with a husband who had to *work* at being married to her!

CHAPTER TEN

MISERY AND GUILT kept Merry awake for half the night. She had threatened Angel just as he had once threatened her and now it lay like a big rock of shame on her conscience because she had witnessed the depth of his attachment to Elyssa, had watched it develop, had even noticed how surprised Angel was at the amount of enjoyment he received from being a parent. He did not love his wife but he definitely *did* love his daughter.

All her emotions in free fall after the sensitive family issues that had been explored at Sybil's house, she had been in no fit state to deal with Angel. She had drawn up battle lines for a war she didn't actually want to wage, she acknowledged wretchedly. A divorce or separation didn't have to be bitter and nasty and she hadn't the smallest desire for them to fight like cat and dog over their daughter. Angel was a good father, a *very* good father and she would never try to deprive him of contact with his child. Just because she couldn't trust him with the Roulas of the world didn't mean she was blind to his skills as a parent or that she wasn't aware that Elyssa benefitted as much as Angel did from their relationship. She wasn't that selfish, that prejudiced against him, *was* she?

Anguish screamed through her as she sniffed and blew her nose over her breakfast in the dining room. She was a garish match for her elegantly furnished surroundings, clad as she was in comfy old pyjamas and a silky, boldly patterned kimono robe that had seen better days. She had left her fancy new wardrobe behind on Palos as a statement of rejection that she wanted Angel to notice. She had wanted him to appreciate that she didn't need him or his money or those stupid designer clothes, even if that was a lie.

Her real problem, however, was that pain and hurt magnified everything and distorted logic. She had told Angel that she was leaving him because pride had demanded she act as though she were strong and decisive rather than betray the reality that she was broken up and confused and horribly hurt.

The thwack-thwack of a helicopter coming into land made her head ache even more and she gulped down more tea, desperate to soothe her ragged nerves. She heard the slam of the front door and she stiffened, her head jerking up as the dining-room door opened without warning and framed Angel's tall, powerful form. She could not have been more appalled had he surprised her naked because she knew she looked like hell. Her eyes and nose were red, her hair was tangled.

'Will you come into the drawing room?' Angel asked grimly. 'There's someone here to see you.'

'I'm not dressed,' she protested stiltedly, her head lowering to hide her face as she stumbled upright, desperate to make a quick escape from his astute gaze.

'You'll do fine,' Angel told her callously, dark eyes cold and treacherous as black ice.

'I can't see anyone looking like this,' Merry argued vehemently, striving to leave the room and flee upstairs by sidestepping him, but she found him as immoveable in the doorway as a rock.

'You'll be in very good company. I swear she's cried all the way from Greece,' Angel informed her incomprehensibly, gripping her elbow with a firm hand and practically thrusting her into the room next door.

Merry's feet froze to the floor when she saw the woman standing by the window. It was Roula, looking something less than her usually sophisticated and stylish self. Her ashen complexion only emphasised her swollen eyes and pink nose and she was convulsively shredding a tissue between her restive fingers.

'I'm so...*so* sorry!' she gasped, facing Merry. 'I lied to you.'

Angel shot something at the other woman in irate Greek and she groaned and snapped something back, and then the door closed behind Merry and when she turned her head again, Angel was gone, leaving them alone.

'You *lied* to me?' Merry prompted in astonishment.

'I was trying to frighten you off. I thought if you left him he might finally turn to me,' Roula framed shakily, her voice hoarse with embarrassment and misery.

'Oh,' Merry mumbled rather blankly. 'You're not his mistress, then?'

'No, that was nonsense,' Roula framed hoarsely. 'We've never had sex either. Angel's never been interested in me that way, but because we were such good friends I thought if you broke up with him he would confide in me and maybe start seeing me in a different light. But it's not going to happen. He said the idea of me and him ever being intimate was disgusting, *incestuous*. I wish I'd worked out that that's how he saw me years ago. I'd have saved myself a lot of heartache.'

Merry experienced a very strong desire to pat the blonde's shoulder to comfort her and had to fight the weird prompting off. She could see that the other woman felt humiliated and guilty and very sad. 'Did Angel force you to come here and tell me this?'

'Well, it wasn't my idea, but he said I owed him and he was right. From the moment he told me that he was marrying you I was so *jealous* of you!' Roula confessed with a sudden wrenching sob, clamping her hand to her mouth and getting herself back under control again before continuing, 'Why you? I asked myself. Why *not* me? You worked for him and he never ever sleeps with his employees and yet he slept with *you*…and you've got a great figure and you're very pretty but you're not exactly supermodel material…and then you totally freak him out by having a baby and yet somehow he's now crazy about the baby as well!'

'Have you always been in love with him?' Merry mumbled uncomfortably, grasping that, by Roula's reckoning, Angel deciding to marry her qualified as an unbelievable and quite undeserved miracle.

'When I was a teenager it was just a crush. He was my best friend. I knew all the rotten things Angelina has ever done to him and it broke my heart. I learned how to handle her to keep her out of his hair, to try and help him cope with her. That's why she likes me, that's why she decided that he should marry me if he ever married anyone. I've had other relationships, of course,' Roula told her wryly. 'But every time one broke down, I told myself it would've been different with Angel. He was my ideal, my Mr Right…at least he was until he dragged me onto that plane and shouted at me half the night!'

'His temper's rough,' Merry conceded while frantically trying to work out how she had so badly misjudged the man whom she had married. It was obvious that Roula was now telling her the truth. Bitter jealousy had driven the blonde into an attempt to destroy Angel's marriage.

'And he's like the elephant who never forgets when you cross him. He'll never forgive me for causing all this trouble,' Roula muttered with weary regret.

'He'll get over it,' Molly said woodenly, wondering if he would ever forgive her either.

'I'm sorry. I'm truly sorry,' the blonde framed guiltily. 'I know that's not much consolation in the circumstances but I deeply regret lying to you. I didn't think it through. I told myself you'd probably got deliberately pregnant and planned the whole thing to trap him. I could see he was happy on your wedding day but I wouldn't admit that to myself and if anyone merits being happy, it's Angel.'

'I think we can forget about this now,' Merry commented uncomfortably. 'I can't put my hand on my heart and say that I forgive you, but I am grateful you explained why you did it and I do understand.'

'Fair enough,' Roula sighed as she opened the door to leave.

Merry tensed when she saw Angel poised across the hall, straightening to his full predatory height, shrewd dark eyes scanning her like a radiation counter.

'I told the truth,' Roula told him flatly. 'Can I leave now?'

'You're satisfied?' Angel demanded of Merry.

She nodded in embarrassed confirmation.

'I'll have you returned to the airport,' Angel informed Roula curtly.

Merry took advantage of his momentary inattention to head for the stairs at a very fast rate of knots. She wanted to splash her face, clean her teeth, brush her hair and ditch the pyjamas with the pink bunny rabbits on them. Then she would work out what she had to say to him to redress the damage she had done with her lack of faith. Possibly a spot of grovelling would be appropriate, obviously a heartfelt apology…

She was caught unprepared and halfway into a pair of jeans when Angel strode into the bedroom. He thrust the door shut, leant his long, lean frame sinuously back against it and studied her with brooding dark eyes.

'I'm sorry… I'm really sorry,' she muttered, yanking up the jeans. 'But she was very convincing and I don't think she's a bad person. I think she was just jealous and she got a bit carried away.'

'I don't give a damn about Roula or why she did what she did,' Angel declared impatiently. 'I care that even after being married to me for weeks you were still willing to threaten me with the loss of my daughter.'

Merry lost colour, her eyes guiltily lowering from the hard challenge of his. 'That was wrong,' she acknowledged ruefully. 'But you used the same threat to persuade me into marrying you…or have you forgotten that?'

'My intentions were good. I wanted to persuade you to give us a chance to be a proper family. But your intentions were bad and destructive,' Angel countered without hesitation. 'You wanted to use Elyssa like a weapon to punish me. That would have damaged her as much as me.'

'No, I honestly wasn't thinking like that,' Merry argued, turning her back to him to flip off the despised pyjama top and reaching for a tee shirt, having decided for the sake of speed and dignity to forgo donning a bra. 'Even when I was mad at you I accepted that you are a great father, but I assumed you would make any divorce a bitter, nasty battle.'

'What made you assume that?' Angel asked drily. 'I didn't even ask you to sign a pre-nuptial agreement before the wedding. That omission sent the family lawyers into a tailspin but it was a deliberate move on my part. It was an act of faith formed on my foolish assumption that you would respect our marriage as much as I did.'

Merry reddened with more guilt. He really knew what buttons to push, she reflected wretchedly. It hadn't occurred to her that he hadn't asked her to sign a pre-nup before the ceremony, but in retrospect she could see that that had been a glaring omission, indeed a very positive statement, in a marriage involving a very wealthy man and a reasonably poor woman. His continuing coldness was beginning to unnerve her. He had never used that tone with her before. He sounded detached and negative and he was still icily angry. She glanced up, scanning his lean, strong features for another, more encouraging reading of his mood, and instead noted the forbidding line of his wide, sensual mouth, the harsh angle of his firm jaw and the level darkness of his accusing gaze.

'But the instant we hit the first rough patch in our marriage you were ready to throw it all away,' Angel condemned.

'A long-term mistress is more than a rough patch,' Merry protested helplessly. 'I believed Roula because you introduced me to her as a friend that you trusted.'

'She's the sister I never had,' Angel asserted with sardonic bite. 'The thought of anything of a sexual nature between us is…repellent.'

And the last piece of the puzzle fell into place for Merry, who, while believing Roula, had not quite been able to grasp why Angel had never been tempted into having a more intimate relationship with her. After all, Roula was a beauty and had to share a lot with him. But if he saw the blonde in the same light as a sibling, his indifference to her as a woman was instantly understandable and highly unlikely to ever change.

'I've seen a lot of divorces,' Angel admitted. 'In my own family, amongst friends. Nobody comes out unscathed but the children suffer the most. I don't want my daughter to ever suffer that damage, but neither do I want a wife who runs like a rabbit at the first sign of trouble.'

'I did *not* run like a rabbit!' Merry argued, hot-faced. 'Maybe you're thinking of what you did after I told you I was pregnant!'

'I took responsibility. I ensured your financial needs were covered.'

'But you weren't there when I was throwing up every morning and trying to drag myself into work to keep my job.'

'You didn't need to keep on working. Your allowance would have covered your living costs.' Angel hesitated before asking with a frown, 'Were you sick that often?'

'Every day for about four months, often more than

once a day. And then one evening I started bleeding and I assumed I was having a miscarriage. After that, I resigned from my job and went home to stay with Sybil.'

Angel levered his long, lean frame lithely off the door, moving with that innate grace of his towards her, his lean, dark face troubled. 'You almost lost Elyssa?'

'Well, I *thought* I was losing her and I panicked and went to the hospital, but it was just one of those pregnancy mishaps that seem more serious than they are. It was very frightening, though, and very upsetting.'

'And I wasn't there when I should've been,' Angel registered for himself, studying her grimly. 'Can't turn the clock back and be there for you either, so that can't be changed. Do you think you will always hold my absence during those months against me?'

'I try not to dwell on it. If you didn't want a relationship with me at the time there would've been no point in you coming back into my life,' she conceded simply. 'It would've been too awkward for both of us.'

Angel winced. 'I didn't even realise that I *did* want to be in a relationship with you back then. I would have to admit that I was completely blind to my own hang-ups. Growing up I only saw shallow, chaotic relationships, which is why when I was an adult I avoided anything that could have been construed as a relationship. I had sex and that was that, end of…only then I met you and my blueprint for a relaxed and unemotional life went up in flames.'

'How could you have an unemotional life when you're so full of emotion?' Merry asked him incredulously.

'I keep that side of me under control...at least I did until you and Elyssa sneaked through my defences,' Angel reasoned wryly. 'You know, you may not have been a happy camper while you were pregnant but I wasn't any happier. You shook me up. You made me want more and that scared me because I had no experience of a normal relationship.'

'You don't do relationships,' she reminded him drily.

'What have I been doing with you for the past month?' Angel shot back at her. 'There's nothing casual about our connection. Do you really think it's normal for me to be content to spend so much time with one woman?'

'I didn't ask you to do that.'

'I'm a selfish bastard. I did it only because I wanted to.'

'For your daughter's sake, you *worked* at being married to me,' Merry paraphrased with pained dismissiveness.

Angel shook his arrogant dark head in wonderment. 'I've got to admit that right now I'm having to *work* at being married to you because you are so stubbornly determined to think the worst of me.'

'That's not true.'

'You don't trust me. You're always waiting for the roof to fall in! I used to think that was cute but now I'm beginning to wonder if you'll ever recognise that, even though I've made a hell of a lot of mistakes along the way, I do love you,' he completed almost defiantly.

Merry stared at him in astonishment. 'You don't.'

'Even when you're wearing the bunny pyjamas you were wearing the night I got you pregnant,' Angel assured her with confidence. 'I didn't recognise it as love until after we were married. Even though I'm always worrying about you, I'm incredibly happy being with you. I wake up in the morning and everything feels good because you're there beside me. When you're not there, everything feels *off* and I feel weirdly lonely...'

Merry's lower lip parted company with her upper and she stared at him in wide-eyed consternation.

'And the most extraordinary thing of all is that I thought you loved me too until you walked out and accused me of cheating on you,' Angel admitted ruefully. 'I thought that for the first time in my life I was loved for who I was, not for what I can do or buy or provide. You know I'm flawed and you accept it. You know I'm still finding my way in this family set-up.'

'You're not the only one. Yesterday I discovered that Sybil is not my aunt but my grandmother,' Merry told him in a sudden surge. 'That's another reason why I was so upset and over the top with you yesterday. I was already all shaken up. My mother was adopted by Sybil's parents and only learned the truth when she was eighteen. Oh, never mind, I'll explain it all to you later, but finding out that Sybil and Natalie had been keeping all that from me all my life made me feel deceived…and you're right, I *do* love you,' she completed almost apologetically. 'I have almost from the start. Don't know why, don't know how, just got attached regardless of common sense.'

Angel rested his hands down on her taut shoulders. 'We had an electric connection from the first day. Somehow, we match. I just wish I hadn't wasted so much time staying away from you when I wanted to be with you. I was existing in a sort of fog of denial that everything had changed and that I wanted the sort of relationship that I had never trusted or experienced with a woman.'

'And I let you down,' she whispered guiltily. 'I did think the worst at the first sign of trouble. I wasn't strong and sensible the way I should have been.'

'It's sort of comforting that your common sense leaves you when you're upset. When I arrived and saw you'd been crying, obviously upset, it gave me hope that you did care.'

'I'll always care,' she muttered softly, turning her cheek into the caress of his long fingers.

'I've never trusted love. I know my father cares about me but my mother lost interest the minute I grew beyond the cute baby stage,' he confided. 'What you said about Sybil and your mother? Take it back to basics, *agape mou*. You may not have known the whole story but you were *always* loved. That's a blessing. It's much harder to love without that experience and the confidence it gives you.'

Merry stretched up to him and buried her face in his shoulder, drinking in the musky familiar aroma of his skin like a restorative drug. He caught her chin in his fingers and tipped up her mouth to taste her with hungry urgency.

'You taste so good,' he ground out, walking her back towards the bed with single-minded intent. 'Tell me you love me again… I like hearing it.'

'How did you guess how I felt?' Merry pressed. 'I thought I was hiding it.'

'You put up with all my unreasonable demands and still smiled at me. I didn't deserve it so there had to be some other reason why you were being so tolerant and sometimes I couldn't help testing you to see if you'd crack.'

'I don't crack. I'm loyal and loving…as long as you don't take on a mistress.'

'Where would I get the energy?' Angel growled, his attention elsewhere as he slid his hand below the tee shirt to mould it to a plump breast with satisfaction, and then wrenched her out of its concealment with unashamed impatience. '*Thee mou*, I want you so much it hurts… I thought I was losing you.'

'And then I disappointed you.'

'You're not supposed to walk away, you're supposed to stand and fight for me,' Angel told her. 'I fought for you.'

'I was hiding behind my pride.'

'I don't have any where you're concerned and I have even fewer scruples. I was willing to drug and kidnap you to get you back to Greece. You don't want to know the things that ran through my mind when

I thought I was losing you,' he assured her. 'A large helping of crazy, if I'm honest.'

'That's because you love me,' Merry told him happily. 'You're allowed to think crazy things if you want to fight to keep me...'

And their clothes fell away in a messy heap as Angel moved to make her his again and satisfy the last lurking stab of insecurity inside him. Merry was his again and all was right with his world, well, almost all. He shifted lithely against her, holding her close.

'When you feel up to the challenge, we'll have another baby and I will share the whole experience with you,' Angel promised, jolting her out of her drowsy sensual daydream.

'*Another*...baby?' Merry gasped in disbelief. 'You've got to be kidding! Elyssa's only seven months old!'

'You could consider it...eventually, hopefully,' Angel qualified. 'Although I'll settle for Elyssa if you don't want another child. It's not a deal breaker.'

'Are you sure the threat of that extra responsibility won't make you run for the hills again?' Merry asked snidely.

'No, set me the challenge of getting you pregnant and I assure you that I will happily meet every demand, no matter how strenuous or time consuming it becomes.' Dark golden eyes alive with tender amusement, Angel gazed down with a wide, relaxed smile. 'In fact I find the concept quite exciting.'

Merry punched a bare brown shoulder in reproach. 'Anything to do with sex excites you!'

Angel looked reflective and a sudden wicked grin lit his darkly handsome features. 'I'm sure if we had about six children, six very *noisy* and *lively* children, I could persuade my mother to find her own accommodation. You see, expansion could be a complete game changer in the happy-family stakes...'

'I do hope that was a joke,' Merry sighed, warm and contented and so happy she felt floaty. He loved her and it shone out of him. How had she not seen that? How had she tormented herself for so long when what she desperately wanted was right there in front of her, waiting to be claimed?

And now Angel was hers, finally all hers, and equally suddenly she was discovering that she was feeling much more tolerant and forgiving of other people's frailties. Her mother was trying to show her that she cared and perhaps it was past time she made more of an effort in that quarter. And then there was Roula, unhappy and humiliated—possibly she could afford to be more forgiving there as well. Happiness could spread happiness, she decided cheerfully, running a seeking hand down over a long, sleek male flank, keen to increase his happiness factor too...

'Well, I have to confess that I never saw this coming,' Natalie admitted, studying her mother, Sybil, and Angel's father, Charles, as they stood across the room graciously receiving the guests at the wedding reception being held at Angel and Merry's home on the island of Palos. 'I thought it would fizzle out long before they got this far.'

'He's daft about her and she has made him wait six years to put that ring on her finger,' Merry reminded the small blonde woman by her side. 'I think she's just finally ready to settle down.'

'Well, she took her time about it,' Natalie pronounced wryly. 'Angel's mother isn't here, is she?'

'Hardly, considering that she was Charles' first wife,' Merry remarked.

'Not much chance of *her* settling down.'

'No,' Merry agreed quietly, reflecting that they saw remarkably little of Angelina these days. Angelina had bought a Manhattan penthouse where she now spent most of her time. Occasional scandalous headlines and gossip pieces floated back to Angel and Merry, but Angel was no longer forced to be involved in his mother's life and now found it easier to remain detached.

Elyssa rushed up, an adorable vision in a pink flower girl's dress that already had a stain on it. 'Keep this for me,' she urged, stuffing the little wicker basket she had carried down the aisle into her mother's hand. 'Cos and I are going to play hide and seek.'

Merry bent down. 'No, you're not. This is a very special party for grown-ups and children aren't allowed to run about.'

Her son, Cosmas, four years old to his big sister's almost six years, rushed up, wrenching impatiently at the sash tied round his waist. 'Take this off.'

'Not until Sybil says you can,' Merry warned. 'There are still photos to be taken.'

'Where's the rest of the horde?' Natalie enquired curiously.

Their two-year-old twins, Nilo and Leksi, were chasing Tiger through the hall. Merry hurtled in that direction to interrupt the chase before it got out of hand. Tiger was a mere shadow of the fat and inactive little dog he had once been. Living in a household with five children had slimmed him down. His first rehoming hadn't worked out and when he had been returned to Sybil soon afterwards, after shaming himself and stealing food, Merry had scooped him up for a rapturous reunion and brought him back to Greece. As she hovered Angel appeared, a baby clutched securely below one arm, and spoke sternly to his youngest sons. Atlanta beamed gummily across the hall at her mother and opened her arms.

'I don't know where you get the energy,' Natalie confessed, watching Merry reclaim her eight-month-old daughter. 'Either of you. You produce like rabbits. Please tell me the family's complete now.'

Colour warmed Merry's cheeks because their sixth child was already on the way, even if they had not yet announced the fact, and Angel grinned down at his tongue-tied wife with wicked amusement. 'We haven't decided yet,' he said lightly.

Atlanta tugged on her mother's long hair as Merry walked out onto the terrace to take a break from the festivities. It had taken weeks of careful planning to organise the wedding and accommodation for all the guests. She had wanted everything to be perfect for Sybil and Charles, both of whom were frequent visitors to their home. After all the years of feeling short-changed in the family stakes, Merry had come full circle and now she was surrounded by a loving family.

She was even happier to have achieved a more normal relationship with her mother, who had returned to the UK and started up a very successful yoga studio. These days she regularly saw Natalie when she went over to London with Angel. Her mother had mellowed and Merry had put the past behind her in every way.

A year earlier she had acted as Roula's matron of honour when the other woman had married the island doctor in a three-day-long bout of very Greek celebration. Roula was still a friend of the family, and sometimes Merry suspected that the trouble the other woman had caused with the mistress lie and the truths that had then come out had actually helped Roula to move on and meet someone capable of loving her back.

But then Merry was willing to admit that she had learned from the same experience as well. Discovering that she was married to a man who loved her so much that he was willing to do virtually anything it took to hang onto her and their marriage had banished her insecurity for ever. She liked being a mother and Angel revelled in being a father. The rapid expansion of their family had been exhausting but also uniquely satisfying.

Lean brown hands scooped the slumbering baby from Merry's lap and passed her to Jill, Sally's co-nanny, for attention. Angel then scooped his wife out of her chair and sank back down with her cradled in his arms.

'You are very tired,' he scolded. 'We've talked about this. You agreed to take afternoon naps.'

'After the meal,' she murmured, small fingers flirting with his silk tie as she gazed up at him, loving and appreciating every line of his lean, startlingly handsome features and thinking back lazily to the poor beginning they had shared that had miraculously transformed over the years into a glorious partnership.

'*Thee mou*,' Angel intoned huskily. 'Sometimes I look at the life you have created for all of us and I love you so much it hurts, *agape mou*. My wife, my family, is my anchor.'

Happy as a teenager in his public display of affection where once she would have wrenched herself free, Merry giggled. 'You mean we drag you down?'

And Angel gave up the battle and kissed her, hungrily, deeply, tenderly while somewhere in the background his mother-in-law snorted and said in a pained voice, 'You see...like rabbits.'

* * * * *

THE GREEK'S
ULTIMATE
CONQUEST

CHAPTER ONE

WHEN HAD HE actually last slept…?

The medication that the medic had administered to him in the field hospital had only taken the edge off his agony and since he'd got on the military air transport to Germany it hadn't even done that, despite the copious amounts of alcohol he'd downed in an attempt to self-medicate.

But now he was finally about to fall sleep, the moment was delayed as a half-burnt log in the open grate disintegrated, sending a star burst of sparks outwards and pulling him back from the brink. He watched through heavy half-closed eyes as the flames flared briefly before fading, leaving dark specks on the sheepskin stretched over the wood floor.

The woman lying across his arm stirred gently before burrowing into his shoulder. He flexed his fingers to relieve the numbness that was creeping into his hand, and with his free hand pushed back a hank of hair tinged silver by the moonlight shining through the open window. He glanced down, the soft light caressing her face revealing the smooth curve of her cheek.

She was, simply, beautiful. It wasn't just the bone structure and the incredible body, but she had something else about her…a *glow*, he decided, smiling at the uncharacteristically sentimental thought as he rubbed a strand of her hair between his fingertips. She was the sort of woman that at any other time in his life he would have gravitated towards. But even though he'd picked her out immediately when she had entered the bar earlier—with a noisy, youthful après-ski group oozing the confidence that came with privilege and intent on having fun and spending money—he had not reacted. Instead shutting out the sound of upper-class voices, he'd turned back to the drink he'd been nursing as he'd sunk once again into his black thoughts.

Then she'd come over to him. Up close she was even more spectacular, and she clearly had the self confidence that went with knowing it as she approached him. A real golden girl complete with golden glow, long gorgeous legs, her lithe body lovingly outlined in tight-fitting ski gear that was suited to her sinuous, athletic body. Her fine-boned face had perfect symmetry, the full lips and the deep blue of her wide-spaced eyes made him think of an angel, a sexy angel with a halo of lint-pale hair that glittered in the reflection of the beaten copper light shade suspended over his table.

'Hello.'

Her voice was low, accentless, and had a slight attractive husk.

A flicker of uncertainty appeared in her eyes when he didn't respond, then after a moment she repeated the greeting, first in French and then Italian.

'English is fine.'

She took the comment as encouragement and slid onto a stool beside him. 'I saw you from…' Without taking her eyes from his face—*they really were the most spectacular eyes*—she nodded towards the group she had arrived with, who seemed to be involved in a noisy shot-down-ing game. The sight of the bunch of spoiled socialites giving the bar staff a hard time twitched his lips into a contemptuous sneer.

'You're missing the fun,' he drawled.

She glanced back at her friends, giving what appeared to be a wince before training eyes that were a shocking shade of blue on him. 'It stopped being fun about two bars ago.' Her soft lips still smiled but a quizzical groove appeared between her brows and her head tilted a little to one side as she continued to stare at him. 'You look...*alone*.'

He gave her a look then, the one that made ninety-nine out of a hundred people back off. The hundredth was generally drunk, although it was obvious this woman wasn't; her blue stare was clear and candid, unnervingly so. Or maybe what unnerved him was the electric charge he could feel in the air between them, a low-level thrum but undeniably present.

'I'm Chloe—'

He cut her off before she could introduce herself fully.

'Sorry, *agape mou*, I'm not good company tonight.' He wanted her to go away, he wanted to be left alone to slide back into the darkness, but when she didn't, he wasn't really sorry.

'Are you Greek?'

'Among other things.'

'So what do I call you?'

Nothing worse than he'd called himself. 'Nik.'

'Just Nik?'

He nodded and after a moment she gave a little shrug of assent. 'Fair enough.'

When her friends had left she had stayed.

This was her room, an apartment in an upmarket chalet—not that they'd made it as far as the bedroom. A trail of their clothing traced their stumbling path from the door to the leather sofa where they lay.

He had always enjoyed the physical, sexual side of his nature but last night… Nik still couldn't quite believe how raw it had been, a true sanity-sapping explosion of need, and for a few moments he had felt free, free of grief, guilt and the oily taint left by the things he had witnessed.

He trailed a hand down her back, letting his fingers rest on the curve of her smooth bottom. As he breathed in her scent he desperately wanted to close his eyes, but for some reason every time he thought about it his glance was drawn across the room to where, he knew, even though the light was too dim to see properly, his phone lay after it had fallen from his pocket.

How did he know it was about to vibrate?

Then it did.

He glanced down to see if the sound had disturbed the sleeping woman and every muscle in his body clenched violently in icy horror and shock, trapping the cry of visceral terror in his throat. He was staring down, not at a warm, beautiful woman, but at the pale, still face of his best friend. The body he held was not warm and breathing but cold and still, the eyes not closed but open and staring up at him, blankly empty!

When he suddenly awoke, gasping, he was not in his bed but beside it on the floor on his knees, shaking like someone in a fever, sweat dripping from his body as he gulped for air. The effort of drawing oxygen into his lungs defined each individual sinew and muscle in his powerful back as he rammed his clenched fists against his rockhard thighs. The scream that clawed at the edge of his mind remained locked in his raw throat as he struggled to reclaim reality from the lingering wisps of his dreams.

It finally came, and when it did he felt...well, he felt no better or worse than he had on any other of the countless times previously he'd woken out of exactly the same nightmare.

Slowly Nik got to his feet, the normal fluidity of his actions stiff, the athletically honed body so many envied, and even more lusted after, responding sluggishly to commands as he lurched across the room to the bathroom, where he turned on the cold tap of the washbasin full blast and put his head under the stream of cold water.

Fingers curled over the edge of the basin hid the fact he refused to acknowledge, that his hands were shaking, but as he straightened up he was unable to avoid a brief view of his own reflection in the mirror before he turned away, knowing that although the blinding visceral fear was temporarily back in its box, the shadow of it remained in his eyes.

The shower did not entirely banish the shadow either, but it did revive him. He checked the time; four hours' sleep was two hours too little but the idea of returning to bed, probably only to relive the nightmare yet again, held little appeal.

Five minutes later Security buzzed him out of the building, the concierge dipping his head and wishing him a good run when he exited, while privately probably thinking that the guy from the penthouse who regularly took a pre-dawn run was insane. Maybe, Nik reflected grimly as he pulled up the hood of his sweatshirt against the rain, he had a point.

The exercise did the usual trick of clearing his head so by the time, shaved, suited and booted, he skimmed through his emails the night horrors had been banished, or at least unacknowledged. He had other things to focus on, things that were nothing to do with the message on his phone. After noting the caller identity with a grimace, he slid it into his pocket.

He knew without looking at the content that it would be a reminder about the dinner party his sister was hosting that evening, the one he had agreed to attend in a moment of weakness. With Ana it was easier to say yes, because *no* was not a word she understood, neither was single or unattached, at least where her younger brother was concerned.

He slowed as he reached another set of traffic lights that had sprung up overnight, and smothered a sigh as he struggled to push aside the thoughts of his evening entertainment and the inevitable candidate for the position of wife, or at least serious girlfriend material, who would be seated beside him.

He loved his sister, admiring her talent and the fact she juggled a career as a designer with being a single parent. He was ready to admit she had many good traits but unfortunately conceding defeat was not one of them!

Part of his mind on the increasingly heavy traffic he was negotiating, he tried to put the evening ahead out of his mind, but maybe due to his disturbed night the prospect of being polite to one of the perfectly charming women his sister produced on a regular basis to audition for the role of potential mate weighed more heavily on his mind.

He knew that as far as Ana was concerned all his problems would be solved the moment he found a soul mate. He still couldn't decide if she really believed it and though there were occasions when he found her rosy optimism sweet, usually after a bottle of wine, mostly it was intensely irritating.

Hell, if he'd thought love was a cure-all he'd be out looking for it now, but as far as Nik was concerned the search would be in vain. It was a stretch but he was prepared to suspend disbelief and concede that it was possible that there was such a thing as true love, but if this was the case, the way some people were born colour-blind, he was love-blind.

It was a disability he was prepared to bear. At least he was never going to be in the position of having to experience the falling *out* of love process. It would be hard to find two people more civilised, more genuinely nice than his sister and her ex, but he had watched their break-up and eventual divorce and it had been toxic! The worst aspect of the split had been the child stuck in the middle. It didn't really matter how hard you tried to protect them from the worst, and they had tried, a kid had to be affected by it.

Give him plain and simple lust any day of the week, and as for growing old alone, surely it was better by far than growing old next to someone you couldn't stand the sight of!

He was prepared to concede that there were happy marriages around but they were the exception rather than the rule.

The car moved five yards before he came to another halt, and someone farther down the line of stationary cars sounded their horn in frustration. Nik raised his eyes heavenwards, the frown lines in his brow smoothing out as his glance landed on the neon-lit face on the advertising billboard across the road.

The advertising agency had clearly gone old school. There was nothing subtle about the message they were sending, just a straightforward fantasy for men to buy into. Use the brand of male face product clutched to the generous bosom of the woman in the bikini and you too would have similarly scantily clad and gorgeous women throwing themselves at you.

Not this one... His mobile mouth twitched into a sardonic smile; he was probably one of a handful of people who knew that this particular object of male fantasy was in a secret same-sex relationship. Secret, not because Lucy was concerned about any negative impact on her career, but because of a deal the couple had struck with her partner Clare's soon to be ex-husband. The guy wouldn't contest the divorce if the women waited to go public with their relationship until after he had landed the contract worth multi millions he was in the middle of negotiating with a firm who had built their brand on family values and a squeaky-clean image.

Maybe, Nik mused, if the guy had spent as much time on his marriage as he did on nurturing business deals he might still be married...? After all, if you believed everything you read, maintaining a good relationship took time, energy and hard work. Well, he definitely didn't have the time. As for energy, he was quite prepared to be energetic, but not if the sex seemed like hard work... No, marriage really was not for him.

He was jolted from his reverie by another blast on a horn, from behind him this time. It had a knock-on effect...not *quite* a eureka moment but pretty damn close and, like all good ideas, it was perfectly simple. Actually he couldn't quite figure out why it had not previously occurred to him to counter his sister's relentless matchmaking by turning up with a date of his own choosing and acting like a man in love.

He smiled up at the inspiration for the idea looking down at him...was Lucy Cavendish in town? And if she was, he wondered if the idea would appeal to her sense of humour; failing that he'd appeal to her conscience. After all, she did owe him one as he was the person who'd introduced her to Clare.

The caterers were carrying boxes through the open front door when Chloe arrived. Tatiana had asked her to be early but maybe this was *too* early?

'Go through to the office. Mum's in there.'

Chloe did a double take and realised that one of the caterers holding a box was Eugenie, Tatiana's teenage daughter.

The girl saw her expression and nodded. 'Yeah, I know...not a good look, but Mum insisted I work at least half the holiday to reduce the danger of me being a rich spoilt brat who thinks money grows on trees. You look great!' she added, her eyes widening as she took in the full effect of the sleeveless silk jumpsuit Chloe wore. 'Of course, you have to have legs that go on for ever to get away with it.'

Chloe laughed as the girl whisked away.

The door of the study was open and after a brief tap Chloe went inside. The room was empty except for the dog that was curled up on top of a designer silk jacket that had been flung over a chair. Even crushed and underneath a Labrador the distinctive style of the design made the label it bore unnecessary. *Tatiana* had become famous for her use of bold, brilliant colours and simple wearable designs.

The animal opened one eye and Chloe went over, drawn by a silent canine command. As she stroked his soft ears she looked curiously at the drawings set up on the massive draftsman table that took centre stage in the room.

'Oh, don't look at those. I was having a bad day,' Tatiana exclaimed, walking into the room. In one of her own designs, the petite brunette projected an air of effortless elegance. 'Down, Ulysses!' She gave a little sigh when the dog responded by wagging his tail and staying put. 'Nik says a dog needs to know who's master, but that's the trouble—you already do, don't you, you bad boy?' she crooned.

Chloe gave a smile that she hoped hid the fact that her first thought whenever she heard the name of Tatiana's younger brother was, *Oh, God, not brother Nik again!*

Nothing Tatiana said about her brother challenged Chloe's growing conviction that the man thought he was an expert on everything—and was not shy about sharing his expert opinion.

But then, being reticent and self-effacing were probably not the most obvious characteristics for someone who was the head of a Greek shipping line, and though Chloe knew that Nik Latsis had only stepped into his father's shoes relatively recently, it sounded to her as though they fitted him very well indeed!

Tatiana didn't seem to question or resent the fact that her younger brother had inherited the company simply because he was male, so why should Chloe?

Maybe because she wasn't Greek.

And there was no doubt the Latsis family considered themselves Greek even though they had been London based for thirty years. They were part of a large, well-heeled Greek community that had settled in the British capital. Rich or nouveau riche, they all had the rich part in common, that and being Greek, which seemed to be enough to make them a very tight-knit community where everyone knew everyone and traditions were important.

As she gave the dog one last pat she caught sight of her

reflection in the mirror that made the generously sized room appear even larger, and made a conscious effort to iron out the frown lines that the thought of Tatiana's invisible brother had etched in her forehead.

The invisible part was no accident. It was eighteen months since his father's stroke had brought forward the younger brother's ascension to the 'throne' of Latsis Shipping and he had kept a very low profile, something you couldn't do unless you had loyal family and friends, limitless resources and, she supposed, an inside working knowledge of how the media worked that being an ex-journalist would bring.

The point being, Chloe, she told herself sternly, *is that he is invisible. You've never met the guy, and yet here you are making all these judgements on the basis of a few comments and gut instinct.* Something that she'd have been the very first to condemn in anyone else.

'You're being a hypocrite, Chloe.'

The softly voiced self-condemnation caused Tatiana, whose eyes had drifted with a distracted expression to the fabrics pinned on one of the boards, to look up. She directed an enquiring look at Chloe, who shook her head.

'Those colours are beautiful,' Chloe said, nodding to the fabrics, and lifted a finger to touch one piece of silk that was a shade or two deeper than the blue wide-legged jumpsuit she was wearing.

'It would suit you, but I'm not sure…' Tatiana stopped and shook her head. 'Sorry, I just struggle to switch off sometimes.'

She smiled ruefully as she moved to kiss Chloe warmly on her cheek.

'The trials of being artistic,' Chloe teased.

'I don't know about that, but I do know that I am a bit of a workaholic…the work-life, home-life balance always did elude me.' A wistful expression crossed her face. 'Maybe that's why I got divorced…' She shook her dark sleek head slightly and smiled. 'But never mind about that tonight…just look at you!'

Hands resting lightly on Chloe's slim upper arms, she pushed the taller woman back a little. The sombreness of earlier drifted across her face when her glance stilled momentarily on Chloe's legs covered in loose folds of sky-blue silk, but it was gone by the time her eyes reached Chloe's face.

'You look stunning, as usual. I'm not saying it's all about a pretty face, but it definitely helps when you're trying to get men to open their wallets for a good cause… and before you ask you have my permission to put the hard sell on everyone here tonight.'

'People are usually very kind,' Chloe said.

'Especially when they are being guilted into it by the sister of a future queen. But why not use your connections? That's what I always say, and, while I might not have the right sort, your sister certainly does.' She sketched a curtsy and Chloe laughed. Her sister might be a princess and one day destined to be the Queen of Vela Main, but Chloe could not imagine anyone less *royal*. Both sisters had been brought up to believe that what a person did was more important than their title.

'I'll do my very best for the charity,' Tatiana continued in earnest now. 'In my book, I owe you.' She walked across to the mantel where the marble surface was covered with framed photos. She selected one and held it up in invitation for Chloe to see it. 'For what you did for Mel,' she finished, looking fondly at the photo she held.

Chloe shook her head, uncomfortable with the praise. As far as Chloe was concerned, the young Greek girl was her inspiration. 'I didn't do anything.' She took the frame that Tatiana offered and looked at the photo it held. It was a snap taken the previous month in a pavement café on a girls' trip to Barcelona. 'She's a brave girl.'

Chloe had known Tatiana by sight and reputation before the other woman had boosted Chloe's career by mentioning her blog in an interview she'd given covering London fashion week, two years ago now, Chloe realised, though it seemed more like a lifetime. Back then the interview was pretty much responsible for her blog becoming a profitable overnight success.

Chloe had contacted Tatiana to thank her for the plug and they had exchanged the odd email but they had never met in person.

That had happened in a very different context a year ago, after the designer's god-daughter was moved into the room next to Chloe's own in the specialist burns unit. Chloe had already been in there for three months; she'd known every crack in the ceiling and had been living vicariously through the love lives of the young nurses designated to her care.

Though the burns Chloe herself had received in a road traffic accident had been severe and painful and the healing process long, her own scars were easy to hide from view under her clothes. But the young woman in the next room had not been able to hide the damage done to her face by the fire caused by a gas explosion. Then, as if life hadn't already thrown enough rubbish at her, the day after she had arrived at the burns unit her boyfriend had dumped her, at which point Mel had turned her face to the wall and announced she didn't want to live.

As she'd listened through the partition wall Chloe's heart had ached for the other girl. Their first conversation later that night shouted through the wall had been a one-sided affair, but it had been the first of many.

'You got her through it, Chloe,' Tatiana choked. 'I'll never forget that day I arrived and heard her laugh—you did that.'

'Mel helped me as much as I did her. Did you see the information sheet she put together for me on make-up techniques?' she asked, placing the photo back on the shelf. In doing so she accidentally nudged the one next to it and straightened it, admiring the frame; it was an antique one, the ebony wood delicately carved and rather beautiful.

Chloe was admiring the craftsmanship, running her fingers across the smooth indentations, when her glance drifted across the photo it held. Her mouth tugged into a smile; with a white-knuckle ride in the background, a younger Eugenie smiled back at her, complete with braces, from under the peak of a baseball cap with the logo of an adventure park emblazoned on it.

The jeans-clad man crouched down beside her in the shot was wearing the same cap, and he was… Chloe's smile vanished like smoke as brutal stinging reality hit her like a slap across the face. Pale as paper now, she stared at the male in the picture, wearing jeans, a tee shirt, and a teasing, carefree expression on his hand-some face, a face that bore no signs of a tortured soul. There were no shadows that she felt the need to banish; he was just a regular guy…well, only if the *regular* guy in question was more handsome than any man had a right to be with a body that an Olympic swimmer might dream of possessing.

She stood like a statue staring at the photo she held in a hand that quickly developed a visible tremor—the tremor penetrating past the skin level and moving deep inside her.

By sheer force of will she released the breath she was

holding in her lungs, but not the avalanche of questions whirring in dizzying succession through her brain. She felt as though a dozen people were inside her shouting so loudly she couldn't make out the individual questions.

Obviously it couldn't be him but, equally obviously, it was! The man in the photos was the same man who she had spent a never-to-be-forgotten night of lust with. If all learning experiences were as brutal as that one had been, it would not be worth getting out of bed in the morning—happily they weren't and she had moved on.

But that didn't mean she'd forgotten any of it. Forgotten the feelings of emotional hurt and humiliation that had made her physically sick the next morning when she'd realised he'd slipped away during the night. And the worst part was, she had no one to blame but herself. Because she had been the one who had followed her instincts when she'd approached him in that bar, telling herself that what she was doing was somehow meant to be… If they had been handing out awards for naivety and general stupidity that night, she would have walked away with an armful of prizes!

She'd wondered if his name really was Nik. It seemed utterly incredible to her now that she'd ever thought it part of the romantic fantasy element of their night together that she hadn't even known his full name! Time had stripped away the romantic gloss and revealed it for what it truly was—a cheap and tacky one-night stand, even if the sex had been utterly incredible.

Keeping her voice carefully casual, she half turned to Tatiana, as yet unable to tear her eyes from the snapshot. 'How old was Eugenie in this one?'

Tatiana came across and looked at the photo of her daughter and she gave a nostalgic sigh. 'Oh, that was taken on her tenth birthday, although just five minutes afterwards she was throwing up. Nik let her eat a bag of doughnuts then took her on some white-knuckle ride.'

Chloe's own knuckles were bone white where her hand was pressed to her chest. Her poor heart was vibrating against her ribcage, her insides were quivering as she told herself sternly to get a grip, not to mention a sense of proportion. It was only a photo after all, and he was old history.

Note to self, she castigated herself, *the next time you decide to make love, don't do it with a complete stranger! No, Chloe, let's be grown up and honest here—it wasn't making love, it was having sex.*

It hadn't been until she'd accepted that particular fact and realised that what they had shared that night had had absolutely nothing to do with a spiritual connection but everything to do with blind lust that she had been able to move on.

Move on—really? So why was she shaking?

She put the photo down carefully and smoothed her hands down over the fabric of her jumpsuit. She would not let that man do this to her again; she was not that silly naive girl any longer.

It had been a painful learning experience, but once her pride had stopped stinging and she had stopped feeling basically stupid she'd understood that while empty sex with anonymous strangers could obviously be physically satisfying, it probably wasn't for her. She wasn't exactly holding out for the love of her life, but she did think maybe a bit of mutual respect might be nice.

'So that's your brother Nik,' she said flatly. Sometimes it seemed as if fate had a very warped sense of humour.

Her eyes skimmed the mantel. The same man, she recognised now, was in several of the photos. It wasn't just the time difference that made him look younger, it was the absence of the cynicism and dangerous darkness she had sensed in him that night they'd had sex. What had happened to the man in these photos to turn him into the one she'd met only a few years later?

She dug her teeth into her plump lower lip as she squared her shoulders. Nik Latsis, *her* Nik—it was *so* weird to finally be able to put a full name to the man who had introduced her to sex and the fact it really was the only thing that some men were interested in. Well, his name was actually pretty irrelevant and she couldn't care less what had happened to turn him into such a cold bastard.

Not that she wasn't totally prepared to take her fair share of the blame. After all, 'naive closet romantic meets utter bastard'—it was never going to end well, was it? But she was not that person any more.

'I forgot, you haven't met Nik...have you?' Tatiana asked.

The truth or a lie?

Chloe settled for somewhere in the middle. 'He does look a little familiar...'

It's the clothes that threw me.

She brought her lashes down in a concealing sooty curtain and fanned her hot cheeks with a hand, causing the bangles she wore around her wrist to jingle. 'I think summer might finally have arrived,' she commented, ignoring the house's perfect air-conditioning system.

'You might have seen him on the television, perhaps?'

'Television?' A puzzled frown drew Chloe's brows together above her small straight nose. 'I don't think so...' Then it clicked; Tatiana wasn't talking about the present day but her brother's previous life. 'Oh, when you said he was a journalist I thought you meant he was in print...'

His sister nodded. 'He started out in print journalism

but Nik was a war correspondent, and he was on the telly quite a lot actually. He won awards.' Tatiana's pride in her brother's achievements was as obvious as her distress as she enlarged. 'He spent the last two years of his journalistic career embedded with the military, in the worst war zones you can imagine. Nik has always been the sort of person who doesn't do half measures.'

He had certainly been no half-measure lover or, for that matter, halfway callous!

'On his last assignment his cameraman, his best friend, was shot.'

Chloe blanched in shock. 'Did he…?'

Tatiana nodded. 'He died in Nik's arms, but the worst part—at least for the families—was that for three days we knew that there had been a fatality. There were about ten journalists, all from different media outlets pinned down, but we didn't know their identities or who had died.'

Chloe gave an empathetic murmur of sympathy and touched her friend's hand as the older woman closed her eyes and shuddered. 'We all loved Charlie, he had just got engaged…but at the same time we were all so incredibly relieved that it wasn't Nik. It made everyone feel so guilty.'

'Survivor's guilt,' Chloe said, thinking of her sister who, after the accident from which she had escaped unscathed while Chloe had not, had been helped by a therapist. Well, Nik Latsis could afford the best help money could buy.

'You've probably seen him, although professionally he used Mum's maiden name, because he didn't want to be accused of using the family name. Does Kyriakis ring a bell…? Nik Kyriakis?'

Chloe shook her head. 'I've never watched much TV.

There was a rule when we were growing up, half an hour's television a day, and then when I could decide for myself I suppose it had become a habit I never really broke. Even now I listen to the radio rather than switch on the box. It must have been hard for your brother going back to work after what had happened…?'

She had gone back to the spot where the accident had happened—had it been therapeutic? Only in the sense that she had proved to herself that she could do it?

That had been how she had privately charted her recovery: the things she was able to do, the things she could move past—looking at her scars, showing them to her family, getting into a car, driving a car…going back to the winding mountain road where the accident had happened.

'He didn't go back. A day after he returned, our dad had his stroke and couldn't run the company any more; the plan had always been for Nik to step up when the time came.' She stopped, an expression of consternation crossing her face. 'Nik doesn't ever talk about what happened to Charlie, so don't mention it tonight, will you?' she finished anxiously.

If he wanted to bottle things up in a stupid manly way, that was fine by her; she definitely wouldn't be getting him to unburden himself to her. In fact, the idea of seeing him, let alone passing the time of day with him, made the panic gathered like a tight icy ball in her stomach expand uncomfortably.

Ironically there had been a time when she would have paid good money to confront her runaway lover, but that time was long gone; she had no intention of having any sort of conversation with Nik Latsis.

He was history, a mistake, but not one she was going to beat herself up over any more, and one she really didn't want to come face to face with, but, if she absolutely had to, she was going to do it with pride and dignity.

Well, that was the plan anyway.

'I won't,' she promised as the voice in her head reminded her once again that her plans often had a habit of going wrong…

CHAPTER TWO

'YOU'RE LATE.' TATIANA kissed her brother's lean cheek, grimacing a little as the sprinkling of designer stubble grazed her smooth cheek before one eyebrow rose. She struggled to hide her surprise as she shifted her gaze from her impeccably turned-out brother to the woman who stood with one hand possessively on his dark-suited arm.

'You know Lucy Cavendish?' Placing a hand across her shoulders, he drew the model, her famous dazzling smile firmly in place, close into his side. The redhead tilted her head. Unusually for a woman, in her heels she topped his shoulder.

'I did Tatiana's last catwalk show in Paris. What a lovely home you have.' Lucy's expertly made-up green eyes moved admiringly around the entrance hall with its chandeliers and dramatic staircase.

Tatiana inclined her dark head and delivered an air kiss. 'Thank you. You're looking well, Lucy...' Tatiana looked up at her brother. 'You growing a beard, Nik?'

'With your views on facial hair, Ana, would I dare?'

'Oh, I just *lurve* the moody, broody look.' Lucy's eyes sparkled with teasing amusement as she stroked his cheek, letting her red fingernails slide familiarly over the stubble.

Nik removed the hand firmly from his cheek where it

had lingered and whispered so only she could hear him, 'Don't overdo it, angel.'

As they moved across the hall the sound of voices and laughter drifted out through the open double doors of the drawing room.

'Anyone I know here?' Lucy asked.

'Just a small gathering of friends.'

Letting Lucy go ahead of them, Nik fell into step beside his sister. 'Hope you didn't mind me bringing Lucy.'

'Why should I mind?'

'I thought you might have had me paired off with some good breeding stock…?'

'I don't—' Tatiana stopped and gave a shake of her head, admitting ruefully, 'I suppose I do, but I just want you to be happy and…like you used to be…before…'

Impelled by an inconvenient spasm of guilt, Nik stepped in to hug his sister as suddenly the charade with Lucy seemed less of a good idea. 'I am happy.'

'I like Lucy. Are you two together?'

Nik's glance slid away. She looked so hopeful that, although this had been the idea, he felt reluctant to raise her hopes, knowing full well they were false ones. 'Early days,' he prevaricated slickly.

'I just hope Lucy won't be bored silly,' Tatiana fretted, glancing towards the model who was walking through the double doors. 'It so happens that there is a woman here who might interest you—'

'Just when I thought I might have misjudged you,' he began sardonically.

'Not in that way!' Tatiana cut back. 'She's a good friend of mine.'

'And you wouldn't wish me on a friend?'

She slung him an irritated look. 'I just want you to set a good example when you meet her, and give a *really* generous donation to the charity—set a good example for the others.'

'Another of your worthy causes, Ana?'

'This is important to me, Nik.'

'Fine, I'll be generous.'

Chloe glanced at the clock…maybe he was a no show? Annoyed with herself for caring one way or the other, she turned her back on the doorway and focused her attention fully on the man beside her, a middle-aged Greek man who ran a property development company and seemed genuinely interested in the charity.

'I admire your enthusiasm but, and I don't want to be negative, aren't you being a little overambitious? Have you costed it up properly? The premises alone would—'

'Yes suitable premises, especially here in London, will be difficult.'

'Which is where I come in?'

Her smile glimmered. 'Your specialist knowledge and advice would be much appreciated.'

'And my money?' he added shrewdly.

Chloe's dimples appeared. 'I know that Tatiana has already spoken to you about…sorry, I really can't do this.'

The recipient of her half-empty glass of champagne looked startled and then amused as Chloe popped the finger food she had been holding into her mouth, swallowed, then smiled. 'That's better!' she said as she held out her hand for her glass.

Tipping his head, her companion replaced the crystal wine cup in it.

'Mostly I can multitask,' she told him cheerfully. 'I can do food or drink but not both at the same time. You wouldn't believe how many outfits I've emptied glasses of wine down, which makes it sound as though I always wander round with a glass of pinot in my hand, which I don't.' She delivered another smile. 'I can assure you that your donation will be in sober and sensible hands.'

The older man gave an appreciative chuckle at her tactics. 'Nice try, but I don't recall saying yes.'

Chloe conceded his point with a nod. 'But you didn't say no either and I'm an optimist.'

This time the man's chuckle was loud enough to divert some of the attention currently being given to the model who was making her entrance. 'So let me get this right, you'd like me to let you have the lease on several buildings for a fraction of what they are worth, and what do I get?'

'A warm glow knowing you've done the right thing? Or, failing that, the sort of publicity that money can't buy? The sort of publicity that comes from having your company represent the caring face of capitalism,' Chloe said, thinking wryly that she was getting quite good at this.

The man gave her an approving look tinged for the first time with respect. 'I think we should schedule a meeting, Lady—'

'Call me Chloe,' she cut in quickly.

He tipped his head in acknowledgment of her request. 'Right, Chloe, how about…?'

As the man's eyes moved over her head and his voice trailed away Chloe turned to see what had snatched his attention. The answer was immediately obvious in the shape of a glamorous redhead in a glittering gown more suited to a red carpet event than a dinner party.

Immediately tolerant of her companion's distraction, she turned to study the new arrival with some curiosity. In her experience people you had only previously seen beautifully lit on the screen or airbrushed in magazines rarely lived up to expectations, but Lucy Cavendish did and then some.

She looked beyond her hostess and the model to see if Lucy had come with someone. The woman's past boyfriends had included not one but two Hollywood A-listers, a Russian oligarch and the heir to a banking fortune, so Chloe was expecting a handsome face or serious money, someone who might be interested in donating to a good cause, perhaps?

She got neither...or rather actually what she got was both!

What she also got when she saw that Lucy's date was Nik was a jolt similar to the occasion her hairdryer had given her an electric shock, times a hundred. A home-made and dangerously uncontrolled defibrillation that felt as if a hammer had landed on her chest and made her limbs feel weak.

But this was fine; she could totally deal with it...

Not dealing with it, Chloe!

Ignoring the mocking voice in her head, she took a deep breath, straightened her slender square shoulders, cleared her throat and readjusted the chunky necklace of raw amethyst slices that hid the pulse pounding at the base of her throat.

Breathe...she told herself, so she did, and for good measure she focused on the positive.

The worst was over and, as *worsts* went, seeing the man you'd made the mistake of sleeping with without knowing his full name was, on the scale of things, pretty low-key. A couple of minutes and her nervous system would catch up with the message and by tomorrow she'd be laughing—all right, maybe *smiling* about it.

But that was tomorrow; being realistic today, as in the

next sixty seconds, she was aiming for a less ambitious goal. Her legs stopping shaking would be a good start.

She stifled a stab of impatience; her nervous system was getting this situation way out of proportion. After all, what was the worst that could happen?

And what was the worst anyway: him remembering her or him not?

Her mobile lips quirked into a smile as she considered the alternatives. An awkward reunion or a hit to her ego?

Did it really matter?

The fact that she could even ask herself the question was a sign of how much she'd changed in a little over a year. There had been a time when, despite the outward confidence she projected, what people thought about her had mattered, and she wanted the right people to like her...she wanted to fit in.

The journey to where she was today had not been easy, but everything had changed. Well, maybe not *everything*, she conceded, watching the new arrival above the rim of the glass she raised to her lips. Still, even at a distance, he had the ability to make the muscles deep in her pelvis quiver...so it was lucky she could consider this phenomenon in an objective way, wasn't it?

She might not be able to achieve total physical indifference to the male magnetism he oozed, but she was more than a bundle of hormones...despite the fact that he was, she thought, studying him through the protective sweep of her lashes, just as incredible-looking as she remembered.

They said you always remembered your first and it turned out they were right. The self-mocking glint in her wide-spaced sky-blue eyes faded and a tiny pucker appeared between her darkly defined feathery brows as she realised how intact her memory of him was, not just the way he looked, or moved, but the texture of his skin... the smell of his... She took a shaky breath and straightened her shoulders, slamming the door on that particular memory. *It was just a lapse of judgement, ancient history, Chloe,* she told herself. *Do not revisit.*

'What a stunning woman!'

Chloe started slightly at her companion's comment and tore her eyes from the tall figure whose dominant presence had made her forget about the woman he'd brought with him, although they made a pretty magnificent couple. 'Yes, she is.' Stunning was probably an understatement.

'But I'd say she's high maintenance, and I can't see her climbing Kilimanjaro.

The comment startled a laugh from Chloe. 'It sounds to me like you measure all women by some pretty high standards.'

He smiled and nodded. 'My wife is an extraordinary woman.'

Chloe stood and listened as the man launched into what was clearly his favourite subject. An emotional lump settled in her throat as he talked about his wife. What would it feel like to be the centre of a man's universe? she wondered wistfully.

Nik walked past his sister and moved to where Lucy stood.

'Maybe this isn't such a good idea,' he muttered.

'I was the one who told you that,' the model reminded him. 'But you've been my beard on more than one occasion, darling, so I kind of owe you. Do you realise how much money is in this room tonight?'

His eyes moved over the heads of the fellow guests assembled; most were members of the Greek expat community, and all of them would have considered not having a private yacht as being poverty-stricken. 'That figures. Ana is raising money for one of her causes again.'

'So you're not in danger of meeting Ms Right here. Does that mean you're dumping me already, darling?'

'Funny… God, I need a drink.'

He placed a guiding hand under Lucy's elbow, and she immediately exclaimed mockingly, 'Ooh, darling, I do so love it when you're masterful. Ah!'

She staggered a little as Nik suddenly released her arm without warning.

It was an automatic response to a soft peal of laughter that made Nik turn his head. Although it hadn't been loud, there was something attractively infectious about the sound that tugged his lips into a smile.

As his eyes surfed across the heads of the other guests to the source of the sound, his smile snuffed out as recognition crashed through his nervous system like a tsunami, and for several seconds his mind went a total blank, the effect of sheer shock colliding with serendipity.

He took a deep breath and decided he'd call it something more mundane—*convenient*. Or he would once he got his rampant, raging libido under control. It took another few deep breaths to think beyond the heat that had streaked down his body and settled painfully in his groin.

His cognitive powers were clearly working on the reserve battery. He had no idea how long he stood there paralyzed, it could have been a second or an hour, before, like a man waking from a trance, he finally shook his head.

The air trapped in his lungs hissed out as in a single urgent sweep his dark, penetrating stare took in every single detail of her. The soft shiny blonde hair falling from a slight widow's peak down her back and cut shorter at the sides to frame a vivid beautiful face, the sinuous curves of her lush body outlined by the flowing lines of blue silk.

She was stunning.

He'd sometimes wondered, generally around two a.m., if he exorcised the woman, would he finally exorcise the nightmare? The two seemed so intrinsically linked, maybe they were interdependent? It had been an intellectual exercise he'd never really taken seriously as he hadn't expected their paths to cross again.

Well, it was no longer intellectual, and neither was the roar in his blood, and he knew that not to explore the theory now that he had the opportunity would be insane!

Chloe knew Nik was standing there even before Spiros's glance moved past her, alerted by the fine invisible downy hairs on her body rising in reaction to his invisible presence.

She emptied her glass carefully, wiped her expression of anything that could be interpreted as a desire to dig a big hole and jump in it and mentally circled the wagons against attack.

If she refused to be defined by the scars she wore, she was definitely not going to be defined by a past mistake, even if he was six foot three and sinfully gorgeous!

Her defensive stance wasn't against anything he might say or do, as there was a very strong possibility that he wouldn't even remember the night they had spent together, but against her own indiscriminate hormones, which still, it seemed, responded independently of her intellect to his rampant animal magnetism.

Oh, for God's sake, Chloe, you need to get a life!

While she was silently chastising herself Nik had moved level with her. 'Spiros.'

His voice had the same rough velvet, almost tactile quality she remembered…but this time she was only shivering because she was standing in a draft, she told herself stubbornly.

They were actually standing level, side by side as he stretched out a hand to the older man, but Chloe didn't turn her head. She didn't need to, because she could already feel the sheer physical power of his tall, muscled frame.

'No Petra tonight?'

'No, she's resting up. She sprained an ankle during training.'

Nik made a sympathetic noise in his throat. 'For *another* marathon?'

The older man gave a rueful nod. 'I think it's addictive.'

'You not going to join her?'

'I know my limitations.' Chloe, who felt as though her *casual* social expression could do with some work but needed all her focus to control her too rapid breathing, took encouragement from the fact that Spiros didn't seem to notice anything amiss as he touched her arm and looked at Nik. She was still working her way up to it. 'Do you know Chloe?'

She held her breath.

'Of course; we go way back,' Nik said smoothly.

'Royal connections—you kept that quiet, Nik.'

No longer able to delay the moment, Chloe turned her head, her features arranged in a smile that was intended to project polite indifference, although she had a horrible feeling that a touch of the hunted animal had crept in!

Her first hope had been that he wouldn't remember her; the second was that up close he would have some flaw she had forgotten, but again her fairy godmother had not granted her wish.

So Plan B it was, then: be polite, be distant, be… Oh, God, on an intellectual level the dark, predatory, raw animal magnetism stuff did nothing for her, only it seemed the message hadn't filtered through to the non-intellectual parts of her that were only listening to the hormonal clamour—but then it was pretty loud.

His male beauty, and beauty was no exaggeration, hit her at a purely visceral level. She had never experienced anything like it before—well, just the once.

His high knife-sharp cheekbones, strong aquiline nose, and angular jaw even dusted with stubble gave his face a patrician cast, though this was offset by the overtly sensual outline of his mobile mouth, twisted at that moment into a faintly cynical smile. The same emotion was reflected in his eyes, his quite simply spectacular eyes; deep set and heavy lidded, and fringed with dense, straight, spiky lashes, they were a stunning dark chocolate brown.

Pinned by those dark eyes, she experienced a 'rabbit in the headlight' moment and froze.

'How are you… *Chloe*?' He seemed to roll the word over his tongue as though he were tasting it.

As *he'd tasted her*… Chloe pushed the thought away but not before her body's core temperature had raised a few uncomfortable degrees. She lifted a hand to her neck to feel the dull vibration of her heavy pulse, and she fingered the uncut gemstones that felt cold compared to her skin.

From somewhere she manufactured a smile but the effort made her cheek muscles ache while she silently struggled to keep the door locked against forbidden memories. It wasn't about wanting to forget him, she thought, but more not wanting to remember and be reminded of the things she strongly suspected she might never experience again.

And maybe that was a good thing, she rationalised. Yes, head-banging, uninhibited sex was good—it was pretty excellent—but so was waking up with someone who actually cared for you, or for that matter was physically still there in the morning.

Refusing to acknowledge the sense of loss that still lay like a heavy weight in her chest, she reminded herself that she was looking, or she would be when the time came, for more in a man than his knowledge of the female anatomy... Hell, clumsy with feeling was infinitely preferable to the refined torture of a skilled touch with no emotion behind it.

'How long has it been?' he asked coolly.

'I'm not sure,' she lied, thinking, *Eighteen months, eight days and thirty-one minutes...not that I'm counting.*

She stiffened when without warning he bent his head and brushed her mouth lightly with his. His lips were warm, reminding her of when they had been even warmer, when he had tasted of her... The muscles low on her pelvis cramped as she stood as still as a statue, fighting with all her might the shameful urge to lean in and kiss him back.

The gasp she locked in her throat ached as she breathed in the warm male scent of him through flared nostrils.

It wasn't until he lifted his head that she realised she was holding his sleeve, though she had no memory of grabbing it. Disturbing, but there was no point reading too much into it, she decided as she let it casually fall away, ignoring the tingling sensation in her fingertips.

Nik smiled. The quiver he'd felt run through her body as he'd kissed her reminded him of just how receptive she'd been that night…how *giving* she'd been. And he'd taken… He countered the irrational slug of guilt with a reminder that she was the one who had taken the initiative that night, she'd made all the running and she hadn't acted like a woman who would take no for an answer.

His smile, the glimmer of dark danger glittering deep in his eyes, elicited an involuntary spasm of excitement in her belly that made Chloe feel ashamed.

'You look well.' She looked incredible, though up close there was less of the outdoorsy golden glow he remembered. Her skin was creamy, the faint touch of colour in her cheeks highlighting the smooth contours, the freckles along her cheekbones paler too, but she was, if anything, even more delicious than he remembered.

'Thank you, and how are you—sorry, Nik, wasn't it?'

The composed words aimed somewhere close to his left ear were prim, but the message shining in her deep cobalt-blue eyes as they glittered up at him was neither prim nor polite.

They said quite clearly, *Go to hell!*

Her reaction threw him off his stride, in the same way he realised he'd have been thrown if he'd reread a favourite book and found a main character had suddenly been given a different personality.

Except the woman in his dreams had never had a personality beyond being warm, giving, passionate and available when he had needed her, and he had not been curious about what lay beyond those qualities.

Realising that there *was* a beyond came with a sense of shock as Nik struggled to consider her negative reaction to him dispassionately, but got sidetracked by his own reaction to her.

The problem being there was very little room left for dispassion after the explosive blast of primal desire that obliterated everything else when he looked at her. It was like walking…no, *running* full pelt into a ten-foot wall of lust.

The time it took his stupefied brain to push past this fresh blast of raw hunger was only moments but it felt longer, and the mere fact that he *had* to make the effort deepened the frown lines in Nik's broad forehead.

In his previous life, he had cultivated dispassion until it required no effort, and it was second nature. He'd seen men and women in his old line of work who hadn't managed to do that, and the personal toll it had taken on them had not been good to see. You needed to be able to keep an emotional distance.

He had witnessed acts of bravery and self-sacrifice that were humbling, but for every one of those inspiring acts there were a hundred acts and images of suffering and inhumanity. You carried those nightmare images around with you and they ate you from the inside.

The sheer absurdity of comparing a war zone to a dinner party where people were toting glasses of wine instead of automatic weapons almost dredged up a smile. *Almost.*

CHAPTER THREE

'I'M—'

'With Lucy Cavendish…' Chloe paused, head tilted in challenge, to let the reminder sink in and had the satisfaction of seeing an expression of shock chase across his handsome face.

'Lucy…hell, I forgot about her!' A quick glance located the model, who was deep in conversation with another guest. Nik dragged a hand across his hair-roughened jaw in annoyance; he must have left her standing there looking like… He gritted out a curse. 'I'm never going to hear the end of this.'

The wrathful, choking gasp of sheer disbelief that escaped Chloe's lips drew his attention back to her face.

If there had been even the *faintest* suggestion of guilt in his reaction, she thought it would have gone some way to redeeming him…actually, no, it wouldn't!

Wanting to make excuses for him made her even angrier—as if there could be any excuse for a man who arrived with one woman and then came on to another with all the subtlety of a sledgehammer!

It made her wonder whose bed he had walked straight into after being in hers.

There had been a time when the thought would have hurt…now it simply made her stomach quiver queasily.

'It's so inconsiderate of a woman to expect you to remember that you came with her.' She produced a saccharine-sweet sympathetic smile, waiting until he frowned slightly in response to her comment before slinging out sarcastically, 'I suppose she even expects you to be there when she wakes up in the morning.'

The words hung there, every syllable oozing with exactly the sort of subtext Chloe had wanted to avoid. She sounded just like what she hated most: a victim.

Someone to pity.

Her narrow-eyed glare dared him to show it, but, although her comment had surprised a flicker of reaction, it was something else she saw move at the backs of his eyes. Fine, she could deal with something else, actually *anything* else, but *pity*.

'You were asleep.' This was the reason he avoided one-night stands; there was the potential for the stranger you went to bed with assuming that one night of sex connected you in some deep and meaningful way.

'I'm not talking about me.' She lifted her feathery brows in an attitude of mild surprise that he should think otherwise, then, willing herself not to blush, she pronounced bluntly, 'We had sex but we were not in a relationship. Although it would have been useful if you had woken me as I had somewhere I needed to be.' She wrinkled her brow, giving the impression she was trying to recall the sequence of events—events that couldn't have been more indelibly imprinted on her had someone branded them into her soul. 'I'm pretty sure I was late.' In her head she clutched the invisible award to her chest as a voice pronounced, *And the award for most convincing liar goes to... Chloe Summerville!*

The dream had once more become a nightmare before he'd ever reached the moment where he'd made the choice to leave her sleeping, not that waking her had ever really been an option. Good manners versus getting to his dying father's bedside after receiving the call about his stroke had been a no brainer.

And yes, he'd been relieved not to have to speak to her again.

Relieved to avoid the potential morning-after awkwardness and recriminations. It hadn't been his first one-night stand, but those other encounters had all been with fellow journalists, and there had been some mutual respect on a professional level between him and the smart, independent women who had shared his bunk. There had been no need to explain the desire he had felt to escape the sights and sounds of war for a few hours and let passion drown it all out. The connections had been brief, pleasurable, but nothing deeper remained.

He wouldn't have cared if any of them had forgotten his name, or implied that the memory they'd walked away with after sleeping with him was that they'd had somewhere else to be but had overslept! His ego took a few startled seconds to recover from the blow while recognising the irrationality of his reaction. Chloe Summerville's cool attitude was *exactly* what he looked for in women he gravitated towards. Women who had a male approach to sex; women who did not expect or even welcome sentiment in their liaisons, but enjoyed sex in an uncluttered and simple way.

'Sorry, I had someplace I needed to be too...but unlike you I wasn't too late.'

His father's prognosis had been grim. The doctors had been all for calling time and letting nature take its inevitable and cruel course, but his mother had insisted they try a third lot of clot-busting drugs. When Nik had walked into the room, his father had been sitting up with nothing but a slight hesitation in his speech to show he'd even had a stroke and people had been talking about miracles.

'Well, it's…nice to see you again, lovely to catch up…' Chloe said absently, adopting the tone you used when you bumped into someone whose name you kept forgetting. 'But if you'll excuse me, tonight is about work and I need to circulate.' Giving her best impression of a woman with her priorities firmly sorted, she flashed him a generic smile and turned back towards where Spiros stood talking to a small group of guests.

Even if he'd taken everything else out of the equation the dismissal would have awoken his interest, if only for the fact that it was new territory for Nik. Women did not usually walk away from him. His curiosity overcame his irritation… So, all right, it was something a lot stronger than irritation, but he didn't need to waste energy trying to identify it as it morphed seamlessly into the much easier to deal with lust and his eyes became riveted on her long, sinuous curves and the gentle sway of her hips.

If sleeping with her again was the way to finally lay his nightmares to rest, great. If not, the trying was going to be fun. Not trying at all had stopped being a possibility the second he'd set eyes on her.

The frustration raging through his veins made it hard for him to formulate a plan of action, as there had been no plan required in his dreams. On a conservative estimate he'd been making love to Chloe every other night for the past year…except this wasn't a dream, it—*she*—was the real deal! And Chloe Summerville was *more* in every way than the woman he remembered. A halfwit could have worked that out in thirty seconds.

And Nik was accounted to be quite intelligent.

She had been pulled into a group several feet away

from where he stood alone, and he watched like a hawk as she lowered her lashes over a smile in response to something Spiros had said. In profile he could see the little quiver of the fine muscles in her throat and along the delicate line of her jaw, and he wondered why he found it so fascinating.

Was he finally losing his mind?

Chloe's legs were still shaking but, as there was no longer any imminent possibility they would give out beneath her, she let go of the image of herself lying on the floor and people staring down at her. Sad, they'd say, she used to be able to stand on her own two feet… She suddenly realised a moment too late to avoid awkwardness that the extended silence was one she was meant to fill. Chloe gave an apologetic smile.

'Sorry. I wasn't following; I was just trying to remember if I put an aspirin in my bag.' She delved into the limited depths of her bag, her hair falling in a concealing curtain around her face.

Still she couldn't quite escape the conversation replaying in her head… When he had asked her how long it had been since they'd met, she'd had a nasty shock. Up to that point she hadn't known that she knew the answer even to the day and hour, but she clearly did… God, but it was terminally depressing.

What, she asked herself, had she ever seen in him?

Beyond of course the face, the body, the high-voltage charge of raw, scalp-tingling sensuality he had oozed… Beyond that, nothing at all!

Other than the dark brooding aura tinged with danger and a touch of vulnerability.

Well, he wasn't vulnerable now and she was no longer the romantic little fool she had been, but, considering her reaction to Nik just now, it was lucky that she had decided celibacy was the way to go… Not for ever—just short term. Who knew what the future held?

But one of the advantages of celibacy was that she could stand here now and look at this incredibly…really incredibly sexy man, and remember, in a way that sort of felt as if it had happened to someone else, how it had felt to have his warm, no, *hot* flesh slide over hers and it wasn't a problem.

God, you are such a liar, Chloe Summerville.

In fact, if she had truly believed she was cut out for celibacy long term, it would have simplified life in general, she concluded, studiedly ignoring the scornful voice in her head.

'You have a headache?' a woman whose name Chloe couldn't recall, despite being normally good about that sort of thing, asked.

'It's not that bad.'

Then Nik touched her arm. She knew it was him without even looking at his long fingers brown against her skin, and suddenly it was *extremely* bad. The thump, thump in her temples was keeping time with her heartbeat as Chloe felt a primitive thrill run along her nerve endings. Deeply ashamed, she waited for the fluttering inside her to subside and, under cover of looking in her bag again, calmed her breathing.

'Lost something?' he asked.

'Just an aspirin; I'm getting a headache.' *And I'm looking at it.* But she wasn't. She looked everywhere but at the tall dynamic figure towering over her, which was not something that happened often when you were five feet ten.

Eyes she had control over, but not her thoughts that drifted back to the moment she had first seen him, as if she were stuck in some sort of mind-destroying time loop. The last thing she had anticipated when they had crowded into the almost empty bar was that she would leave with a total stranger. She'd never been a person who was led by her hormones and, while she'd had any number of male friends, she'd not had a lover.

She had dated, obviously, but things had usually ended in an *it's me not you* sort of way. And she had started to think it was—that she was simply one of those women who weren't highly sexed.

Until that night.

Whatever had been lying dormant within her had surfaced with a vengeance!

'Oh, Chloe, have you met Olivia?' Spiros asked, oblivious to any atmosphere, drawing a striking middle-aged woman into the group.

Chloe shook her head, welcoming the opportunity to turn her back on the biggest mistake of her life to this point.

'Olivia, this is the young woman I was telling you about. Olivia was very interested when I told her about your project; her husband, who isn't here tonight, is a plastic surgeon.'

Chloe beamed. 'That's why you look familiar!' she exclaimed. 'I've seen the photo of you that your husband has on his desk at work.'

Listening to her, Nik twisted his lips in a cynical smile. The plastic surgeon must be very good at his job because you really couldn't tell Chloe had had any work done at all. Whatever it had been, he decided, watching her expressive face as she chatted with animation to the older woman, it hadn't been Botox.

Though now he thought about it there were changes, though not those he associated with surgical intervention. Some of the youthful softness he remembered in her face had gone, had become more *refined*, revealing a breathtaking bone structure. As he continued to study her the therapeutic benefits having sex with her might bring to him slid to the back of his mind, leaving having sex with her as soon as possible just because he wanted to very much in the forefront.

'So sorry,' he interjected.

This time with the touch of his cool hand on her wrist Chloe couldn't stop herself turning towards him; the intention was defensive, the result was not!

He was standing very close to her and she stiffened, her chest lifting as she took a deep breath and held it while, inside her ribcage, her heart rate climbed like that of an athlete waiting for the starter's pistol.

Fighting the impulse to cover her mouth with her hand as his eyes drifted to her lips and stayed there, she waited until he had stepped back far enough for her to escape the heat from his body to release the air trapped in her lungs, but unfortunately his aura of sexuality had a wider radius.

'You don't mind if I steal Chloe, do you?' he asked, taking her elbow. To an observer his attitude as much as his body language was suggestive of a long and intimate relationship with her.

The suggestion might have drawn a smile from her if her facial muscles were not locked in what she sincerely hoped was an expression of indifference. What they had shared had been little more than a collision! Granted, an extremely *intimate* collision... As a series of freeze-frame images flashed through her head they had an almost out-of-body quality to them.

She had fallen asleep in his arms, and as she'd drifted off she'd found herself thinking that she had never felt more comfortable with anyone in her life.

Comfortable was something she didn't feel right now as he half dragged her across the room; if she could, she would happily have crawled out of her skin. But pulling away would have made her look even more conspicuous.

He came to a halt in one of the deep window embrasures where the half-drawn curtains gave it an element of privacy that Chloe could have done without.

She immediately pulled away, retreating as far as physically possible. He countered her action by raising one sardonic brow.

Chloe embraced the anger that prickled through her with something approaching relief, while simultaneously ignoring the worrying excitement that popped like champagne bubbles in her bloodstream, making her feel light-headed, which probably made the little head toss with attitude she gave a mistake, but she did it anyway.

'What the hell do you think you are you doing?' she muttered under her breath.

The silky fair hair that streamed down her slender back settled into attractive waves around her face. As he watched the process he suddenly remembered it had taken a long time to gather it all up in his hand and each time his fingers had brushed her skin she had shivered.

Good question, Nik. What the hell was he doing?

He said the first thing that came into his head. 'So you're a royal of where?'

'Do you mind? I was having an important conversation back there!'

He shrugged his magnificent shoulders. 'So have a conversation with me.' *So I can look at you.* 'And if by important you mean you were about to get a donation for whatever charity it is… I'll double it,' he said casually.

She expelled a hissing sigh. 'Am I meant to be impressed by your altruism, seeing as you don't even know what the money is for?'

'Does it matter?'

She gritted her teeth and fought the impulse to slap him—anything that would break through his armour of sheer selfishness.

'Clearly not to you!' she countered contemptuously.

'You still haven't told me…'

'Told you what?'

'Royal how?'

She gave a growling sound of aggravation through her clenched teeth. 'My family,' she said finally in a bored, reading-the-telephone-directory voice, 'lives on East Vela; it's an island.' Most people didn't have a clue where it was, though most had watched the recent royal wedding on the television.

Nik proved a little more informed.

'The Vela that has just been reunified.'

She nodded.

'So where do you fit in?'

Chloe used her stock reply. 'I'm the sister who hasn't married the future King.'

'Lucky you.'

It was not the usual stock response and Chloe bristled defensively at the slightest suggestion of criticism of her brother-in-law. 'Lucky me? Most people envy my sister!'

'Do you?' The speed with which she had jumped to the man's defence made him wonder if there wasn't a personal element to her reaction, and the possibility tugged his lips into a cynical sneer.

The sheer unexpectedness of his response made Chloe blink and shake her head. 'What sort of question is that?'

He ignored the spiky question and reverted to his original comment. 'I meant lucky because a queen with any kind of history has to be a nightmare for the PR people-lovers with kiss-and-tell stories coming out of the wood-work,' he explained, pointing out the obvious.

She was tempted, but only for a moment, to retort that her *only* lover was more concerned about keeping a low profile than she was, so that was problem solved. But what would he say if he knew that? The question cir-cling in her head jolted her back to her usual common-sense mode.

Unable to adopt a sufficiently *shallow socialite* tone while she was looking at the outline of his disturbingly sensual mouth, Chloe switched her focus to his hard, stubble-covered jaw. 'Yeah, it really was a lucky escape for me,' she began, and then stopped, her eyes darken-ing as the memories of feeling cheap and used, still fresh and raw, surfaced once again. Why was she pretending to be someone she wasn't? She didn't care what he thought of her and her chin lifted a notch in defiance. 'Oh, why don't you just call me an easy lay and have done with it?'

His half-closed eyes lifted from the heaving contours of her breasts and collided with her blue shimmering glare. She pulled in a deep breath and, lower lip caught between her white teeth, took a moment to control the quiver in her voice before she drove home her point.

'Just because you treated me with zero respect, Nik, do not assume that I don't respect myself!'

She was lecturing him! Nik was too astonished to immediately react to her accusation and too ashamed to admit anywhere but in the privacy of his own thoughts that he probably deserved it.

'And for the record this is the twenty-first century; no-body expects a prince to marry a virgin bride these days!'

'Again, that's lucky or the European royalty would be a doomed species...' As he spoke the gaps between his words extended as he almost lost track of what he was saying. Her currently outraged attitude meshed with the images and little snatches of memory from that night in his head, flickering faster and faster until he could hear his own thoughts from back then—*so deliciously tight*, so *excitingly shocked…* As if everything *was* new to her, shockingly new! Had she been a virgin?

'We are a doomed species anyway, I suspect,' she was saying. 'They call it evolution, but I suppose royals are a bit like dinosaurs. In the future there will be entire floors of museums displaying our fossilised remains in glass cases.'

'Evolution is preferable to revolution… How didn't I treat you with respect?' he suddenly shot at her, trying to catch her by surprise so she would answer him truthfully.

She said nothing.

'So you *did* have a problem with me walking out on you?'

Her eyelids half lowered. 'It was a first for me, I admit.'

A first? A first of what, exactly? The idea that she could have been a virgin, considering the way she'd approached him that night, was totally crazy, and even if it were true, did he actually want to know? Didn't he have enough guilt in his life without adding any more? The problem was that now the idea was out there, swimming around in his brain, he had to voice it, even if he did end up looking like a fool.

'The first time you'd woken up with the pillow beside you empty, or the first time for you full stop?'

She felt a trickle of sweat trace a sticky path down her back and decided to deliberately misunderstand him. 'First one-night stand? You really haven't read any of the surveys in the magazines, have you? Everyone's doing it.'

'The thing about those surveys is that people lie.'

His intent stare made her feel as though he were looking directly into her head and she could feel the blush she was willing away materialise until she felt as though every inch of her skin were on fire.

'And I'm not talking about one-night stands,' he added flatly.

Pushed into a corner, she reacted with cool-eyed hauteur. 'I really don't think there's any need for a post-mortem…but if you're asking what I think you're asking, I don't think I owe you any explanation.'

'So you *were* a virgin.'

'Weren't we all once…even you?' Hard as it was to imagine. 'How old were…?' Her eyes flew wide. 'Oh, God, I said that out loud, didn't I?'

'I was sixteen and she was…older.' The glamorous, bored stepmother of one of his friends at boarding school, and he'd been very willing to be seduced. 'But even at sixteen I would not have thought it the greatest idea in the world to pick up a total stranger in a bar and have sex with them.'

'It wasn't exactly planned!'

'Look, I'm fine with youthful rebellion. I've been there and done that, but I sure as hell don't much like being the unwitting partner of it.'

Chloe felt her embarrassment slip away, incredulous anger rushing in to fill the vacuum; his hypocrisy was staggering. 'So now you're the victim and *I* should apologise? Not that there is a victim, I mean… I just saw you that night and…' She met his eyes and looked away. 'Oh, for heaven's sake, it's not as though you were fighting me off with a stick, is it?'

A laugh was wrenched from Nik's throat before he closed his eyes and wondered how a man could feel like a defiler of innocence and incredibly turned on at the same time.

'I guess I crushed a few of your romantic illusions,' he said heavily.

She sucked in a deep breath. 'Well, it had to happen sometime so relax; after the therapy I'm totally fine.' She stopped suddenly, remembering that she was talking to someone who might really have needed therapy for something more than making a poor choice. She'd slept with the wrong man; he'd seen his friend die in his arms. 'Not that there is anything funny about therapy...in fact, it's a very useful tool,' she told him earnestly.

A nerve began to slowly clench and unclench in Nik's jaw, and it had a mesmeric effect on Chloe.

'What has my sister been saying to you about me?'

Chloe began to shake her head, thinking his sister's opinion of him proved that love really *was* blind... *Lust*, however, was a completely different proposition... She tilted her chin and refused to acknowledge the shameful ache of arousal she felt just looking at him, but in her own defence this man took the term eye candy to a whole new level! 'Absolutely nothing...except of course that you are an expert on just about everything. To be totally honest with you, I'd got sick and tired of hearing the sound of your name.'

All the time she had been ripping up at him he'd stood there looking at her in that disturbing way. When she finally stopped talking he placed a finger against her lips just to make sure he was not interrupted. 'You are really, truly *perfect*! Hell, I so want to take you to bed right now.'

The raw driven declaration, barely more than a husky whisper, made her catch her breath, the air between them shimmering with suppressed sexual tension. She could only stand there, her eyes wide as he moved his finger down her cheek, the light touch, barely there, making her shiver with delicious sensation.

Her eyes had half closed in drugged pleasure when from somewhere a sliver of sanity shattered the sensual haze.

What the hell are you doing, Chloe?

'Does that line really work for you?' She was pretty sure it did, and she'd have been yet another of the women who'd fallen for it if it hadn't been for that one word… *perfect*! He still saw her as the woman with the perfect body he remembered from eighteen months ago.

The ugly reality would surely have him running for the hills.

'It isn't a line.' His heavy-lidded eyes moved in a slow approving sweep from the top of her glossy head to her feet in kitten-heeled slingbacks. 'You look fantastic.'

'Yes, I know.' But *looks*, she reminded herself, were cruelly deceptive. Even if she had been tempted to accept the offer he was making, she knew that it wasn't about her; it was only the perfect body that he wanted.

The body that no longer existed.

Loss was something she didn't normally allow herself to feel but it slammed through her now.

'I'd forgotten how direct you were. It's really refreshing,' he said.

The memory of how direct she'd been brought a flush to her face. If she ever regained the sort of confidence she'd once had, then it wouldn't be with a man like Nik Latsis. It would be with a man who could see beyond her scars, and who would want her for the woman she really was.

'Ah, well, I'm so glad to have refreshed you, and speaking of which, if you'll excuse me, I'm going to refresh my glass. I'm not interested—is that direct enough for you?'

'I'd be devastated if I believed you,' he returned with a level look.

'Believe me, you are the *last* man in the world I would be interested in!' Interested, no, she was *fascinated*...but equally she recognised it was an unhealthy 'moth to the flame' sort of fascination. One that would only lead to her being burnt up, and not in a good way.

'Never mind, Nik. If I was interested you'd be the first man to know...or maybe the second,' Lucy Cavendish corrected. 'My dentist has the loveliest eyes.' Her smile deepened as she looked at Chloe. 'So have you.'

Chloe's face burned with embarrassed heat.

Just how long had the model been standing there listening to them? And yet she didn't seem even a jot put out by what she'd heard... Maybe because she had heard it all before? Chloe speculated. Maybe she was fine with sharing her man? Or even...? *None of my business,* she told herself, swiftly closing down this lurid avenue of speculation.

'Dinner is served and I'm starving,' Lucy drawled, then, turning to Chloe, she added, 'I loved your blog, by the way. If you want to know any of the dirty details on this one, I'm the girl to come to.' She gave her a conspiratorial wink before leading Nik away.

CHAPTER FOUR

DAZED AND BEWILDERED, Chloe experienced a quite irrational sense of abandonment as she watched the couple walk away arm in arm. She hung back as the guests made their way through the double doors, which had been flung open revealing a long table covered in white linen and groaning with antique crystal and fine china. The last to enter the room, Chloe saw that Eugenie was directing guests to their places. As she watched Nik bent down and kissed his niece's cheek.

'I'm working, Uncle Nik,' she remonstrated, kissing him back despite her protest.

Chloe watched him throw a quizzical glance at his sister. 'Child labour, Ana?'

'Laying the foundations for a healthy work ethic, you mean,' Tatiana shot back.

'You were right the first time.' Eugenie raised her voice as her uncle moved away. 'No, you're down that way, Uncle Nik,' the girl called, pointing in the opposite direction from where her uncle was heading.

'No, kiddo, I think I'm sitting here.' Nik picked up one of the place cards and held it up to show her his name.

His niece frowned, pulling a slim tablet from her pocket. 'But I thought...'

Her mother leaned in and closed the tablet. 'It's fine,

love,' she said drily, picking up a card from the floor and, glancing at the name on it, placing it at a gap on another table.

Her brother reacted to the pointed look she sent him with an unrealistic innocent expression.

Watching the interplay, Chloe had a sinking feeling, and so she was unsurprised when the teenager smiled at her and directed her towards where Nik was holding out a chair next to his place.

Chloe's eyes brushed his and her stomach vanished completely!

The prospect of spending the entire meal next to him made her feel nauseous. *Oh, get over yourself, Chloe,* she told herself sternly. *What's the worst that can happen—you get indigestion?*

'Now, isn't this nice?' The innocence was gone and instead there was a feral gleam of challenge in his steady stare as he stood behind the chair waiting for her to take her seat. 'So cosy,' he murmured, pushing in the chair neatly behind her legs before taking his own seat.

Cosy? Huh. Chloe decided, nodding to the woman seated to her right, that was the last word she would use where Nik Latsis was concerned, so she didn't voice any of the half-dozen sarcastic responses that trembled on her tongue. The best way to cope with this situation was simply not to rise to the bait; instead, she would rise above it.

'Thank you,' she murmured, rather pleased with her aloof little nod, a nice combination of condescension and coldness. Yes, she decided, the high ground was *definitely* the route to take in this situation. Right but not very easy when even without looking at him she could feel the male arrogance he was radiating.

He set his elbows on the table and looked at her. 'You're dying to ask me, so go ahead.'

She squared her shoulders, and took a long swallow of the very good wine, looking at the plate that had been put in front of her; it smelt fantastic but she had virtually no appetite. 'Sorry, I don't know what you mean.'

'I'll put you out of your misery, then. You're right, Lucy and I are not a couple, just, as they say, good friends.'

'Well, that's a relief. I wouldn't have been able to sleep tonight if you hadn't explained that to me.'

Far from annoying him, her sarcastic riposte drew a broad grin. 'Ana often invites potential mates to her cosy little dinners.'

'This dinner isn't little or cosy or, as it happens, all about you.'

A smile quivered across his lips. 'Ouch!'

'You could always try dating agencies, which would be a bit more scientific than relying on your sister to set you up,' she suggested.

'I've always thought a sense of humour is overrated, especially when I'm the joke. Ana wants to see me settled down; she thinks that marriage is the magic bullet that will solve all my problems. She means well but it can get…tiresome. But you don't want to know all that; the point is… Lucy isn't my girlfriend.'

'Why are you telling me this?'

'Because I want you to say yes when I ask you to come home with me tonight.'

Having delivered this conversational dynamite in the same manner a normal person would discuss the weather, he calmly turned to the man on his right and inserted himself into the conversation concerning the most recent banking scandal.

Chloe couldn't hear what they saying, because she couldn't hear anything much beyond the static buzz inside her own head. Of course, she was going to say no to him.

She rested her hand on her thigh, running her fingers lightly across the raised damaged skin under the fine blue silk. The outline of the ugly ridges beneath her fingertips had an instant mind-clearing effect, and the doubts fluttering around in her head vanished. A man who hadn't bothered hanging around to say goodbye the morning after they'd had mind-blowing sex wasn't interested in her emotional journey; he only wanted perfect.

'I used to be a fan of your blog...is there any chance of you resurrecting it?'

Chloe snapped clear of her reverie before it reached self-pitying territory and smiled at the woman sitting across from her who'd just asked her a question. 'Well, never say never, but at the moment I can't see it happening.'

The woman looked disappointed. 'You were very successful and you had so many followers, but I suppose you've got your hands full at the moment.'

Nik had disengaged from the conversation he was involved in and took an indulgent time out to study Chloe, watching as the fine muscles along her firm jawline quivered beneath the smooth creamy skin. Her long fingers tightened around the stem of her wine glass, and he noted the absence of rings.

'So what is this blog I keep hearing about?' Nik asked curiously.

He had just announced his intention of inviting her to spend the night in his bed and now he was making small-talk! Did he compartmentalise his life as neatly as he did his conversations? she wondered, envying him the ability.

'It was a fashion blog. I started out just writing about things that caught my attention, fashion tips, current style trends, that sort of thing, and it took off after your sister—' she glanced towards Tatiana '—gave me a plug.'

'Was?'

She nodded and directed her gaze to the wine swirling around in her glass. The crystal caught the light of the chandelier that hung over the table, sending little sparks of colour through the flute. 'I've moved on to other things.'

Dreams were not reality, they were an exaggerated, distorted form of it, and Nik had assumed his memory had been guilty of making some editorial cuts, smoothing out the flaws and adding a rosy tinge to the reality of the woman who had shared her body with him. *Sharing* hardly seemed an adequate description for the lack of barriers that had existed between them—but actually sitting beside her now, he realised that the reality was even better than his memory. And she'd been a virgin— her cagey reaction had virtually confirmed his stab in the dark—but it still didn't seem possible.

'I suppose a lot of people would get bored quickly if they didn't have to worry about paying the rent, *Lady* Chloe.'

His efforts to needle her into a response were rewarded when she slung him an angry glare and drained her glass in one gulp.

It was not the first time that someone had added the title and her background together and come up with the totally inaccurate conclusion that she was a lady of leisure who didn't have to work for a living.

They weren't to know that, although her family had the aristocratic family tree and the castle that came with it, they didn't have any money, which accounted for the holes in the roof, the ancient plumbing and the fact she and her sister had always been expected to work for their living. Of course, it didn't make them poor by most people's standards but the man sitting there judging her was not *most* people.

Even at this table, where conservative estimates of all the guests' wealth were eye watering, he was probably worth more than them all combined.

Her indignation fizzed hot under the surface as she fixed him with a smile of dazzling insincerity and batted her lashes like the social butterfly he seemed to think she was.

'Oh, and how I envy the *little* people with their *simple* lives… I've even heard that some people don't bathe in ass's milk or have anyone to put toothpaste on their brushes for them.'

'Did I say something to annoy you?' His glance slid from her blazing eyes to her tightened lips and his body stirred involuntarily as he remembered kissing them, tasting her… The need to do so again as soon as possible made his body do more than stir.

She shuddered out a breath and their gazes connected. Chloe was aware that she was breathing too fast as she fought to escape the message that seemed to vibrate with a palpable force in the air between them.

'You breathing annoys me!' *Too much honesty, Chloe,* she thought, aware she had lost her moral high ground the moment the childish admission left her lips, but at least she was no longer thinking about kissing him, which was good. Taking a deep breath, she glanced around to see if anyone had heard her comment. Greatly relieved when it seemed they hadn't, she directed a straight look at him. 'Look, Tatiana is a friend and I don't want to be rude to her brother.' *Or go to bed with him.*

'Or alienate a potential donor?'

Chloe realised guiltily that the sobering reminder was

necessary. She *was* in danger of forgetting that tonight was about getting the charity off the ground. Tatiana had done her bit, inviting people with deep pockets who were sympathetic to Chloe's aims, but the rest was up to her.

It was a crowded market; there were so many good causes around Chloe knew that she needed to make a positive impression on these people if she was going to make a difference.

'True, and all donations are gratefully received.'

'You already have Ana on board, so how long have you two known one another?'

'She took an interest in my fashion blog, but we'd never met. We actually met in person only a year ago, a few months after the—' She stopped abruptly, her lashes lowering in a protective sweep.

'After what?' Against his better judgement, her sudden impersonation of a clam made him curious, and, even though he knew on one level that this should be an exercise in exorcising his demons, he found he really wanted to know what made her tick.

'After I got bored with it,' she countered, deliberately not analysing her reluctance to discuss the accident with him. She applied herself to her starter, trying to simulate an interest in her food, which she couldn't even taste.

Nik, who continued to ignore his own food, propped an elbow on the table and studied her. 'So what do you do now, besides selling raffle tickets?'

'I'm working to raise the profile of the charity.'

For *working*, Nik translated, she had probably arranged a charity fashion show or a masked ball, which was fine, but hardly enough to stimulate someone of her obvious intelligence. His dark brows flattened as he recognised but struggled to explain a sense of disappointment.

It wasn't as though he had any expectations of her, and God knew she wouldn't be the only titled socialite who didn't hold down a real job. Maybe it was just that he was surrounded by strong, driven women. His mother was a partner in a law firm, who had raised brows when she had continued to work after she was married, and his sister juggled a successful career with motherhood. Ana might be in the fashion industry, but he knew that his sister would have been appalled if her daughter had thought being decorative was more important than getting an education, which made this friendship with Chloe all the more puzzling. He really couldn't see what the two women had in common.

'I don't have my wallet with me, but I do have my chequebook and I am a dutiful brother,' Nik said.

Before Chloe could react to the patronising undertone that brought a sparkle of annoyance to her eyes, across the table an elderly silver-haired Greek businessman began to laugh.

'I wouldn't be so quick to give her a blank cheque, my boy. If that young lady gets you in a headlock, she's relentless.'

Nik elevated a dark brow. 'I thought that was just a rumour.'

'She's cost me more than my wife.'

'Which one, Joseph?'

The question caused a ripple of laughter around the table.

'It's all in a good cause,' Tatiana said, patting his hand. The soft murmur of agreement that followed her words left Nik feeling excluded, as he seemed to be the only one who didn't have a clue what the old man was talking about.

'And what *cause* would that be?'

The rest of the table had returned to their own conversations and Nik's curiosity was the only thing left to distract himself from the ache in his groin. Messing with the seating arrangements had seemed like a good idea at the time, but he really hadn't factored in the painful strength of the hard throb of need, which was becoming increasingly impossible to think past.

Insane... When had a woman made him feel like this? He looked at her mouth, remembering how it had tasted, and wondered. Last night about three a.m. she had vanished from his dreams like mist, as she always did. What if he woke up with her in his arms for real? Would she and the nightmares be gone for ever?

Chloe shifted in her seat before looking up from her contemplation of her empty glass. Strands of blonde hair fell across her cheek and she brushed them away, puzzling at her own reluctance to discuss the subject so passionate to her heart. It struck her as ironic considering she'd spent the evening selling the cause, and in all honesty she felt she was pretty good at it.

'Helping burns victims. Originally the idea was to raise money for specialised equipment for the NHS that under normal circumstances they can't afford.'

It was the last thing he had expected to hear. 'And now?'

'Oh, we'll still do all those things, but, in conjunction with that goal, we are also aiming to set up centres where there is access to physical therapy like physiotherapy, rehabilitation and so forth, alongside psychotherapy and counselling, plus the practical stuff like learning how to apply make-up to cover scarring and job retraining. In essence it will be a one-stop shop where people can access what they need or just come in for a cup of coffee and a chat.'

He watched her face change as she spoke and the animation was not something that could be faked. She was truly passionate about this charity. 'That is a very ambitious scheme for someone so young.'

She lifted her chin. 'I really don't see how my age has anything to do with it, and I was always brought up to aim high.'

'So you're saying positive thinking works miracles?'

'I'm not after miracles. Everything we are aiming for is achievable and I have the facts and figures to prove it. As for positive thinking...well, that is helpful, but there comes a point when action is needed. This isn't some sort of game to me.'

'I can see that.' His admission came with some reluctance. He didn't want to admire her; he wanted to bed her. *Liking* was not a prerequisite for compatibility in the bedroom. In fact, it was a complication.

'So why this particular cause?' he asked.

'I met someone in hospital...'

'You were ill?' He visualised an image of her lying in a hospital bed and didn't dare analyse the emotion that tightened in his gut.

She dodged his interrogative stare and looked down at her fingers, watching as they tightened around the stem of the wine glass she held. She had recovered her composure by the time she responded, explaining in a quiet measured voice wiped clean of any emotion, 'I parted company with a motorbike.' The shaky laugh was less planned. 'Or so they tell me.'

The how and why remained a blank to this day. In fact the only thing she remembered that might not have been a dream was climbing on the bike calling to her sister to follow her, and then nothing until the smell of burning and sirens. If it hadn't been for her brother-in-law she wouldn't even remember that.

She wouldn't be here at all.

Some people needed their drug of choice to be happy, but she was alive and that was all the buzz she needed. The knowledge that life was so fragile had made her determined to do something with her life that would leave something tangible behind.

'I hope the driver didn't get off scot-free.' The corners of his mouth pulled down in disapproval as he imagined her slim arms around some leather-clad idiot, her lithe body pressing into him.

'I wasn't riding pillion.' It occurred to her that her pride was misplaced; after all, how well had the going-solo scenario been serving her so far?

The problem with being so independent was that when you messed up there was no one else to share the blame with.

'So you like to be in charge?'

'In charge? If by that you mean do I like to make my own decisions, then, yes, I do,' she told him calmly. 'It's never been my fantasy to be dominated by a male chauvinist.' *Just a bit too much protesting there, Chloe!*

'You're a risk taker, then?'

Holding his gaze and reacting to the challenge glittering in the ebony depths was about the most dangerous thing she had done in a long time. 'I'm not the one who made a living dodging bullets.'

He stiffened, and their eyes connected once more. The shadows in his gaze belonged to a man who had seen far too much trauma for one lifetime. A moment later his expression shuttered and the change was so abrupt that Chloe was momentarily disorientated.

'It's a phase I grew out of.'

It was the bleakness in his voice that made her realise she hadn't imagined it. For a few seconds she was back in the bar, turning without really knowing why and seeing him sitting there, the most handsome man she had ever seen or actually imagined. In the confusing mesh of emotions—attraction colliding with empathy—she'd felt the pain he was unconsciously emanating.

Dragging her thoughts back to the present, she extinguished the ache of empathy with a large dose of objectivity. *You don't need another cause,* she warned herself, *and you definitely don't need this man.*

'So was anyone else hurt in the accident?'

'Several people, including my brother-in-law, though he wasn't then…my brother-in-law, that is. Apparently there had been an oil spill earlier on a blind bend and… it just happened. There was no one to blame but me and fate.'

He tipped his chair back to look at her, though it was hard to read his expression thanks to the thickness of his long lashes. 'So you believe in fate?'

She shrugged. 'I believe you make choices and have to live with the consequences.'

'Well, you don't seem to have suffered too many long-lasting consequences.'

He really had no idea. She struggled not to touch her leg again, and instead let her eyelids lower, shading her expression with her own long, curling lashes. 'I was very lucky,' she agreed quietly.

'So what else do you believe in?' He believed in very little and he found himself almost envying her her idealism, but equally he was disturbed by the idea that it might have been some form of this idealism that had first led her to his bed, or him to hers… Had she seen him as some sort of romantic hero or had it meant nothing to her beyond a rite of passage?

He wasn't actually sure which possibility disturbed him more.

'I believe in the resilience of human spirit, I believe that you should never take anything for granted and I believe…' She gave a sudden self-conscious laugh, her eyes sliding from his. 'I believe that I'm in danger of boring you.'

It came as a shock to realise that they had reached the coffee stage.

'I'd prefer to be dead!'

The horrified exclamation by one of the female guests coincided with a lull in the conversation.

'So what is it you prefer death to, my dear?' The man to her right voiced the question on everyone's mind.

'Being a size fourteen!' She gave a theatrical shudder. 'Can you imagine?'

Chloe sat there and imagined what this woman would say if she saw the scars on her thigh. She knew full well that her reaction would not be unique.

'She's an eating disorder waiting to happen and the sad thing is she has a daughter who she'll probably pass on her neuroses to.'

Anger struck through Chloe; while she might have agreed with the sentiment Nik had privately voiced in her ear, she doubted he had ever dated a woman who carried any extra weight.

'So I suppose appearances don't matter to you,' she charged bluntly. 'You'd date someone who wasn't perfect, would you? You honestly wouldn't care if your wife gained a hundred pounds or suddenly went bald.'

His brows lifted at the heat of her accusation. 'That

sounds rather personal. Were you an ugly duckling before you became a swan? A fat child with acne...or is that a wig you're wearing...?'

She reared back as he went to touch her hair.

'You switched the place cards, didn't you? So you could sit next to me and drive me around the bend.'

'You didn't answer my question.'

'You didn't answer mine.'

He tipped his head in acknowledgment. 'I have some skills,' he admitted modestly. As he spoke he held out his hand and turned it over, extending his long brown fingers. Then with a flick of his wrist he produced one of the place cards from the sleeve of his opposite hand. 'Distraction and sleight of hand. I have other skills.'

She compressed her lips and made a point of not asking him what they were.

'Have you thought about what I said about you coming home with me tonight?'

She choked gently on her mouthful of wine before giving him a direct look. 'I assumed you were joking.' She was quite pleased with the compromise; it was a way of saying no without injuring his male ego.

Unfortunately, he didn't appear to appreciate the favour she was doing him. 'Then I'll have to think of a way of showing you that I'm not.'

Her nerve ends tingling in response to the throaty purr of his challenge, she gave a little gasp and knocked over a glass as she bolted to her feet. Aware that people were looking at her, she calmly folded her napkin and dabbed at the damp spot on the snowy cloth. 'Send me the dry-cleaning bill,' she joked.

People responded to her quip with smiles and barely looked at her as she walked around the table to where Tatiana sat.

'I promised to ring the palace to check on…'

Tatiana's sympathy was instant. 'Of course. Use my office if you want some privacy, then join us for coffee in the drawing room.'

CHAPTER FIVE

SHE LISTENED TO her sister, who spoke at some length on the joys—*not*—of morning sickness. It wasn't until she hung up that Chloe identified the odd achey tightness in her chest as envy, but she refused to acknowledge it. Her sister deserved her happiness; it just made her aware of the things she didn't have and maybe never would.

Catching the self-pitying direction her thoughts were taking, she got to her feet, but halfway to the drawing room she chickened out and slipped into the bathroom, where she spent a great deal of time admiring the decor.

Sometimes discretion was *definitely* the better part of valour. Hoping no one had sent out a search party for her, she waited there long enough to be sure that her arrival would coincide with people leaving. Hopefully she could slip away unnoticed without any further confrontations with Nik.

She had just stepped out into the hallway when she heard Lucy's voice and ducked back into the bathroom. It was instinctive and she felt foolish the moment she locked the door. It wasn't Lucy she was hiding from, but that didn't matter; it was the fact she was hiding at all that filled her with self-disgust.

With a sigh she turned, dumped her bag on the vanity

unit and, palms flat on the marble surface, she looked at herself in the mirror.

Her face illuminated by the spotlights above looked pale and her eyes were too bright. She leaned in and touched the fine skin under her eye; the make-up helped but did not quite conceal the blueish half-moon, which was the result of a week of disturbed nights that had preceded her decision not to continue with further surgery.

The decision had felt liberating, she'd felt completely in control and yet what had it taken to throw that equilibrium into chaos? One single encounter with Nik Latsis. She made a sound of disgust in her throat and turned her back on the mirror.

She sighed. She hadn't felt in control tonight, she'd felt… She shook her head, unable…unwilling to examine her emotions as she turned, taking care not to look in the mirror, and twisted the cold tap onto full.

She stood there with her wrists under the running water, waiting for her heart rate to slow, wanting to reject outright the idea that she was attracted to Nik Latsis. The lie would have been easy, easier than admitting a man like him would never want someone less than perfect, but she couldn't.

It was a fact.

She turned off the tap, lifted her chin and looked at herself in the mirror.

'It is what it is, Chloe.'

She made her way back downstairs, where the hallway was empty but the door stood open. There was no sign of Tatiana, so she decided to call for a cab before saying goodbye to her hostess.

She had started to punch in the number when a voice at her elbow made her jump.

'Have you been hiding?' Nik asked.

'*What?*'

He was wearing a long tailored dark overcoat that hung open, his hair glistened wet and the same moisture glistened on his face. He had brought the smell of outdoors and rain into the room.

Chloe struggled to hide her dismay and the illicit excitement that made her stomach muscles quiver. 'You haven't gone yet.'

'Ever the gentleman, I have been escorting the ladies to their cars.' He held up a large umbrella.

Chloe clenched her fingers over her phone, ignoring the little ribbons of warm electricity making her aware of the tingling nerve endings in her skin. 'I'm just ringing for a taxi.'

He watched as she began to punch in a number, noticing that her face had a fresh scrubbed look as though she'd taken off her make-up. She still looked good, very good, but she looked more vulnerable...delicate, even. He felt an emotion swell in his chest but refused to acknowledge it as tenderness.

'You don't need a taxi.'

The harshness in his voice drew her glance upwards. 'Thanks, but no, thanks,' she said firmly, ashamed of the moments of self-pity she had indulged in.

'You're still here!' Tatiana's relieved voice rang out before Nik could respond.

Chloe was glad of the interruption but puzzled by the older woman's sense of urgency. 'I was just ringing for a taxi before I came to say goodbye, but did I forget something?' She nodded to Lucy who had appeared behind her host; the redhead was wearing a denim jacket over the slinky red dress and carrying off the contrast in considerable style.

Tatiana shook her head. 'Spiros just rang to warn anyone left not to try taking…well, just about any road, I think. The peaceful protests apparently turned out not to be so peaceful, and the police have closed down half the streets. Spiros is stuck, and he saw a car alight too. I really think it would be better if you all stay here for the night. There are reports of the disturbances spreading and even looting.'

'I'm walking home, so it's no problem,' Lucy said.

Tatiana looked alarmed.

Lucy put her hands on the older woman's shoulders. 'Relax, I'm not going to my home, I'm booked into the new boutique hotel around the corner. It's only a hundred yards, so I think I'll be safe.' She air-kissed Tatiana and thanked her, landed a kiss on Nik's cheek and waved to Chloe. 'Interesting night.'

Chloe didn't even try and translate this cryptic utterance.

'And I'm going Chloe's way so that's her problem solved,' Nik announced in a tone that brooked no argument.

Not from where she was standing!

'How do you know which way is my way? That is,' she continued, lowering the levels of antagonism in her voice, 'I wouldn't dream of bothering you.'

'Nonsense!' Tatiana sent her brother a warning glare. 'He's fine with it, aren't you, Nik?'

Chloe clenched her teeth as, with a totally unconvincing display of meekness that made him look even more like a wolf, he tipped his dark head.

'Absolutely.' Slower than Tatiana to jump back squealing when he shook the umbrella, sending a spray of cold water droplets that hit everything in the immediate area, Chloe was the only one close enough to hear his not at all meek-sounding addition. 'My way is whichever way you're going.'

She brushed her ear where the sensitive flesh still tingled from the touch of his warm breath and glared at him, while he continued to look smugly satisfied with himself.

'Well, that's sorted, then,' Tatiana said, looking relieved. 'You will text me when you get home safely?'

Chloe promised.

She gave a sigh and rubbed the tip of her nose with her finger. The truth was, there was a part of her, a clearly twisted part of her, that had…*enjoyed* their flirtation. No, that was the wrong word. It hadn't been flirtation; that was far too gentle. Combat probably better described the heart-thumping, skin-tingling adrenaline charge of their exchanges tonight.

She had felt what…? *Like a woman.* Her eyes flew wide with shock as the recognition of her too-long-suppressed sexuality crashed through her.

'Are you all right?' Nik asked.

'I'm fine!' she lied.

She read criticism in his eyes as they swept her face. 'You look like you're in pain.'

'The only pain around here…' at the last second she managed to apply the brake to her runaway tongue and lowered her eyes, muttering '…is a slight headache.'

Actually pain was pretty accurate for what she felt, as though the circulation were returning to a limb deprived of blood. It hurt and so did this—the part of her that had been in hibernation since the accident had finally woken up and it was tingling!

She wasn't ready yet; she wanted that part to go back to sleep. It was such awful bad timing! At this point an affair of any kind, let alone the sort of superficial no-strings fling Nik Latsis had in mind for them, was the last thing she needed.

She lifted her chin, defiance sparking in her eyes, as she thought, *I deserve more than that! I deserve better than Nik Latsis!*

Even if she had been in the market for a man, which she wasn't, he would not have made the shortlist. If she had needed reminding, and she didn't, how shallow he was, tonight would have driven the point home to her.

Yes, she was attracted to him, it was actually too exhausting to try and pretend otherwise, but in her defence he had more sexual charisma in a single hair follicle than most men had in their entire bodies. Although *attraction* hardly came close to describing the visceral reaction he evoked just looking at him… *Then don't look!* she told herself.

She needed to stop over-analysing everything. Nothing was going to happen between them because it couldn't. She brushed her leg with her hand, not that the numbed scar tissue registered the touch. She found herself wishing fiercely for a moment that the numbness went even deeper, that she could anaesthetise the emotions that tonight had reawoken in her.

She squared her shoulders. If he had been the Nik who had vulnerabilities, and not this insensitive, slick predator, she might have been in trouble, but he wasn't, so she was completely safe.

As safe as being circled by a tiger, she thought, injecting as much grateful insincerity into her smile as she could.

'I hope it's not too far out of your way, Nik.'

It was Tatiana who replied. 'Don't be silly, Chloe…'

'Looks like that's settled, then.' Nik walked ahead and left Chloe to walk beside his sister. When they reached the open front door she realised with a stab of shame that she didn't have a clue what the other woman had just been saying to her.

This had to stop, she told herself. Nik Latsis was the past, not a mistake because the last few months had taught her that thinking about mistakes meant you couldn't move forward. She had moved forward and she would continue to do so.

'It's stopped raining.' Nik, who had walked outside ahead of the women, lowered the umbrella he had raised and held up his hands to the sky. He grinned, twirled the umbrella and stamped in a puddle.

Fighting the urge to run out and join him, Chloe was conscious of an ache in her chest. She snatched a quick breath, knowing that the image would stay with her, but not knowing why…or at least not asking herself why.

'You're welcome to stay over if you like.'

Her friend was looking concerned as she reiterated her offer; if Tatiana had picked up on her distress, Chloe just hoped she hadn't picked up on the cause! She was tempted, she really was, but accepting the offer would mean she was afraid to be alone with Nik. And she wasn't, because nothing was going to happen between them. Chloe gathered herself and turned with a smile that felt stiff and forced, although she was unwilling to admit that even to herself.

'Thanks, but no, it would be good to get home.' She raised her voice a little to make sure that Nik could hear what she was saying and get the message. 'I'd like to sleep in my own bed.' The way her mind was working overtime she doubted there would be much sleep for her tonight.

After a pause, Tatiana nodded and kissed her cheek. 'Take care…and drive carefully, Nik,' she called after her brother, who lifted an arm and waved.

* * *

Chloe trudged on head down, Nik beside her, not touching her but close, close enough for her to be aware of the tension that stopped him dead in his tracks at the sound of distant sirens.

He stood there, head sharply angled, his lean, tense stance making her think of a wolf sensing danger, nostrils flared, scenting it in the air.

The sound retreated and he shook his head as though clearing it before glancing down at her. 'I'm parked over here.'

It took Chloe a moment to recover from the expression she had glimpsed on his face before she fell into step beside him.

'Are you all right?' she asked softly. Haunted; he had looked haunted.

He glanced down at her, the sounds of war, the explosions, the disembodied screams and the discordant staccato peal of shells still sounding in his head. 'The silences in between the shelling were the worst. Somehow they tapped into a man's primitive fears…the calm before the storm.' He stopped and the street light above them showed the shock reflected on his face…as if he'd only just realised he'd spoken his thoughts out loud.

Then it was gone, as quickly as it had appeared.

Another time his car, a low, gleaming monster, would have drawn a sarcastic remark from Chloe about macho power statements, but all she did was slide into the passenger seat when he opened the door.

She ached for his pain but she knew she couldn't let him into her life…every instinct of self-preservation told her this. The memory of that morning waking alone, when she'd waited for him, imagining the reasons for his absence—he'd stepped out for coffee, he'd gone to find a red rose—made her cringe, but even worse was when the penny had finally dropped and she had acted like someone heartbroken.

The memory she filed away as water under the bridge. Mistakes were fine—it was repeating them that was unforgivable! He was a fragment of her history and, after all, you were never supposed to forget your first lover. Well, only time would tell and she was an optimist.

'I need to stop off at the office first...there are some contracts I must sign tonight,' he said.

Any delay, any reason to prolong the time she spent in this enclosed space with him filled her with dismay, although it was mitigated with a relief that he was sounding normal again. If he was acting she was glad...she simply couldn't deal with his trauma and her own reaction to it. A vulnerable Nik was a very dangerous Nik to her peace of mind!

'At this time of night?' Her voice sounded calm but her agitation revealed itself in the smooth stroking motion of her hands as she moved them up and down over her silk-covered thighs.

'I think they'll let me in,' he said, thinking about how her legs had wrapped tight around him as he'd thrust inside her.

'Of course,' she said, feeling stupid...then something more uncomfortable than stupid when she realised his eyes were following the mechanical motion of her hands. She stopped and folded her arms defensively across her chest.

He cast a glance across her face and was distracted for a moment because she was chewing her plump lower lip and all he had to do was bend in a little closer to taste it for himself.

'Look, Nik, tonight I think I might have... If I seemed

like I wanted you to…' She swallowed and stopped; if she really hadn't wanted Nik to flirt with her, why hadn't she just told him straight out about the scars that remained after the operations, the puckered, discoloured patches of flesh on her right thigh? It would have been amusing to see how fast he retreated.

Except it wouldn't have been *amusing*.

She told herself that people's attitudes to her scars were their problem, not hers, and most of the time she believed it, but there was a world of difference between theory and fact, not to mention a world of humiliation, and she wasn't ready for that yet.

'You were saying…?' he prompted, wondering if she knew how expressive her face was. The drift of emotions across it was almost like watching a silent film.

'I think it's a very bad idea to try and relive something that happened in the past. Much better to remember it as it was.'

'So am I a happy memory or a bad one?'

'A bit of both,' she admitted, thinking that she had reached the stars with him and discovered the depths of despair. She buckled her belt, reminding herself that self-pity was for people who did not have a life and she did. She was not going to waste her time thinking about what she'd lost; she was going to celebrate what she had.

Nik watched her, the knot of frustration in his belly tightening the muscles along his jaw. He enjoyed a challenge as much as the next man but this was different… He swore under his breath as he started the engine.

'So how long have you lived in London?' he asked in an attempt at a normal conversation.

'I went to college, but I wasn't very academic…'

'You dropped out?'

'More like I was invited to leave, which was fine because I had begun to make money with the blog, which seemed so amazing at the time. I've always been lucky.'

'And accident prone,' he commented.

'People died in that accident so I was still lucky,' she retorted.

'I'm guessing you are a glass-half-full kind of person.'

'I really hope so…' She turned her head to look at the glass-fronted building he had pulled up in front of.

'I won't be long.' He leaned across and snatched the phone she was nursing on her knee.

A moment later he tossed it back to her. 'My number's in it, and if you see or hear anything, call me,' he directed sternly.

It took her a few moments to realise what he meant. Some of her antagonism faded, but she remained sceptical that his caution was warranted.

'I think Spiros might have been exaggerating the danger.' Other than the initial couple of distant sirens, which was not exactly unusual, they had encountered nothing that suggested widespread rioting.

'You might be right.' He gave a concessionary nod and slid out, closing the door behind him with a decisive click.

Chloe leaned back in her seat, relaxing enough for her shoulder blades to actually make contact with the leather, and she watched him walk away, his hands thrust deep in his pockets, up the shallow steps to the building. He paused for a moment and she heard the decisive click of the car doors locking.

'I don't believe it!'

There was no one to hear her exclamation, and her angry bang on the window went unnoticed. Then there was nobody but the uniformed security guard, who'd come out when Nik went in, who just stood there ignoring her, his eyes constantly scanning the areas to left and right.

When Nik reappeared exactly three minutes fifteen seconds later, the two men shook hands and exchanged a few words before the man walked back into the building and Nik got into the car.

Chloe stared stonily ahead as he flung some files onto the back seat. 'You locked me in.'

'I didn't want any looters stealing my car.'

She compressed her lips. 'That man ignored me—'

'That man is an ex-marine. He knew what you were doing.'

'Oh. Do you have a lot of ex-marines working for you?'

'The transition is not always kind to men who have given their lives to protect us. Dave, back there, flung himself on a landmine and saved three others in his squad, but he lost a leg below the knee.'

Their eyes connected and in his dark gaze she saw something she didn't want to acknowledge. In seconds the heat banked inside her burst into life, starting low in her pelvis and spreading out until her entire body was suffused by the same blazing fire. The instant conflagration scared her witless... It was a warning, she told herself, a warning that said if she had an ounce of self-respect she'd get the hell out of that car right now.

Panic hit her hard. 'Stop the car.' She used the anger when he ignored her to drag herself free of the last of the dangerous languor that lingered in her brain. 'I said, stop the car,' she said calmly.

He took his eyes off the road to briefly glance at her face and she could hear the irritation in his voice. 'Don't be stupid.'

The only stupid thing she had done so far was getting

into this car with him and Chloe had every intention of keeping it that way.

'You're acting as though we have unfinished business, but that's not the case. Look, I spent the night with you, end of story. It is not something I have any wish to repeat.'

'So you want to pretend it didn't happen at all.'

The suggestion, his tone, his attitude they all struck a jarring note inside her, so she counted to ten and fought to dampen the resentment she knew she had no right to be feeling.

'I'm not pretending it didn't happen; I'm admitting it shouldn't have.'

'I—'

'Get down!'

It was the tone as much as the terse instruction that made her stomach clench. 'What's wrong?'

'Just do it. There's a blanket there, cover yourself with it and duck down.' The odd instruction was delivered in a light, calm tone, but when she leaned forward and saw what he had already seen, she didn't feel very calm at all.

Ahead of them the road was filled with crowds of people. Some had banners and some carried dustbin lids, which they were banging.

He wound down the window and the suggestion of noise became a loud, discordant din.

'They sound mad.' Fear fluttered in her belly.

'They are a mob.' And it was the nature of the beast, anger and unpredictability, the pack-animal mentality, that could make the whole group do things that as individuals they would never dream of doing.

'I don't like this,' she said, once again gnawing at her plump lower lip, a nervous habit she'd never managed to break.

'I would be more concerned if you did. Duck down and pull the cover over your head.'

If he had faced this situation alone he would not have broken a sweat, not because he was brave or fearless, but because he had been in far worse situations, and as far as he could see the only thing he stood to lose was a car.

But he wasn't alone, and knowing that Chloe's safety was his responsibility changed everything. He had talked his way out of much worse situations, but with Chloe here he wasn't prepared to take even a calculated risk.

'No, I'm not hiding and leaving you exposed,' she stated, but her fists were clenched tightly.

'Why does beautiful so often go with stupid?' He sighed.

Her wrathful gaze met his in the mirror and he smiled. If she was angry, at least she wasn't afraid. 'Relax, *agape mou*, I will not let anything hurt you.'

She believed him, although it seemed that she ought to be more concerned about her mental well-being than her physical! She caught his arm and he paused, his eyes going from her fingers curled into the fabric, to her face. 'You're not going to do anything stupid, are you?'

'Could you be more specific?' he asked.

'I don't know…like fight them.'

He let out a loud throaty laugh. 'Me against fifty, sixty people? I don't much like those odds, but I'm sorry if I disappoint you in the hero stakes.'

'I promise you I never thought you were a hero.'

One corner of his mouth lifted in a lopsided grin and there was something about him…a combustible quality that made her think it would have been a brave person who bet against him, even if the odds were stacked against him.

'But I do think you're capable of doing something stupid.'

'Like they say, a good general chooses his field of battle. I am not good or a general but the concept holds true.'

'Are you going to drive on through them?' she asked nervously.

Nik had been going to reverse, but a glance in the rearview mirror made it clear this was a now-or-never choice. The street on one side—he adjusted the mirror and silently corrected himself—on both sides of the road were full of people streaming towards the main artery road. It was hard to be accurate but he suspected that their options would close in seconds, not minutes.

'Hold on, this might be a little bumpy.'

She connected with his eyes and made a shocking discovery. 'You are enjoying this, aren't—?' She let out a shriek and closed her eyes as the car went into sudden reverse, travelling at what felt like the speed of light. It continued backwards even when it hit obstacles, objects in the road flung down by rioters.

The banner-waving maniacs followed initially, but they quickly fell away and by the time the car reached the gaggle of police cars the protestors were nowhere in sight.

'Wait here.'

She narrowed her eyes, tilted her stubborn little chin and thought, *Oh, yes that is* really *going to happen!* Who did he think he was, issuing orders to her? She opened her door and got out.

Two uniformed officers were already moving towards the car, and Nik walked towards them, looking calm and confident.

By the time she was within hearing distance, the police were complimenting Nik and shaking his hand.

'Thank you, sir. If all witnesses could be so clinically precise it would make our job a lot easier.'

'More resources,' the younger one said, 'would too.'

In response to a look he received from his colleague, he added a defensive, 'It's no secret that we're over-stretched.' Then he stopped as he saw Chloe coming to-wards them, his eyes widening.

Before he could speak to her, Nik moved, cutting off her approach. With a firm hand on her elbow, he turned back to the men. 'We won't get in your way, officers, and thank you. Come on, Chloe.'

She was hustled back to the car with equal ruthless efficiency. 'You didn't let me say a word to them! What did you think I was going to do?' she demanded as Nik folded his long length in beside her.

'Distract them from their job,' he replied succinctly.

'So what happens now?' she huffed.

'Now I take you home. The police have given me a route that should be clear and, before you ask, the Tube stations are closed, so don't even think of asking me to stop the car again.'

The rest of the journey was completed without inci-dent and in total silence.

She waited until he had neatly reversed the car into a parking space clearly marked reserved outside her build-ing before releasing her seat belt.

'I should thank you.'

'But you won't.'

'That's not what I…' A sound of irritation rattled in her throat. He drove her insane! 'All right, I *do* thank you.'

'It was my pleasure.'

He moved to open his door and she shook her head. 'No, don't get out; I'm fine.'

'I will see you to the door.'

'I'm not going to be ravished or kidnapped between here and there,' she said, nodding to the Georgian building behind them. Once it had housed one family; now it was split into twenty one-bedroom apartments, a bit down at heel, or, in estate-agent speak, ripe for improvement. Chloe had no cash to improve hers as she had poured all the money her blog had made into buying the place.

'Looking like that, I would not be so confident.'

'You mean I would be asking for it?' she countered crankily.

His exasperation increased. 'I mean that you are a very beautiful woman, this is a fact, and it is also a fact that a man who forces himself on a woman is no real man.' His nostrils flared in distaste. 'And a man who excuses the actions of such a person is no less of an inadequate loser.'

He got out and walked around to her side of the car, standing there silently as she got out.

She tilted her head to look at his shuttered face. 'I've offended you.'

He arched an eloquent brow.

'Sorry.'

He bowed slightly from the waist. 'Accepted.' A glimmer appeared in his eyes. 'Friends again?'

Chloe looked at the hand extended to her as if it were a viper. It was news to her that they ever had been friends, but he had got her home so she reached out.

He took her hand but not to shake it. Without his seeming to exert any overt pressure, she found herself colliding with his body.

His dark face lowered to hers. 'It's all about sleight of hand and distraction,' he whispered before his mouth came crashing down on hers.

The kiss was hard, hot and hungry as he plundered her mouth with ruthless efficiency. For a split second, shock held her immobile, then as his dark head began to lift something snapped inside her. Chloe felt it, even heard it, as she dragged his dark head back down to hers, parting her lips to invite a deepening of the slow, sensual exploration.

It was an invitation that he accepted, driving his tongue deep into the warm recesses of her mouth.

She was distantly conscious of the throaty, mewling little sounds but didn't make the connection between them and herself. Her hands curled into his jacket to stop herself falling as tongues of flame scorched along her nerve endings, and she felt a deep shudder ripple through the hard, lean body pressed close to her.

'Oh, God!'

Her shaken gasp seemed to break the spell.

The thud that Chloe heard when she fell back to earth seemed almost as real as the searing humiliation she felt as, still shaking, she looked up at him, to see that he was perfectly fine. Standing there as though nothing had happened, she thought, her indignation going supernova... then cooling slightly as she noticed the streaks of colour along his cheekbones and the fact he was breathing pretty hard.

At least he had put enough distance between them to make the basic stuff like breathing a whole lot easier. She tilted her head but it was impossible to make out his expression. Even with her eyes narrowed, his face was just a dark blur, which was probably a blessing of sorts because he no doubt looked as smug as a man who had just had his point proved could look.

She took a deep breath. 'I am not sure what that was meant to achieve.'

'Achieve?'

She ignored the interruption and didn't even register the odd strain in his voice.

'I already knew that you were a good kisser.' He was a good everything, that was the problem.

'So the problem is…?'

Arms crossed over her chest, she rubbed her upper arms with both hands. 'I enjoyed the night I spent with you, but I happen not to be quite as casual about sex as you are. That's not a criticism,' she hastened to assure him. 'I mean, as far as I'm concerned, each to his own.'

'So now you have developed a puritanical streak?'

She slung him a look of simmering dislike. 'Last time you looked…hurt…lost…' *And what's your excuse this time, Chloe?* 'I don't know, but—'

'You are saying you had pity sex with me.'

'No.'

'So are you looking for a deep and meaningful relationship?'

The sneering tone of his voice set her teeth on edge and tightened her expression into a glare, though she fought to keep the edge of antagonism from her voice. 'I'm not actually looking for any sort of a relationship just now, but when I am… I'd like to find a man who will accept me for who I am inside, and not care about the way I look.'

He gave a hard, incredulous laugh. 'Well, if that's the kind of man you're looking for, I'd start looking for a couple of nice cats instead, if I were you. What's so wrong with being beautiful? It's not exactly a curse; women spend their lives and fortunes trying to look like you and they never will. How is noticing you're beautiful an insult to you?'

She stuck out her small determined chin. 'I'm a hell

of a lot more than that, not that you're ever going to know, and, believe you me, that's your loss!' she flared, secreting the security card she'd extracted from her bag in her palm.

She widened her eyes and looked into the middle distance. 'Oh, my!'

As soon as he turned his head to see what she was staring at, Chloe ran to the door. Her security card swiped first time and she stepped into the foyer, slamming it shut a split second before he reached it.

She pressed the button on the intercom. 'It's all about sleight of hand and distraction.'

A reluctant smile fought its way to his lips. 'I thought you never hid.'

She might not know about distraction, but she understood about odds. Her father owned the leg of a racehorse and she knew the odds were good that if Nik kissed her again and she got another taste of that raw power, if she felt the impression of his erection grinding into her belly, instinct would take over and reason would fly out of the window.

And everything would be hot and marvellous until he got an up-close-and-personal look at the part of her that once had been perfect and now wasn't. Did she want to carry the memory of his look of disgust or embarrassment as he pulled away from her? That was a no brainer.

'I'm not hiding from you. I'm walking away. There's a difference.' The moment she turned away from him the tears she had been holding back began to fall, and, running up the stairs, she swiped at them irritably.

Just sex was really not worth it!

CHAPTER SIX

IT WAS NOON when Chloe got back to her flat, but the first thing she did was strip off, push her clothes in the linen basket and step in the shower. The act of washing was purely symbolic; she knew the scent of hospital was in her mind, because the only thing the doctor's consulting room on the top floor of the rather beautiful Georgian building it occupied had smelt of was his expensive aftershave.

Hair still damp, she tightened the belt of her robe around her waist and flung herself down on the sofa, keying in her sister's number on her phone…but it went straight to voicemail.

With a sigh she dropped the phone in her robe pocket and padded barefoot over to the kitchen. Of course, if her sister had known about the hospital appointment she would have been waiting for the call—no, she would have come with her—but she didn't know. Chloe deliberately hadn't told anyone about it, *especially* her family.

They had been through enough during the long months after the accident—not that her choice not to tell them was entirely selfless. She knew that they, or at least her parents, would struggle to understand her decision not to have further cosmetic surgery. Down the line who knew how she'd feel about it? While it certainly was an option, right now she'd had enough of hospitals and she felt that to go through all that again was unbearable, especially as there were no guarantees regarding exactly how much improvement there would be, as the doctor would not give any promises.

She had taken a sip of her scalding coffee when her phone rang, and she lifted it to her ear and said hello.

It was not her sister who replied and, stifling a surge of disappointment, she said, 'Can you just hold on a second?' and reached out to shut the door of the fridge, which was buzzing to remind her she'd not closed it. 'Hi, Tatiana.'

'S… Sorry, is this a bad time?'

Chloe's reaction was immediate; elbows on the counter, she leaned forward, concern furrowing her brow. 'No, it's fine…is anything wrong?' When they had spoken earlier today, Tatiana had sounded relaxed and happy, issuing an invitation that Chloe had refused, which had been to join her on the family estate on the Greek island of Spetses. But now, only a few hours later, she was obviously close to tears.

'I told you, didn't I, that I agreed to Eugenie spending the first week of the holiday with her friend Pippa in Hampshire…?'

'Yes…has something gone wrong?' Chloe asked.

Tatiana gave an unamused laugh. 'You could say that. Pippa's parents in their wisdom decided that two fifteen-year-old girls were mature enough to be left alone in the house while they went away for the night.'

'Oh, dear!'

'Oh, yes, definitely *oh, dear*. The girls decided to have an impromptu party with supposedly just a few friends but, to cut a long story short, it was gatecrashed by lots of other kids, the place was wrecked and the neighbours called the police! Eugenie has been cautioned by the police and she is waiting at the local police station to be picked up. Pippa's parents have decided she is a bad influence—can you believe it? The problem is, my grandmother has a really high temperature, so I can't leave her, and my brother's not picking up his phone and no one seems to know where he is.'

'What can I do?'

A sob of relief echoed down the line. 'Could you pick her up for me and take her to the airport?'

'Of course.'

'The Gulfstream jet was in Frankfurt; I have no idea what my parents are doing there. Anyhow, I made some excuse up to say I needed the plane, but I really don't want them to know about this. It should be there by the time you arrive.'

'Don't worry, I'll drop her off safely.'

'Drop her off? Oh, no, Chloe, I need you to travel with her to Spetses, and sit on her if necessary! I'm not risking her pulling another stunt.'

It was only the rising hysteria in her friend's voice that stopped Chloe pointing out that there seemed little possibility of her daughter coming to any harm on a private flight to a Greek island. 'Fine, I'll sit on her.'

'I knew I could rely on you. Thank you so much, Chloe. I'll never be able to repay you.'

Actually, Chloe realised as she picked up her car keys, it was Tatiana who was doing her a favour. Left to her own devices she'd have spent the evening brooding over her decision and planning how she broke the news to her parents. Instead, she had plenty to distract her.

A cloudburst proved to be one of the distractions she hadn't figured on.

Chloe was drenched to the skin as she sat in the police

station studying a poster on the wall that proclaimed in large letters *Don't be a victim,* a sentiment she agreed with wholeheartedly, when Eugenie appeared walking alongside a fresh-faced policewoman who barely seemed older than the teen.

The girl's face dropped when she saw Chloe.

'I thought Uncle Nik was coming to get me.'

'Your mum couldn't contact him.' Chloe struggled not to sound judgemental about that as her imagination kicked in, supplying a slide show of selfish reasons for Nik being off the grid, all revolving around beautiful women and bed.

Well, you declined his offer to spend the night with him, Chloe reminded herself. *Did you expect him to go back home and weep into his beer, or did you expect him to pursue you?*

He clearly hadn't done either, which reinforced the obvious: it had been an opportunist offer, made in the heat of the moment, and when she'd refused he had chalked it up to experience and moved on.

A circumstance she told herself she was relieved about.

'Uncle Nik would understand…*he* wouldn't lecture me,' the girl said, her defiant expression suggesting that Chloe couldn't even begin to do so.

In contrast to the girl's dramatic pronouncement Chloe kept her voice light and friendly. 'I'm not here to lecture you,' she returned, thinking, *Thank God, it's not my job.* 'Just get you to your mum.'

The girl pouted and tossed her head. 'Well, you took your time.'

Chloe smiled and counted to ten. 'Yes, I thought I'd take the scenic route as it's such a lovely day for a drive.' She gestured to the window, where the rain was falling from a leaden summer sky. 'And obviously I had nothing better to do.' Without waiting for the girl's response, she turned to the policewoman. 'Thank you very much for looking after her.' She glanced at Eugenie. 'Ready...?'

The girl nodded. Minus the truculent attitude, she looked so miserable and very young standing there shifting her weight from one spiky heel to the other that it was all Chloe could do not to hug her.

Instead she slipped off her jacket and draped it over the girl's bare shoulders. 'It's a bit chilly out there.'

Eugenie turned her head to look up at Chloe. 'Is she really mad? Mum, I mean?' she muttered.

'I'm afraid I'm just the chauffeur.' Chloe hesitated, choosing her words with care. 'I've zero experience of being a parent, but I have been a daughter and when my parents were angry with me it was usually because they were worried about me.'

'There was no reason for her to be worried.'

'If you say so.'

'You don't believe me, do you?'

'I'm parked just over there.'

'Uncle Nik would believe me—he'd understand.'

Well, bully for Uncle Nik, Chloe thought, keeping her lips sealed over her resentment. Uncle Nik, who would no doubt have beautiful babies, and was, as far as she knew, somewhere right now trying to make one.

She frowned, rubbing her upper arms through the silk of her already drenched blouse, and pushed the accompanying image away. Wherever he was too busy to pick up his phone, it was bound to be some place nice and warm while she was drenched to the skin and walking on eggshells with a teenager who made her feel about ninety!

Just as she was on the point of deciding that parenthood was clearly a mug's game, her sulky charge stopped. Impatient, Chloe turned back.

'Thank you for coming for me,' Eugenie said in a small quivery voice.

'You are very welcome.'

Chloe fished her keys from her pocket and opened the passenger door of her own utilitarian hatchback. 'Sorry you're slumming it today.'

'*That* is your car?' The girl's astonishment was almost comical, as was her horror. Chloe strongly suspected that the idea of being seen in anything so uncool worried her more than the idea of parental ire or a jail cell.

'So what does it do, thirty with the wind behind it?'

'If we're lucky.' *Speed* had not been a priority when she had first got behind the wheel of a car after the accident, but safety had. Not that she expected the girl, or anyone else for that matter, to understand that this car represented a personal triumph for Chloe.

She could have rationalised it and it would have been easier than admitting her fears. Far easier to pretend that she was doing her eco bit for the planet by using public transport, asking how convenient actually was it to have a car in the City?

Instead she had admitted she had a problem, and her family had been proud when she had conquered her fears, but the truth was her honesty had certain limitations. She'd never told them that her hands still got clammy when she slid into the driver's seat and her heart rate took a few minutes before it settled into a normal rhythm.

Time, she hoped, would eventually finish the healing process.

'I thought you were meant to be royal or something...'

'Or something,' Chloe admitted with a laugh. 'You can always duck down if you see anyone you know—'

The sound of a car that was neither safe nor slow made them both turn as a limousine complete with blacked-out windows drew up behind them.

The girl's pale face lit up. 'It's Uncle Nik.'

Chloe already knew that. As he got out of the car her minor palpitations suddenly became critical.

'He'll understand.' The relief in the girl's face faded away to uncertainty as she realised what Chloe already had. The man striding towards them was furious.

His face set in hard lines, his dark brows drawn into a straight line above his hawkish nose, he stopped a couple of feet away from them. He was breathing hard and looked like a well-dressed version of a dark avenging angel as the wind caught the hem of his long coat, making it billow out behind him.

'What the hell did you think you were doing?'

As the teenager shrank into her side Chloe wondered if Nik knew he had gone from hero to villain in just one short sentence.

Nik's narrowed eyes followed the protective hand Chloe slid around the girl's shoulders, and his jaw tensed as he flashed her an arctic glare.

'Thank you for your...*help*.' The word emerged reluctantly through his clenched lips. 'I'm assuming that Tatiana contacted you?'

Her chin lifted in challenge. He had managed to make the statement sound like accusation. *No, I just happened to be passing.*

It took an effort but she managed to keep her lip buttoned on the snarky retort that hovered on the tip of her tongue, and she dipped her head in acknowledgment, reflecting that surely *one* of them had to act like an adult in front of Eugenie.

'Well, I'm here now.'

As if that could have slipped anyone's notice! So this was Nik in business mode; impressed hardly covered her reaction. His designer-cut business suit didn't disguise the hardness of the body it covered, but it did emphasise the effortless power he exuded.

Nik dragged his eyes away from the outline of the lacy bra covering Chloe's breasts, clearly outlined beneath the drenched silk, just in time to see her roll her eyes at him. He wondered why, of all the people she could have turned to for help, his sister had chosen this woman, who was nobody's idea of a responsible adult. Hell, she didn't even have the basic sense to leave the house with a coat in a storm!

'Get in the car,' he ordered his niece.

'I'm not going anywhere with you!' was the response.

If his scowl was any indicator, he only saw the surly expression on Eugenie's face, and not the fact that her defiance only went about a cell deep despite the dramatic pronouncements. Clearly it wasn't his incredible insight into female behaviour that got him the girls, Chloe thought sourly.

'I hate you!'

Chloe sighed. It was a long shot, but she felt obliged to at least make an attempt to smooth things over.

'Look, clearly you're both feeling pretty intense...'

Two pairs of antagonistic eyes zoomed in on her face.

She cleared her throat and attempted a smile. As far as feelings went, her own were pretty much all over the place and had been from the moment she'd identified the person getting out of the car and her heart had started fibrillating madly. It had not even begun to calm down when he'd stalked towards them looking deliciously sexy, hard and... She gave her head a tiny shake. This wasn't about her, or her hormones; it was about Eugenie and Tatiana.

'Maybe now…' she continued, channelling sweet reason and calm while wondering if it was all right secretly wanting to do the wrong thing just so long as you actually resisted the weakness.

'Now what?' he bit out.

She dragged away her eyes, which were showing a disastrous tendency to drift up and down his long, lean, loose-limbed frame without her permission, and cleared her throat. What she needed right now was cool thinking, logic and maybe a bit of inspiration. What she didn't need or, for that matter, want was this animal attraction, insane sexual chemistry or a vivid imagination supplying her with memories of how he'd looked naked.

'Now is not the right time to—'

The teen shrugged off the arm across her shoulders and, with hands on her hips, took a defiant step towards her uncle. 'It wasn't my fault.'

Chloe sighed and wondered why she had even bothered to try. If she had any sense, which she did, she would get in her car, drive off and let these two slug it out, but then she reminded herself that Tatiana was her friend, and she had promised her she'd look after Eugenie.

Nik felt his grip on his temper slipping, but he breathed through the moment.

It had not been a good morning. He'd had a breakfast meeting with a guy the normally reliable firm of headhunters had sent, and in the space of thirty minutes the candidate had broken every unwritten rule in the book: drunk too much, confided personal problems, bad-mouthed colleagues and talked politics. Then Nik had returned to the office and found all the messages on his machine his stand-in secretary had not seen fit to respond to.

But compared to his present situation, faced with a

niece who appeared to loathe him while challenging his authority, and the woman who hadn't been out of his head for more than three consecutive seconds ever since they'd parted company nearly forty-eight hours ago, he was extremely frustrated and close to snapping point!

He'd spent the last two days considering the best way to seduce Chloe Summerville. Seduction had never had much to do with the kind of recreational sex he enjoyed; usually it wasn't about anything but slaking a hunger and for a short space of time blocking out everything else. Mutual attraction was certainly involved, but comparing it with what had sparked into life between himself and Chloe would have been like comparing a light shower with a monsoon!

And the attraction between them was mutual, he knew that without question, which made her rejection of him all the more teeth-grindingly frustrating.

He didn't make the mistake of reading anything deep and meaningful into their attraction; it was more to do with the timing and circumstances of their first meeting than anything else. Those circumstances had just intensified the chemistry that existed between them, that was all—a chemistry that would inevitably fade.

If when it did, so did his nightmares, that was only an added bonus. Getting her into bed was definitely going to happen; it was just a matter of when. His instincts could not be that far out, surely?

'Get in the car,' he repeated to his niece, digging into reserves of tolerance that had already been seriously depleted.

Chloe took a deep breath and came to a decision. Stepping forward, she put herself between the angry male and his niece. 'Actually, I promised Tatiana that I would deliver her personally, so, Eugenie, get in my car.' The slam of the car door told her that the girl had obeyed. Chloe felt a stab of relief; she would have looked pretty silly if Eugenie had ignored her.

Nik growled. He wasn't used to having his decisions challenged or his instructions ignored and suddenly the emotions that ran rampant through him had nothing to do with their natural chemistry and everything to do with the fact that Chloe was a pain in his backside! He made to move past her but Chloe mirrored his move.

She held up her hands, her expression determined.

'You think my niece needs protection from me?' he demanded incredulously, his voice pitched to a low, private rumble.

Not half as much as I do, Chloe thought, despising the part of her that couldn't help but notice how incredibly good he looked clean-shaven. 'Don't be absurd!' she snapped, fighting the urge to follow his lead and respond in kind. Instead she modified her tone. 'Of course I don't! It's just that in a situation like this—'

'And how many times have you been in a situation like this, *Lady* Chloe?'

'You might be surprised,' she retorted, but as the antagonistic glitter faded from his eyes she admitted, 'Fair enough, I've never been arrested, but I think you're the last person in the world to be throwing my life of imagined privilege in my face.'

'You're encouraging Eugenie to think this is a joke.'

She flung him a pitying look; for an intelligent man he was being pretty dense. 'She doesn't think it's a joke. She was scared stiff. I just think you're making a big thing out of this when—'

'My niece has been arrested. I call that a big thing!'

'She was only cautioned, and according to the sergeant I spoke to—'

A hiss of impatience left his clamped lips and she changed tactics.

'Look, Tatiana wants to keep this low-key, so you could force Eugenie to travel with you, but what would be the point? I mean, do you even know what you're letting yourself in for? Teenage girls tend to have a taste for melodrama and, I can assure you, she'd make the journey hell for you.'

'Is there a problem here?'

Chloe turned to see the policewoman from earlier standing looking at them. Well, actually she was looking at Nik and her mouth was ajar.

Chloe cleared her throat and gave the girl time to recover, as she had some sympathy for her dilemma.

'You know what it's like—you wait for a bus and two come along at once. This is Eugenie's uncle and we were just discussing it.' She turned to Nik. 'So is it OK if Eugenie comes with me?'

He didn't miss a beat. 'Absolutely and we can catch up on the way. Fred, my driver, can follow us.'

Her air of complacence vanished in an eye blink. 'You want me to give you a lift to the airport?' she squeaked, forgetting to avoid his eyes. They were shining with malicious amusement as if he knew perfectly well that the very thought of being confined inside her car with him for an hour was already making her break out in a cold sweat.

She closed her eyes and breathed out through her nose as she subdued her panic; he'd called her bluff and now she'd have to live with it. An hour was only sixty minutes, she reminded herself, yet somehow the maths wasn't particularly soothing so she decided not to work out the seconds as she watched him speak to the driver of the car.

* * *

Maybe it was wishful thinking but lately she liked to think that she was not quite as tense behind the wheel, but either way this journey was going to put her back months.

Nik was not a relaxed passenger; she could feel the tension rolling off him. Maybe he didn't like women drivers...or perhaps it was just her... He certainly couldn't be comfortable as he had to draw his long legs right up in order to squeeze himself into the space.

Served him right, she decided uncharitably as she stared doggedly ahead, ignoring him and the subtle spicy notes in the male fragrance he used.

The expression on her face when Nik had invited himself had seemed worth it at the time...but the decision had come back to bite him. The physical discomforts aside, and there were several—he had intermittent cramp in his left leg, and was losing the feeling in his foot, and the torture didn't look like being over any time soon, if ever—she drove at a maddeningly slow speed that he found at odds with her personality.

He suspected that if he mentioned it she'd go even slower just to annoy him, but when a caravan overtook them he lost the battle with exasperation. 'You drive like an old woman.'

'Sexism and ageism in one sentence...wow, impressive.'

'You haven't even got out of second gear yet.'

'Enjoy the scenery. Is he going to follow me the entire way?' She glared into the rear-view mirror that reflected the limo that was following close behind.

'That's the idea.'

'Is your driver ex-army too?'

The question startled a surprised look from him. 'What makes you say that?'

She shrugged. 'He has that look, you know, tough, hard…the catch-a-bullet-in-his-teeth type.'

Nik grinned, thinking Fred might quite like the description. 'He's a veteran.'

'You do employ a lot of ex-servicemen.'

'I'm not being charitable…'

He said it as if being considered charitable was an insult.

'I simply employ people I can rely on.'

And where he'd lived and worked, she supposed, you had to trust and rely on the people around you. 'Do you miss it…?' She bit her lip. 'Sorry, I didn't mean to remind you of…anything…'

'So Ana has been talking.'

'She mentioned what you used to do and—'

'Relax, you haven't reminded me. Losing a friend is not something you ever forget.' *Or forgive,* he thought as once again the familiar sense of guilt settled its suffocating weight over him.

She glanced in the rear-view mirror again. Eugenie had her eyes closed, and even over the engine the muffled bass boom coming from the music she was playing through her earphones was audible. 'Of course not… sorry.' She winced—the response to what he'd said seemed painfully inadequate and she pressed a hand briefly to the base of her throat where a blue-veined pulse was pounding in the hollow.

The action drew his eyes to the vulnerable spot, and the arrow-piercing thrust of raw desire caught him off guard and fed into the resentful anger he was feeling. 'If Ana has recruited you to her cause, please don't bother—'

'What cause?' She felt the suspicious brush of his dark hostile eyes over her bewildered face.

'It doesn't matter,' he said after a moment. 'My sister

is overprotective and a great believer in *talking* about everything.'

Comprehension dawned. 'Oh, she wants you to talk through your…experiences with…someone.' And for a proud man, a man used to being in control all the time, that would be anathema. She wished Tatiana good luck with that endeavour, but she didn't envy her the task of persuading her macho brother it was not a sign of weakness to talk about his feelings.

Nik's lips twisted into a cynical smile. 'How delicately put,' he mocked. 'But I don't want to forget.'

'Therapy isn't about forgetting. It's about living with the memories.'

'What would you know about it?' he jeered.

'We plan to use the services of therapists in our centre; it's an intrinsic part of the recovery process.'

'An *intrinsic* part of *my* recovery process is a glass of whisky and a night of f—'

'*Nik!*' Pretty sure what he'd been going to say and equally sure he wouldn't want to risk his niece hearing him say it, she jerked her head towards the back of the car, her eyes wide in warning.

Dark strips of colour stood out darkly against the uniform gold tones of his olive skin, emphasising the slashing angle of his high cheekbones.

In the back Eugenie began humming off-key to her music, her eyes still closed. The sound broke the awkward silence that had settled in the front of the car. 'She'll probably be deaf before she's twenty. I don't know why Ana allows her to use those things,' Nik muttered.

'Maybe you won't sound quite so disapproving when you're the parent of a teenager.' Her smile faded. The idea of Nik with children of any age was quite a depressing thought.

'Ana's a great parent,' he agreed.

Chloe was surprised to hear an unusual tone of humility in his voice, and she was even more surprised when he added, 'So is Ian.'

'I've never met him.'

'He's a nice guy, and they made a great couple. If they couldn't make it work I really don't know why anyone tries.'

'Love, maybe?'

His laugh was hard and cynical…leaving little doubt in her mind about his opinion of love.

For some reason the sound brought back a memory of another laugh, soft instead of harsh, a laugh she'd heard when her tongue had been moving across the hard pebble of his nipple, his fingers tangled in her hair, his body hot as he'd collapsed onto the bed, pulling her on top of him.

Then a minute, an hour, a lifetime later—time had stopped having much meaning—that laugh had come again as he'd rolled her onto her back, pinned her hands above her head with one hand and slid the other between her legs…

'You should be careful—you almost hit forty miles an hour then.'

His voice jolted her free of the images playing in her head and she drew her bottom lip over her upper one to blot the beads of moisture there. She felt the heat that suffused her body travel up her neck, threatening her with the mother of all blushes, so she dealt with it by choosing to pretend it was happening to someone else and it was this anonymous person who was feeling the shameful ache between her legs, not her.

'I'm trying to concentrate,' she snapped, glancing guiltily in the rear-view mirror, relieved when she saw that Eugenie was busy texting on her phone.

He looked at her fingers, which were locked, knuckles bone white, on the wheel. 'Do have you points on your licence or something?'

'Or something,' she said in a flat little voice.

He glanced in the mirror. 'She's texting again.'

'You don't know many teenagers, do you?'

'It's a day for new experiences, it seems. Is there a reason you drive this old thing?'

'Reliability.' A very underrated commodity.

'I have a reliable lawnmower but I don't go to work on it.'

'You could always get out and thumb a lift with your friend Fred.'

'That's a difficult choice. He has terrible taste in country and western music…anything involving heartbreak and tragic lives and he's happy. But if I stay with you, I might never walk again.' He grunted as he attempted to stretch out one leg in the confined space, while beside him she released her death grip on the steering wheel long enough to push a strand of hair behind her ear. Though her hair was almost dry now, the scent of her shampoo still permeated the enclosed space.

Seeing the action out of the corner of her eye, Chloe permitted herself a smirk, which she suddenly doused, feeling ashamed. Maybe she should have allowed him to take Eugenie; after all, he was her uncle.

Had she done the right thing?

The obvious thing would have been to check with Tatiana, but the thought vanished as a sharp pain made her wince and she moved her head to try and ease it. Reluctant to take her eyes off the road, especially as they had just passed a road sign that announced they were approaching a series of tight bends, she twisted her head sharply in the hope that the action would free the earring that had got tangled in her hair, but instead it just tugged harder, bringing tears to her eyes.

'Let me help…'

'I'm fine!' she snapped, unable to keep the note of panic from her voice, but then his long fingers brushed her neck and she flinched, desire clenching like a fist low in her belly.

It was crazy, she knew that, but recognising this fact did not lessen the physical impact, although she didn't have to embrace it!

'These things are lethal,' he said, lifting the weight of her hair to lessen the tug of the earring on her earlobe.

One element of her discomfort eased, Chloe stared straight ahead. Having her earlobe torn or her hair wrenched from her scalp would have been a hell of a lot more comfortable than feeling the warm waft of his breath on her cheek.

'They're one-offs, hand forged, the silversmith is a friend…' She spoke quickly, trying to distract herself.

She remembered reading somewhere that the ear had a lot of nerve endings, and all of hers were definitely screaming right now.

His brows drew together in a dark line of disapproval. 'Your earlobe is bleeding; you must have one hell of a high pain tolerance.'

An image floated into her head of her in hospital, repeatedly pressing the pain-relief button that for weeks had never left her hand. 'Not really.' Actually, not at all, she corrected silently, thinking of the lovely floating feeling after she'd pressed that button. The pain had still been there in the background, but she had been able to float above it.

She felt rather than saw him looking at her.

'I fainted when I had them pierced, although that might have been the...ouch, be careful!'

'Sorry. Hold on, I've almost finished...'

Almost was not soon enough. It seemed to take for ever for him to unwind the silver spiral. Her relief was so intense when he gave a grunt of triumph and leaned back in his seat that she would have punched the air in triumph had she not had such a tight hold of the steering wheel. Instead, she contented herself with heaving a huge sigh.

'Cool!' Eugenie, her earphones now dangling around her neck, leaned forward and snatched the silver spiral that dangled in her uncle's fingers. 'Where did you get them from? I'd love a pair.'

'A friend of mine makes them.'

The girl moved forward asking eagerly, 'Boyfriend?'

Aware that beside her Nik was now sitting with his head bent, fingers pressed to the bridge of his nose, she shook her head. 'Her name is Layla.' She slid Nik a sideways glance and lost the fight against her concern. 'Do you have a headache? There should be some painkillers in the glove box and a bottle of water—'

'I'm fine.' He let his hand fall from his face and exhaled slowly. The headaches hit without warning, but he never took medication. Perhaps he deserved the pain, not that it ever left him feeling cleansed of his sins.

'Uncle Nik is never ill. He's bulletproof *literally*,' she enthused with awe. 'He never got a scratch when he was working in war zones,' she chattered on, lifting the earring to her own ear and craning her neck to admire the effect in the rear-view mirror. 'Mum says the only thing he's got is survivor's guilt...' She stopped abruptly as her uncle caught her eye. 'Well she might have said something like that but I don't quite recall.'

Chloe couldn't see Nik's face but she could feel the raw tension vibrating off him.

In the back seat Chloe gave a sigh. 'How much longer? It's not mine,' she added when the audible sound of a vibrating phone suddenly echoed through the car.

Nik swore. His phone had fallen in the gap between the seats and, eyes still closed, he reached out a long arm for it.

Chloe gave a grunt as an elbow landed in her ribs.

'Sorry,' he muttered and, delving further, he gave a grunt of triumph as he managed to get his fingers around it.

'Your mother,' he said to Eugenie after reading the text message, before switching his attention to Chloe. 'Telling me not to bother, not to worry, that she arranged for someone else to pick you up... I contacted her when I started out but she must have sent this straight away. Looks like you're calling the shots here.'

Embarrassed, Chloe shook her head. 'You're Eugenie's uncle.'

'My sister must really trust you, but it might take me a while to work my way back into her good graces.'

'She'll understand.'

He huffed out a laugh. 'Why should she?'

'It's what family do. Where were you anyway? Not that I have any right to ask, I know...'

'My secretary has the flu and her stand-in hadn't charged my phone.' Louise always did it for him. 'And when I said I didn't want to be disturbed I made the mistake of assuming she would know that didn't include family emergencies. She let all Ana's calls go to the messaging service and when I tried to ring her back there was no signal. Then when I asked her why she hadn't put the calls through she just burst into tears.'

'Poor woman, she was probably scared of you.'

He gave a snort of disbelief. 'Then she'll be much happier working elsewhere.'

Chloe was shocked. 'You didn't sack her!'

'My father would have, whereas I'm a much more tolerant employer and, employment laws being what they are, I just shipped her back to the department she came from.'

'You're afraid to let anyone see you have a heart,' she charged and, expecting to see him discomfited by her discovery, she turned her head to look at him, but found a very different expression on his face.

She looked away quickly, but not before the need she had seen shining in his eyes had awoken the same feeling in her belly.

He shot a quick furtive glance in the back before announcing very quietly, 'I have a heart and I am very anxious to prove it to you.'

'It's not your heart you're offering me.'

'All parts of my anatomy are on offer.'

She shivered and stared ahead. 'I'm not discussing this with you now.'

'Later, then.'

A hissing sound of frustration escaped her clenched teeth.

'Chloe…'

Chloe started guiltily at the sound of the curious voice from the back seat. 'Do you live in a castle?'

'My sister does, but where my mum and dad live is more properly termed a fortified home.'

'Normal people do not live in castles.'

'Normal people do not have a rota for the shower because there's never enough hot water to go around! Trust me, we are not at all glamorous—in fact, we're just a little bit last century. I was at college before I ordered my first takeaway pizza.'

'God!' Eugenie breathed.

'Take the next exit,' Nik said suddenly as they approached the roundabout. 'You just went past it,' he said with an air of resignation.

'Roundabouts are made for going around.' On this note of logic she did so for the third time.

CHAPTER SEVEN

THEIR PROGRESS THROUGH the private airport was swift. Once they were on the plane one of the male attendants drew Nik apart as Chloe and Eugenie were seated.

Their conversation in rapid Greek lasted a few moments.

'I'm travelling up front,' he said to Chloe as he moved past her.

'Can I come too?' Eugenie cried in the act of unclipping her belt.

'You're grounded, or I'm assuming you will be, so no…behaving badly doesn't get rewarded, kiddo.' He flicked her nose affectionately with his finger and walked on, vanishing through the cockpit door.

'I'm going to get my pilot's licence as soon as I'm old enough. Uncle Nik got his when he was seventeen.'

Did that mean he was flying the plane now? Chloe wondered, tensing a little as the plane started taxiing; she was fine with flying but the take-off and landing always tied her stomach in knots.

Once they were in the air, Chloe accepted the offer of tea but refused anything to eat. Eugenie, who seemed to have recovered from her brush with the law, tucked into some hot beef sandwiches.

She finished and sighed in pleasure. Chloe pointed

to her chin and the teen wiped away the spot of relish there.

'So how long does it take to get to Spetses airport?'

The girl looked surprised by the question. 'Oh, there isn't an airport on the island. We land at the small private airport just on the mainland opposite and then we'll fly over on the helicopter.'

Questioning her decision not to simply hand Eugenie over to her uncle when she'd had the chance, Chloe took a sip of her tea. The return flight might not be as simple to organise as she had imagined.

On the helicopter trip over from the mainland Chloe sat next to Eugenie, who went into tour-guide mode the minute they took off. By the time they landed Chloe felt pretty well informed about the island of Spetses and its aristocratic heritage; she could have written a paper about the colourful mansions, the history of blockade running, its significance in the Napoleonic wars, and its long association with the master sailors.

While Chloe was being educated, Nik sat next to the pilot in the cockpit. The two men obviously knew one another pretty well and, with his sleeves rolled up and his dark hair tousled, Nik looked relaxed and very different from the man she remembered from that night in the bar.

Or for that matter from any time since.

It would be very easy, she mused, to let her defences down with this Nik. Just as well she was only here to chaperone Eugenie.

She turned her head at the sound of a phone ringing, struggling to make itself heard against the noise of the helicopter.

'It's Mum, for you,' Eugenie said, holding her own phone out for Chloe.

Chloe pressed the phone close against her ear, raising her voice above the background noise. 'Hello.'

'How can I ever thank you, Chloe?'

'No thanks required. I'm glad I could help.'

'How is she?'

'Fine.' She gave the worried-looking teenager a thumbs-up signal. 'I know a great deal about Spetses now. Did you know that Spetsiots were heroes of the War of Independence?' Chloe was pleased to hear the older woman laugh, then listened to her friend launch into another fulsome apology for imposing on her. 'Eugenie was no problem,' she said honestly, adding when Tatiana made sceptical noises, 'It was good practice for when I have my own children…' She lifted the phone away and waited for the static crackle to subside before shouting, 'I said it was good practice for when I have my own children!'

It was only when she realised the signal had cut out and she lowered the phone that she realised Nik was standing right beside her, so there was zero chance he'd not heard every word she'd said. But if she'd had any doubts his first comment dispelled them.

'Thinking of starting any time soon?'

Working on the assumption that if she ignored her blush he might not notice, she managed a small laugh. 'My body clock is not ticking too loudly just yet.'

'Just wanted to say, another five minutes and we'll be landing.' He turned away and moved back to the cockpit.

Once he'd gone, Chloe closed her eyes and pushed her fist against her mouth to stifle her loud groan. The other hand was pressed to her chest, where her heart was performing all sorts of life-threatening gymnastics.

It was ridiculous…bewildering and humiliating. Why did she react this way to him? What was it about him that seemed to tap into something inside her…a *need*…

a *hunger*…? An image of the answering hunger she had glimpsed in his eyes flashed into her head and her heart gave a heavy traitorous thud then started cantering crazily again.

She was complaining a hell of a lot, Chloe reflected, but if she really didn't want Nik chasing her, throwing temptation in her way, why hadn't she done something about it?

She could.

And she knew it. There was a fail-safe way, a one-hundred-per-cent-guaranteed method to make him back off at her disposal… It wasn't as if she'd even have to show him; just using the words would have the desired effect. She could casually throw into the conversation that she had some ugly scars and always would have.

In Nik's head she was perfect. She inhaled and lifted her chin, a little smile playing across her mouth. She had been perfect and she had taken it for granted. Strange how you didn't appreciate something until it was gone.

The smile vanished and along with it the enduring sadness; she'd been lucky and she knew it. She no longer wallowed in self-pity or asked herself why it had to happen to her.

She contented herself with imagining that one day there would be a man in her life; of course, he might not make her think of passionate, all-consuming sex the moment she saw him but there were other, more important things in a relationship…deeper things that lasted the test of time.

It would be nice to have both, but she was a realist and she knew few people were that lucky.

They had disembarked the helicopter when Nik joined them, his tall, broad-shouldered figure drawing glances from the handful of fellow travellers that hovered nearby. Watching his approach through the shield of her lashes, Chloe had to admit it was not surprising he drew every eye; he might be the most irritating man on the planet with an ego to match, but he was also the most supremely elegant and by far the sexiest.

'If you don't mind I'll hang around for a bit and hand Eugenie over to her mum personally,' she said.

There was a slight time delay before he responded and the enigmatic smile that briefly tugged at the corners of his mouth troubled her, but as she'd been geared up for an argument his non-reaction was a bit of an anticlimax.

'The car should be waiting; it's this way.' His gesture invited Chloe to step ahead of him.

The waiting car was another long, shiny monster, and as they approached the driver jumped out, a Greek version of Fred.

Nik called out to him in Greek, the man called something back in response and walked around to the passenger door, but before he had a chance to open it an open-topped Jeep driven at speed drew up behind it. Chloe stepped back from the cloud of dust it threw up, but before it had even settled Tatiana, wearing a cotton shirt over a tee shirt and shorts, her shiny bell of dark hair pulled back off her make-up-free face in a severe ponytail, jumped out.

Chloe felt the teenager beside her tense and heard her sharp intake of breath, before she stuck out her chin and quavered out defiantly, 'Before you say anything—'

'How could you?' her mother ground out.

'I...' Without warning the youngster's belligerence vanished and she started to sob heartbrokenly. A second later she was in her mother's arms being told everything would be all right. Chin resting on her daughter's head, a shiny-eyed Tatiana shot a look of gratitude in Chloe's direction.

'We are so, so grateful to you, Chloe.'

'It's fine. I'm glad I could help.'

The image of Chloe sniffing into a tissue at the scene in front of her while she blinked hard made something tighten in Nik's chest, but he ignored it and drawled out sarcastically, 'Are you going to cry too?'

'I am not crying!' Chloe snapped back, blowing her nose hard.

'Do you mind travelling back with Nik?' Tatiana asked, glancing at her brother for the first time. 'I could do with talking one to one with this one.' She kissed the top of her daughter's head. 'Alone.'

Chloe minded very much. In fact, the idea of sharing the back seat of the limo with Nik filled her with horror, but she hid her feelings behind a smile and shook her head.

'Actually I don't mind waiting here to catch a lift straight back to the mainland.'

Tatiana looked blank and then shocked. 'You don't think we'd let you go straight back, do you? Heavens, you're here as our guest for as long as you like.'

'I couldn't possibly stay.' Chloe tried to sound firm, but all she sounded was tired as she lifted a hand to her ticcing eyelid.

'Perhaps Chloe has other places to be.' And other people she'd rather be with, he thought sourly, and the silent addition caused the line between his dark brows to deepen.

'You can't fly straight back,' Tatiana argued.

'Not unless she sprouts wings,' Nik inserted drily. 'Marco is refuelling the jet and then heading straight off to Düsseldorf.'

He slid effortlessly into Greek as he added something to Tatiana, who nodded in agreement.

'Well, that settles it, then, you'll stay with us…at least for tonight…to let me say thank you…?'

'But your grandmother is unwell…' Chloe began searching desperately for a legitimate reason to refuse their hospitality, or at least a reason that wasn't, *I really can't be around your brother because I don't want to be reminded of something I want but can't have, and shouldn't even want to begin with!*

It sounded convoluted even in her own head, but then so was her relationship with Nik. Except she didn't have a relationship with Nik. She closed one eye as the eyelid tic started up again.

'She's a lot better.'

'Yaya is a tough old bird,' Nik said gruffly, the warmth in his voice when he spoke of his grandmother unmistakeable.

And I'm sure there are some serial killers who love their grannies too, Chloe reminded herself as she fought hard against any lowering of the levels of antagonism that she felt were essential to maintain. Bad enough that she lusted after him, liking him as well would be too, *too* much to take.

'Well, that's settled, you'll follow us,' Tatiana announced.

Chloe, who was pretty sure that she hadn't agreed to anything, not that that seemed to bother anyone in the Latsis family, opened her mouth to protest but Tatiana was telling Eugenie to throw her bag in the back. 'Or, better still, Nik can take the scenic route and show Chloe…oh, no!' Her eyes slid past her brother and her enthusiasm morphed into dismay. 'Get in the car,' she said sharply to her daughter, then, after adding something urgent-sounding in Greek to Nik, she climbed in beside the girl and slipped back into English, saying hastily, 'Sorry, Nik, but I don't want Eugenie to get caught up in this.'

Nik, who had turned to follow the direction his sister was looking, nodded. 'You get going. Chloe, get in the car.'

Tatiana was already starting up the engine and Chloe couldn't help turning round to see what had caused her friend to rush off.

There was a woman approaching them, about fifty feet or so away now, who was by turns running then walking, or rather stumbling, towards them, her uncoordinated gait suggesting she'd been drinking.

Chloe didn't have a clue what was happening, but she was the only one, it seemed. Even the driver, who had murmured something in Greek to Nik and got back behind the wheel after receiving a nod in response, seemed to be in the know, but she did recognise an order when she heard one. She told herself she wouldn't have obeyed him on principle, even if she hadn't been eaten up with curiosity to discover what was going on!

'I said—' Nik began, still not looking at her, but Chloe could feel the tension coming off him in waves. His taut profile looked grey and grim, and the muscles along his clenched jawline were set like iron.

'I heard you, which isn't the same as obeying you,' she said calmly.

He turned his dark head then, flashing her a look of seething impatience, and ground out, 'I really don't have time for this now.'

The woman was close enough now for Chloe to see that she was correct in surmising that the woman was drunk; she could smell the alcohol from yards away. So, it seemed, could Nik, who set his shoulders and turned back with an air of forced resignation as he waited until she was within hearing distance.

'Hello, Helena.'

The woman was probably pretty when she remembered to comb her hair and her eyes weren't lost in black-smudged circles of mascara that had been washed by tears running in dark rivers down her face.

The sound coming from her was half sob, half breathless pant as she walked straight past Chloe, her attention totally focused on Nik, her eyes burning with hatred.

Nik didn't move an inch as the woman staggered up to him, glaring.

'I wake up every morning wishing you were dead!' she slurred. 'I wish I was dead!'

The mixture of venom and despair in her voice sent an ice-cold chill down Chloe's spine but Nik just stood there. What made it all the more bizarre was that he didn't look angry, he looked…sad, compassionate and, most telling of all, guilty.

Chloe's imagination went into overdrive. What had he done to this woman?

'I'm so sorry,' he said finally.

The woman's face screwed up and an anguished high-pitched shriek left her open mouth as she pulled back her arm and aimed a closed-fisted blow that made contact with Nik's cheek.

Chloe gasped in alarm, her hand going to her own cheek, but he just stood there and continued to do so as the woman started to pound his chest with her flailing fists, shrieking hysterically the whole time.

As the frenzied attack showed no sign of abating, although God knew where the woman got the strength from, the shock that had held Chloe immobile abated.

'No!' She wasn't even aware that she'd voiced her protest or had moved forward until Nik looked at her and moved his head in a negative motion.

It was the total absence of anger in his austere, strong-boned face that hit her, that and the profound sadness. It added a deep ache of empathy to the already present confusion and horror—too many layers of emotion for Chloe to comprehend.

His headshake coincided with the woman running out of steam and she finally slumped her head against Nik's chest, weeping in a way that hurt to listen to.

After a moment Nik lifted a tentative hand to her head, smoothing the tangles of hair down in a gentle stroking motion.

'I'll take her.'

Her focus totally on the tableau before her, Chloe hadn't heard the approach of a man wearing a harassed expression. 'Come on, honey, that's it. I didn't know where you'd got to.' The woman lifted her head slightly at the sound of his voice.

'The bastard should be dead!'

For all the reaction Nik showed to this venomous declaration he might as well have been, the skin drawn tight across the prominent bones on his face giving them the appearance of stone.

The stranger took the weeping woman, who reminded Chloe of a puppet whose strings had been severed, and pulled her against him, wrapping a supportive arm around her ribs as he half dragged, half lifted her away from Nik. 'Sorry, you know she doesn't mean it; she doesn't know what she's saying.' The woman continued to weep uncontrollably as she slumped up against him.

The stranger looked from the woman he held to Nik with an expression that brought a lump to Chloe's throat. 'It's not always this bad, but it's particularly hard today...'

Nik nodded, his face still granite.

'She's been drinking all morning. I thought maybe being here with family would help.' He stopped and shook his head. 'Bad idea. I stopped for gas and she must have seen you... I had no idea that you'd be here.'

'Neither did I. It was an unexpected visit. Is there anything I can do...?'

The woman's head lifted at that. 'Haven't you done enough already?' she slurred, before pressing her face back into the man's shoulder as he turned and began to walk away down the road.

Nik watched for a few moments before he looked at Chloe. Some of the rigidity had gone from his tense posture, but not the lines of tension bracketing his mouth or the shadow in his eyes. 'Have you seen enough now?'

She flinched, but didn't react to the unspoken accusation, which was both harsh and unjust, that she had taken some voyeuristic pleasure at the scene she had witnessed.

'Are you all right?' she asked, wincing inside at the crassness of her words, and she wasn't surprised when he just flashed her a look.

The muscles along his taut jaw tensed as he turned away. He didn't want or deserve Chloe's sympathy.

Are you *all right*? she'd asked. Well, he was certainly more all right than the man who would have been thirty-five today if he'd lived. An image floated in his head, of Charlie grinning as he delivered the punchline of one of his terrible jokes, Charlie looking guilty when he explained this would be the last time they worked together because he was letting his lovely Helena finally make an honest man of him.

Nik remembered feeling pleased that he'd managed to

guilt Charlie into one last assignment, though he hadn't succeeded in planting a seed of doubt in his friend's mind when he'd predicted that Charlie wouldn't be able to live without the adrenaline buzz.

You know when it's time to quit, Charlie had said.

CHAPTER EIGHT

CHLOE WAS LEFT standing there when without a word Nik got into the front seat of the car beside the driver. She blew out a breath and for once in her life wished someone would tell her what to do or at least what to think.

A reel of the terrible scene still played in her head. She had only witnessed it and she felt shaken and physically sick; she couldn't begin to imagine what Nik was feeling and she had the distinct impression he wouldn't be telling her any time soon.

She gave her head a tiny shake and slid into the back seat. In the front Nik was speaking to the driver, issuing instructions, she assumed, but she didn't know for sure because it was literally all Greek to her.

Apart from that, they drove in absolute stony silence. A couple of times Chloe cleared her throat to ask how long it would take to reach their destination or for that matter where they were heading but chickened out at the last moment. So silence reigned until about maybe ten minutes into the journey when Nik suddenly spoke in Greek once again.

The driver responded in the same language and pulled onto the side of the road. The car had barely stopped when Nik flung himself out, and, leaving the door open, he strode off into the scrub at the side of the deserted road up an incline, immediately disappearing from view as he went down the other side.

So what did she do now?

Did she sit here and wait, or did she follow him…? She caught the eyes of the driver in the rear-view mirror, and his expression was sympathetic but he just shrugged.

'I think I'll stretch my legs,' she said, not sure he understood her or if he'd try and prevent her from leaving the car.

He didn't.

Grateful her shoes only had moderate heels, she stumbled her way across the steep slope of the rough ground, waking up tiny little things in the undergrowth as she picked out a path between the rocks, following roughly— she hoped—the route she had seen Nik take. The linen trousers she wore were of a loose style that ended mid-calf, protecting most of her legs from the razor-sharp ends of the long tough grass that poked through the rocks. But her calves already ached; the incline was steeper than it looked.

She had lost track of time today but the sun overhead was still high in the sky that was a uniform blue. It was very hot and she became uncomfortably aware of rivulets of sweat trickling down her back. Pausing to rest, she turned her head to make sure that she had not lost sight of the car.

Getting lost really would add the finishing touch to this day. Nik had seemed to vanish from view after only moments, so either he was astonishingly fit or she had somehow gone off course and attacked the slope at a wider angle.

Probably both, she decided, pausing again, this time just below the top of the incline. She ran her tongue over her lips; they felt dry and she was thirsty. Without the crunch of her footsteps, she could make out a distant whooshing sound above the softer constant buzzing of the bees that smothered the sweet-smelling wild thyme that filled the air with a deep sweet fragrance.

She closed her eyes and inhaled.

What are you doing? she asked herself wearily. *So you find him—what then? Does he strike you as a man who needs a shoulder to cry on?* Like a wounded animal, he'd gone away to lick his wounds; he clearly wanted privacy and she was going to crash it. It had seemed like a good idea at the time—but *why* exactly?

She puffed out a gusty sigh. This was starting to feel like a very bad idea, but, torn between turning back and pushing on, she hesitated only momentarily before tackling the last few feet of slope.

As she crowned the hill her efforts were rewarded by a view that made her catch her breath. In contrast to the steep slope she had just climbed, the other side was a very gentle incline, the vegetation spare where it grew out of the sandy ground, but she barely noticed as her eyes went to the horseshoe curve of a bay ringed by rocks. Alternating stripes of pebbles and silvery sand ran down to the water. Beyond the gentle waves that frothed white as they broke on the beach, the blue of the sea deepened, interspersed with iridescent swirling areas of deep green and dark turquoise before it met the sky.

The view was so unexpected and so soul-soothingly beautiful that for a long moment all she did was stare, but the moment of spiritual peace shattered into a million shards as her eyes reached the figure standing at the farthest point of the beach before the rocks rose up out of the water.

Nik stood, his tall, remote figure a dark silhouette against the backdrop of bright blue. The strength of the empathetic sympathy that swelled in her chest took her by surprise, and, without pausing to examine it or the need to be with him right now, she began to jog towards him, the downward journey on the smooth, gentle slope far less taxing than the climb up it.

Once she reached the sand she slowed until finally pausing to remove her shoes. Swinging them from the fingers of one hand, she continued slowing as she picked her way across the bands of smooth stones that were sandwiched between the wider bands of powdery sand.

The closer she got to the water, the more she felt the breeze, warm but very welcome as it lifted the damp strands of hair from her neck. She stopped a few feet away from Nik, suddenly unsure what to do next, which seemed to suggest she'd ever known. The thought that she actually knew what she was doing or had any sort of plan when it came to Nik tugged her lips into an ironic, self-mocking smile.

Blind instinct had got her this far and if she had any sense, Chloe reflected, it would take her straight back the way she had come.

She never had had much sense.

'It's very beautiful.'

He didn't react to her comment, so she assumed he already knew she was there. She took a few more steps towards him, in the shade cast by the rocks, which meant it was pleasantly cooler underfoot. But not as cool as standing ankle deep in the water, which Nik was doing in his beautiful handmade leather shoes, although he seemed utterly oblivious.

'Don't worry; I'm not going to ask you if you're all right.'

'Are you moving on to *you probably deserve it*?' he tossed back, thinking grimly that if so, she was right.

Digging his hands deep into the pockets of his tailored trousers, he stared sightlessly in front of him, eyes narrowed at the horizon, trying to remember what it felt like not to carry this constant weight of guilt around with him.

He swivelled around, his short hair catching the breeze as a sudden spurt of stronger wind made it stick up in sexy tufts.

As their eyes connected it struck Chloe with the force of a blow that his expression was exactly the same as the first time she had seen him, dark and tortured. The sight made her heart squeeze in her chest.

The expression he caught on her face stung his pride into painful life, but he didn't want her concern, genuine or otherwise. He didn't deserve concern, and certainly not from her... Hell, life had been easier when she had been filed in his memory banks under the heading of a typical shallow, narcissistic socialite. He had used her once to distract himself from his past and he was doing the same thing now; why didn't she seem able to recognise a lost cause when she saw one?

'No, I don't think you deserved it.' Chloe's first thought had been that she was seeing an ex-lover he'd done the dirty on seeking revenge, and to her shame she had been prepared to be the cheering squad, but the impression had only lasted for seconds as it had almost immediately become obvious that she was seeing something much more complicated.

An expression she couldn't interpret flickered across his face. 'Well, I do.' He flung the words at her like a challenge.

'You must have done something really bad, then,' she said calmly.

A sense of deep self-loathing rushed through him with the force of a forest fire. His chest heaving, he heard a roar inside his skull before the feelings he'd kept locked inside for years finally exploded out. 'I killed a man— my best friend.'

'I'm sorry.'

His head came up with a snap.

'*Sorry!*' he echoed as he began to walk out of the water towards her with slow deliberate steps. Confession was supposed to be good for the soul but he didn't feel good or cleansed; he felt furious with himself for losing control, especially in front of the last person he wanted to see…see what?

The question brought him to a halt when he was six inches away from her, so close that she had actually closed her eyes to shut out the awe-inspiring image he presented.

She could feel the heat of his body through the narrow gap between them but it was nothing compared to the anger and frustration that the air was practically coloured with that rippled off him in almost tangible waves.

He dragged a frustrated hand roughly across his forehead, but as he scanned her face for a clue to what she was thinking his own expression was cloaked. 'Did you hear what I just said?'

'You said that you killed your best friend. I have no idea what actually happened but, as they put people in jail for murder and you are not there, I'm assuming—'

He interrupted her, speaking through clenched teeth. 'He is dead.' His shoulders sagged as the anger drained away leaving a desolate hollowness inside his chest. 'I am here.'

The emptiness in his flat delivery brought an ache to her throat. Watching him through her lashes, Chloe struggled to hide the dangerous rise of emotions that made her chest tight.

'I know, Nik, I'm not deaf or blind.'

The hand he was dragging back and forth through his hair stilled at the mild reproof. He shot her a look and wondered for the tenth time in as many seconds why, if he was going to have some sort of meltdown, he had to do it in front of this woman who did not seem to have any concept of personal boundaries.

'I am not one of your charity projects!' he snarled, the very idea offending his masculine pride deeply.

Taken aback by the outraged charge, she just blinked.

'Has it ever occurred to you that people who put so much of themselves into worthwhile causes are compensating for something that is missing in their own lives?'

Anger at this outrageous statement replaced her bewilderment. Face flushed, she compressed her lips and arched a brow. 'Let me guess what you think is missing in my life—a man,' she drawled. 'Why do all men assume that they are essential for a woman's happiness and fulfilment? If there is anything missing in my life I'll get myself a dog. They're far more reliable.'

Eyelids half lowered so that all she could see was a glitter of dark brown, he let the silence that developed between them stretch out taut before breaking it with a thoughtful, 'I obviously touched a nerve there.'

He'd managed to change the subject from his own trauma, she realised, which she was assuming had been his intention all along. 'Your friend is dead and I'm sorry. You might feel responsible, you might *be* responsible in some way, I have no idea, but I do know for definite that you didn't kill anyone.'

'How can you possibly know that?' he jeered. 'You don't know me.'

She found herself wondering if anyone did. Did he push the world away or was it just her? 'Who was that woman?' she asked quietly.

He turned to look at the sea again. 'Her name is Helena and she was engaged to Charlie, my best friend.'

'Do you mind if I sit down?' Without waiting for him to respond, she brushed a piece of silvered driftwood to one side with a foot, set down her shoes and sat down on the sand, stretching her long legs in front of her, crossing them at the ankle.

Nik turned as she was leaning back on her hands, just as the breeze lifted her hair, blowing it across her face before it settled in a fine silky mesh down her back except for a few errant strands that stuck to her face. Wrinkling her nose, she pursed her lips and huffed them away.

There was something about her beauty that could touch him in a way he hadn't known he was capable of even at a time like this. He made an effort to resurrect a scowl but gave up on the attempt, deciding instead to sit down beside her.

'Charlie was a cameraman, the best there was. People often forget when they see some correspondent standing there in the middle of a gun battle that there's a man behind the camera too, taking the same risks without the same recognition. We'd worked together for two years in the sort of environment where...well, let's just say that you get to see the best and worst of people.'

Chloe glanced sideways at his face...and wondered what he was seeing as he stared out to sea. For a while there was nothing but the hissing sound of the waves breaking a few feet away, and she had the impression he had forgotten she was there.

When he finally spoke his deep, strong voice held a rusty crack.

'He met Helena through me. Her family are part of the London Greek expat community too, but like us they have relatives who still live here on the island. When I was a kid staying with my grandparents I used to hang around with her brothers. That was one of them with her back at the airport—Andreos. Helena used to tag along with us,' he recalled. 'A nice kid.'

And the nice kid had grown up to be a beautiful young woman with everything to live for, except now she didn't want to live.

'She and Charlie hit it off straight away. I was surprised as they were total opposites. Charlie was an extrovert and she was thoughtful, quiet and...' He swallowed hard, the muscles in his brown throat working.

It really hurt her to see him struggle. 'So it was a whirlwind romance?'

'Actually more of a slow burner,' Nik recalled. 'They had an on-off thing that lasted eighteen months or so, the sort of thing that often fizzles out. But then something changed... I don't know what it was, but they got engaged.'

She watched as he silently wrestled with the emotions inside him. Finally, she prompted softly, 'You were surprised.'

He turned his head, his dark eyes glittering with self-contempt as he contradicted her. 'I was irritated. We were a team and Charlie had announced that he was quitting and moving to a safe job where there was no risk of being kidnapped or shot.

'It was me who persuaded him to take that one last assignment together. I was convinced that he'd realise that he couldn't survive without the adrenaline rush, that he'd resent Helena if he gave up a life he loved for her. Oh, I was a *really* caring friend.' Nik squeezed his eyes closed, still seeing Charlie's dead eyes, his nostrils flaring at the remembered metallic iron scent of blood. 'So it did turn out to be his last assignment after all, and he was only there because of me.'

Chloe swallowed the lump in her throat and turned her head to hide the tears that filled her eyes before picking up a handful of sand and letting the silver particles slide through her fingers, watching them vanish into the billions of identical grains. Risking a look at him through her lashes, she saw his expression was completely remote as though he'd retreated to another place entirely.

She didn't attempt to react to his words until she had full control of her emotions again. Nik didn't want her tears or her sympathy; he'd made that obvious. The only thing he wanted from her was her body, which rather begged the question as to why she was getting involved with his problems, seeing as it was the one thing she couldn't give him.

'What happened was a tragedy.' She winced at the triteness of her comment. 'But how exactly is it your fault?'

He vented a hard laugh and looked at her incredulously. 'Have you listened to a word I said?' He still didn't know why he'd said those words—any of them.

He was already regretting it.

He was a private man living in a world where people were tripping over themselves to expose their innermost thoughts and feelings, mostly for public scrutiny. You couldn't turn on a television or a computer, or open a newspaper, without finding some celebrity *revealing all*, but the idea of turning your personal tragedies and failings into entertainment for the masses made his blood run cold.

Getting to his feet, he brushed the sand off his clothes

and stood there looking down at her. 'Tatiana will be wondering what has happened to us.'

Chloe uncrossed her legs and raised herself gracefully to her feet. 'Do you think you're honouring your friend in some way by beating yourself up for being alive? The way you talk about him, it doesn't make it sound as though your friend Charlie would have approved.'

'Helena might disagree.'

'Come on, you're an intelligent man—it doesn't take a professional to see that the poor woman needs help. She's attacking you because she wants someone to blame.' She shook her head in disbelief as he turned and walked away. 'Nik!' Cursing softly under her breath, she picked up her shoes from the sand and ran after him. 'Fine,' she said, falling breathlessly into step beside him. 'Deal with it by ignoring the problem. That always works, doesn't it? It's very adult of you!' How the hell could you help a man who was too stubborn to admit he needed it?

He stopped and swung around to face her, feeling a twisting feeling in his chest as he looked down into her angry face. 'I did not invite you into my head, so stay out!'

'Or what?' she charged, pitying the woman who one day actually wanted to reach him, whose heart ached to help him.

He reached out and cupped a hand around the back of her head, drawing her up onto her toes until their lips were a whisper apart. 'Or this.'

Her gasp of shock was lost in the warmth of his mouth as it came crashing down hard on hers. He kissed her like a man starving for the taste, kissed her as though he'd drain her. One big hand slid down the curve of her back, coming to rest on the smooth curve of her bottom, dragging her up against the grinding hardness of his erection.

His free hand moved to the back of her head to hold her face up to his as the kiss continued on and on until her head was spinning.

Her body arched against him as her shoes fell from her nerveless fingers. Mouths still sealed, they took a few staggering steps together as the ferocity of their desire intensified. Chloe's knees were on the point of buckling when without warning he suddenly let her go.

She slid down to the sand and sat there, arms wrapped around herself as she looked up at him, her big eyes wide and shocked. Bleeding control from every nerve ending, Nik's hands clenched by his sides... He wanted to shed the pain, lose himself inside her—but he knew he would be using her in exactly the same way he'd used other women...using sex to gain a few moments' oblivion.

Why couldn't he bring himself to use Chloe?

'*That's* my way of dealing with it, *agape mou*,' he told her harshly, staring at the pouting line of her lips, which were still swollen from his kisses. 'So if you're feeling sorry for me and fancy a bit of pity sex...?'

Even as she winced at the deliberate crudity of his suggestion, shameful excitement clenched low in her belly.

'It was just a thought,' he drawled.

She watched him stalk away, wondering how anyone managed to look rock-hard, tough and vulnerable all at the same time, but then he was a man of massive contradictions. Her energy levels felt as though they'd moved into negative territory as she began to slowly slog her way through the sand after him. It wasn't until the car came into view with Nik standing beside it looking impatient that she realised what the tight feeling in her chest was—fear. She had never felt more scared in her life, which was saying something.

She couldn't be in love with Nik. She lifted her chin in defiance at the idea… She *refused* to be in love with him.

As she approached he opened the back door for her.

She tipped her head in acknowledgment and murmured sarcastically, 'What a gentleman,' before slamming the door behind her just in case he thought he was going to ride in the back with her.

CHAPTER NINE

'Do you like it?'

'It's beautiful,' Chloe said honestly as she walked around the room that Eugenie had guided her to. 'What a view,' she exclaimed, walking over to the open French doors. Three steps away was the infinity pool and beyond that the sea.

'It used to be a little tiny cottage, and Granny was born here,' the teenager confided. 'She was poor. That must be awful, I think. When she married Grandpa he wanted to knock it down but she wouldn't let him so he built around it. There wasn't any beach here then, so he brought the sand and made one.'

'What about the big place on the hill?' It had looked Venetian and just gorgeous set against a backdrop of pines.

'Oh, we own that too. Grandpa bought it but Yaya wouldn't live in it and he preferred modern so...' She gave a shrug that made Chloe think of her uncle. 'It's pretty much falling down now.'

'That's sad,' Chloe said, glancing through the doors of a walk-in closet, realising that she didn't have even so much as a toothbrush with her.

The girl seemed to read her thoughts. 'Don't worry. Mum will organise you some stuff.'

'No, really—'

'It's fine. She has closets full of samples.' She looked at Chloe with envy. 'They wouldn't fit anyone else here. Are you sure you won't join us for dinner?'

Chloe resisted the pleading tone and gave a firm shake of her head, adding, 'I'm really whacked.' She escorted Eugenie to the door and closed it behind her reluctant-to-leave guest.

She released a sigh and leaned back against the wall, willing the images that were flashing through her head to stop or at least slow down because they made her dizzy.

Finally summoning the energy to kick off her shoes, she flopped onto the bed and lay there staring at the fan that was whirring silently above her head.

She had pleaded exhaustion when she had been given the option of a tray in her room, which suggested she looked as bad as she felt. The bone-deep weariness felt as if it were crushing her; even lifting a hand to her head was an effort, as was closing her eyes. But when she'd managed it, opening them again was just not an option.

She suspected her weariness was as much emotional as physical. Lack of sleep was the reason, she decided, unwilling to admit the truth even to herself.

She touched her lips, a silent sigh rippling through her body as she remembered the moment Nik's eyes had dropped to her mouth and she'd known he was thinking about kissing her... Had he been able to feel how much she wanted him to? Oh, God, why was she even wasting her time thinking about it? It was just a damned kiss; there was nothing deep and meaningful about it!

She sighed, thinking, *I'll get up in a minute and shower the day and the memories away...* There was no hurry.

* * *

Fighting her way out of sleep was like fighting her way through layers of gauze, convinced when she finally broke through the veil of sleep that she had heard someone crying out.

She lay there listening but it was silent except for the sounds of the night coming in through the open door.

Night!

She sat up abruptly, looking around the room. It was dark but not inky black, as the sky outside the door was tinged faintly with red. She reached for the lamp switch and found it, illuminating the room and revealing a tray on a table, the food covered by domes.

She swung her legs over the side of the bed and the first thing her glance lighted on was a full-length silk kaftan hanging on a hook of the door to the bathroom. She smiled as she got stiffly to her feet. She picked up her phone and glanced at the time, her eyes widening as she saw it was five-thirty in the morning!

She picked up one of the domes and looked at the food, but she was not hungry enough to be tempted by the sad, cold remains of what had, she had no doubt, been a delicious meal.

There were more clothes neatly folded and stacked on the shelves in the wardrobe and hanging on padded hangers. Tatiana had clearly crept in while she was asleep like a petite Greek Santa. She yawned and stretched, wondering about Greek Christmas traditions.

She spent a long time in the shower and emerged feeling half human. Laying out a towel on the bed, she sat down and began rubbing the oil one of her physiotherapists had recommended into the tight tissues of her scars with light but firm strokes.

Maybe its effects were just a placebo but it smelt good

and, while it was no magic cure-all, her skin always felt more supple after she'd applied it. She had got into the habit of carrying it in her handbag.

She waited for it to dry before she put on the kaftan, enjoying the feel of the silk against her skin. She lifted an arm and performed a swishing motion, smiling. Tatiana really was talented. Drawn by the smells and sounds of early morning, she wandered to the open door and pulled aside the mosquito curtain that someone had pulled across while she slept.

Eyes closed, she breathed in deeply before she walked out, the soft scented breeze blowing the kaftan against her body. A tiny lizard disturbed by her tread emerged from a crack in the stone and vanished beneath the glossy, well-trimmed shrubbery.

The swimming pool lit by underwater lights that reflected the mosaic tiles drew her like a magnet; she loved water. She'd learnt to swim at school and if she had been prepared to put in the sort of dedication that involved a relentless early morning training schedule and no social life she might have been able to compete at a high level.

Physical ability and natural talent were no good unless you had the dedication that went with them and Chloe didn't…but she really loved to swim. Apart from the times she had stayed with her sister, as camera lenses and shocked stares were really not an issue in the royal palace, she had not ventured into the water since the accident.

She liked to think that one day she would be brave enough to swim in a public pool and not care about the stares, but that day had not yet come.

Walking to the edge, she hitched the folds of silk around her knees and sat down, dangling her feet in the warm water, thinking about the lovely feeling of it on her skin.

It was tempting to go in for a swim, it really was... Who was around to see?

Nik had been swimming lengths for ten minutes, pushing his body to the limit in an attempt to wash away the personal devils left in his head after the nightmare had visited him yet again. He neared the wall at the deep end, flipped over and had lifted his head to gulp in air when he saw Chloe approach the pool through a watery haze.

He paused, his head just breaking the surface as he trod water, the shimmering image solidifying. He was unable to take his eyes off her as she walked towards the water, the thin floor-length robe she wore blowing tight against her, outlining every supple curve of her long, luscious body.

She obviously wasn't wearing a stitch underneath.

The sound of blood drumming in his ears became deafening as in his head he saw her opening the garment and slipping it off, then standing there naked on the side before diving in... All she actually did was trail her toes in the water, pretty tame by most standards, but Nik felt his dormant libido once more kick into life—hard.

He took a deep breath and slid silently down under the surface of the water.

Her dreamy thoughts drifted as she continued to inscribe circles in the water with her toes.

The sheer unexpectedness of the sudden tug on her foot drew a shrill shriek from her throat. She pulled against the pressure and scooted back, fighting against the restraint and kicking out wildly.

There was a grunt of pain followed by a curse and she was suddenly free. She had curled both legs up protectively against her body when Nik's sleek dark head appeared, water streaming down his face.

'What the hell did you think you were doing? You nearly gave me a heart attack!' she accused shakily.

'I was swimming…it's good; come in and join me.'

The invitation sent a slam of hormonal heat through her body. She shook her head, her heart thudding like a metronome as she stared at him.

'Fair enough.' It took him two lazy strokes to reach the side. 'Then I'll join you.' Hands flat on the mosaic tiles, he casually heaved himself out of the pool, pausing for a moment on the balls of his feet before straightening up to his full impressive height.

Chloe had no control over her stare, and her skin prickled with heat as her helpless gaze travelled up the length of his long legs, taking in the ridges of his flat belly and broad, hair-roughened chest. His shoulders were muscle packed and powerful but he wasn't bulky. There was a streamlined strength to him, no excess flesh at all to blur the symmetry. Each individual muscle stood out defined and perfect beneath the surface of his gleaming golden skin.

Her eyes reached his face and his white grin flashed, making him look like a very smug fallen angel as he lifted one hand and rubbed it hard across his hair, causing more water to stream down his face.

He tilted his head to one side in an enquiring attitude. 'Sure I can't tempt you?' asked her personal embodiment of temptation, the gleam in his eyes suggesting that this was no secret to him.

Even though it was frustrating it was also true— she had zero control over the colour that rushed to her cheeks—but she refused to drop her gaze, or was it she couldn't escape the grip of his black, heavy-lidded stare?

Her insides clenched as she ran her tongue across the outline of her dry lips.

'No, you can't,' she lied, struggling to inject a note of amusement into her response. 'But don't let me stop you.' Hearing the quiver of something near to desperation in her own voice, she half turned and gave an elaborate yawn. 'I was just going back inside.'

He reached for a towel that was slung over a chair, rubbing it over his dripping hair, then blotting the moisture off his face. 'You really should take a swim.' His eyes went to the wet hair that was slicked back to reveal her smooth, high forehead and perfect pure profile. 'Or have you already?'

She lifted a self-conscious hand, dragging it down the damp surface of her wet hair. 'I showered.'

He swallowed, the muscles in his brown throat visibly working, a nerve spasmodically clenching in his lean cheek as his darkened eyes drifted slowly over her face, then down over the soft curves of her lush body outlined beneath the folds of iridescent fabric, his imagination peeling away the fabric, seeing the water streaming down her smooth skin.

It took Chloe a few moments to realise that the noise she could hear was her own breathing, as she struggled to breathe through the sexual tension that hung in the air.

She wasn't sure that Nik was breathing at all. He just stood there, the bands of dull colour running along the slashing angles of his cheekbones emphasising their razor-edged prominence as the moments ticked away. Each passing second made her heart beat faster until she could feel the thuds vibrating throughout her entire body.

'I… I need to go.' Her voice sounded as though it was coming from a long way away.

'Why?'

'I need to book my flight.'

'It's six a.m.'

'Online.'

'Eugenie will be disappointed; she was looking forward to showing you the sights.'

'I need to get back.' There was a hint of a plea in her voice.

He shrugged and looped the towel around his middle, drawing her attention once again to his flat, ribbed belly and the thin directional line of dark hair that vanished into the waistband of the black shorts he wore. 'Are you sure you won't join me for a swim? It'll take the edge off it.'

She didn't make the mistake of asking what *it* was.

How would he react, she wondered, if she pulled the kaftan open and stood there scars and all? *Why are you even asking the question?* she asked herself.

He's not interested in your heart or soul; he only wants the beautiful body—or the one he thinks you still have.

'I don't have a swimsuit.'

His eyes dropped. 'You've never skinny-dipped?'

She stiffened and lowered her lashes over an expression that tugged his dark brows into a straight interrogative line above his hooded stare... *Sadness* seemed an inexplicable reaction for her to have.

'Are you afraid of the water?' he asked gently.

Her eyes slid longingly over the still surface of the pool, but she shook her head.

'Do you often swim at this time of the morning? Are you in training or something?' She'd only been changing the subject, but now that she'd thrown the idea out there she found it wasn't actually a struggle to see him competing in a triathlon or something; he had the body, the fitness levels and undoubtedly the competitive streak it took for such an endurance event.

'No, I usually run.' He bent and picked up a second towel before rubbing his still-wet hair vigorously with it.

'So you are in training?'

He dropped the towel. 'I don't sleep.'

The confession evoked a rush of sympathy in Chloe.

Midway through her hospitalisation, when the heavy doses of analgesia she'd been prescribed for pain had been reduced, she'd suffered badly from insomnia. Though it was not a time she thought about often, choosing instead to focus on the fact she had survived, the experience had left her wary of taking even an aspirin and she'd gained a personal appreciation of the negative impact insomnia could have on a person's daily life.

'I suppose it's hard to switch off sometimes.' *Especially when you have chosen to carry around guilt the size of a planet... Not your problem, Chloe,* she reminded herself, rejecting the stab of empathy that made her chest tighten. People who deserved sympathy were those who actually tried to do something about a problem. 'I settle for warm milk—not very cutting edge, I know, but that usually does the trick for me.'

He gave a sudden hard laugh. 'I don't want to sleep.'

'You mean you don't *need* much sleep?' He fitted the profile of the driven alpha type you generally associated with surviving on two or three hours a night.

'I mean I have nightmares.' The hand he was dragging across his face stilled, shock flickering in his hooded gaze as he asked himself why the hell he had just told her that.

His nightmares were something he had never discussed with anyone. Did he suffer from some form of post-traumatic stress disorder? He was sure there were any number of so-called experts who would be happy to tell him. In Nik's view the label didn't matter. Sharing was not his style and the idea of being an object of pity was something that he rejected on a visceral level.

Charlie was dead because of him and no label was going to change that. He didn't want to feel better... He didn't *deserve* to feel better, he accepted that, but the nightmares were a punishment too far.

She blew out a long fatalistic sigh. She knew that she was issuing an invitation to have her head bitten off but she couldn't bring herself to do *nothing*. *Story of your life, Chloe.*

'So do you want to talk about it?'

He turned his head and glared at her. 'Can you turn off the empathy for a minute? That's not what I want from you.'

Chloe held her ground. 'You're not responsible for what happened, Nik. Charlie made his own decisions.'

'How the hell can you say that? I told you...' He stopped, his eyes narrowing over an expression of angry bewilderment. Why *had* he told her when he hadn't told anyone else? He didn't like that he couldn't answer the question. He was at her side in three strides, his hand closing around her upper arms as he dragged her into him until their bodies collided. 'Why do you have to be different?'

The emotions pouring off him made her dizzy, or was that the contact with his hard, lean body? The sexual pulse emanating from him and the feverish glitter in his dark eyes made her head spin.

His eyes stayed open and connected with her own as his lips moved across her parted lips, the contact a mere whisper, the progress agonisingly slow.

She shuddered and sank deeper into the suffocating excitement that caused her breath to come in short, shivery little gasps. His face blurred before she closed her

eyes and the ache of hunger low in her pelvis dragged
a sob from her aching throat as she whispered fiercely.

'Please!'

The hoarse, hungry plea snapped whatever shred
of control he retained as, with a moan deep in his own
throat, Nik plunged his tongue into her mouth, plunder-
ing the warm recesses. The kiss grew wild, teeth clashed,
tongues tasting with an escalating passion.

Rising up on her toes, Chloe put her arms around his
neck to hold on for grim death. She could still hear alarm
bells ringing but they were almost drowned out by the excited clamour of her own heartbeat. Her fingers dug into
the smooth muscled skin of his shoulders and back as she
pulled him closer, craving the connection of their bodies.

He'd still been clinging to the idea that making love to
her was some sort of therapy to drive his devils away, but
that illusion burned away the moment his hands began to
move over her body, exploring the soft curves.

This wasn't therapy, this was survival—he felt as
though his life depended on this. He *needed* this; he
needed her. No, it was just sex, he amended as he cupped
one warm breast in his hand and held it, his thumb rubbing across the engorged peak as he kissed his way up
the curve of her neck.

'You make me want you!' he growled, thinking that
all she had to do was breathe and he was out of his mind
with lust. 'I just want to feel your skin on mine. I have
to kiss and taste every inch of you.'

What was she doing? Your skin on mine, he'd said...
In her mind's eye she suddenly saw the puckered flesh of
her thigh and imagined the shocked disgust on his face
when he discovered it. And she couldn't bear it.

'No...no!' She pushed hard against him and his arms
fell away. He stepped back, his chest lifting and falling

dramatically as he appeared to struggle to draw enough air into his lungs.

'What is happening here, Chloe?'

She gave a tight little smile and thought, *I'm dying*. 'Nothing is happening. I just…changed my mind.'

'You changed your mind?' The lines of colour along his cheekbones stood out starkly against his blanched, sweaty pallor. He looked like a man in shock and he felt like a man in purgatory!

She took a deep, controlling breath. 'You come with too much baggage for me… I like to keep things simple.'

His head went back as though she'd struck him; he was aching and hurting and mad as hell. She thought he was some sort of emotional cripple who needed taking care of and she didn't want the job! The injury to his pride was almost as painful as the frustration that raged through his body. 'It's only sex, *agape mou*; I'm not asking you to marry me.'

She knew it was irrational to let the words hurt, but they did anyway. 'Maybe, but *just sex* can get complicated.'

'I'm a man of simple needs.'

She gave a bitter smile. 'You don't need to tell me that. As I recall you didn't even manage to say a simple goodbye…' She regretted the words even before she registered the speculation in his eyes and rushed into further speech. 'I really think you should talk to someone qualified, about the nightmares, I mean. It's good that you don't drink to excess now, but the way you were that night…'

'The night we had sex, you mean.' He saw her flinch and was glad; she deserved to flinch after her harsh rejection of him just now. 'There hadn't been any nightmares that night because I hadn't been to sleep.'

There was a beat of silence before a look of shocked comprehension slid across her face, taking with it any trace of colour that had been there. By the time she breathed again even her lips were bloodless and the only colour in her entire face was the burning blue of her eyes.

'Charlie's death had just happened, hadn't it?' But it wasn't a question… Suddenly it all made sense: the darkness in him, the combustible quality of their chemistry, the driving need of his lovemaking—he'd been trying to burn away the pain of his memories in the fire of passion.

He tipped his head in acknowledgment, the weight in his chest painful as he looked at her standing there, frail and defenceless. Wasn't there already enough guilt in his life?

'You used me.' Anger and hurt shimmered through her and she didn't care if she was being rational; she didn't feel rational.

'I was too tired to fight you off,' he shot back.

Chloe flushed. At what point had she thought he would *ever* let her in? 'You really are a bastard.'

He didn't deny it. How could he? It was true. She turned away. 'Where are you going?' He had to clamp his lips tight over the word *stay*! He had never begged a woman in his life, and he wasn't about to start now.

'Going?' She turned back and lifted her chin. 'As far away from you as I can get!' she flung childishly. 'And who knows? If I'm lucky I might find a man who is not afraid to admit he's not perfect.'

'*Agape mou*, you're not looking for a man, you're looking for a cause!' he sneered contemptuously.

'Maybe I am, but you're a *lost* cause,' she flung back. 'You'll never have a future until you forgive yourself for the past. And you don't want me, you want a memory of something perfect… Well, I'm not that. I'm…' Breathing hard, she fought her way out of the kaftan, ripping the silk as she tore it off her body and stood there naked in the light of the breaking dawn.

He sucked in a deep breath, his eyes moving down over her body. She watched his face and saw the exact moment when he reached the area where the skin was badly scarred, saw the shock and horror he couldn't conceal.

That tiny flame of hope died right then and there.

'You see, I'm not what you need. I'm not perfect any more.'

She had no idea how she managed to walk the few steps back to her room, oblivious to the fact he had followed her.

CHAPTER TEN

THE VIOLENCE WITH which she'd slammed the door behind her made it swing back open, but she seemed oblivious to that as he stepped over the torn silk robe that lay crumpled on the floor.

It took him a few dazed seconds to label the emotion that broke loose inside him as tenderness when his gaze lifted to the slim figure standing there, staring blankly straight ahead like a beautiful, flawless marble statue... Except she was not stone, she was blood and flesh and nerve endings, and the flaw on her body that stood out only emphasised how stunning she really was.

He could only imagine what was going through her mind. This woman had more guts in her little finger than a regiment of marines.

'Haven't you seen enough?' she asked, staring at a point over his left shoulder. If he hadn't, she certainly had!

She would never forget that look of horror in his eyes.

Every resource he had was needed to retain his control, but he was straining at the leash so hard he could barely form the word. 'No!'

Her eyes flew to his face as he walked towards her, the fierce tenderness in his eyes making her tummy flip and her throat tighten, as she had no defence against it.

'But...'

'I want to do more than look at you,' he growled out, lifting a big hand to curve his fingers around one side of her face. 'And I think we can do better than just sex!' he declared with arrogant confidence. Holding her startled gaze, he bent his head, closing his eyes only when their mouths were sealed together.

When he raised his head they were both breathing hard, her eyes were bright, her skin was feverishly hot, and every skin cell on her body was bursting with painful awareness.

'Let's even things up a bit, shall we?' he suggested, stepping away but only far enough to slide his wet shorts over his hips.

She swallowed, her eyes dropping to watch his actions, helpless to resist the desire that flowed through her as she observed how the lowering of the fabric revealed the level of his arousal. He flashed a grin at her, but his features were hard and fierce as he held her eyes.

'Come here!' he demanded.

She did and he took her hand, directing it straight onto his groin and curling her fingers around the hardness of his erection. 'That is what looking at you does to me.'

'But… I'm not…'

'You're perfect to me…and you are perfect for me.'

At the stark declaration the muscles deep inside her fluttered and the rapid rise of desire swept over her like a wave, wiping away the last shreds of her self-consciousness. As she tightened her fingers experimentally over his crotch, excitement swirled through her.

'Amazing!' she murmured.

He gave a low, sexy rumble of laughter that made the hairs on the nape of her neck tingle.

Nik caught hold of her hands, raised them to his lips and pressed kisses into each curling palm before lowering his mouth to hers once again.

The kiss began as a slow, sensual tender exploration and then suddenly it became something else, his tongue driving deeper inside her mouth and eliciting an explosion of raw need and desperation as teeth clashed and tongues collided. Chloe moaned deep and raised herself up on her toes, gasping as her aching, sensitised breasts flattened against his iron-hard chest.

By the time they broke apart, they were both breathing as though they'd just crossed the marathon finishing line, and he hooked a hand behind her neck, sliding his fingers into her hairline, the fingertips gently massaging the skin there.

Then he kissed the swan curve of her neck and Chloe's head fell back in rapture, her eyes squeezed closed on a long sigh that became a groan as his hand claimed first one quivering breast and then the other, stroking then kneading... Her head fell back further to allow him greater access, her spine arching back, supported by the iron strength of the arm across her ribs.

Her passion-glazed blue eyes flickered open as he scooped her up as though she weighed nothing and walked towards the bed.

She stroked his face, touching his mouth, his fascinating, pleasure-giving mouth, thinking that she honestly wouldn't have cared if he had laid her down on the floor and taken her there and then... The thought was both shocking and incredibly exciting to her.

As he strode towards the bed, although she wasn't small or delicate he made her feel both, yet at the same time powerful and strong.

He laid her down on the tumbled sheets and stood there looking down at her, nostrils flared, breathing hard, each breath lifting his ribcage.

His body was hard and tanned, warm, bone, sinew

and muscle all so perfect that the desire low in her belly clutched hard as she stared at him, unable to look away.

'You're beautiful,' she whispered. 'Perfect.' Her eyes suddenly filled with tears as she choked out, 'I wish I still was for you too—'

The rush of emotion he felt when he interpreted the expression in her eyes was shocking in its intensity.

She was grieving.

His expression was both stern and tender as he came down beside her, lowering his long body so that they lay thigh to thigh.

'Listen to me. You are beautiful.'

She gave a teary smile, loving him so much it hurt. 'Inside, maybe.'

'Everywhere,' he contradicted. 'Inside and out. And I want to love every part of you. You have lost something, I know, but let me give you something to fill the space...' He took her hand and laid it on his chest where she could feel the heavy thud of his heartbeat, strong and steady. She could feel it vibrating through her own body; it was as if they were one...but she craved an even more intimate joining.

'I want you,' she said simply.

His eyes darkened in response to the husky plea. 'Then, *agape mou*, you shall have me.'

Arms braced above her head either side, he leaned down and kissed her, and she sighed into his mouth, eager for his taste, wanting to fill her senses with it. The heat was searing and she whimpered as she was swept away on a tidal wave of primitive need.

The erotic exploration of tongue against tongue continued as he lowered his body beside her and turned her onto her side to face him. He lifted his mouth from hers, but only to kiss his way down her neck and then over the quivering mounds of her breasts.

A keening cry escaped her lips at the first brush of his tongue over first one nipple and then the other, then when he took one into his mouth and sucked on it sensuously she gasped.

Her damp nipples continued to ache from his ministrations as he slid lower, his tongue leaving a wet trail over the slight mound of her belly while his fingers moved into the soft curls at the apex of her legs, stroking the damp folds gently and then parting them until he found the tight nub nestling inside.

She was so focused on the new, agonisingly blissful sensations he was creating that she didn't realise at first where he was kissing.

She stiffened, rejection making her eyes fly wide open, hating that he was touching the ugly scarred tissue on her thigh, imagining the disgust he had to be feeling. She didn't want him to have to pretend to be enjoying it. 'No!'

'Yes!' he insisted.

For the space of a heartbeat their eyes connected, and she was the first to look away.

Quivering but quiescent now, she lay there as he gently kissed the damaged skin, her face wet with silent tears that slid unnoticed down her face.

'You can't want to do that.'

Her broken whisper felt like a tight fist around his heart. In response, he loosed a low growl and dragged himself up her body until they were face to face. Holding her gaze, he took her hand and curled her fingers around the hard, silky shaft of his erection. His whole body was trembling with need as she stroked him, breathing in the male musk of his warm body.

She looked into his eyes and the desire blazing there burnt away her last doubts and inhibitions; she suddenly felt free.

Kissing her passionately once again, Nik pulled her on top of him and held her there, his hands curved over her bottom, continuing to kiss her into mindless submission until he finally rolled them both over, reversing their position.

Lying beneath him, Chloe gave herself over to the sensations bombarding her. She surrendered to the feelings, as she surrendered to him.

Then he parted her legs and she held her breath and released it in a low, slow sigh when he finally slid into her. She grabbed his hips, her back arching to deepen the pressure, wanting more.

With a groan he obeyed, giving her everything he'd got. 'Put your legs around me, Chloe.'

She did and he sank deeper into her, each strong movement of him inside her sending her deeper into herself, into him. It became one and the same, and they were both at the core of a firestorm, and when it broke the effect on every nerve cell in her body was electric!

She turned her head on the pillow, where beside her Nik lay gasping for air, his chest heaving and the sweat on his skin cooling.

She began to worry that he was cooling towards her because he suddenly seemed so far apart from her, but before the fear could take root he reached out and dragged her against him, as close as possible.

'What are you doing all the way over there?' he asked, propping his chin on the top of her hair-rumpled head as he pulled up a sheet to cover them both.

'Does it still hurt?' he asked quietly when they were both lying still.

She sat up then, dragging the sheet up to her chin, and looked down at him. 'My leg?'

He nodded.

'Only when I laugh… No, seriously, not really, it's kind of numb because the nerve endings were pretty damaged.'

He was pretty sure that her matter-of-fact delivery covered a world of hurt and pain.

'The skin can get tight sometimes.' She reached out and took a bottle from the bedside table. 'If it does, I usually massage this stuff into it.'

'Were you in hospital for a long time?' The image of her lying alone in a hospital bed enduring such pain produced a fresh surge of protectiveness in him.

'Longer than expected, because the grafts didn't take. There was an infection so they had to start all over again. That's why I'm not going back.'

He stiffened. 'They want you to?'

She nodded. 'They have offered me another op, but that's what they said last time…'

'Shouldn't you listen to expert advice?'

'The surgeon says he *might* be able to improve the appearance, but there are no guarantees, and I've had enough of being poked and prodded.'

The way she said it, the defiance in her tone, made his throat ache with emotion, and his arms tightened around her narrow ribs as he rocked her against him.

'But wouldn't it be worth it if they could improve it?' he said against her neck.

She pulled away, her expression wary. 'I still wouldn't be perfect, and it's not about other people, it's about *me*. *I* have to be able to look in the mirror and know I'm still me…' she pressed a hand to her breasts '…inside.'

He watched the tears slide down her cheeks and felt as

if someone had reached a hand into his chest and pulled out his heart. 'Don't cry, *agape mou*.' He smoothed down her hair with a hand and pulled her back into his arms.

Nik felt regret when he saw the warm rays of sunlight filtering through the blinds, certain to wake Chloe up. The irony of his dismay was not lost on Nik, as for a long time he hadn't been able to wait until he could get out of bed.

But morning was already well established now, which meant that he'd have to let her go and lose the incredible sense of peace and *rightness* he'd felt holding her, a peace that had been better than the sleep his body craved, sleep that he had denied himself out of fear that in the grip of a nightmare he might hurt her. It was a fear with foundation, as there were reported incidents of men suffering from PTSD acting out their nightmares and injuring their partners in their sleep.

If he hurt Chloe, even unconsciously, he knew it would kill him.

The time had come to get up, but on the plus side the bright sunlight made it possible for him to study the face on the pillow beside him. Half obscured by the tangle of silky blonde hair, she lay with one arm across his chest and the other tucked under her head like a pillow. He could make out the fact that her eyelashes fanned out lush and curving against her smooth cheek.

If anyone had told him before yesterday that he would say a woman's name just because he wanted, no, *needed* to hear it he would have laughed them out of the building and yet...

'Chloe.'

It was barely a whisper but she must have sensed it because she stirred, whimpering a little and shifting restlessly, then, eyes still closed, she shouted, 'No!' She opened her eyes suddenly, and blinked as the haziness vanished. 'I was dreaming...' she whispered sleepily.

'It sounded like a nightmare.'

'I forgot about my leg and had put on shorts, which is silly because I never forget...' she murmured sleepily. 'People were laughing and pointing at my scars...'

Nik flinched inside. 'I won't let anyone laugh,' he promised fiercely.

Chloe smiled happily as he turned onto his side and pulled her to him, running a hand in long soothing strokes down her back again and again until her breathing evened out once more.

It was a long time since he had spent more than an hour or so in bed with a woman, partly because he didn't want anyone to witness his nightmares. It was ironic, really, that the nightmares this time had been Chloe's.

You don't have exclusive rights on nightmares, Nik.

The memory of her pathetic whimpers cut right to his heart, and he kissed her forehead gently, pleased that her breathing was now soft and easy.

She bore her scars so bravely but how many times had she lifted her chin and pretended not to care...as she had with him earlier this morning? Carefully he leaned across her and pressed the phone that lay on the bedside table, so that the time appeared; it was already nearly ten a.m.

His throat was dry and the glass of water remained out of reach.

He moved, sliding a hand from under her, careful not to disturb her, and levered himself from the bed. Walking through to the kitchen, he closed the door to muffle the sound and turned on the tap. He downed the glass of water greedily.

Then he retraced his steps, making a detour to retrieve his own phone, which was in his jacket pocket, before he stood there gazing at the sleeping figure. While he respected her decision not to have further surgery he wondered if there wasn't another way to help her...a way that would leave her free of nightmares about people pointing at her.

A sense of deep grinding impotence rose up inside him. There *had* to be a way to protect her from all the cruelty out there, the people prepared to gossip and mock.

Chloe woke up and wondered why she felt so good, then she remembered and she felt even better. Eyes still closed, she patted the bed beside her, realising that the sheets were almost as cold as the sudden tightness behind her breastbone. Nik had left her again.

No, Chloe, this is how paranoia starts.

'Good morning.' Nik must have been back to his own room, as he was now wearing an unbuttoned shirt—a very good look on him—and cream linen shorts... Well, you couldn't have everything, she thought naughtily, knowing she preferred him naked. He was carrying a tray that held a cafetière of coffee, buttered toast and some fresh fruit.

'Hello.' She hid the sudden surge of paralysing shyness by grabbing for a piece of toast.

'Hello to you too. Black or white?' Nik asked, nudging the bedside lamp out of the way to balance the tray on the little side table. He sat down on the bed beside her and scanned her face.

She pushed a hank of hair from her eyes. 'Black and thank you, for earlier on.'

'I'd say it was a pleasure, but I hope that was perfectly obvious.'

She blushed, taking a sip of strong, fragrant coffee, and peeped at him over the rim. 'For me too.'

'I've been doing a bit of research online.' He was buzzing with the information he'd discovered and couldn't wait to share it with her.

She took another sip of coffee and thought ruefully that he had more energy than she did, as she felt tired in places she hadn't even known existed!

'I don't know who your consultant is but there is a team of medics in New York who are working on some new plastic surgery techniques. They're still at the trial stages but the results are nothing short of miraculous.'

She listened to him in silence but he had lost her after *your consultant*.

'I'm not interested.'

The coldness in her flat voice acted like cold water on his enthusiasm. He regarded her in frustration but when he spoke to her his tone was all gentle patience. 'I don't think you understand.'

She put down her cup and tightened her grip on the sheet she had gathered across her breasts. 'No, it's you who doesn't understand, Nik. It's you who hasn't been listening.' Or at least understanding. She felt a fool now for believing that he had. 'You really think there is anything you can tell me about possible treatments? Do you think I haven't looked into absolutely everything available?' She pushed her bare leg out from under the covers, shocking a small grimace from him. 'I've been living with this for a long time.'

He shook his head. 'I realise that—'

'Do you think I came to this decision lightly?' she asked him, her anger growing steadily. 'Do you think I didn't agonise over it? I came to a decision that is right for me and I need you to respect it.'

'Obviously, this is an emotional subject,' he began, 'but—'

Her lips tightened. 'Don't patronise me and don't try and change me. You need to accept me as I am, or walk away.'

He held his hands out flat in a pacifying gesture; this conversation was not going at all the way he had anticipated! 'There is no need to overreact.'

She arched a brow. 'No? Well, how would you feel if I brought you a cup of tea and told you all about the PTSD that you are suffering from?' She saw his flinch and ignored it. 'That I suddenly became an expert on your *problem*.' Her mouth tightened as her resentment rose.

'We are not talking about me.'

'Yeah, because unlike you I'm not in denial about my problem…and it isn't a problem for me. The only problem is the attitude of people like you!'

While she had been speaking the colour had gradually leaked from his face and by the time she'd finished his warm skin tone was ivory.

'I'm trying to help you!' he ground out, getting to his feet.

'How about helping yourself first? *I* don't need fixing. You're the one who won't even admit he has a problem!' she flung back, wanting to hurt him as much as he had her. A strange sense of calm settled over her as she looked up at him…this damaged, beautiful man she had grown to love in such a short space of time. This thing between them, whatever it was, had been doomed from the outset. It had never been going to work; she had only been fooling herself.

Why drag it out? she asked herself sadly.

'Until you sort yourself out… I don't want anything to do with you!'

CHAPTER ELEVEN

SHE'D KNOWN THE event was being filmed live but Chloe hadn't expected the cameras to be outside as well.

She could hear the young woman speaking into the mic as she stepped out of the car that bore the royal crest of Vela. She squared her shoulders. If her sister, who absolutely hated being the centre of attention, could do this then so could she…all she had to do was channel her inner show-off.

'And this…yes, that is Lady Chloe Summerville, who is standing in for her sister, the future Queen of Vela. We understand,' the reporter continued with a coy smile for the camera, 'that the princess was unable to attend tonight, and, though there has been no *offi-cial* confirmation, I'm sure you recall how the Princess suffered terrible morning sickness during her first pregnancy…?

'Lady Chloe is wearing…' she consulted a sheet of paper she was holding '…yes, I believe she is wearing a creation by Tatiana… Lady Chloe, hello.'

Chloe paused in front of the mic that had been pushed into her face, and smiled. 'Hello.' The personal touch would have been nice but she didn't have a clue who the other woman was.

'That is a beautiful cape,' the reporter said, gazing

at the floor-length velvet fur-trimmed cape Chloe wore. 'Real fur?'

'No, it's not real.'

'You are presenting one of the awards tonight, I believe, to the little girl who, I'm sure our viewers will remember, ran back into a burning house to save her baby sister and was injured herself. Humbling...so humbling...'

'To *Kate*, yes, I got lucky being able to present that particular award.'

'Standing in for your lovely sister? And how is the princess?'

Sabrina was where she spent most evenings at the moment, hanging over a toilet bowl...still asking anyone who'd listen why they called it *morning* sickness.

'She is really sorry she couldn't be here as it's a cause very close to her heart. Heroes so often go unsung and it's good to redress the balance just a little.'

'So why was she—?' The fortuitous arrival of the cast of a famous reality TV programme saved Chloe from fielding any more questions, and as the camera moved to the new arrivals she made her way quickly up the steps and into the theatre's foyer, which was filled with small gaggles of well-dressed people chatting. Tatiana immediately peeled off from one of the nearer groups and came across to where Chloe stood.

Chloe bent to kiss her when almost immediately her phone began to bleep and, fishing it from the minuscule bag she carried, she glanced down. 'A text from Sabrina,' she explained, skimming the message her sister had sent her.

Good luck and chin up! If you change your mind that's fine either way. We'll be cheering you on, so have a glass of fizz for me! And hurry back, please. If my husband asks me if I'm all right one more time I might have to kill him.

Chloe's smile was tinged with wistfulness as she switched her phone off and slipped it back into her bag. What would it be like to have a man be as crazy about you as her brother-in-law was about her sister?

Swallowing the emotional lump in her throat, she knew how lucky she was to have a family like hers, who were aware of her plans and supported any choices she made. It had been a struggle to stop her parents from flying over to offer moral support, and she suspected they were a bit hurt by the rejection, but she knew it was something she had to do alone.

'Is everything all right?' Tatiana asked.

'Fine if you discount the fact that Sabrina can't keep anything down. The doctor says if things don't improve by the end of the week, they'll have to give her IV fluids.'

'Oh, the poor thing!'

'So what happens now?' Chloe asked.

'Well, you're up first so they want you to go straight backstage, and after you've presented the award you'll see Kate back to her table, where they've seated you there for the rest of the dinner.'

Chloe nodded. 'That sounds good.'

'You sure about this?'

'Quite sure.' Chloe was surprised by how calm she felt now the moment was almost here.

'You know there are going to be headlines.'

Chloe nodded again, refusing to give mind space to fear and doubts. Producing headlines was the idea. You couldn't challenge common perceptions from a position of fear. She'd been going around telling the world that they should accept people with scars while hiding her own.

Which made her a big fat hypocrite.

'Tonight is the night of the big reveal.'

'I think you're very brave,' Tatiana husked emotionally.

Chloe felt uncomfortable with the praise. 'No, the people being awarded tonight are brave.'

She'd never thought of herself as brave but she had thought that she had come to terms with her injury. However, watching a filmed conversation with the little girl she was due to present a bravery award to tonight had destroyed that particular illusion for Chloe.

'So what do your friends think about your scars, Kate?' the reporter had asked.

The little girl had put down the doll she was playing with and thought about it.

'Well, I think they thought my arm looked funny at first, and some kept staring. A few people, not my *proper* friends, were mean and made me cry, but everyone's used to it now, so they don't even notice it cos they see it every day and I'm still me.' She'd picked up the doll, applied a comb to its hair and added thoughtfully, 'I still cry sometimes cos I liked my arm the way it was.'

The hard-nosed reporter had had tears in his eyes as he'd wound up the segment and Chloe doubted anyone watching would not have been similarly affected.

She herself had wept gallons but her tears had been partly out of shame. She had been hiding, Chloe realised that now, and if she hadn't, if she'd been truly honest with herself and everyone else, that devastating scene with Nik a few weeks ago on Spetses would never have happened.

Now she'd have to live with the memory for ever, all because she had preferred to be treated like a woman with no imperfections. Of course, there had been a price to pay for her deceit: she'd fallen deeply in love. Flaws and all, she loved Nik Latkis, but he didn't love her in return. Unrequited love had seemed much more romantic when she was a teenager with a lurid imagination, but the reality actually sucked.

It didn't help that her youthful imagination was still hanging in there inventing implausible happy-ever-after scenarios, not that she was ever in any danger of identifying her fantasies as anything other than what they were.

It was the thought of Nik's far more sinister dreams that continued to haunt her. She wondered and worried about the demons that visited him in the night and the eventual toll they would take on his health, both emotional and physical. She longed to comfort him but knew that was never going to happen after what had happened between them. She didn't blame him for that; he'd tried, but her scars were obviously an issue for him and he wasn't interested in helping himself, either.

Would he be watching the awards ceremony?

Would he disapprove of her decision?

She knew full well that her big reveal would go viral on social media, sparking thousands of debates, which was good, and an equal number of cruel comments, which was not, from people who thought anonymity gave them the freedom to say vile things about people they had never met.

She was prepared for the impending blaze of publicity as much as it was possible to be prepared.

'Lady Chloe.' One of the organisers, an efficient-looking woman in a blue evening dress, appeared. 'You look lovely,' she gushed. 'Has Tatiana explained the format to you? Excellent. You really do look amazing. Oh, excuse me.' She stepped to one side as, at a nod from Chloe, Tatiana moved forward to remove her floor-length cape.

'It's OK,' Chloe whispered when the older woman hesitated.

Chloe smoothed down her hair, which tonight she was wearing gathered in a simple jewelled clasp at the base of her slender neck. Her dress was the same bold red as her lipstick, a silk sleeveless sheath cut high at the neck and low at the back, the reverse cowl open almost to her waist, and plain except for the pattern traced in hand-sewn beads along the daring slit that was cut high on the left side that fell open to reveal her thigh.

It wasn't accidental; she had asked Tatiana to do it that way.

'Stunning!' the woman began then stopped; she'd clearly reached the revealing slit. There was a pause before she lifted her eyes and during the slight hiatus Chloe fought the urge to twitch the fabric over the scars.

When the woman did finally speak, her voice was husky. 'That,' she said, looking at Chloe as though she were seeing her for the first time, 'is *beautiful*.' Then, clearing her throat, she waved away the assistant who had clearly been allocated to escort Chloe. 'I'll take Lady Chloe in myself.'

The lift was empty as they stepped in.

As the lift whooshed silently upwards the woman cleared her throat. 'My sister was born with a cleft palate and lip; it's fine now and you'd never know, but I re-member the comments she'd get when my mum used to take her out in the pushchair. People can sometimes be very cruel and what you're doing is…good, very good. I'm Jane, by the way.'

Backstage was actually pretty crowded, but Jane found Chloe a seat in a corner that wasn't occupied by what seemed to be the entire cast of a hit West End musical, who were waiting to go out and do the opening number.

Jane left but returned almost straight away with a glass of wine, and stayed with her while the comedienne who was hosting the event introduced the musical stars.

'Your turn.'

Chloe jumped at the touch on her arm.

'Don't worry. Pretend the cameras aren't there.'

Chloe straightened her shoulders and walked out onto the stage.

Nik arrived late, but he was there. He entered the back of the hall and surveyed the tables that had replaced the normal seats in the auditorium, searching for his sister and niece. He had just located them and plotted a course towards them when a ripple of applause made him decide to hang back until there was a break in proceedings so he could slide unobtrusively into his seat and no doubt get an earful for being late.

Maybe he'd slip out to the bar…? He hated this sort of occasion and he'd have been much happier to just make an anonymous donation, but he'd been guilted into coming, not by his sister for once, but his niece, who had gone into Bambi-eyes mode and reminded him that he'd never taken her to the show he had promised for her birthday.

He was in no position to deny it, although he didn't remember the promise or the birthday, so here he was. He hadn't smelt a set-up, not until he heard Chloe's name announced, followed by another ripple of applause.

Nik only heard the name.

Theos, she looked magnificent!

Lust struck through his body as his glance moved from the woman standing on the stage to the larger image on the screen at the side of the stage. Elegant, assured, with the glamour of a siren of the bygone golden Hollywood era, she was wearing a dress that had to have sent every male temperature in the room sky-high… The thought of anonymous males lusting after her drew his brows into a straight line of disapproval above his eyes, but they relaxed when she began to speak.

A sigh of pleasure left his lips…he had missed that sound. The simple admission sent a shock through his body and he didn't catch what she said as he focused instead on the sound of her voice.

She had a beautiful voice; pleasingly low and clear, it filled the room. She must have said something amusing because there was a soft ripple of laughter…except he didn't feel like laughing. There was nothing humorous about the way he was feeling, the *things* he was feeling.

Did an alcoholic feel this way when they found the innocuous orange juice they'd just swallowed was laced with vodka?

What did they say about recovery? Something about the first step was accepting you had a problem…but what if you didn't want to recover—*ever*?

Frustration burned through him as he stood there staring at her, a multitude of clashing emotions swirling inside him. He desired her, he resented her…he had *missed* her.

He had been only trying to help her and she had thrown his actions back in his face, accusing him of being the one with the problem, assigning the worst possible motives to his actions.

Why should he defend himself to this woman?

The woman who had tapped into his deepest fears, the weaknesses he despised in himself, and exposed them all to the light, and she'd made it sound as though he had a choice…?

She was wrong. Knowing it was enough, challenging her mistakes would have made it seem as though he needed to defend his actions, or, as she saw it, his lack of action... Move on, she'd said, but where was he meant to move on to? He couldn't rewrite the past.

A man takes responsibility for his own actions, Nicolaos.

The memory of his father's comment surfaced, smoothing out the creases of uncertainty at the edge of his mind.

Strange how some memories stuck. How old had he been? He couldn't even remember what lie he'd told, or what childish rule he'd broken. Maybe the moment had stood out for him because it was outside the norm. His father had not had a hands-on parenting style; he had seemed as remote a figure as the portrait of his stern-looking great-grandfather that Nik always felt disapproved of him.

He remembered the shame he'd felt and the determination never to disappoint his father again; he'd be a man.

The idea that he hadn't lived by that adage ever since was ludicrous. As for feeling guilty about how he'd handled matters with Chloe, she was the one who had seduced him that night they'd met!

Ah, poor you, the unwilling victim!

His inner dialogue was interrupted by a sudden roar of applause, and Nik realised that he was the only person in the room still looking at the figure in red on the stage. The spotlight, along with everyone else, was focused instead on a table near the front.

The big screen showed a little girl with a woman kneeling beside her, obviously her mother, encouraging her to go up on stage to receive her award, but the little girl was shaking her head emphatically.

There was an awkward silence as the child began to sob loudly then, and it was a heart-rending sound.

He was relieved and pleasantly surprised by the show of sensitivity as the camera moved off her face. No, not sensitivity, he saw then, they were just following the story. It focused on the tall figure in red who was now walking down the steps of the stage.

A murmur of approval went round the room that faded to a silence as Chloe began to weave her way through the tables towards the child. A silence Nik didn't understand until he saw the image of her body on the screen. The camera had dropped to show the long legs, the daring slit and…everything inside him froze.

The lighting was harsh and the camera picked out every detail of the discoloured, twisted flesh.

'*Theos…!*' His stomach muscles clenched, not in reaction to the sight of the ugly marks, but the pain they represented, the *months* of pain they represented. The explosion of pride he felt drew a raw-sounding gasp from a place deep inside him he hadn't known existed. An emotion he had stubbornly refused to acknowledge.

Like everyone else he watched as she dropped down into a graceful crouch beside the little girl, the big screen showing her smile as she spoke.

There was another faint ripple of sound around the room when the little girl lifted her teary face from her mother's shoulder. Chloe nodded and pointed to her own leg.

The room held its collective breath as the child reached out and touched Chloe's leg, then released it on a sigh as the camera recorded the smile that bloomed on her face.

Chloe said something that made the kid laugh, then she got to her feet and held out her hand. The room erupted when the child took it, and together to the sound of applause they walked back up onto the stage.

Nik wasn't applauding, he was barely breathing… He

felt a maelstrom of pride, shame and an aching desire to run up there and take Chloe in his arms, but he knew that even if he had earned the right to do that, which he hadn't, this was her night.

As the tall, beautiful woman walked onto the stage and turned to face the audience they rose to a man and gave a foot-stamping ovation, which the excited child joined in with…and Nik knew he was looking at tomorrow's front-page headline.

He also knew he was looking at the love of his life.

And he'd blown it.

For once, no heads turned his way when Nik Latsis left the room.

CHAPTER TWELVE

It was nearly one in the morning when Chloe got back to her flat.

She rarely received a call on her landline these days, but the red light on her answer machine was flashing, showing her it was full of messages.

She ignored it, as she had already spoken to everyone who mattered, and her mobile phone lay switched off in her bag. She massaged her temples with her fingers to alleviate the tension she could feel gathering behind her eyes.

She could feel the exhaustion bearing down on her like a lead weight, but her mind remained active, not in a productive, problem-solving way, but more of a febrile, hamster-on-a-wheel way.

She kicked off her heels, conscious of a sense of anti-climax. She had been building up to tonight for days, not quite admitting how nervous she was about it, and now it was over and it couldn't have gone better, she should be feeling elated. But instead she felt…oddly flat, and not at all the inspiring figure that people had lined up to tell her she was this evening.

Easing the beautiful cape off her shoulders, she walked through to her bedroom, where she hung it on a hanger before covering it in a protective bag. Hopefully a few people would bid for it at the charity auction her sister had planned for next month.

When Chloe had suggested the timing might not be good for Sabrina to organise an auction, she had quipped, 'Trust me, I'm a doctor. I'll be feeling fine by then.'

As she stripped off the beautiful red gown and ran a bath for herself, she debated having a nightcap, but on balance decided against it, worried it might compete with the champagne she'd drunk earlier that evening.

Lighting the scented candles around the bath, she eased herself into the sweet-smelling water and lay there drifting, feeling deliciously decadent. Slowly the tension began to ease out of her shoulders.

Then the doorbell rang.

Her eyes peered through the open bathroom doorway to the clock on her bedroom wall, and she squinted to make out the time. Who on earth could that be in the middle of the night?

Everyone had warned her to expect some press intrusion after tonight and she thought that was realistic but this was ridiculous. It was getting on for two a.m.!

She decided to ignore it.

But her late-night caller was not giving up, and Chloe lay there, teeth gritted as the tension climbed back into her shoulders. And then the answer to her earlier question popped into her head.

Who did knock on doors at this time of night? The police with bad news.

Leaping out of the water, her pulse racing in panic and still dripping wet, she fought her way into a thick towelling robe and ran to the front door, leaving a trail of wet footprints in her wake. By the time she reached the door her imagination was cranked up to full volume and she was on her fourth awful possible scenario!

Cinching the belt a little tighter, she checked the safety chain was fastened and, as an extra precaution, picked up a heavy pale wood Dala horse from the console table and opened the door a crack.

Her late-night callers weren't wearing uniform and it was one visitor, singular, although she couldn't make out who it was.

Caution replaced dread, though on the plus side if this was a homicidal maniac standing there the walls were very thin in the apartments. Someone would be bound to hear her being murdered, and hopefully report it to the police.

'My neighbour is a black belt in karate!' she called through the crack.

She could only see a sliver of the man standing outside her door in the communal hallway, but as he stepped closer the partial view was more than sufficient to make the colour in her face recede, leaving her dramatically pale, and then return as quickly, dusting her cheeks with rose pink as she stood there frozen.

Her first thought was that she had fallen asleep and this was a new version of her recurring dream. In all the other versions, Nik had been wearing black swimming shorts and nothing else, not a dinner jacket that hung open and a white dress shirt that was pulled open at the neck and seemed to have several buttons missing. There were the remains of a bow tie sticking out of his breast pocket too; he really did not look his usual immaculate self.

'Hello.'

This Nik, with dark shadows under his eyes and stubble on his chin, still looked more sexy than any man had a right to be.

'I need to lie down,' she mumbled, thinking, *And then I need to wake up!*

'Can I come in first?' His mild tone was at stark variance to the glitter in his eyes as he stared at her.

'I thought you were the police! I thought Sabrina had lost the baby or my mum had fallen and broken her hip, or my dad had—'

'Sorry I scared you.'

'You can't really be here because you don't know where I live. I moved.' She'd rented out her old place as part of the entire new change she had decided to adopt on her return from Greece.

'Then you should consider going ex-directory, you know.' He dragged a hand across his hair and sounded tired as he added gruffly, 'Let me in, Chloe, please.'

'All right.' It took her longer than it should to remove the chain. Her hands, she noticed, viewing the phenomenon with a strange out-of-body objectivity, were shaking violently.

Finally she released it.

She stepped back as Nik walked in; he was real after all. Dreams didn't smell this good, carrying with them the scent of outdoors underlain with a faint scent of whisky.

'Beware Greeks bearing gifts,' she murmured.

Especially tall, lean, gorgeous Greeks with pride etched onto every inch of a classically perfect profile and with explosive tension locked into every muscle.

He held out his empty hands and turned them over. 'I don't have any. I wasn't sure if you'd even let me in.'

'I wasn't sure you were real,' she countered huskily. Then, shaking her head to clear the static buzz, she tried to inject a little normality into what was a very surreal situation.

'Do you know what time it is?' She flicked back the

hair from her face, the soggy ends dusting her cheek with dots of moisture.

'I couldn't wait until morning,' he said simply.

Struggling to convey a calm she was a million miles from feeling, Chloe met his eyes. The combustible quality in his heavy-lidded stare dried her throat and made her heart thud harder against her ribcage. She cinched the belt even tighter, suddenly very conscious of the fact that she was naked underneath her robe.

'Why are you here, Nik…?' Her eyes fluttered wider. 'Has something happened to Tatiana… Eugenie…?'

'No, they're fine,' he soothed immediately.

Panic subsiding, Chloe let out a relieved little sigh and arched a brow, folding her arms in an unconsciously protective gesture over her chest as she asked again, 'So why are you here?'

'Why didn't you tell me…?' He stopped and spread his hands. 'Tonight, you… No, you don't have to tell me. I know I've got no right to encourage your confidence in me.' He was the last person she'd turn to for support.

'You saw it on television?'

'I was there,' he said heavily. The pride he had felt for what she'd done was still there but overlaying it now was apprehension for her future. For every voice raised in admiration there would be another writing crude, cruel insults, but he'd be there for her, regardless.

She refused to jump to conclusions. 'Where?'

'At the theatre, for the bravery awards.'

The muscles along his jaw tightened as he realised with a sudden startling insight what she really wanted. She didn't want to be protected from people; she wanted to be released to be the brave, beautiful heroine she was. She might make those who cared for her sick with worry on her behalf, but it was a price they'd have to pay.

Nik knew with a total certainty that he wanted to be one of them, even though the idea of anyone hurting her by word or action left a sour taste in his mouth, and rage in his heart.

All he could do was be there for her—if she'd let him.

'Oh.' What else could she say? 'You didn't stay around for the party, then.' Her attempt at levity fell flat in the face of his grim-featured non-reaction.

For a big man Nik moved very fast.

The weight of his body made her take a staggering step back as he framed her face with his hands and turned it up to him.

'It was the bravest thing I have ever seen,' he rasped in a throaty whisper. 'Can you ever forgive me? I don't want to change you, I swear, but I'll change who I am. I'll—'

'I like you the way you are…'

His kiss silenced her. When he finally lifted his head his forefinger replaced his lips. 'Let me speak without putting words in my mouth…' She nodded dazedly, and he took his finger away. 'Tonight I saw the bravest, most beautiful woman I know…do the bravest, most beautiful thing.'

Her eyelids lowered over the haze of tears that shimmered in the swimming azure depths. 'I was scared stiff,' she admitted. 'I thought you'd be angry with me.'

The expression drawn on his chiselled face was one of astonished incredulity. 'I *am* angry.'

Her head began to lower but he placed a finger under her chin and drew her face inexorably up to his. 'But not with you, *agape mou*. Never with you. I'm furious with *myself* for wasting so much time!' he rasped out throatily. 'I know I have a problem with PTSD, and I'll get help for that. I might never be the man you deserve but, so help me, I'll do whatever it takes, so long as you take me back?'

She blinked in shock as she stared at him. 'Did I ever really have you?'

The shaky laugh dragged from her throat cut off abruptly as she encountered the hard, hungry, slightly unfocused look in his stare.

'From that first moment I met you, I think, but I was too stupid, too much of a stubborn, proud fool to realise it.' He dragged a hand through his hair. 'I really don't have any pride left, Chloe, and there hasn't been a day gone by since that morning in Greece that I haven't hated myself for making you think I was ashamed of your scars.'

She put up a hand and cupped his cheek. 'I see now that wasn't the case.'

'It's *my* scars I'm ashamed of,' he admitted heavily. 'Everything you said to me that morning was absolutely right. I knew it then, but I just couldn't admit it. Now I'm asking you to take me, Chloe, scars and all, for better or for worse… I love you, *agape mou*, and I need you.'

He took a deep shuddering breath. 'I know I walked away from you—twice—but I promise that will not happen ever again. Let me into your life and I will always let you be you. I don't want to stifle you. I want to watch you fly.'

With a little sigh, she laid her head on his chest, her eyes squeezing shut as she felt his strong arms close around her. She stood there listening to the thud of his heartbeat, feeling the weeks of loneliness slip away.

Finally she lifted her head. 'I love you too, Nik.'

The kiss he gave her went on and on, his hungry passion leaving her feeling limp yet very happy when they finally came up for air.

She stroked his face lovingly. 'I feel as though a weight has been lifted from me the last few weeks.'

He took her face between his hands. 'I love you, I love every part of you, and, yes, I admit I did want you to reconsider the plastic surgery, but not,' he emphasised, 'for me. For you…'

'I realise that now,' she admitted.

'I don't know if you've fully considered this,' he began tentatively, 'but what you did tonight will make you the target of—'

'Internet trolls and other low-life, yes, I know.' She dismissed them with an impatient click of her fingers.

It took a few moments for the information to filter through to his brain…but when it did his hands fell from her face in astonishment.

'Of course I know that; I'd need to live on Mars not to know,' she said with a rueful smile.

'And you still did it.' He shook his head and gave a laugh. 'You really are the most incredible woman,' he declared with husky pride.

'Is there stuff out there already?'

He nodded.

'We're not going to read it,' she declared.

'I think that is a good move.'

He cleared his throat.

'Nik, why are you looking shifty?' she demanded.

Without a word he picked up his phone, scrolled down the screen and handed it to her. 'There are some other things out there you should probably know about.'

With a puzzled frown Chloe took it and began to read, her expression changing from bemusement to anger as she progressed. 'Oh, my God, who did this? Do you know who the source is? It has to be someone close to you to know all these details. It's a gross invasion of privacy!' she declared indignantly.

'Me!'

Her eyes flew wide. It made no sense. Nik was an intensely private person so why would he feed this story about himself to a journalist? 'I don't understand.'

'I gave this story, this evening. You made me so proud tonight, seeing how courageous you were, not hiding in any sense of the word... You were marvellous and it made me feel completely ashamed of myself. You were right: I've been hiding like a coward. Your name is going to be out there all over the media, and I knew I couldn't stop that, but I could show some solidarity so... I decided to join you and—who knows?—reading about what happened to me might even help someone else. I'm definitely going to do something about it, I promise you.'

'I know you will.'

'I wanted to prove to you that you could give me your heart and I would keep it safe and I am hoping that you would accept mine.'

Chloe's breath caught in her throat.

'And for the record I don't want to change a single thing about you.'

Tears pouring down her cheeks, Chloe flung herself at him, sobbing with sheer joy, and he swung her up into his arms.

Eyes locked on his, she took his hand and placed it on her heart. 'I know you'll keep it safe.'

Three months later

'Another builder has quit,' Nik said, wandering into the office where Chloe was working. 'At this rate we'll never move into the house on Spetses. You have to do something about her.'

'Me!' Chloe echoed. 'I don't think so. She is your grandmother.'

'She is counting nails! We are in the middle of multi-million-pound renovation of a classic sixteenth-century mansion and my grandmother is counting nails.'

'She is thrifty.'

'She is insane, and you know it.'

'She's *your* grandmother…' she reminded him, coming around the table and looping her arms around his neck. Nik kissed her hard.

'At this rate we're not going to be able to move in after the wedding.'

Chloe shrugged. 'I don't care if I start married life in a shoe box, so long as it's with you.'

'Now you tell me, after I've already had to cope with planning officers from hell, contractors who never answer their phones and, of course, let's not forget Yaya.'

'She's excited about us being her new neighbours… well, for some of the time.' Nik had not given up his London house.

'It will all be worth it in the end, you'll see, waking up to the smell of pines and the sound of the sea,' she said dreamily.

'So long as I can see you when I wake up, I don't care. Which reminds me, have you got the shortlist for the new team leader for the charity? I don't want my wife—'

Her eyes widened as she pressed a finger to his lips and looked over her shoulder. 'Hush! You'll give the game away! Imagine how upset everyone will be if they find out we already got married after they've been to so much trouble to arrange this massive wedding.' Somehow she didn't think that people would be that understanding about their impulsive elopement.

He looked at her, eyes glowing with pride and love. 'I couldn't wait to make you my wife. I just wish I saw more of you.'

'I know,' she admitted, stroking his cheek with a loving hand. 'But who knew that the charity would take off this way? We're interviewing for a team leader next week and there are some very strong candidates.' She squeezed his bicep and pretended to faint. 'Obviously not as strong as you, darling.'

Their kiss might have gone on longer if Nik's ninety-five-year-old grandmother, all four feet five of her, hadn't suddenly appeared. 'A man came who said he was a building inspector. In my day there were no such thing; we just build a house with no paper.'

'The good old days,' Nik murmured. 'So where is the building inspector, Yaya?'

'Gone. I told him my grandson and his woman were busy making babies, and if they weren't doing that, then they should be.' Chortling at her own joke, she shuffled out of the room.

'Well, they do say that with age comes wisdom.' Nik extended a hand towards the door through which his grandmother had just exited. 'How about it, wife? Do you fancy a little baby making?'

'Only if you lock the door. If Yaya walks in on us, I might be scarred for life…' As the unintentional play on words hit home she released a loud laugh.

Nik felt pride swell in his chest once more. His wife laughed when others might weep. She had a gift for living life to its utmost, and looking at the world through her eyes had finally brought him the peace he'd never thought he'd feel again.

'Have my children, Chloe.'

Her throat closed up with sheer happiness. 'It's a big house, Nik, and there are lots of bedrooms to fill.'

'So maybe we should get started.'

'You read my mind!'

* * * * *

MILLS & BOON

Coming soon

**BOUND TO THE
SICILIAN'S BED**
Sharon Kendrick

Rocco was going to kiss her and after everything she'd just said, Nicole knew she needed to stop him. But suddenly she found herself governed by a much deeper need than preserving her sanity, or her pride. A need and a hunger which swept over her with the speed of a bush fire. As Rocco's shadowed face lowered towards her she found past and present fusing, so that for a disconcerting moment she forgot everything except the urgent hunger in her body. Because hadn't her Sicilian husband always been able to do this—to captivate her with the lightest touch and to tantalise her with that smouldering look of promise? And hadn't there been many nights since they'd separated when she'd woken up, still half fuddled with sleep, and found herself yearning for the taste of his lips on hers just one more time? And now she had it.

One more time.

She opened her mouth—though afterwards she would try to convince herself she'd been intending to resist him—but Rocco used the opportunity to fasten his mouth over hers in the most perfects of fits. And Nicole felt instantly helpless—caught up in the powerful snare of a sexual mastery which wiped out everything else. She gave a gasp of pleasure because it had been so long since she had done this.

Since they'd been apart Nicole had felt like a living statue—as if she were made from marble—as if the flesh and blood part of her were some kind of half-forgotten dream. Slowly but surely she had withdrawn from the sensual side of her nature, until she'd convinced herself she was dead and unfeeling inside. But here came Rocco to wake her dormant sexuality with nothing more than a single kiss. It was like some stupid fairy story. It was scary and powerful. She didn't *want* to want him, and yet . . .

She wanted him.

Her lips opened wider as his tongue slid inside her mouth—eagerly granting him that intimacy as if preparing the way for another. She began to shiver as his hands started to explore her—rediscovering her body with an impatient hunger, as if it were the first time he'd ever touched her.

'Nicole,' he said unevenly and she'd never heard him say her name like that before.

Her arms were locked behind his neck as again he circled his hips in unmistakable invitation and, somewhere in the back of her mind, Nicole could hear the small voice of reason imploring her to take control of the situation. It was urging her to pull back from him and call a halt to what they were doing. But once again she ignored it. Against the powerful tide of passion, that little voice was drowned out and she allowed pleasure to shimmer over her skin.

Continue reading
BOUND TO THE SICILIAN'S BED
Sharon Kendrick

Available next month
www.millsandboon.co.uk

LET'S TALK

Romance

For exclusive extracts, competitions
and special offers, find us online:

f facebook.com/millsandboon

⊙ @millsandboonuk

🐦 @millsandboon

Or get in touch on 0844 844 1351*

For all the latest titles coming soon, visit
millsandboon.co.uk/nextmonth

Calls cost 7p per minute plus your phone company's price per minute access charge